"ABOUT SATURDAY NIGHT . . ."

Matt dismissed Saturday night with a single crude expletive, then, before Carol could unlock the door to her car, he pulled her into his arms and kissed her, not as gently as before but with a demanding, consuming passion that brought an enthusiastic cheer from a teenager riding by on his skateboard.

"Does that convince you I'm not confusing you with my late wife?" he asked in a husky whisper against her hair.

Carol closed her eyes to shut out the sights and sounds of the traffic. She could feel Matt's heat through her clothes, and caught the faint scent of "Antaeus" on his cheek. She raised her hand to his temple and caressed his springy curls. When he finally stepped back, all she could do was regard him with a befuddled stare.

"I'll pick you up at seven-thirty on Saturday," he told her before turning away.

Carol leaned against her BMW, grateful for the solid comfort and chrome and steel; the kiss had turned her legs to jelly. How had she gotten herself into this situation? All she'd wanted was a date for the reunion—but she had gotten a lot more than she'd bargained for. She drove home, humming the chorus of Cortéz High's fight song and praying she would survive her next scrimmage with Matt . . . with her heart intact.

IT'S NEVER TOO LATE FOR LOVE AND ROMANCE

JUST IN TIME (4188, $4.50/$5.50)
by Peggy Roberts
Constantly taking care of everyone around her has earned Remy Dupre the affectionate nickname "Ma." Then, with Remy's husband gone and oil discovered on her Louisiana farm, her sons and their wives decide it's time to take care of her. But Remy knows how to take care of herself. She starts by checking into a beauty spa, buying some classy new clothes and shoes, discovering an antique vase, and moving on to a fine plantation. Next, not one, but two men attempt to sweep her off her well-shod feet. The right man offers her the opportunity to love again.

LOVE AT LAST (4158, $4.50/$5.50)
by Garda Parker
Fifty, slim, and attractive, Gail Bricker still hadn't found the love of her life. Friends convince her to take an Adventure Tour during the summer vacation she enjoyes as an English teacher. At a Cheyenne Indian school in need of teachers, Gail finds her calling. In rancher Slater Kincaid, she finds her match. Gail discovers that it's never too late to fall in love . . . for the very first time.

LOVE LESSONS (3959, $4.50/$5.50)
by Marian Oaks
After almost forty years of marriage, Carolyn Ames certainly hadn't been looking for a divorce. But the ink is barely dry, and here she is already living an exhilarating life as a single woman. First, she lands an exciting and challenging job. Now Jason, the handsome architect, offers her a fairy-tale romance. Carolyn doesn't care that her ultra-conservative neighbors gossip about her and Jason, but she is afraid to give up her independent life-style. She struggles with the balance while she learns to love again.

A KISS TO REMEMBER (4129, $4.50/$5.50)
by Helen Playfair
For the past ten years Lucia Morgan hasn't had time for love or romance. Since her husband's death, she has been raising her two sons, working at a dead-end office job, and designing boutique clothes to make ends meet. Then one night, Mitch Colton comes looking for his daughter, out late with one of her sons. The look in Mitch's eye brings back a host of long-forgotten feelings. When the kids come home and spoil the enchantment, Lucia wonders if she will get the chance to love again.

COME HOME TO LOVE (3930, $4.50/$5.50)
by Jane Bierce
Julia Delaine says good-bye to her skirt-chasing husband Phillip and hello to a whole new life. Julia capably rises to the challenges of her reawakened sexuality, the young man who comes courting, and her new position as the head of her local television station. Her new independence teaches Julia that maybe her time-tested values were right all along and maybe Phillip does belong in her life, with her new terms.

Available wherever paperbacks are sold, or order direct from the Publisher. Send cover price plus 50¢ per copy for mailing and handling to Zebra Books, Dept. 4400, 475 Park Avenue South, New York, N.Y. 10016. Residents of New York and Tennessee must include sales tax. DO NOT SEND CASH. For a free Zebra/Pinnacle catalog please write to the above address.

Phoebe Conn

TANGLED HEARTS

ZEBRA BOOKS
KENSINGTON PUBLISHING CORP.

This book is dedicated to Los Angeles poet Julian J. Edney, who graciously provided Casey's poem, Aluminum Moons.

ZEBRA BOOKS are published by

Kensington Publishing Corp.
475 Park Avenue South
New York, NY 10016

First Printing: December, 1993

Printed in the United States of America

One

Pasadena, California, Spring, 1992

"Whatever happened to love?" Suzanne paused to take a bite of spinach tortellini, but she didn't miss the exchange of pained glances passing between Carol and Aimee. They were seated on the patio at Papagallo, one of the most popular restaurants in Pasadena's newly refurbished Old Town. The spring day was so gloriously clear that in the distance the craggy peaks of the San Gabriel Mountains stood out in sharp relief. A redhead as vibrant as the dazzling day, Suzanne struggled to make her point.

"All anyone talks about is *relationships*. People report whether or not they're in a relationship, or just ending a disastrous relationship, or hoping to meet someone for a committed relationship, but no one ever mentions love. I don't think it's a matter of sophistication either. I think everyone's scared to death to admit what they really want is a lasting love."

Carol pushed a crouton aside before spearing another forkful of Caesar salad. "We're fifty-two years old, Suzanne. We've had a lifetime to become disillusioned with love."

"It's not just us, though," Suzanne complained. "It's everyone. I know neither of you is home in the afternoon to watch Oprah or Phil, but the few times a week I see their shows I can count on them having troubled couples, or lonely people longing to become part of a couple, and some expert who's written the latest book on how to have a fulfilling relationship with the ideal mate."

"All right," Carol confessed, "I'll admit to occasionally going up to the fifth floor to catch Oprah on one of the television sets on display. She's become a cultural icon and while she doesn't wear the clothes I buy for my department, many of her guests do. I can justify watching her show to survey fashion trends. I'll agree with you, there are a lot of unhappy people in the world, and they habitually turn up on the talk shows."

Aimee revealed her own tastes with a careless shrug. "If Oprah's on on a bank holiday, I usually watch, but problems make for more interesting shows than blissfully happy couples would. You can't blame her for choosing guests who'll boost her ratings."

Suzanne had to finish chewing a piece of roll before arguing. "Ratings aren't the issue," she insisted. "It's the focus on relationships, rather than love that I think is so sad, and everyone seems to feel so emotionally battered. Just look at us. You've been divorced twice, Carol. Aimee's been widowed and divorced, and I stayed in a loveless marriage for more years than I care to count before I divorced Frank. Was everything we were taught about love and marriage a farce? Am I wrong to expect more out of life than an endless series of tepid relationships? Doesn't love really exist?"

Aimee's hair had turned prematurely gray in her early thirties and she had never bothered to color it. She curled a silvery strand behind her right ear, a gesture she had developed in grade school where the three of them had met and sworn to be best friends forever. "I know it exists because I had it in such wonderful abundance with Steve," she replied. "Because I missed it so bad, I was an easy mark for Bill. I wish I'd realized what a phony he was before we were married rather than after, but I've learned my lesson. The kind of love I had with Steve comes only once in a lifetime and I can't tell you what a relief it is to no longer wait for it to happen again."

Suzanne sighed. "I don't think life is worth living without passion. I don't know what I'd do if I thought I'd never make love again."

Carol gave a lemon wedge a vicious twist and dropped it into her iced tea. "Please, you're depressing me. Tell us about Perfect Match, the video dating service you joined. It has to be a far more amusing topic than our marital failures."

"It was Perfect Match that got me thinking about relationships," Suzanne insisted. "I joined because I wanted someone to love and while I've met a lot of nice men, if I like them, then they don't care for me. The ones who've liked me have been so enthusiastic I've felt smothered, and not wanted to see them again. I find dating so difficult at our age, and the men are equally ill at ease.

"Each member of the service has a profile describing their interests and the type of person they'd like to meet," Suzanne went on. "The problem is, everyone says they love walks on the beach and romantic picnic suppers at the Hollywood Bowl, but when you meet in person, you quickly discover that's not enough in common to get you through a single date, let alone a lifetime. I had one date with a man, he was bright and attractive, but we struggled through a miserably awkward evening before discovering the one thing we had in common was a love for Clavell's KING RAT."

"That was a great book," Carol agreed, "but definitely not much in the way of common ground."

"No, it wasn't. The problem is, so many of the men are looking for women who share their interests rather than being willing to explore new ones. They'll say they're looking for an independent career woman, but then they'll add that she ought to love golf, or tennis, and be available to take extended vacations."

"I know the type," Carol remarked. "What they really want is an independently wealthy woman with plenty of free time, who'll cater to their every whim."

"Yes, I'm afraid you're right, but still, I keep hoping to meet someone special. I divorced Frank because I wanted a real marriage rather than a sham and it's so depressing to get dressed up, excited about meeting someone new, and then continually be disappointed. I'm beginning to feel like a really clumsy trapeze artist who goes out each night hoping to complete a triple somersault to thunderous applause, but who keeps on landing face down in the sawdust."

"Ouch, what a painful image," Aimee murmured. She had finished her minestrone and set her bowl aside. "I can't believe all your dates have been disastrous. Haven't any at least been amusing?"

Suzanne stopped to think a moment and then nodded. "How's this? One man suggested we meet for half an hour to have dessert. He said then if we didn't like each other, we wouldn't have wasted an entire evening."

"He actually said that?" Carol asked.

"He was one of the first who asked to meet me, and he sounded interesting so I recommended Beckham Place because they have a friendly atmosphere and delicious desserts. The fellow was actually quite handsome, but a salesman, lots of showy gestures and insincere smiles. Our opinions clashed on every topic he introduced. Then, just before our thirty minutes were up, he reached into his pocket, withdrew several slips of paper, and asked me to draw one."

"Now that's original," Aimee exclaimed. "What did it say?"

"That I'd won an additional thirty minutes!"

Carol laughed. "He must have picked up that trick in junior high. Well, what happened then?"

"I made the mistake of staying," Suzanne admitted. "That second half hour was even more uncomfortable than the first after I told him I bet all the slips said the same thing. He denied it, but jammed them back into his pocket without showing them to me. Things went downhill rapidly after that and we got into a ridiculous argument about whether or not it's wise for couples to live together before marriage.

"Now remember, this is a man I knew I'd never want to see again, and he wanted to debate modern living arrangements. I told him every study I'd read proved couples who lived together first divorced in greater numbers than couples who hadn't and that I had no intention of increasing my chances of going through another painful divorce."

"Spoken like the true scientist you are, Suzanne." While amused, Aimee had a sympathetic smile for her friend.

"You're missing the point," Carol insisted. "By offering you the slips, he admitted that he wanted an additional half hour with you."

"Really? I didn't even consider that, but I didn't hear from him again, and frankly, I was relieved. A great many men say they're looking for petite blondes. They'd love you, Carol. Why don't you give Perfect Match a try?"

Carol was dressed in a stunning black and amber print outfit by her favorite designer, Carole Little. A size ten, she often bought samples from the designer showrooms in the Los Angeles Merchandise Mart. She had excellent taste, and as one of the buyers of women's fashions for Russell's, a prestigious Southern California department store chain, she felt an obligation to dress well. Finished with her salad, she pushed up her sleeves and set her plate aside.

"I loved both my husbands dearly," she swore with her right hand raised. "They were wonderful providers in terms of material goods, but so consumed by their careers neither had the emotional energy to devote to a family. Bob was a perfectionist I could never please, while Cliff always put his law firm first, leaving the boys and me to finish a poor second. I didn't expect Cliff to spend more time with Bob's sons than Bob did, but even if Cliff and I had had children together, I doubt things would have been any different.

"So, I've had ample opportunity to see what marriage has to offer, and frankly, as far as I'm concerned, it's nothing but heartbreak. I'll pass on that, thank you, but I certainly hope for the best for you. I'm surprised you haven't met someone exciting at the university."

"There are some gorgeous men in my classes, but unfortunately, none is over twenty-five."

"I'll bet you'd enjoy dating younger men."

"Not that much younger!" Tickled by the idea, Suzanne couldn't help but laugh, but she went on to describe her situation more fully. "Cal State is predominantly a commuter school," she reminded them, "so it has little sense of community either among the students or the faculty. With the legislature constantly cutting our budget, much of the staff is too anxious about their jobs to have any interest in social life. As a tenured professor, my job appears to be safe, temporarily at least, but Anthropology, like most of the departments, now has a sizable number of part-time faculty.

"Some of those poor instructors teach a single class at several colleges and have such tight schedules they dash off campus the minute their office hours are over. While I still love my job, there's little of the comradery between professors that used to make it so much fun."

Envying her friends' svelte figures, Suzanne left the last two tortellini on her plate and sat back to brush the crumbs off her ample bosom. She preferred wearing loose-fitting separates in earth tones to show off the magnificent silver and turquoise jewelry she had collected over the years, but she would have loved to look as good in a red linen sheath as Aimee did.

Carol noticed Aimee checking her watch, and glancing at her own, realized they were nearly out of time. "I don't mean to change the subject abruptly, but the reunion is a week from Saturday and—"

Suzanne let out an anguished moan. "How can it possibly have been thirty-five years since we left dear old Cortéz High?"

"Easy," Aimee replied. Her memories of

high school were a colorful blur, but she still recalled college vividly. She had met Steve in the student union her first semester at San Diego State. They had married two years later, the day after his graduation, and had spent seven of the happiest years of her life together. Then one night he had been killed in a fiery freeway crash on his way home from work. He left two beautiful daughters, and a widow who never stopped loving him. Tears stung Aimee's eyes, and she hurriedly wiped them away.

"Forgive me," she begged. "I didn't mean to allow my thoughts to become so maudlin."

"No, you needn't apologize," Carol assured her. "That we're fifty-two rather than eighteen is painful for us all. That's why what I have to say is so important. I volunteered to be on the reunion committee to make certain it would be as enjoyable an event as it should be, but it's also given me an opportunity to learn who's made reservations, and as of the first of the week, we're the only ones planning to attend alone."

"I thought we were going together," Suzanne said.

"I swear for a woman with a doctorate, you're maddeningly dense at times, Suzanne. Of course we can ride to the reunion together. We can lock arms and walk through the door together, we can sit together for what should be a delicious dinner, but the major portion of the evening is reserved for dancing. The committee has hired a marvelous band which specializes in songs from the fifties and I know everyone will want to dance until the manager of the Ritz Carlton turns out the lights. The only problem is, the three of us are going to be left sitting on the sidelines.

"Now I'm not suggesting that we can find love, or even a *relationship,* in little more than a week, but I do think we can find presentable men to serve as escorts so we can have a good time at the reunion rather than slap silly smiles on our faces and pretend that we are."

Aimee gestured with both hands. "Oh no, I've had plenty of years to be on my own and I'm positive that's a better alternative than just glomming on to any available man. We haven't seen our classmates in ten years and it will be fun to catch up on everyone's news. That will be more than enough entertainment for me."

Carol had to hold her argument as their waiter appeared to clear their table. She had no interest in seeing the dessert menu, and neither did Aimee. They both ordered coffee, but Suzanne sent a longing glance toward the pastry cart.

"Would you care for some dessert, ma'am?" the young man asked.

Ashamed to be so transparent, Suzanne

shook her head. "No, thank you. I'll just have coffee too." As soon as he had left to bring it, she lowered her voice to a whisper. "Don't you just hate being called ma'am? I don't know when it happened, so it must have been gradual, but I can still recall when waiters used to call me miss. Ma'am sounds so damn old."

"When I'm ninety, maybe I'll admit to being old, but certainly not now," Carol exclaimed. "Let's concentrate on the reunion. I'm thinking of inviting one of the men I know at work. Casey's one of the housewares buyers, and we're good friends. I think he'd enjoy the evening, and it would save me from getting a wallflower complex. Isn't there someone you've met through Perfect Match whom you could invite?"

"No. The men I've liked haven't called me again, so I wouldn't dare ask them to something as special as a reunion. There are other men whose invitations I've refused, and I know one or two who'd be thrilled to go, but it would be cruel to mislead them into thinking I have a romantic interest in them when I don't."

The waiter returned to pour their coffee and Aimee spoke as soon as he moved on to another table. "I agree with you, Suzanne. Women ought not to use men, any more than men ought not to use women."

"I'm not talking about using anyone," Carol

insisted. "All I want is for us to have friendly escorts so we can enjoy the party. At the twenty-fifth reunion, I was still married to Cliff. Suzanne was with Frank, and what was the name of the man you were dating?"

"Mark Simmons, but that might have been the last time we dated, and he soon married someone else."

"All right, so he won't do, but don't you have some male friends at the bank?"

"Yes, I do, but like Mark, they're all married, so they're unavailable even if I were interested in them, which I'm not. You two can take dates. I've had years of practice and won't feel out of place going alone."

Carol pounded her open palm on the glass-topped table. "I don't think you realize what's at stake here, Aimee. We're talking about having a great time, rather than a depressing evening. We're bright, attractive, successful women, and we ought to have bright, attractive, successful dates. If you two can't find them among your acquaintances, perhaps you ought to hire them."

"Hire *gigolos?*" Suzanne gasped.

Carol looked around quickly to make certain no one else on the crowded patio had heard Suzanne's outburst. Only one elderly woman was observing them, but she appeared to be merely befuddled rather than shocked. Carol smiled at her before turning back to her friends. "No, certainly not *gigolos.* I'm taking about escorts, there's a difference."

Aimee placed her napkin on the table. "I doubt it."

Fearing Aimee was a lost cause, Carol renewed her efforts to win Suzanne to her side. "Do any of the part-time professors look interesting when they're dashing by? Or maybe there's a man in your neighborhood you've longed to meet. This is the nineties. Women ask men for dates all the time."

"Younger women," Aimee argued.

"Who's the most attractive man you know?" Carol persisted.

Suzanne looked off toward the mountains and was amazed to discover she could actually count the individual pines growing along the crest. "An attractive man," she repeated absently, and then began to smile with delighted surprise. "Matt Trenerry, my plumber."

Carol put her hand over her eyes and moaned.

"Don't be so hasty," Aimee warned. "Didn't you notice how Suzanne's face lit up when she mentioned his name?"

"Suzanne has a Ph.D.," Carol countered. "Do you sincerely believe she ought to date a plumber?"

"I don't think whom she chooses to date is

any of my business. Now tell us about him, Suzanne."

Embarrassed, Suzanne needed considerable coaxing before she gave in. "Matt's about our age, maybe six feet tall, with a trim build. His eyes are as blue as yours, Carol, and his hair is silvery gray like Aimee's, but curly rather than straight. He's very good looking, but so unassuming in his manner I doubt he's aware of it."

"Is he single?"

"I really don't know. He doesn't wear a wedding band, but lots of men who work with their hands don't as a safety precaution."

Carol listened in amazed silence as Aimee encouraged Suzanne to invite her plumber to their reunion. While she doubted anyone would be particularly impressed with Casey, he was at least a buyer for a major department store chain. She touched up her lipstick, and fluffed out her short curls. Finally she got an inspiration.

"Why don't I host a barbecue this Saturday afternoon? I'll invite Casey, you bring the plumber, and Aimee can come by herself if she wants to. It will be a rehearsal for the reunion, and if it doesn't go smoothly, we'll have a week to straighten things out."

Again, Suzanne took a while to come up with her answer. "Well, I do have a dripping faucet on my service porch; so I have a legitimate reason to call Matt when I get home."

"Do you have anything else that needs repair?" Aimee prompted. "After all, the longer you keep him working, the more time you'll have to decide if you'd really like to date him."

"No, I don't think so, but I'll look."

Aimee took out her wallet. "I have to get back to the bank. Assuming you have the barbecue on Saturday, what can I bring?"

"How about that luscious chocolate cake of yours?" Carol pulled out a twenty dollar bill. "Do either of you have change?" She waited while Aimee added up what each of them owed, plus a tip, and then left her twenty and collected change from the pile of ones and fives Aimee and Suzanne had contributed. She rose and pushed her wrought iron chair back into the table. While her plan to find dates for the reunion had not gone nearly as well as she had hoped, it was at least a start and she was smiling as they walked out to the parking lot. It wasn't until a valet greeted her as ma'am that she began to cringe.

Suzanne had to run an errand on the way home, but came through the front door by two o'clock. She carried in the mail, zigzagged around a carton of Pre-Columbian artifacts she had used in a class earlier in the week, and dropped two new magazines on the heap growing by the couch. She intended to read every one, but they arrived at a faster pace than she read and so the stack continually outstripped her best intentions to dispose of it. She tossed the mail on the dining-room table and went into the kitchen to look up Matt's number.

She got his machine, then took a quick inventory but failed to find anything other than the dripping faucet to report. Her breakfast dishes were still in the sink, and she rinsed and slipped them into the dishwasher, straightened the day's edition of the *Los Angeles Times* so it occupied only a small portion rather than the whole top of her kitchen table, and sat down to sort through the mail.

Perfect Match sent postcards whenever someone asked to meet her and she was disappointed to find none tucked among her bills. She stopped by the center each time a card arrived, but so far, she had had more disappointments than pleasant surprises when she had viewed her prospective dates' videotapes. When she had joined, she had been confident she would be one of the lucky ones the service featured in their advertising—women who met their ideal mate after only a few dates—but she was fast losing heart. She jumped when the telephone rang, and then, ashamed to be asking Matt to stop by her house under essentially false pretenses, downplayed the severity of her problem.

"It's just a small drip," she explained, "not an emergency that needs immediate attention." When Matt said he would be right over anyway, she thanked him, hung up, and sent another worried glance around her kitchen. It wasn't that she was a poor housekeeper. It was just that she had nowhere to store most of the materials she used in her classes, so they ended up in brown cardboard banker's boxes stacked wherever she found room. The kitchen was free of the clutter marring the rest of the downstairs, however, and grateful that Matt always came to the back door, Suzanne poured herself a glass of water and tried to relax.

With Perfect Match, she had the advantage of not having to meet a man face-to-face until she had accepted his request to meet, or he had replied favorably to hers. Standing there waiting for Matt to arrive, she felt the same fluttering anxiety she had experienced whenever she had had to ask a date to a dance in high school or college. In high school, she had never succeeded in overcoming her fears to actually ask a boy for a date, and in college, she managed it only a time or two before she met Frank.

"That was such a long time ago," she murmured wistfully and before she had managed to reassure herself that asking Matt for a date wouldn't be as difficult as she imagined, he knocked lightly at the back door. She hurried to let him in.

"It's just the faucet here on the service porch," she explained and he walked on by her to check the problem. He tried both faucets, and noted the annoying drip. "It just needs a washer, doesn't it?"

"Yes, that's all. I'll have this fixed for you in a minute."

Suzanne moved back into the kitchen as Matt went outside to his van to get his tools. Asking him out had seemed easy enough when she had been with Carol and Aimee, but now that she had to confront him on her own, she was terrified. What if he turned her down? She was sure he would do it politely, perhaps even regretfully, but it would be a rejection all the same. She would be so embarrassed she would never be able to call him again. She'd have to find a new plumber.

She heard him come in the back door and begin working, but she remained leaning against the tile counter. Matt had always been friendly, but watching him work would be torture. Afraid she was going to spoil everything, she rehearsed a dozen different descriptions of the reunion, but she doubted she could make it sound so tempting he would want to accompany her.

"Mrs. Marsh?" Matt came into the kitchen. "Do you have anything else you'd like me to look at? I hate to bill you the trip charge for just replacing a washer."

While Matt's hair had a silver cast, his brows and eyelashes were still dark brown, providing a handsome frame for his blue eyes. Appreciating his relaxed smile, Suzanne tried to reply in an equally casual tone. "No, the drip was the only problem, but despite the March rains, apparently our drought isn't really over, and I didn't want to keep wasting water."

Suzanne wore her hair long and tightly permed. The sunlight streaming in behind her made the red waves glow with a golden shimmer and while Matt had always considered her attractive, there was something especially appealing about her that afternoon. She looked rather lost, and considering the fact they were standing in her kitchen, that made no sense at all to him. He had been called out on an emergency early that morning and had almost let his son, Dan, take her call. Now he was glad he hadn't.

"Are you sure there isn't something else?" he prompted.

"No, not a thing," Suzanne insisted. As Matt wrote out his bill, she went into the dining room to pick up her purse and brought it back to write a check. She noted the amount he had charged, quickly filled in the figure, and handed it to him. He thanked her, slipped it inside his clipboard, and turned to go.

In that painful instant, Suzanne had a sudden premonition that even if he turned her down, it wouldn't hurt her pride nearly as much as letting him go without making the effort to ask him to the reunion. "Matt?" she called.

His hand was already on the doorknob and he turned to look back over his shoulder. "Yes?"

"I was just wondering, well, are you married?"

Startled by such an unexpected question, Matt started to laugh, but he quickly caught himself. He came back into the kitchen and leaned his shoulder against the refrigerator. "How long have we known each other, Mrs. Marsh?"

Suzanne frowned slightly. "The first time you did some work for us was just after we'd moved here in 1968. A pipe was leaking beneath the garage and it took you all of a Saturday afternoon to repair it."

Matt nodded. "I remember that job. If that was in '68, then we've known each other more than twenty-five years. In all that time, has my marital status been a concern to you?"

Suzanne blushed as red as her hair. "No, never. It has absolutely nothing to do with your ability to perform the job."

Matt could tell he was making Suzanne exquisitely uncomfortable, and he straightened up and adopted a more serious tone. "Good. I'm single, and since you asked, should I assume you've a reason other than plumbing for wanting to know?"

Matt was wearing a blue work shirt and Levi's. Had she met him at Cal State, she would have mistaken him for a fellow professor, but that he was confident as well as attractive didn't make her task any easier. She cleared her throat, and tried her best to sound as though whether or not he accepted her invitation meant very little to her.

"I had lunch today with a couple of friends I've known since grade school. We went to Cortéz High together too, and our thirty-fifth reunion is next week. We decided it would be a lot more fun if we had dates, but if you're busy, or don't want to go with me, that's all right."

Matt was too shocked to give a coherent reply for a long moment, but during that uncomfortable pause, he saw Suzanne's lower lip tremble and he realized just how difficult asking him out had been. "I didn't go to Cortéz High myself," he replied, "but I'd be honored to take you to your reunion."

Suzanne wasn't certain she had heard him correctly. "You would?"

Matt laughed again, he had a rich, rolling

laugh that encouraged others to join him. "Of course, you're one of my favorite customers and I wouldn't dream of disappointing you."

"Really? I had no idea."

Matt had been teasing her again, but she looked so pleased by his compliment he wasn't even tempted to admit the truth. "Yes, you certainly are."

Encouraged by his praise, Suzanne told him about Carol's barbecue. "It's so we can all get acquainted. Then we'll be going to the reunion as a group of friends. It won't have to be a real date."

"Fine, that sounds like fun too." He asked what time she would like him to pick her up on Saturday, and after thanking her for the invitation, left for home. Dan badgered him constantly about dating, but frankly, he just hadn't been interested. Now he was tempted to call his son and tell him he actually had a date, even better, two. Then again maybe it was too soon to brag.

Two

Carol hung up the telephone with a weary sigh; now that Suzanne had a date for the barbecue and reunion, she could no longer delay speaking to Casey. Russell's buyers operated out of the downtown Los Angeles branch, an ultramodern brick building Carol referred to as the "fortress," and not merely because of its architecture. The office of Russell's CEO was located on the top floor, where he and his staff worked in mahogany-paneled splendor while she and her fellow buyers had offices scarcely larger than dressing rooms.

Carol had come into work that morning intending to ask Casey about the reunion as soon as she had checked over yesterday's sales reports. She had been interrupted by department managers in several branch stores who had called requesting reorders on the latest Liz Claiborne separates and it had taken most of the morning to place them. Now, after an enthusiastic nudge from Suzanne, she couldn't justify putting off seeing Casey a moment longer.

Picking up her coffee mug, she made her way through the back hall of the women's fashion floor to the freight elevator. Out on the sales floor, Russell's customers saw only the elegantly clad mannequins and beautifully designed displays, but the cool corridors, cramped offices, and crowded stockrooms behind the scenes composed the true heart of the department store. She rode up two flights to the fifth floor and maneuvered her way past stacked cartons of newly arrived Farberware two wiry stockboys in blue smocks were struggling to unpack.

Casey's door was open, but Carol paused to rap lightly on the jamb. "You have the best coffee in the store. May I please have a cup?"

Casey welcomed her with an expansive wave. "Only if you promise to drink it here."

"Fair enough." Carol filled her mug from the Krups Coffee Time Plus machine conveniently placed on a lateral file cabinet, added tiny amounts of artificial sweetener and cream, then sat down in the chair beside Casey's desk. Casey was in his shirtsleeves, and he had loosened his tie, but as always, everything in his office was in immaculate order. A large bulletin board covered with designers' sketches, fabric swatches, and copies of orders dominated Carol's office, but

Casey had only a single stylish print of a chrome teakettle from New York's Museum of Modern Art.

Blue-eyed, he wore glasses with attractive wire frames, but kept his brown hair cut shorter than the menswear buyers who cultivated a more sophisticated image. Carol considered him cute rather than handsome. He was slightly younger than she, but age had never been a factor in their friendship. He had been poring over a stack of catalogs and she turned one toward her.

"What's the latest in housewares?" she asked.

"I'm making up my Christmas orders and I want to make certain I have enough Presto Tatertwisters to make curly fries. There was a time when I couldn't keep pasta makers in stock, then it was the bread bakers. Espresso coffee machines and Aeromatic ovens are selling well to the yuppie crowd, but I'm betting we'll do a big business in Tatertwisters this year."

"I thought most people had given up eating fried foods."

"That may very well be true, but they'll still want to have an occasional binge on curly fries. Or at least I'm hoping they will. How are things for you, sales still good?"

"Yes, thank God, but as long as they're down storewide, I'll hold my breath every morning until I've read the latest sales report. Russell's used to have a dozen competitors but in the last year, look how many of the department stores have either merged or have gone out of business altogether." She quickly ticked off the names on her brightly polished red nails. "Some couldn't compete with the discount stores, others couldn't survive the slow economy. What's your prediction for Russell's; are we going to last?"

Casey leaned back in his chair and propped his hands behind his head. "I think the board may very well be forced to close the branches with marginal profits, but Russell's has been in California since the gold rush, and we're strong. We'll survive."

"That's encouraging. Whenever I have a spare minute, I like to prowl the store to gather opinions and I always value yours."

"Well, thank you." Casey got up to pour himself another cup of coffee and refilled Carol's mug before he sat down.

"Are you dating anyone special?" Carol asked as casually as she could, but Casey still choked on his coffee. "I'm sorry, I didn't mean to pry."

Casey swallowed and wiped his mouth on the back of his hand. "No, you're not prying. You just surprised me is all. The answer is no. I'd certainly like to be, though."

Now afraid her next question would shock him more than her first, Carol chose her words with care. "My thirty-fifth high school reunion will be at the Ritz Carlton in Pasadena a week from Saturday. It should be fun, but I don't want to go alone. I was hoping you might like to go with me."

"Well sure, I'll be happy to, but now I'm embarrassed that in all the time we've known each other, I've never asked you out."

Carol didn't want to mislead him. "We're friends, Casey. If we go to an occasional party together, it doesn't have to change anything between us."

Casey nodded, but he looked slightly pained. "Sure, I understand. We wouldn't want to ruin a perfectly good friendship with anything more intimate, would we?"

"No, we most certainly would not." Afraid she had hurt his feelings, however unintentionally, Carol described the barbecue as an opportunity for him to meet her friends before the reunion. "They're very nice. I'm sure you'll like them. Suzanne's bringing her date, but Aimee will probably come alone. It'll just be a friendly get together, nothing terribly special."

"What can I bring?"

"The menu's all set, so all you need do is arrive at three." Carol wrote her address on a Russell memo, and drew a simple map. "It's in Arcadia near the Santa Anita Fashion Park, and

I know you've visited the Russell's store there often enough to know how to find it."

Casey tucked the memo in his shirt pocket. "It'll be no problem. I'll see you at three on Saturday if not before."

"Thanks for the coffee."

"Sure, any time."

Carol left Casey's office with the uncomfortable feeling she had just made an incredible blunder. She replayed their conversation as she walked to the elevator, and was positive she hadn't misled Casey about her intentions. But she couldn't shake the lingering suspicion she had disappointed him somehow.

Casey rang Carol's doorbell at ten minutes to three on Saturday and greeted her in an excited rush. He gestured with a bouquet of spring flowers. "There's a peacock standing right out there in the street. I had to drive around him to park. Should we call Animal Control to come get him?"

Carol opened her screen door and drew Casey inside. "He's an escapee from the Arboretum. It's just up the street and we have peacocks strutting through our gardens all the time. He'll wander back home when he's ready. How thoughtful of you to bring me flowers.

Come on in the kitchen and talk to me while I put them in a vase."

Casey had expected Carol to live in an exquisitely decorated condo. To find she occupied a sprawling ranch style home had amazed him. The kitchen had the latest built-in appliances, dark wood cabinets, and sparkling white tile. "Do you live here all alone?"

"Yes. Tom, my younger son, he's a chiropractor, lived here with me until last fall, and frankly, I'm so glad to finally have the place to myself, I'm never lonely."

"This was your family home then?"

Carol opened the cupboard above the refrigerator and removed a tall crystal vase. She didn't recall Casey ever being interested in her personal life, but she was happy to indulge him. "Bob, my first husband, is my sons' father. We lived in Pasadena, but after we divorced, and I remarried, we moved here. My elder son, Rob, is a dentist and in practice with his father. Would you like a free toothbrush? I have plenty."

"No, thanks, my dentist gives them away too. Say, didn't you put too much water in that vase?"

Carol had been reaching for her kitchen shears to trim the stems of the daisies, spider chrysanthemums, and iris he had brought, but her hand froze in mid-air. Bob had been meticulous, and not merely in his dental practice, where it was required, but at home as well. He had never been openly critical, but as Casey had just done, he had subtly undermined her confidence by questioning everything she did. It had never mattered how carefully she did things either; he had always had a better way.

For an instant she wanted to hurl the heavy vase at Casey and tell him to get out, but she curbed the impulse and picked up the shears. It was her vase after all; was it unreasonable to assume that she had used it on numerous occasions without slopping water over the edge when she added the flowers? "We'll soon see," she replied with forced cheerfulness.

Leaning over the sink, Carol trimmed a half inch from the crisp stems with a vengeance. She was annoyed not so much with Casey as with herself for not realizing a man who kept his office spotless and his hair short would be of the same perfectionist ilk as Bob. The signs had been clear, had she only stopped long enough to read them. She supposed she had not bothered because it had not really mattered when they were just two buyers who occasionally shared a cup of coffee and a few minutes' conversation about business.

Carol took enormous delight in arranging the mixed bouquet without spilling a single drop of water. "There." She picked up the vase to show it off proudly and then carried it outside to the umbrella table she had already covered with a bright yellow cloth.

Casey followed her out on the patio. It was bordered with a deep green lawn, while bright pink azaleas, camellias loaded with white blossoms, and vivid fuschia bougainvillaea lined the walls separating her property from her neighbors'. "You've a lovely yard."

"Thank you, but my gardener deserves all the credit. My friend, Suzanne—she should be here soon—is incredibly talented where plants are concerned, but I'd be afraid to raise anything other than cactus, which thrive on neglect. I still have the vegetables to prepare, but why don't you make yourself comfortable out here?"

Casey chose to follow her back inside. She had iced tea, soft drinks, and beer chilled. He took a soda. "Are you sure there isn't something I can do?"

Carol wished she had a dog so she could ask him to walk it. "Thank you, but no. It won't take me a minute to slice the carrots and celery."

Casey watched Carol a moment, and then offered a suggestion. "Rather than just chopping off rounds, you ought to slice the carrots on the diagonal. It will make for a more attractive presentation."

Carol's head came up. Casey was dressed in Levi's and a madras shirt, but his expression held the same strained intensity she had often glimpsed at work and had, unfortunately, discounted. There was an old joke about a farmer giving a mule three chances before he shot him, and as far as she was concerned, Casey had just used up two of his. She held out the paring knife. "Here, if you like them a certain way, why don't you do it?"

Casey jammed his hands into his hip pockets. "I didn't mean to insult you. It was just a suggestion."

"I'm not insulted," Carol assured him a bit too emphatically. She waited, and finally he came forward to slice the remainder of the carrots. "I suppose you'd like to make little rosettes out of the radishes?"

"Sure, why not?"

"Fine." Carol flopped a bunch of radishes on the counter. "Is there any particular way you like to have the celery prepared?"

"Yeah, do you have any peanut butter? It's good stuffed with that."

Carol laid the celery on the counter along with a jar of crunchy peanut butter. "There you are, fix it any way you like."

"I was just trying to be helpful."

"Yes, I know." Carol removed a bowl of potato salad from the refrigerator. "Would you like to sample this?"

Believing she was serious, Casey accepted the

fork she offered and took a bite. He chewed thoughtfully, and then frowned slightly. "That's rather bland. Do you have any curry powder?"

"Why, of course. What kitchen would be complete without curry powder?" She opened the cupboard beside the stove and removed a jar. "Here you are."

Casey used the serving spoon she handed him and measured out what he thought would be the right amount and mixed it into the potato salad. He sampled it again, added a bit more curry powder, and then gave her the fork. "Now you have a taste. Isn't this better?"

Carol was surprised to find it really was delicious. "Yes, it is. I had no idea you enjoyed cooking."

"I used to be a chef. Why did you think Russell's hired me to buy housewares?"

"I don't know. I just supposed you'd worked your way up through the organization the way I did. There's the doorbell; excuse me a minute."

Carol hurried out of the kitchen, but paused in the living room to catch her breath before opening the door. After reminding herself she only had to put up with Casey for the afternoon and the reunion, not the rest of her life, she managed to find a smile. She took Suzanne's salad bowl as she greeted her, but she nearly dropped it when her gaze locked with Matt's.

Despite Suzanne's flattering description of the man, she had never imagined he would be better looking than the male models Russell's featured in their menswear ads. Although she was positive they had never met, a sizzling jolt of recognition shot clear through her and she clutched the wooden bowl as though it were a life preserver and she were in mortal danger of drowning. She could not even remember the last time she had been so intrigued by a man. This particular man was her friend's date, however, and therefore way off-limits.

Matt stared at the petite blonde a moment too long. She was dressed in white pants and a T-shirt with a nautical design. He preferred to see women in dresses, and had complimented Su-zanne on her aqua blouse and skirt, but despite her casual attire, Carol struck him as being one of the most delightfully feminine creatures he had ever met. Boyish curls framed blue eyes that danced with a pixy's charm but her lips were most definitely a woman's. He tripped coming in the door, but caught himself without bumping into Suzanne.

"How do you do?" he asked, then silently cursed the fact he hadn't said something more clever.

Matt's aftershave smelled so delicious Carol didn't even know what she said, but somehow she got Suzanne and him into the kitchen and after providing them with drinks, sent them on out to the patio. Aimee arrived before anyone had taken a seat and without consciously arranging places, Carol took a chair opposite Matt's. She had always enjoyed entertaining, and had never had any difficulty putting her guests at ease, but that afternoon her mind refused to cooperate. After passing the relish tray Casey had prepared, she couldn't think of a single thing to say.

Without a date to distract her, Aimee watched Carol and Matt gawk at each other, while Casey kept eyeing Suzanne with a curious sidelong glance. Suzanne, eating a piece of peanut-butter-stuffed celery, seemed not to notice the direction of her companions' interest. Rather than feeling like an outsider, Aimee enjoyed having a dispassionate view of the party.

"We didn't have nearly enough time to talk at lunch the other day. Have you been doing any more traveling, Suzanne?" Aimee asked. "Suzanne's an anthropology professor at Cal State LA and visits all sorts of interesting places," she added for Casey's benefit, but Matt nodded as though he had just learned something too.

"I made another trip to Vancouver at the end of the last quarter," Suzanne replied. "It's such a beautiful city. Have any of you been there?"

When none had, she wiped her hands on a cocktail napkin, and did her best to describe it.

"It's built right on the coast with the thick cedar forests of the Coast Range providing magnificent scenery. There's a great deal of new construction downtown, lots of modern architecture with glass walls which must provide the office workers with sensational views of the sea or mountains. They get a great deal of rain, but it isn't terribly cold there. In fact, most of the Indians, or aboriginals as they prefer being called, didn't bother with clothes before the arrival of the white man.

"At Cal State, I teach classes on native cultures. We offer several courses on Mexico and the Southwest, but the Indians of the Northwest Coast have always been my special favorites and the Museum of Anthropology located on the campus of the University of British Columbia has a marvelous collection of their work."

Drawing a complete blank, Matt looked perplexed. "Which Indians are those?"

"There are quite a few, but the Tlingit, Haida, and Kwakuitl were among the largest tribes. Do any of those sound familiar?"

Matt shook his head. "Not a one, sorry."

"Well, they had a marvelous culture. They had an abundance of food from the sea and streams and vast cedar forests to supply wood for their homes and canoes. The chiefs took great pride in their wealth and had contests to see which one could give away the most goods, or at times, simply destroy them."

"Sounds like an extravagant crowd," Matt ventured.

"Yes, they certainly were, but they lived with such incredible abundance they could easily replace whatever goods they had lost."

"Didn't they make masks?" Casey asked.

Pleased by Casey's interest, Suzanne grew more effusive. "Yes, they did, and wonderful ones too. I have several excellent examples that I need to find a way to display at home when I'm not using them in class. Some were of their clan animals, the raven, bear, and beaver, while others were designed to be especially fierce to terrify their enemies when they went on raids."

Aimee noted Suzanne's enthusiasm for her subject, and Matt's polite attention. It was Casey who continued to ask questions though, prompting a discussion of salmon fishing that grew into a debate of the best ways to prepare the fish. He shifted his chair closer to Suzanne's as he began to describe how to poach one in a dishwasher. When Matt shrugged and looked toward Carol, Aimee expected their hostess to speak to him and when she didn't, Aimee gave her a gentle poke as she got up to get a handful of carrots.

Carol licked her lips. Matt was dressed in

Levi's, with a blue and white polo shirt. He had an athlete's lean muscular body, and she assumed he must jog, or play a sport of some kind. "I've just learned Casey enjoys cooking. What do you do for fun, Matt?"

Matt winced slightly. "It's been so long since I had any, I don't remember."

Carol waited for him to say more, or perhaps ask her a question, but he didn't. He just continued to regard her with an amused smile. Out of doors, the fragrance of his cologne wasn't noticeable, but the memory continued to tease Carol's senses and she vowed to visit the men's fragrance counters on Monday to identify it. She had not thought a plumber would bother with cologne, or if he did, that he would wear the Old Spice or perhaps Canoe he had received at Christmas, but whatever Matt was wearing had the most haunting appeal she had ever encountered.

"Excuse me a minute, I need to start the charcoal," she said.

"I'll help you," Matt offered. He followed her over to the bright yellow Weber grill, but stood back rather than crowd her.

Carol held her breath waiting for him to start offering directions as she worked, but he didn't. He didn't provide a single hint, nor a word of caution. He just watched until she had finished lighting the brickets. Ashamed for having expected the worst of a man she had just met, she tried to be more friendly.

"I didn't know what you men would like so I thought I'd barbecue both chicken and ribs and hope you'd like one."

"I like everything."

It wasn't what he had said, but the way he had said it that made Carol's knees grow weak. Then her stomach knotted up in a tight curl that was more a result of excitement than fear. Damn! She screamed silently. Turning so her back was to Suzanne, she spoke to Matt in a frantic whisper.

"Please stop doing that."

Matt looked around, as though expecting to find something he had missed. "What are you talking about?" he replied in an equally hushed whisper. "I'm not doing anything but standing here."

Carol gave the smoldering heap of charcoal a savage poke with a barbecue fork. "Look, I think you're very attractive, but you're with Suzanne, and I wouldn't hurt her for the world."

"Neither would I," Matt assured her, "but maybe you should have put Casey on a leash." He nodded toward the others, where Suzanne and Casey were huddled together talking while Aimee sat to one side apparently content to follow along.

"Casey and I are just friends," Carol insisted.

Matt sent her a questioning glance that readily conveyed his doubts.

"We both work at Russell's. That's the only thing we have in common."

"Good."

He let the word hang in the air until it took on a taunting ambiguous quality, but his gaze remained far too direct. Embarrassed, Carol finally looked away and he left to rejoin the others but she remained by the grill and not because the charcoal needed her attention. Since her divorce from Cliff, she had had an occasional date, usually with someone she had met through work, but she hadn't been looking for romance and hadn't encouraged any of the men to want more than an evening or two of her company. None of them had ever eyed her the way Matt did, as though he longed to start licking at her toes and take all night working his way up.

She jabbed the charcoal again, then laid the fork aside and went to get herself more iced tea. Aimee soon joined her in the kitchen. "The charcoal won't be ready for a while yet. I should have had some chips as well as vegetables to munch on. Or I should have thought ahead and lit the charcoal earlier."

"I don't recall ever seeing you so nervous," Aimee observed. "Relax, we're all just friends here, right?"

Carol shook her head. "Matt's every bit as gorgeous as Suzanne said he was, but she was wrong. He knows it."

"And he uses it too, doesn't he? Come on, Carol, I'm not blind. Suzanne and Casey seem to have struck it off so well they haven't noticed the glances passing between you and Matt, but I'd think twice about inviting him into your bedroom while they're eating dessert."

"The man's a plumber!"

Aimee responded with a knowing smile, and carried the pitcher of iced tea out to the patio.

When Carol finally gathered the courage to return to her guests, she found Aimee and Matt talking about current interest rates. Without appearing overly curious, she learned his firm also did kitchen and bath remodeling. Suzanne had referred to him as a plumber though, and had called him to repair a leaky faucet, so apparently he handled a wide range of jobs.

"My bank is still considered sound," Aimee assured them when Suzanne and Casey joined in the discussion, "although the banking industry as a whole surely isn't. Our parents' generation had more confidence in their jobs, and could look forward to a comfortable retirement, but I don't have that sense of security. The bank advises our depositors on a variety of retirement plans, but I know from my own experience how difficult it is to save for the future."

Casey agreed, and Suzanne again lamented the budget crisis that meant cutbacks in higher education. While Carol had considerable doubts on the state of the economy, she found it impossible to voice her thoughts with Matt watching her so closely. He made her nervous, but in the most delicious way.

Embarrassed by the invisible current that flowed so easily between her and Matt, Carol was relieved to find Casey sitting back in his chair, talking amiably with both Aimee and Suzanne. When the conversation turned to politics, Matt and Casey quickly found themselves at odds, but joked about it in good-natured fashion rather than arguing. With the afternoon going well, if not as she had expected it, Carol again went into the kitchen to get the first of the meat she had ready to barbecue. She had just removed the foil topped pan of ribs from the refrigerator when Suzanne joined her.

She was again munching on a piece of celery. "What do you think of Matt?" she asked.

Carol found it far easier to concentrate on opening a bottle of barbecue sauce than on her friend's mischievous smile. "He's definitely everything you said he was."

"I'm glad you agree. I'm also glad we're sitting outdoors, because I sneezed so often on the way over I was afraid he would guess I'm allergic to his aftershave. Not that it doesn't smell good, it certainly does, but I haven't been able to wear perfume for years and whenever I'm near a man who uses cologne, I spend more time sneezing than talking."

"What a shame."

"Yes, it is, especially since I know he wore it to impress me. What can I do to help?"

Carol poured the sauce into a bowl and picked up the brush to apply it. "Would you carry the pan with the ribs?"

Suzanne picked it up but made no move toward the door. "I really like Matt, but the radio in his truck is tuned to a country and western station and I absolutely can't abide that stuff. He's into politics and sports, while I like art and poetry. We talked about the Dodgers on the way over, and I can't name a single player on the team. This has turned out like so many of the dates I've had through Perfect Match. Matt's a great guy, but we've so little in common, I doubt we'll see each other after the reunion."

"Don't be so hasty, Suz, give the man a chance." Carol was proud of herself for being so gracious, but it hurt to think of Suzanne dating Matt when she found him so appealing herself. "I thought passion was your first priority. Doesn't he qualify in that department?"

Suzanne looked out at the group on the patio as she mulled over Carol's question. "Yes, passion is definitely a priority, but is it wrong of me to want both physical pleasure and a friend with mutual interests in one man?"

"Isn't that what Perfect Match guarantees?"

"They can't guarantee anything but the opportunity to meet the right person. As for Matt, give me credit for having sense enough to know when something isn't going to work. Not that we couldn't have a glorious, if brief affair, but that isn't what I'm looking for. What about you and Casey? You described him as just being a friend. Is that all he is?"

Now that Matt was no longer the focus of their conversation, Carol relaxed and confided in her friend. "Yes, but he's begun to remind me of Bob, and I'm sorry I asked him to the reunion. I'm pleased you and he are getting along so well. He's a nice guy, but just not my type."

"Yeah, like Matt isn't mine. How old do you suppose Casey is?"

"Forty-something I suppose. Now let's get everything cooking so we won't have to eat in the dark."

"That might be very romantic," Suzanne suggested slyly.

If the atmosphere on her patio got any more highly charged, Carol feared she really would be tempted to invite Matt into her bedroom during dessert. Aghast at that thought, she shoved it aside as absurd in the extreme. She followed

Suzanne out to the grill and tried to capture the spirit of her guests' light-hearted laughter, but it still eluded her. She was relieved beyond measure that Suzanne hadn't fallen madly in love with Matt, but she could not help but be apprehensive about what lay ahead. Perhaps nothing, she scolded herself. Matt might simply like to flirt and never take it any further where she was concerned. Then again, he might like to do far more than merely tease, and then she would really be in trouble.

She put the ribs on the grill and closed the lid. She had just as easily closed her heart when her marriage to Cliff had failed, but that afternoon, Matt had jarred her comfortably composed life to its very foundations. Trying to convince herself she was simply more lonely than she had realized, she glanced over her shoulder, wanting no more than a glimpse of him to convince herself he was real. Matt had been watching her though, and responded with a barely perceptible nod.

She knew in that instant that the real question wasn't whether Matt liked to do more than flirt, but whether she had the courage to follow his lead.

Three

The ribs hadn't been on the grill more than a minute before Casey came over to help. "How did you make the sauce?" he asked.

Carol had left the empty bottle on the counter, and made no attempt to pass off the popular brand as her secret recipe. "I'm sure you must know how to create a truly sublime sauce, but this will have to do for now."

Casey frowned slightly. "Not necessarily. Do you mind if I take a look at your spices?"

Carol handed him the bowl and brush. "Add whatever you like." Leaving the ribs with him, she sat down with Aimee, Suzanne, and Matt, and tried, somewhat more successfully this time, not to regard Casey as a meddling nuisance. She took a deep breath, had a sip of tea, and ate two pieces of stuffed celery before she felt like talking.

"Shouldn't we put the chicken on to cook?" Suzanne asked.

Carol had completely forgotten the chicken, but as she started to rise, Suzanne stopped her.

"Stay put, I'll get it."

"Thank you," Carol called before apologizing to her remaining two companions. "I didn't mean to interrupt your conversation."

"You didn't," Matt assured her. "We were just talking about you."

Mortified, Carol had to swallow hard. "What about me?"

"We were talking about how unusual it is to find people in California who've been friends as long as we have," Aimee explained. "That's why I'm really looking forward to the reunion. Other than Suzanne and you, I've lost track of everyone else. There were people I no longer recognized at the last reunion ten years ago. I'm sure there will be even more I've forgotten this time. What about you, Matt, have you been to any reunions?"

"I grew up in San Diego, but my parents are no longer living and I don't get down there much. I suppose there must have been reunions over the years, but I've not gone to any. I didn't enjoy high school, so seeing everyone again, doesn't appeal to me. I try not to look back, if you know what I mean."

He glanced Carol's way, and she couldn't help but wonder if he was issuing a challenge to live in the moment without any regard for the consequences. She wasn't that type of person any more than Suzanne was, and found the prospect of a brief affair equally unappealing. "If we're careful about how we live today," she offered, "then there's no reason to fear our memories."

"If you're too careful," he warned, "you won't have any."

Carol knew she wasn't imagining things this time. That comment had definitely been a challenge. The man was as smooth as a porcelain tub and she felt way out of her depth. She picked up a piece of carrot and chewed it to little tiny bits that she had to wash down with tea.

"My last husband was an attorney," she finally said. "He loved verbal sparring. I don't."

Matt straightened up in his chair. "How many husbands have you had?"

"Just two. Now you'll have to excuse me again, I need to warm the rolls."

Matt watched Carol enter the house with a long, swift stride that made her anger plain and while he was tempted to follow her, he feared he would only upset her more. "Is there anything worse than reminding a woman of her ex-husband?" he asked Aimee.

"I'm sure there must be, but off-hand, I can't think of it. I wouldn't worry though, Carol is remarkably even-tempered, and she won't hold a chance remark against you."

Matt turned to survey the colorful yard. He drew in a deep breath and let it out slowly. He knew he ought to make the effort to talk with Aimee, but it had been so long since he had been alone with a woman, other than a customer, that he had completely forgotten how. "This is a real pretty yard," he said when the silencc between them grew more painful than he could bear.

"Yes, it is. Do you have children, Matt?"

Relieved she had thought of something they could discuss, Matt began to smile. "I have a son, Dan. He's my partner. He's married and has a cute little boy of his own. I hate to think of myself as a grandfather though. What about you?"

"My daughters are twenty-eight, and twenty-six. Karen's an artist, and JoAnne's a nurse. Neither is married so I don't have to worry about becoming a grandmother for another year at least."

"You're lucky then. When I was a kid, grandfathers were little old men who liked to fish and play checkers. I just can't see myself being a part of that crowd." He also felt damn silly being out on a date at his age, and wondered just where he did belong. He kept an eye on the back door, waiting for Carol, and was disappointed when she remained inside.

Carol pretended to be attending to the last

of the dinner preparations, but she kept a close watch on her guests. Suzanne and Casey were still at the grill, laughing together and taking turns brushing barbecue sauce on the chicken and ribs. Aimee and Matt were conversing easily, but then Aimee had always had a talent for putting people at ease and Carol wasn't surprised at how quickly she had made friends with Matt.

She tossed the salad Suzanne had brought, and got out a serving spoon for the potato salad. Forcing herself to serve a meal she doubted she would taste, she brought everything outside the instant Casey announced the meat was ready. They moved their chairs to the table, and after passing the meat platter, salads, and rolls, ate with only low murmurs of appreciation for the first few minutes.

As Carol paused to lick the barbecue sauce off her fingers, she looked up to find Matt again watching her far too closely. Self-conscious, she immediately switched to her napkin but Matt then made an exaggerated show of licking his own fingers. He did it very slowly, with just the tip of his tongue, but his eyes never left her face. It was easily one of the most wildly erotic things she had ever seen and she quickly surveyed the table hoping the others were too preoccupied with their ribs to notice Matt's outrageous performance.

Grateful to find they were, she quickly complimented Casey. "This is the best sauce I've ever tasted. What did you add?"

Rather than use his fingers, Casey was carefully slicing the meat from a chicken breast with his knife and fork. "There aren't any secret ingredients, but a bit of ginger will give any bottled sauce a real snap."

"Well, whatever you did, it's wonderful," Carol assured him a second time. She was sorry she hadn't been more gracious to him earlier, but that he reminded her so much of Bob still made it difficult for her to appreciate him.

"Everything about this afternoon has been wonderful," Matt added. "Thank you for asking me, Suzanne."

"You're welcome." Pleased that Matt was enjoying himself, Suzanne made certain he got plenty to eat, but she continued to direct most of her comments to Casey.

The conversation turned to plans for the summer and Carol was able to contribute, but she carefully avoided meeting Matt's gaze. His voice was softer now, but he laughed whenever something amusing was said; he was clearly having a good time. They all left room for a slice of Aimee's chocolate cake, but as soon as they had finished their coffee, she got up and began to clear the table.

"Just leave everything for me," Carol protested. "I never let my guests do dishes."

"I never leave a hostess with a messy kitchen either," Casey insisted and following Aimee inside, he donned an apron, rinsed the dishes, and put them in the dishwasher while Aimee wrapped the leftovers and stored them in the refrigerator. The pair soon finished, and after insisting everyone take home a second piece of cake, Aimee was the first to leave.

Carol brought in the flowers and placed them on her breakfast table. "Thanks again for everything, Casey."

"You're welcome." Casey rinsed out the sink and turned on the garbage disposal, but after an initial whir, it made a horrible clunking sound and he immediately shut it off. "Damn, I must have missed one of the ribs," he complained.

"It just needs to be reset," Matt assured him. "I'll get it."

Casey moved out of his way, but Carol stepped in front of the sink. "You were invited here for dinner, Matt, and I don't expect you to stay to make repairs."

Because resetting the disposal would take only a few seconds, Matt couldn't agree. "It's just a minor problem, not a major repair."

"Come on, Carol," Casey argued. "I'm the one who jammed the disposal, and if he can fix it, let him do it. Of course, if it's going to take awhile, I could give Suzanne a ride home so she wouldn't have to wait."

Rather than demonstrate just how quickly he could get the job done, Matt waited for Suzanne to object to Casey's offer, but she seemed not to mind, and neither did he. He looked at Carol, hoping she had no idea how to reset the disposal herself but she appeared to be too flustered to either ask him to stay or tell him to leave, providing him with the choice of either quickly resetting the disposal and walking out with Suzanne, or staying with Carol. Matt had seldom made up his mind so quickly.

He leaned back against the edge of the sink. "That's real nice of you, Casey. I'd hate to force Carol to go to the expense of hiring another plumber when I'm here and after having such a delicious meal, I'd say it's the least I can do. If you'd rather not wait, Suzanne, why don't you go with Casey and I'll call you next week about the reunion."

In an almost comical exchange of smiles and goodbyes, Casey and Suzanne left. Appalled by how quickly she had been abandoned, Carol yanked open a drawer and hurriedly rummaged through her cutlery. "There's a special wrench that came with the disposal. It should be here somewhere."

Content to watch Carol inventory the entire

kitchen if she wished, Matt remained in a relaxed pose next to the sink. "Whoever did your remodeling did an excellent job. The tile work's especially good."

Carol kept shuffling through the crowded drawer. "The credit belongs to Russell's interior design department. I chose them because of the quality of their work, not just because I'd receive a discount."

"Well, they were a good choice. Do you want me to help you look?"

"No, I'm sure I tossed it into this drawer when I got it, so it has to still be here." She gestured with a rosette iron. "Somewhere."

There was a tremor in her voice, and fearing she was becoming upset, Matt walked up beside her, reached into the cluttered drawer and withdrew a slender aluminum rod. An elongated S-shape, it was stamped with the brand name of the disposal. "This is it."

Had he begun performing magic tricks and conjured up a bouquet of silk flowers, Carol couldn't have been more surprised, or felt more foolish. "I don't know how I missed it."

Matt waited for her to turn toward him. "Yes, you do."

Although he had been sitting outdoors for several hours, Carol still caught a hint of the sweet, musky scent of his cologne. He was right. She had been too distracted to conduct a thoughtful search and it was all his fault. Clearly he wanted her to admit it, but she slammed the drawer shut, crossed her arms over her chest, leaned back against the counter, and stubbornly refused.

Amused rather than annoyed by her defiant stance, Matt considered taking his time resetting the disposal, then decided he ought not to push his luck. He first checked to be certain there weren't any more bones in it, then opened the cupboard beneath the sink, removed the waste basket, bent down, and reset the disposal in the few seconds he had anticipated.

"Come here," he called. "I'll show you how to do this yourself the next time."

Matt's curls brushed his collar, and Carol had to fight the ridiculous impulse to reach out and slide her fingers through the soft, silver waves. She had never met another man she had longed to pet, and certain she ought not to touch Matt, she knelt down beside him. She realized her mistake instantly for now they were so close their noses were almost touching. He smiled, then explained how to use the unusual wrench, but she couldn't have repeated a word of his instructions, let alone followed them, and rose as soon as he finished his brief lesson.

Matt replaced the waste basket, turned on the water, and tried out the disposal to make certain it was again functioning with a powerful hum.

He handed Carol the wrench, but deliberately brushed her palm with his fingertips when he released it. He watched her jump back and couldn't help but laugh.

"You needn't be so afraid of me. I don't bite."

It wasn't a bite Carol feared, but when his sly smile promised a wealth of delicious diversions, she didn't want to invite him to do more than he already had. "Thank you. I didn't realize you'd finish so quickly."

"I did, though, and it's real likely that Casey did too."

Carol took a step back, unconsciously putting more space between them. "What are you saying? That he deliberately jammed the disposal so you'd offer to stay and he could take Suzanne home?"

"No, I doubt it was deliberate. But when it happened, he made the most of it and his ploy worked, didn't it?"

While asking Matt to spend the night definitely crossed Carol's mind, the idea absolutely appalled her. She barely knew him and besides, he was a plumber of all things! she reminded herself in a desperate bid to suppress the desire he aroused with each teasing glance.

"All I know is that my plans for the evening end right here," she announced suddenly. "I'm not interested in casual sex."

"Did I say I was?"

Carol shook her head. "You don't have to put it in words when you lace every word and gesture with an erotic innuendo. While it's flattering, I'd rather not rush into something I'd undoubtedly soon regret. I told you I'd been married twice. What about you? Have you had multiple wives, or don't you believe in marriage?"

While Matt had definitely amazed her on several occasions that evening, she was alarmed by the transformation in him now. In the space of a heartbeat his demeanor changed completely, erasing all trace of the cocky, self-assured attitude that had made her so uncomfortable. The pride left his posture, and his taunting gaze clouded with pain.

"I've only been married once. Deborah and I were together twenty-five years. She died four years ago, after what the papers referred to as 'a lengthy bout with cancer,' but that didn't begin to tell the story of what a courageous woman she was." Carol's question had plunged him into an icy well of self-pity, and disgusted with himself rather than her, Matt turned away. "Thanks again for dinner."

"Matt?" Carol called to him, but he walked out of her house without looking back. She went to the front window and watched him drive away in a white pickup truck. While she now knew it had been a mistake to ask Casey to the reunion, she was positive she had just behaved so badly Matt would no longer have any interest in her, and surely that was a far worse blunder.

Matt got only a half block down Carol's street before he had to pull over to the curb and park. Although he had greeted Deborah's death as a blessed release from pain, it had taken him as long as any widower who had adored his wife to recover from her loss. He had neglected his business while she had been ill, but work had been his salvation once she was gone. He and Dan had increased their profits despite the slow economy, but he hadn't spent anything on himself.

He hadn't taken any splendid vacations, nor made any friends who would have enriched what little spare time he allowed himself. He had stubbornly denied he was lonely, and ignored Dan's encouragement to get out and meet another woman. He had actually convinced himself he was fine and preferred being alone, but Carol's flip reference to marriage had shattered that illusion. Fine man that he was, he had walked out on her.

Wiping the threat of tears from his eyes, he decided he couldn't wait a week and mumble some inane excuse at the reunion. Knowing Carol deserved better from him, he drove back to her house, and rehearsed his excuse as he walked up to the front door. When she answered his knock, he gave it his best shot.

"I owe you an apology and not just for walking out, for the whole evening. I've felt nothing but numb for so long I'm afraid I've forgotten how to behave with a desirable woman and—"

Carol opened the screen door, reached for his hand, and drew him inside. "Kiss me good night, and I'll forgive you anything."

"I haven't ruined things?"

Matt had definitely ruined Carol's complacent view of life, but she dared not admit something so important as that. She raised her hands to his shoulders, and as he began to incline his head, she closed her eyes. Afraid to hope his kiss would be as magical as his glance promised, she held her breath but the instant his lips touched hers with a light caress, she knew he would never disappoint her. His mouth was warm, and his first tentative kiss so enticing she slid her fingers through his curls to encourage more and he gave it so willingly she melted into his embrace.

Her conscience put up such a faint argument about rushing things that it was easily muffled by the pounding beat of her heart. When Matt was the first to pull away, she couldn't hide her dismay. He leaned back against the door, but left his arms draped around her waist.

"Now do you understand why I don't like to look back?" he asked.

All Carol could manage was a slight nod.

"Good. I'd like to see you tomorrow. Are you free?"

"What day is tomorrow?"

Her muddled expression prompted Matt to laugh. "Sunday, but it's hard for me to believe it's been so long since you were kissed that you've forgotten what day it is."

Embarrassed, Carol tried to step back, but Matt refused to release her. She didn't want to admit anything about other men when just looking at him felt so incredibly good. Touching him had been even better, and his kisses had enveloped her in such a delicious heat she didn't want to say or do anything stupid to spoil it.

"I'm sure you must have that same effect on most women," she countered. "I don't have any plans for tomorrow. What would you like to do?"

Matt responded with a suggestively raised brow, and then enjoying her blush, offered a discreet alternative. "It should be a nice day. Let's go over to the Huntington Library and walk around the grounds."

"I'd like that." Carol heard Matt say he'd pick her up at one, but all she really wanted was another kiss which he provided with a lazy insistence that left her clinging to the door long after he had gone.

* * *

Suzanne lived in southwest Pasadena in a charming wood bungalow built in the 1920's. It was too dark by the time Casey brought her home to see her flower-filled yard, but the night-blooming jasmine scenting the warm air gave abundant proof of her gardening talents. As they climbed the steps to the wide veranda, the conversation that had flowed so easily between them all afternoon dissolved into an embarrassed silence.

Occasionally a date from Perfect Match called for Suzanne at home, but at the end of the evening they invariably mumbled something about being busy with work or that Pasadena was too far from their homes to visit frequently. Readily understanding those comments were prompted by a complete lack of interest, she didn't bother to ask them to stay for awhile. As Suzanne fumbled for her key, she wondered if she ought to invite Casey in for coffee. Thinking perhaps he had had enough of her company for one day, she was reluctant to make such an offer and force him to refuse. Casey, however, surprised her.

"If it's not too late," he said, "I'd love to see some of your art collection."

He was carrying her salad bowl, and after unlocking the door, Suzanne took it from him. "Would you really? Come on in then and I'll make us some coffee. There is a path, but you'll still have to be careful where you step. I'm afraid it will take me awhile to unpack things for you. As I said earlier, I really need to build storage and display space for everything."

She had left a light burning, and as he crossed over the threshold, Casey found her home not only decorated with a delightfully eclectic assortment of Victorian furnishings, but also cluttered with stacks of cardboard boxes, a precariously high heap of magazines, and bookshelves so overburdened they appeared in danger of imminent collapse. Shocked that Suzanne could abide living in such grossly disorganized surroundings, he paused, but caught himself before making the type of critical remark he knew had infuriated Carol.

"It must be difficult having to carry all these boxes back and forth to Cal State," he sympathized instead.

Suzanne set the salad bowl on the dining room table, then went on into the kitchen and turned on the light. "It certainly is. I wish I could keep more things in my office, but I'm sharing it with another professor who has as much or more than I do and that makes it impossible."

Casey walked through the dining room, and relieved to find it held no more than an oak table, chairs, and a china cabinet, followed Suzanne into the kitchen. Small by today's standards, it was painted a sunny yellow and spotlessly clean. "Can I help?"

"I'm just making coffee. Are you still hungry? I could fix something more if you are, or there's the cake Aimee gave us."

"No, I'll probably stay full for several days. Coffee will be plenty." Casey debated with himself a moment, and then felt he had to make a suggestion. "If you're really serious about displaying your collection of artifacts, I'd be happy to help you make some plans. After all, it wouldn't be all that different from designing displays for coffeepots and toaster ovens."

Suzanne took two bright blue ceramic mugs from the cupboard and set them by the coffee maker. "I definitely need help," she readily admitted, "but I can't afford to have Russell's design crew do the work."

"I wasn't trying to get a commission for them. I'm offering to do it myself, and if you'll buy the materials, I'll provide the labor for free."

Suzanne filled the mugs with freshly brewed coffee. "Do you take cream or sugar?"

"No, just black." Casey joined her at the kitchen table. The coffee wasn't as strong as he liked it, but he wisely kept that thought to himself. "What we ought to do first is unpack everything. We can just lay it out on the floor, try different groupings, and get some idea of how much space will be required."

"That sounds good," Suzanne agreed. She wasn't certain what had prompted Casey to volunteer his expertise, and didn't want to misunderstand his motives. "You're a very nice person," she began. "But—"

"Thank you, I think you're very nice too, but I don't like the sound of that, 'but.' Is there something wrong?"

Carol had described Casey as cute, but Suzanne thought he was quite good looking. They had formed an easy rapport in the relaxed atmosphere at Carol's, but now that they were alone together, she grew apprehensive. "You seem happy to help with whatever needs to be done, whether it's barbecuing chicken or doing dishes, but I hope you don't regard me as some pathetically needy woman who can't manage on her own."

"Not at all," Casey assured her. "Where did you get such a bizarre idea? I'd like to see you again, but that doesn't mean I want to run your life."

Suzanne was now positive she had said the wrong thing, but with Frank, too much had gone unsaid and she did not want to make the same mistake with Casey. "I'm sorry. I didn't mean to hurt your feelings. It's just, well, how old are you, Casey?"

"I'm forty-six. Is that a problem?"

"It might be. I don't feel any different than I did as a teenager, but I am fifty-two."

"So?"

Since her divorce, Suzanne had dated a number of men, but none had been younger. She turned her mug slowly rather than look at him. "I think it's important for people to understand each other right from the beginning. Otherwise, each might have expectations the other doesn't realize and can't ever meet. I really hope to find someone who'll be eager to share my life with the same wildly, passionate enthusiasm I'll share his. At forty-six, you probably date younger women who can give you children. My daughter's twenty-six, and that's all the family I intend to have."

Searching for a way to respond, Casey sat back and simply stared. With a mass of long red curls and a voluptuous figure, Suzanne had impressed him as being a warmly affectionate Earth mother type, but he could not recall ever meeting another woman who had stated what she wanted in such explicit terms on the first date. He then had to remind himself this wasn't even a date. He cleared his throat, and hoped he wouldn't sound like a complete ass.

"I come from what is now described as a dysfunctional family and I decided long ago that I didn't want to risk repeating my parents' mistakes by having children of my own. I also don't need to prop up my ego with younger women. Besides, you're a remarkably youthful fifty-two, Suzanne, and I doubt anyone who saw us together would guess we aren't the same age. What does six years matter anyway? I don't give a damn how old you are."

He looked quite emphatic about it too, and embarrassed, Suzanne felt very foolish. "Thank you. I've enjoyed meeting you too."

"All right then, let's just worry about your artifacts for the time being, and let our relationship take care of itself."

Suzanne couldn't agree. "I can't abide the word *relationship*. It's such a vapid term."

That Suzanne might have a temper hadn't occurred to Casey, but it wasn't really surprising in a woman who claimed to want passion, and he just shrugged. "You're absolutely right. Shall we just work on being friends?"

"Yes, I'd like that."

Casey checked his watch. "It's too late to start sorting your things tonight. How about tomorrow? If eleven's a good time, I'll bring the ingredients for my favorite omelet and make brunch."

Suzanne walked him to her front door. "That's very sweet of you, but I'd swear you told me you'd probably not eat for days, and I'm too full to think about food tonight. Besides, if you're here helping me, I ought to feed you, not the other way around."

"Well, regardless of how I feel tonight, I know I'll be hungry tomorrow. I enjoy cooking, and it's not much fun to cook for myself."

Suzanne took a deep breath. Casey was nice, but she was beginning to feel smothered and that was a most uncomfortable sensation. That he was so eager to be helpful was touching, but she wondered if he weren't just lonely and she didn't want to be a convenient peg for him to hang his troubles on. She also didn't want to judge him so harshly after only a few hours conversation.

"I've never had a man cook for me. If you'd really like to prepare brunch for us, please do."

Casey broke into a wide grin. "See you at eleven then."

Suzanne hoped she hadn't gotten herself into something she'd regret. Then again, it would be nice to be pampered for a change. She closed her door and surveyed her living room with a troubled gaze. It wasn't really shelves she wanted, but love. She just hoped that if Casey proved to be the right man, she still had enough love to give in return.

Four

Karen opened the back door and bent down to pull an overloaded wicker laundry basket onto the service porch. "Good morning!" she called.

Aimee looked up from the Sunday comics. "Good morning, hon." She got up and went to the kitchen doorway to watch her daughter sort what had to be three weeks' worth of paint-splattered laundry. "Looks like you'll be here most of the day. Want some breakfast?"

Karen had her father's dark curly hair and hazel eyes, and Aimee's tall, lithe figure, but the sweetness of her features was distinctly her own. "Sure. Let's make pancakes."

Making pancakes had been a weekend ritual when her daughters were small and Aimee was glad to continue it. She looked forward to their visits, and never considered their using her laundry facilities an imposition as some parents of grown children did. By the time Karen had her first load of wash in the machine, Aimee had three buttermilk pancakes bubbling on the griddle.

"I had dinner at Carol's last night, so I only made half a recipe."

Karen poured herself a glass of cranberry juice and leaned back against the counter. "What was the occasion?"

"No occasion really. The Cortéz High reunion is next Saturday night and Carol wanted a dry run."

"Why? You and Carol certainly know each other well. Wasn't Suzanne Marsh there too?"

"Yes, but they wanted their dates to have a chance to get acquainted."

Greatly intrigued, Karen moved around the cooking island to face her mother. "Didn't you have a date too?"

Aimee flipped the pancakes with effortless grace, but studiously avoided looking up at her daughter. "No, I don't need a date for the reunion to enjoy it."

Karen sank down into a chair at the table and picked up the comics. "Mother, really, that line is getting old."

"And so am I."

"Is that going to be your new excuse: that you're too old to enjoy a man's company? I'll never be that old!"

Aimee didn't doubt Karen's vow, for from the moment she had entered nursery school at two and discovered little boys existed, she had been enormously fond of them. Aimee put the golden-brown pancakes on a blue-bordered plate and handed it to Karen.

"I doubt that you will, but your life has been very different from mine. At your age, I was a widow with two little girls to raise."

Karen got up to get the bottle of syrup from the cupboard. "Yes, and JoAnne and I turned out beautifully, but I'm worried about you."

Concentrating on cooking, Aimee poured three more circles of batter onto the griddle. With a steaming hiss it slowly puffed into the deliciously light pancakes she and her daughters loved. "I'm the mother here; worrying is my job."

"I disagree. I think you'd benefit from several sessions with a therapist."

Shocked, Aimee gestured with the pancake turner. "Why? Because I'm happy without a man? That's a reason for congratulations, not therapy."

Karen dripped a lacy filigree of syrup over her pancakes. "No it isn't. You're not nearly as well-adjusted as you'd like everyone to believe. I think you're more afraid of men than content to live without them."

"With good reason," Aimee swore under her breath.

"That may very well be true, but you're no coward and you ought to try again."

Aimee flipped the pancakes none too gently. "That's enough, Karen. I appreciate your concern, but I don't need your advice. Besides, I'd rather hear the latest about Roger."

Karen feigned a tortured moan as she scooped up a bite of pancake. "Roger is terminally self-absorbed, and I've finally had it with him. I told him so last night but I doubt he heard me. Then again, maybe he just didn't care."

"You admire his work."

"Yes I do, that's what drew me to him in the first place but I've decided two artists make for a totally incompatible, rather than superb match."

Aimee dropped two more pancakes on Karen's plate, and kept the last one for herself. She took the chair beside her daughter and reached for the syrup. "You're extremely talented. Is he jealous?"

"Very, but it's not just my work that bothers him. It's everything about me. He criticizes me for coming from a rich family and when he's really on a roll, he blames me for all of society's ills."

"We aren't rich!" Aimee surveyed her kitchen

with an amused glance. She still loved the delicate pink and blue floral wallpaper, but after seven years it was beginning to fade. Steve had left enough insurance money for her to remain in their family home in San Marino and raise their girls in a nice neighborhood, but there had been plenty of years when it had been a tough struggle.

Her current challenge was saving the money to repair a garage roof that leaked so badly the structure resembled a carwash when it rained. Working in a bank, she could have easily arranged for a loan, but she took pride in staying out of debt unless it was a life-threatening emergency and a leaky roof just didn't qualify. That Roger assumed she was rich was ludicrous.

"I know we're not," Karen agreed, "but compared to his parents we are. Damn leftist punk. I'm through with him. Thank God I never let him move into my studio."

Keying in on the comforting chugging rhythm of the washing machine, Aimee tried not to shriek her next question. "I didn't realize things were that serious between you. Did he suggest living together?"

Despite Aimee's attempt at self-control, Karen read her mother's expression accurately. "Sorry, I didn't mean to shock you. He brought up the subject a couple of times, but in a sort of teasing way. You know the kind of remark people make when they aren't sure what the reaction will be? If I'd said yes, he would have gone running to get his things, but if I'd said no, he would have sworn he was only kidding. As it was, I didn't respond either way. He's always been difficult, and I just didn't want to have him around full-time."

Relieved, Aimee found a smile. "That's a wise decision, honey. If he's so critical, then he isn't the right man for you." Aimee longed for her daughters to find men as fine as their father.

Karen wiped up a puddle of syrup with her last bite of pancake. "I know he isn't, but it would be a whole lot easier to break up with him if he weren't so damn good-looking. There are times when I feel like I'm trapped in some horrid joke. Roger and I have so much in common that we ought to be one of the great couples of all time, but he's just so damn hostile it's never going to happen and I'm tired of slugging away at an impossible dream. I wish I could remember Dad. Was he really as wonderful as you say?"

"Even better, sweetheart, and he would have been so proud of you."

Karen watched as an all too familiar sheen of tears brightened her mother's gaze. "He shouldn't have been the only one for you, Mom. Bill was simply an aberration. You'll never run into another scumbag like him. Maybe you'll find an exciting man at the reunion."

Aimee had no such hopes. "You're forgetting I knew them all when they were eighteen. If they didn't excite me then, they certainly won't now."

"Not necessarily," Karen argued. "It takes men several years longer than women to mature. Maybe someone will surprise you."

"Well, even if he does, he'll be there with his wife or a date so nothing will come of it. Carol's already warned me I'll be the only one there alone."

Karen looked sincerely pained. "Do you want me to ask Roger to take you? He looks terrific in a tux and if you insist he keep his political opinions to himself, he'll be sure to impress your friends."

For a mere instant, Aimee imagined herself walking into the ballroom of the Ritz Carlton with Roger by her side. The temperamental artist might be difficult, but with an impressive build, thick blond curls, and bright blue eyes, he was definitely a hunk.

"Thank you, but I'm not even tempted, besides, I thought you weren't speaking to him."

"I'm not, but it will take him at least a week to notice." Karen reached out to take her mother's hand. "This isn't right, Mom. Neither of us was meant to be alone."

Aimee folded her hand over Karen's. "Unfortunately life doesn't always have happy endings, sweetheart, but if Roger isn't right for you, you'll soon find someone who is. You're much too young to be alone."

"So are you!"

Aimee shook her head, for while she might still have a remarkably youthful appearance, in her heart, where it really mattered, she was the oldest woman alive, and she knew love wouldn't come her way again.

Casey arrived at Suzanne's house ten minutes early but forced himself to sit in his car until eleven so as not to appear pitifully eager to see her again. A neighbor out watering the ivy bordering his lawn kept eyeing him suspiciously, but Casey just nodded and smiled as though he had every right to be parked where he was. Finally eleven arrived and he walked up to Suzanne's door carrying a cumbersome bag of groceries.

Suzanne greeted Casey warmly, then reached for the bag. "Here, let me get that."

"No, I'll take it into the kitchen," Casey insisted, and without waiting for her to lead the way, he followed the meandering path from the living room into the dining room and on into the kitchen. "It's a lovely day," he called to Suzanne. "Do you have a table outside?"

Suzanne had been right behind him but because the kitchen was too small for both of them to work together comfortably, she paused at the kitchen doorway. Along with a carton of eggs, Casey had brought milk, butter, cheddar cheese, sour cream, an avocado, croissants, his favorite pan, and a pancake turner. She expected him to pull an apron from the bottom of the bag, and was surprised to find he hadn't included one.

"I didn't want you to go to so much trouble," she murmured apologetically.

"It's no trouble. This is what I do for fun."

"Maybe you should have been a chef."

"I was one once, but gave it up. Do you have a mixing bowl and a plate I can use?"

Suzanne entered the kitchen to get him what he needed, but then returned to the doorway to keep out of his way. Thinking they would be busy sorting her collection, she had put on a pair of worn jeans and a purple T-shirt printed with Hopi kachinas but with Casey preparing such a special breakfast, she felt as though she ought to have worn a dress. He was wearing Levi's and a blue and green plaid shirt, and embarrassed she did not look nearly as nice, she tugged on the hem of her T-shirt.

"If cooking is fun for you, why did you quit?" she asked.

Casey glanced over his shoulder. "It's a sad story; are you sure you want to hear it?"

"Not if it will make you sad to tell it."

Casey nodded. "That's very considerate of you. Do you have a grater? I forgot to bring mine."

Again Suzanne left her post to provide the utensil he needed. "Would you like some coffee? I just made it."

Casey had been afraid of that, but again held his tongue about the strength of the brew. "Thank you. I would like a cup." He stopped grating cheese while she poured their coffee, then raised his mug in a mock toast. When his first sip proved to be as strong as he liked it, he broke into a grateful smile.

"I used to live in San Francisco," he began. "The city is noted for its fine restaurants and I had no trouble getting work as a chef. When I married, my wife and I began saving our money in hopes of one day owning a little place of our own in Sausalito. The trouble was, I worked most nights, and while my pay was very good, and our savings were adding up quickly, Melanie got very lonely."

He paused to take a fortifying gulp of coffee. "I'm sure you can imagine what happened. She found someone else, and got most of our savings in the divorce settlement. I decided right then and there that work as a chef and being a husband were incompatible goals, and came down to L.A. and went to work for Russell's. Now I have regular hours, but my hopes for finding another wife haven't materialized, as yet," he added with a grin.

Suzanne set her mug down on the counter. "Do you really mean that you left a career you loved so you'd be better able to please a woman you'd not even met?"

Casey hadn't thought of it that way, but after a moment's reflection agreed. "Does that sound so strange?"

"It's usually women who are forced to make choices between their careers and having families, not men, so I'm just surprised is all." She frowned slightly. "I think you should be able to do whatever work you love, and find a woman who'll support you in that career."

"That's the ideal of course, but I know I'd have gotten lonely if it had been Melanie who worked late every night."

Suzanne was afraid to ask her next question, but did anyway. "Would you have been unfaithful to her?"

Casey shook his head. "No. Like I said last night, I don't come from the ideal family, and having a home and wife meant a great deal to me. I'd not have jeopardized my marriage for anything, but Melanie didn't have the same priorities."

"Obviously not. That must have been a painful discovery."

Casey set his mug aside and went back to grating the thick block of cheese. "Yes, you could certainly say so, but now I don't know which was worse, losing Melanie, or giving up the dream of owning my own place. Love doesn't survive betrayal, but dreams, well, they have a way of hanging on long after the means to make them come true is gone."

Suzanne's voice was warmly encouraging. "You're still a young man, Casey; you can own your own restaurant if that's what you really want."

"Yes, I know, but without someone to share in its success, what would be the point?"

"Pleasing yourself!" Fearing she had stated her opinion far too emphatically, Suzanne went outside to sweep off the deck. She had not thought of eating outdoors until Casey had suggested it, but now wished she had been better organized. Of course, that was her whole problem: she just wasn't organized. That was why Casey was here, but whatever his organizational skills might be, she felt sorry for him. She was just leaning against her broom, gazing out across the backyard when he joined her.

"Oh, I'm sorry," she said. "Are you ready to eat?"

"No, I've not even started the omelets, but I was worried about you. I hope I didn't say the wrong thing."

Suzanne licked her lips. Casey was very attractive, and she thought if he didn't try so terribly hard they would have as much fun as they had had at Carol's party, but now he seemed so desperately eager to please she just ached for him. "Casey, you're such a nice person, but—"

Casey started to back away. "I understand, you've begun to find me tiresome. You needn't go into detail. I'll just get my pan and go. Make whatever you like out of the things I brought."

Suzanne threw her broom aside with a careless toss and it clattered down the steps and landed on the grass. "You aren't going anywhere until you've served me the omelet you promised." She yanked open the back door, and gestured for him to precede her. "When I give someone my word on something, I follow through, and I expect the same from you."

Her cheeks were a bright pink, and thinking anger most becoming, Casey shrugged helplessly. "Wait a minute. I always keep my word too. I was just afraid I was no longer welcome here."

"Why would you think that?"

The answer to her question too painful to

admit, Casey looked away. "It's just an impression I get sometime."

"From whom? Parents who weren't loving, or a wife who let you down? Is that why you try so hard to make people like you?"

Casey had to swallow hard before he found an answer. "I didn't realize I was so transparent."

Suzanne reached out to give his shoulder a sympathetic squeeze. "You're not transparent at all. It's just that every quarter I can count on having several students who'll constantly seek my approval. They might do excellent work, but never seem to be able to appreciate their own worth. I refer them to the campus guidance clinic where the counselors can give them the help they need. Did you have any kind of counseling after your divorce?"

Casey shook his head. "My wife left me for another man; I certainly didn't want to talk about it."

"Well, that was a mistake, and believe me I know because I stayed married to a man with whom I shared nothing except the same mailing address and had I had sense enough to see a marriage counselor I would have left him years before I did. Now come on, let's have breakfast so we can get started on sorting my things."

Casey opened his mouth, then caught himself

before he asked her if she really liked him. After all, she had just insisted that he cook breakfast and help her sort her treasures and for now, that was more than enough to satisfy his need to be wanted.

Carol Hagan couldn't remember the last time she had visited the Huntington Library, but it wasn't the railroad magnate Henry E. Huntington's magnificent collection of rare volumes and priceless art she was anxious to see. She didn't care if she and Matt didn't even leave the parking lot. She just wanted to spend the afternoon with him so badly it frightened her.

She had changed her clothes half a dozen times before deciding on her favorite sundress. A floral print in shades of coral and rose, it flattered her figure as well as her fair coloring and always gave her spirits a boost when she wore it. She had slept fitfully, if at all, and hoped that her conversation wouldn't be punctuated by yawns. Not that she was worried about falling asleep in Matt's company, but she didn't want to spoil the afternoon by appearing bored.

She paced the living room as she waited for Matt to arrive, now uncertain what had possessed her to yank him through the door and kiss him as she had last night, but ever so grateful that she had. Still, as wonderful as that blissful moment had been, she didn't want to hope for more that day. What if it had merely been a fluke? she agonized. What if she didn't find Matt nearly as attractive that day, or God forbid, what if he quickly lost interest in her?

When his truck pulled up in front of her house at one, she ran to the kitchen for a final sip of water so her mouth wouldn't be so dry her lips would stick to her teeth when she smiled. She got back in time to watch him walk up to her door, and felt the same ridiculous rush as when Suzanne had first introduced him. "He's Suzanne's date," she reminded herself as she opened her door, but when he smiled at her, she wanted him too badly to care.

It wasn't until she spotted one of her neighbors watching her climb into Matt's truck that she remembered he was a plumber. At least he didn't have the name of his firm painted on the truck, but she could tell by her neighbor's astonished frown that he had never expected to see her drive off in a pick-up truck. Snob, she whispered under her breath, but it hurt to know how swiftly most people would judge Matt by the kind of car he drove.

"You're awfully quiet," Matt chided.

"Am I? Well, I've not done much this morning other than read the *Times* and I guess that didn't inspire much in the way of conversation."

"What did you think of the president's latest statement on the economy?"

In truth, Carol had been so busy selecting her outfit she hadn't done more than glance at the headlines. "I'm sorry, I didn't really study his remarks in depth. I'll make a point of it when I get home. After all, Russell's sales are dependent on California's economy, and I can't afford to let myself get out of touch."

Matt studied Carol with a sidelong glance. "Am I making you nervous, or do you have something else on your mind?"

Caught off guard, Carol quickly looked away. "You make me very nervous," she admitted.

"Why?"

He was wearing the same delicious scent as before, but she couldn't bring herself to blame her distracted state on his cologne. "You're a very handsome man."

"Really? Well, most women don't faint dead away when I walk by them. It took Suzanne more than twenty years to work up enough interest to ask me for a date. In my opinion, that doesn't say much for my sex appeal."

Sorry he had mentioned Suzanne, Carol stood up for her friend. "She hasn't been divorced long, and you weren't available either until recently. Now could we discuss something other than Suzanne? I'm beginning to feel guilty."

"Why? I'll bet she's with Casey. Do you want to stop and call her?"

"No, that's the last thing I want to do."

"Are you often plagued by a guilty conscience?"

"Never," Carol swore.

"Not until now, you mean."

Carol nodded. The afternoon was one of the absolutely glorious warm and clear kind that seduces tourists and prompts them to make California their home. She had wanted so badly to be charming and witty, but she was rapidly losing what little confidence she had. "I haven't dated much," she blurted out.

"You're still ahead of me. I haven't dated at all."

Carol turned toward him. He held the steering wheel in a relaxed grasp, readily conveying the competence with which he apparently approached all aspects of his life. While she was glad he wasn't seeing several other women, to be the first one to interest him after his wife's death was an uncomfortable burden. Feeling woefully inadequate, she glanced out the window and wished she weren't so damn intimidated she couldn't even think.

Matt reached for the knob to turn on the radio, and then doubting Carol would like country and western music he drew back his hand. He wished she hadn't turned so shy, but just being with her was nice even if she didn't feel like making conversation. When he drove through the impressive wrought iron gates at the Oxford Road entrance of the Huntington, he pulled a ten dollar bill from his pocket.

"Wait," Carol begged as she began to fumble in her purse. "Let me get this."

"No way." Matt took the brochures the guard offered and passed him the bill. "I'm definitely old-fashioned when it comes to money. I don't think much of a man who'll live off a woman."

"That's not the case here. You drove, so it's only fair for me to pay the entrance fee," Carol argued.

"It's just a couple of miles, and I asked you, remember?" The library opened in the morning on weekends, and the artfully landscaped parking lot was already half filled but he soon found a place to park. "Now just stay put and I'll open your door."

Carol did as he asked, but she could not recall the last time she hadn't opened a door herself. When he didn't just open her door, but reached in, took ahold of her waist and lifted her out of the truck, she was more startled than pleased. Then she looked up at him, and his smile was so charming, the complaint that had flown to her mind was forgotten before it reached her lips.

Matt took her hand and started toward the

end of the parking lot where a stream of camera-toting visitors was funneled toward the entrance of the library. "Looks like everyone has brought their relatives from out-of-town today. Do you want to visit the gallery and see *Blue Boy* and *Pinkie,* or just go for a walk?"

"It's too pretty to be inside," Carol urged, but as they walked past the Beaux Arts mansion that housed one of the art collections, she wondered if it wouldn't have been smart to insist upon touring the library's current exhibition. The Gutenberg Bible was always worth seeing, and she knew whatever else had been put on display would undoubtedly inspire far more interesting conversation than she seemed to be capable of producing. As they entered the Shakespeare garden where plants mentioned in the playwright's works are featured, along with accompanying quotes, she seized the opportunity to read them aloud.

Speaking Shakespeare's words rather than her own was an immense relief and by the time they moved on to the rose garden, Carol wasn't nearly so tense. She stopped to savor a lush yellow bloom and Matt laughed easily with her as the petals fell away under her touch. Deciding it was permissible to just be with him rather than having to keep him amused, Carol brushed his cheek with a light kiss.

"Thank you," she murmured softly.

"For what?"

"For just being fun to be with."

Matt had lived in a painful fog for so long, it took him a moment to realize Carol was sincere. They were having fun, and doing nothing more strenuous than strolling Henry Huntington's luxurious estate. He heard someone calling her name, and turned with her to see a striking brunette hurrying their way. "A friend of yours?" he asked.

"An attorney with my ex-husband's firm," Carol whispered. She had never particularly liked the woman, and would not have approached her, but having been seen, she attempted to make the best of it and introduced Matt to her. "It's been a couple of years since I last saw you, Gloria. How have you been?"

"Busy, as always. I'm here with a client I ought not to neglect, but I did want to say hello." Bright red acrylic nails accented her fluttering gesture as she reached out to touch Matt's arm. "You look so familiar. I'm positive we've met somewhere, or perhaps I've just seen you at the courthouse. What firm are you with?"

"Trenerry and Son, we're plumbers, and I don't recall ever doing any work at a courthouse."

Gloria's false eyelashes brushed her brows. "You're a plumber? Well, now isn't that an interesting career choice." She took a step backward. "You'll have to excuse me, I don't want my client to get lost in the underbrush. We should really get together sometime soon for lunch, Carol. I miss our shopping trips. Give me a call."

Carol was angry about the way Gloria had dismissed Matt. "I had forgotten just how much I despise that woman," she revealed as soon as Gloria had turned away.

"Why? Just because she isn't impressed by a plumber? I'll warn you now, no one is. Occasionally someone will refuse to shake hands with me, as though they're afraid I regularly wash mine in a toilet."

There wasn't a trace of laughter in Matt's eyes now and Carol understood he was being dead serious. "The world is filled with pompous fools and Gloria and my ex-husband are among them. I really don't care what you do for a living. I buy sportswear for a department store. That's scarcely an exalted position."

Carol looked ready to back up her words with her fists, and Matt couldn't help but be amused. "I can defend myself, but thanks for trying to make me feel better."

First thing Monday morning, Carol knew Gloria would tell Cliff she had seen his ex-wife with a plumber, and Cliff would call her before noon. He would undoubtedly have a legitimate excuse for the call, but he would be sure to mention he knew she was dating a plumber. She could hear the snicker in his voice now and felt the same sickening wave of dread his sarcastic teasing had always inspired.

She slipped her arm through Matt's. "Let's go bang the gong over in the Japanese garden until we give everyone here a gigantic headache."

"Sounds like my kind of fun, lead the way."

Carol tried to smile but couldn't. She liked Matt; she really did. She was ashamed of herself for being no more generous than Gloria in her views when Suzanne had first mentioned inviting him to the reunion. God, she had completely forgotten about Suzanne, but she sincerely hoped Matt was right about her being with Casey that afternoon. She gave Matt's arm an affectionate squeeze. She didn't feel like she was slumming, but the sorry fact that other people would accuse her of it hurt. She hated being put on the defensive, but as she glanced up at Matt, she couldn't think of anyone she would rather defend.

Five

When Matt brought Carol home, her son Rob's red Porsche was parked in her driveway. "Would you like to meet him?" she asked.

"Sure," Matt agreed, but he left after exchanging no more than half a dozen halting sentences with the young man, leaving Carol feeling both perplexed and disappointed.

Rob crossed to the window and watched Matt drive away. "I didn't realize the rugged outdoorsman type appealed to you, Mom. What sort of work does he do?"

Carol had known that question was coming, and even more surely, how negative Rob's reaction would be to the answer. She had hoped the afternoon would end on a pleasant note, but Matt's abrupt departure had already marred it. Pretending a confidence she really didn't have, she looked Rob in the eye as she replied. "He's a plumbing contractor."

"A plumber?" Rob winced. "You've got to be kidding."

Rob had inherited his father's dark good looks. The quintessential yuppie, he was dressed in a pink Izod shirt and neatly pressed chinos. He kept his hair neatly trimmed, his extensive wardrobe organized by color, and his expensive car washed and waxed. Carol had always been proud of him, but from the hour of his birth he had been more his father's son than hers. That he had followed Bob into dentistry, a profession demanding minute perfection, had not surprised anyone who knew him.

"No, I'm not kidding," she replied wearily. "He's also bright and attractive. You ought to know it's impossible to judge a man's character from his profession, and in the future, I'll thank you to keep your prejudices to yourself."

Carol's rebuke didn't faze Rob. "How did you meet him? The cesspool overflow?"

"You know damn well we don't have a cesspool." Exasperated, Carol walked into the kitchen and opened the refrigerator, but she was too annoyed to have much appetite and removed only a bottle of water. She poured herself a drink, then sat down at the kitchen table and began sorting through the pape[illegible] looking for the article Matt had mentioned o[illegible]
omy.

Rob followed his mother into t[illegible]

"You ought to have higher standards," he cautioned, deliberately repeating her phrasing. "You're a class act, Mom; you shouldn't have to settle for a plumber."

"I am not settling," Carol argued. In her opinion, Rob's tastes ran to bimbos he dropped with ungentlemanly haste. "We're both adults, and ought to respect each other's choices in friends."

"Oh come on, Mom. A plumber can't be your first choice. What will Dad say when he hears about this? Doesn't it bother you that he'll think it's pathetic you can't do any better than a plumber?"

Carol got up from the table. At six feet, Rob was half a head taller than she, but she had never been intimidated by his size. "I'm only going to say this once," she warned, "but whom I choose to date is no one's business but my own. If I cared what your father thought, I'd still be married to him so I'd appreciate it if you left him out of this discussion;"

Rob raised his hands in mock surrender. "Fine, I won't mention Dad again, but I wish you'd just stop for a minute and think things through. You earn an excellent salary at Russell's. Matt doesn't look like the kind of man who'd be pleased to have a wife who earns more than he does."

Carol knew exactly what Rob was doing: shifting focus without losing sight of his original target which was to ridicule Matt to the point she would lose interest in him. It was an attorney's tactic he had learned from his stepfather, but she saw through it. "I've only gone out with him once, Rob, and our respective earnings wasn't one of the topics we covered. I barely know the man, and it's much too soon to start discussing finances."

"I agree, but you've got to consider possible conflicts now because they'll only intensify if you don't. I'll wager a truck-driving plumber has a real traditional view of life and probably wouldn't want you working at all. Are you prepared to throw away your career for a man who carries a wrench to work rather than a briefcase?"

"Matt's occupation is irrelevant to that question, Rob, because I'd not give up my career for any man."

Thinking he had won an important point, Rob broke into a wide grin. He had sparkling white teeth that were an excellent advertisement for his professional talents. "Good, be sure that's the answer you give when he asks you to carry a plunger down the slippery road of life."

Carol glowered at Rob's teasing smirk. He was as tenacious as his father and no matter how an argument ended, he would insist he had won. She knew better than to prolong such a ridiculous exchange. "If you came by to borrow something, I suggest you take it and go."

"Sorry to disappoint you, but this time I came to return the hedge clippers. I put them back in the garage."

"Thank you." Carol returned to the table, but while she found the front page of the *Times*, she still couldn't concentrate on it. She didn't look up as Rob left, but his questions had hurt more than she had let on. What if Matt really did want a woman who would stay home and bake bread and sew curtains? How could she even ask such a question without alienating him for good?

She heard the front door open and close and assumed Rob had forgotten something, but it was her younger son, Tom, who walked in. He had her fair hair, and his blue eyes were dancing with mischief. Unlike Rob, who could have posed for Russell's menswear ads, Tom preferred wearing baggy sweats on the weekends.

"Did you see your brother?" Carol asked.

Tom slid into the chair opposite hers and wiped his sun-bleached curls off his forehead with a careless swipe. "Sure did. What's the story on the plumber?"

Not wanting a repetition of the awful scene she had had with Rob, Carol sighed. "Rob feels I've disgraced the whole family by spending the afternoon at the Huntington Library with a plumbing contractor. Would you care to comment?"

Tom shrugged. "Hell, no. I earn my living with my hands, and so does Rob if he'd just admit it. I'm not going to criticize a tradesman. Is he a nice guy?"

Relieved, Carol found it easy to smile. "Very." She stacked the newspaper into a neat heap before voicing her true misgivings. "But he's a widower, and might still be too attached to his late wife to be able to care for me."

"Give him time then."

Tom was engaged to a young woman who still had another year of chiropractic college. They were a close, loving couple who had plans to one day open their own clinic and she envied them their easy compatibility. "How's Sharon?"

"She has to spend too much time studying, but outside of that, she's fine."

"Good, I've always liked her."

"I'm sure I'd like your plumber too."

"He's not 'my' anything as yet," Carol pointed out. "In fact, I'm afraid I'll jinx any such possibility just thinking about it. Can you stay for supper? There's some barbecued chicken left over from last night."

"Great, I was hoping I'd timed my visit right."

Carol fluffed his curls as she left the table, but it was Matt's silvery hair she remembered.

That he had left without kissing her again struck her as an extremely bad omen. It was going to be a very long week until she saw him again at the reunion.

Monday morning, Casey found Carol at the men's fragrance counter. He stood back watching her sniff her way down the display of expensive colognes and then walked up, and placed one of the testers in her hand. "Trust me. This is it."

He had given her Chanel's Antaeus, and a single whiff was enough to convince Carol she had found Matt's enticing cologne, but she was embarrassed that Casey had caught her trying to identify it. "That is nice. I was just looking for gift ideas for my sons' birthdays."

"And thought they'd like Matt's cologne? Of course you were. Come on up to my office, I'll swap you some coffee for a little advice."

Carol was too depressed to advise anyone on anything, but she accompanied Casey up to the fifth floor. That morning the stock boys were unpacking cartons of Oster rice cookers, and she and Casey had to scoot sideways along the wall to reach his office. Once there, she sat down beside his desk to wait while he made a fresh pot of coffee.

"I want to thank you again for all your help

on Saturday. The food wouldn't have been half as good without your expertise."

"You're being very gracious, but let's face it, I was an overbearing ass.

Carol sucked in a deep breath. "I wouldn't go that far."

"You don't have to." Finished filling the coffeemaker, Casey sat down at his desk. "We're both adults and I think our friendship will survive the truth. I like you a lot, but if there were ever going to be a romantic involvement between us, it would have happened long before this, don't you think?"

While Carol was surprised by Casey's summation of their relationship, she couldn't argue with him. "Definitely, and it's never wise for people who work together to become involved. Everyone knows how difficult that can become."

"Exactly, I couldn't agree more." Casey got up to pour their coffee. He remembered how Carol liked hers and added sweetener and cream before handing her a cup. "I spent yesterday helping Suzanne sort through her artifacts from the Northwest Coast. She has such beautiful things, it's a shame they haven't been on display in her home long before this, but I hope to soon remedy the situation. I just wanted to let you know I was seeing her, so you wouldn't be shocked or hurt, if she mentioned it."

Having decided on Saturday that she and

Casey were completely unsuited to each other, Carol wasn't in the least bit insulted. "I'm glad you like her, Casey. She's one of my dearest friends and deserves a warm, caring man like you."

"Thank you, but I'm working on not swamping Suzanne with attention and I hope she'll want to continue seeing me once the display cases are built. Now about the reunion, I couldn't help but notice the sparks flying between you and Matt, and I was wondering if we couldn't just switch dates on Saturday night without anyone feeling slighted."

Carol took a sip of coffee. She had hoped Matt might call her, but he hadn't. She couldn't go along with Casey's suggestion.

"I won't object if you want to spend the entire evening with Suzanne, but let's keep to our original plan, and just go as a group of friends."

Casey couldn't hide his disappointment. "I'm sorry, I thought when Matt stayed with you Saturday night, that, well, that you two were getting along rather well."

Carol straightened up. "Say, now that you mention it, did you deliberately jam the garbage disposal?"

"How can you even imagine such a thing?" he asked with a chuckle. "It was just stupid, not deliberate, but I chose to make the most of it.

I'm sorry it didn't work out as well as I'd hoped for you."

Carol responded with a careless shrug. "It's really too soon to say. Matt's a widower, and might not be ready for someone new."

"Give him time then."

"That's what my son Tom said, but if something isn't right, no amount of time will make it work."

"That's probably true in our case, but if you like Matt, don't give up on him."

Carol took another sip of coffee. "You make excellent coffee," she murmured.

"Thank you, you've told me that before." He waited for her to say something more about Matt, and then finally realized she had just closed the door on the subject. "Okay, we'll attend the reunion as a group of friends as planned. Then no one will feel pressured into having to impress anyone."

"Yes, if you don't mind, I think it would be best."

"No, I don't mind, but please feel free to monopolize Matt so I'll have to keep Suzanne company."

Carol rose and took her paper cup with her as she started for the door. "I'll do my best, but I can't promise anything."

Casey rose and walked her out into the crowded hallway. "I'm not asking for any promises,

Carol. Lord knows they're much too hard to keep."

Puzzled, Carol wondered to what he was referring but he didn't explain. "I'm sure I'll see you later in the week." She left him then, and just as she had predicted, her assistant had left telephone messages on her desk. Both of her ex-husbands had called. Not wanting to hear any gross references to plumbing, she wadded up the messages and tossed them in the trash.

As usual Monday evening, Aimee came home to an empty house, and although she was used to being alone in the evenings, she felt strangely restless, and found it difficult to concentrate on the television news while she prepared supper. She read the View section of the *Times* while she ate, then went out for a walk, but when she returned home and found no movies worth watching on cable, her thoughts strayed to the reunion. She went to her closet and perused the cocktail dresses she had bought over the last couple of years for parties hosted by the bank. Each was a possibility for Saturday night, but she wasn't in the mood to try them on.

She could recall the last reunion so clearly that it seemed impossible it had been ten years ago. Wandering into her living room, she checked the bookshelves beside the fireplace and found her high school yearbooks. She carried the last one over to the sofa, sat down, and flipped through the photographs of seniors hoping she would be able to recognize her classmates on Saturday night. Except for her gray hair, she didn't look all that different than she did when she was a cheerleader. Carol hadn't changed much either, and while Suzanne might be twenty pounds heavier, her red hair would make her easy to identify.

As she came to the clubs and organizations, a telephone list slipped out on the rug. She picked up the faded sheet, and scanned the names. Most had attended the reunions over the years, but several people were completely lost from her memory. She looked them up, matching names with photos of earnest young men and women, and wondered what had become of them. On a sudden impulse, she dialed Carol's number.

"I just came across an old telephone list," she explained, "and wondered if someone on your committee had contacted the people who've missed our reunions in the past."

When the telephone rang Carol had prayed it would be Matt; she had leapt to answer. Now she had to cover her disappointment. "We used the list of graduates Cortéz High supplied, and put notices in all the local papers hoping to reach everyone we'd missed. Is there anyone in particular you're curious about? I have the list of reservations right here and I can tell you whether or not they're coming."

Aimee read off the names she had found, and not surprisingly, the four people she couldn't place hadn't made reservations for the reunion. "After thirty-five years, do you suppose any of them will still be at these numbers?"

"I doubt it," Carol said, "but why don't you give them a try? There's still time to invite them to the party, and if they've missed the other reunions, they're sure to enjoy this one."

Aimee hesitated a long moment, then having nothing better to do that evening, agreed. "All right, I'll give it a try. I'll call you later if I find anyone who'd like to come." She hung up, and rechecked the photograph of the first girl, Connie Sotherby. Try as she might, she just couldn't remember her, and when she dialed the old number, she got a recording giving the hours of a local laundry. She checked Connie off the list.

The next person was Tad Billingsly, who had played on the football team, but again, if he and she had had any classes together, she couldn't remember them. She found a Chinese family at that number, and apologized for disturbing them. Thinking this a stupid waste of time, she was about to give up, when a second look at the photograph of the next student, Gordon Ashbach, produced the faint memory of a shy young man with thick glasses who had sat at the back of her senior English class.

Checking the index, she discovered his only extracurricular activity had been the math club—all male at the time. She remembered those boys, a clannish lot who preferred trigonometry and calculus to girls and sports. Still, there was a remarkable sweetness to Gordon's smile and she gave his number a try. When a man answered, she asked for Gordon and was amazed to find it was he.

"This is Aimee Reis," she began, "I was Aimee Stewart when we attended Cortéz High. The thirty-fifth reunion is this coming Saturday night, and I called in hopes you might want to attend."

Gordon nearly dropped the telephone, then got tangled in the cord as he made a wild grab for it. "Aimee Stewart, the cheerleader?" he asked as soon as he had recovered from his initial shock.

He had a marvelous voice, deep, and yet edged with humor, so Aimee quickly forgave him for asking such a silly question. "I haven't led a cheer in thirty-five years, but yes, that was me."

"And you want me to go to the reunion?"

"Yes, did you get an invitation?"

Gordon glanced toward the heap of unanswered correspondence on his desk. "I think so, but I can't swear to it."

"Well, if you'd like to go, it isn't too late to make a reservation."

Gordon closed his eyes and easily conjured up a vision of Aimee Stewart. She'd been all legs and had worn her glossy brown hair in a ponytail that had kept time with a bouncy rhythm as she waved her pom-poms at pep rallies. The Cortéz High's colors had been red and white and she had looked as delicious as a peppermint in her white pleated skirt and red sweater. The sound of her voice brought back an incredible wave of longing.

"I wouldn't know anyone," he murmured shyly.

"You remembered me," Aimee pointed out, "and I think we only had one English class together. I'm sure you'll remember some of your old friends from the math club."

"Aimee Stewart," Gordon breathed out softly.

"Yes?"

"I just never expected you to call."

"Would you like to think it over? You can call me tomorrow at the bank if you decide you'd like to go."

"You work in a bank?"

Aimee told him which branch she managed.

"I've been with them more than twenty years, since my husband died."

Gordon strangled a totally inappropriate whoop of joy. "You're a widow?"

"Yes." Aimee hated to admit that she was also a divorcee, but her marriage to Bill Dunham was something best left forgotten. She had never used his last name, and had been grateful she had not had to change all her accounts back to Steve's name when they divorced. "What about you? Is there a Mrs. Ashbach you'd like to bring with you Saturday night?"

"No, I've never married."

"A date then?"

"No, there's no one."

"Well, you needn't worry about going alone. I am. The party's at eight o'clock at the Ritz Carlton in Pasadena. Shall I add your name to the list?"

Gordon's fingers tightened around the receiver. He had thought he had outgrown the painful shyness that had plagued him as a teenager, but an unexpected call from Aimee Stewart had brought back the old paralyzing fear and it took him a long moment to draw a breath. "Yes, I'll go. What time would you like me to pick you up?"

Aimee hadn't meant to give Gordon the impression she was inviting him to be her date, but as she had mentioned she would be going alone, she could understand how he had made that mistake. She hesitated, wanting to correct his error, but then realizing they would be the only two attending the reunion alone, she thought it would be cruel to refuse his offer of a ride. After all, she had called to encourage him to attend, so she could scarcely insist he drive there by himself or spend the evening sitting in a corner all alone.

"How thoughtful of you," she exclaimed before naming a time and giving him her address. "Do you remember Carol Powers or Suzanne Shepard? I'd planned to sit with them and their dates."

Gordon did not ever reminisce about his wretched high school years, but the names sounded vaguely familiar. "I think so. Was Suzanne the redhead?"

"Yes, that's her." After again assuring him it would be an enjoyable evening, Aimee told him goodbye. She tried to remember more about Gordon than the fact he had sat in the back of her English class, but that was all she recalled. "Well, he certainly has a marvelous voice," she mused aloud, and hoping he could not have turned out too badly, she tried the final name on her list. Again reaching the wrong party, she offered a hasty apology and redialed Carol's number.

"Carol? You're not going to believe this, but

Gordon Ashbach was still at his old number and although I'm not quite sure how it happened, we'll be going together Saturday night."

Carol had not allowed herself to hope it would be Matt the second time the telephone rang and she giggled along with Aimee. "I can't remember him at all."

"Check the annual. He was one of the skinny guys who wore glasses and belonged to the math club, sort of a lovable nerd."

"Well nerd or not, you've got yourself a date for the reunion and that's good news. Were you able to talk to any of the others?"

"No, Gordon was the only one I reached."

"Poor guy probably still lives with his mother."

Aimee knew the type and assumed Gordon would still be painfully thin, probably balding, and so bashful she would have to carry the conversation the whole night. "Look, I'll simply count going to the reunion with Gordon as my good deed for the week. If the poor soul is lonely, an evening with us should make him grateful to retire to the dank confines of his mother's house."

"Good Lord, Aimee, you don't think he's turned into another Norman Bates, do you?"

The reference to *Psycho* sent Aimee into peals of laughter. "I can remember the guys in the math club moving around campus in a stumbling huddle, slide rules in one hand, and peanut butter and jelly sandwiches in the other. They were harmless then, Carol, and I'm sure they still are. See you Saturday night."

After putting away her annual Aimee went back into her bedroom and took a second look at her cocktail dresses. The black one was elegant, but too somber for a reunion, and she reached for the red sheath with the beaded top. After all, dressing in the school colors was appropriate, and still hoping to have a good time even if she was stuck with a date she hadn't truly wanted, she hung the dress on the back of her bedroom door where she would see it all week, and look forward to a fun evening.

Casey stopped by Suzanne's late Tuesday afternoon. "I made some sketches and wanted to see what you think."

"Come on in. I'm amazed, I didn't expect you to have them ready so soon." After looking through her pieces on Sunday, they had repacked them and stacked the boxes against the wall where they no longer posed an obstacle course for her and her visitors. She led Casey over to the green velvet couch. "I just got home from my afternoon class. I'm glad I didn't miss you."

"I should have called."

"It's quite all right. Whenever I'm home, I

enjoy having visitors, but it's always a good idea to call so we don't miss each other. I'd hate to have you come all the way out here for nothing."

Casey had purposely arranged his schedule to be in her neighborhood, but he didn't admit it. "I had to visit our West Covina store this afternoon, and your place was on my way home." He removed the rubber band, unrolled his sketches, and laid them out on the marble-topped coffee table. "I deal regularly with the firm that makes our display cases and all I did was combine several of their standard units. What do you think?"

After their initial near confrontation before brunch, Sunday had gone remarkably well, and Suzanne hoped she and Casey would continue to get along. She looked at his drawings, and then got up to judge how the units he was suggesting would look in her living room. Bookcases flanked the fireplace on the south end, windows facing the street cut into the west wall, the dining room was on the north, and the display units would go along the east wall. She tried to envision the glass cases running floor to ceiling, and feared they might be too much.

"Could you put wood doors on the bottom two shelves on the side units, and leave the central one all open shelves?" she asked. "Then I wouldn't have a solid wall of glass."

"Are you worried about earthquakes?" Casey asked. "I'll bolt everything to the wall so you won't have any breakage."

Suzanne pursed her lips thoughtfully. "Thank you, but my concern was merely an aesthetic one. I'm afraid three rows of glass shelves will look too much like a department store."

"I can do whatever you like, but I thought you wanted to display your masks and baskets, rather than hide them."

Suzanne could see where this discussion was going, but she refused to back down. "The shelves are going here in my house, Casey, so I'll be the one to choose the design."

"Yes, ma'am." Casey took out his pen, pulled his carefully detailed drawings close, and with a quick cross-hatch pattern inked in the doors she had requested. "There, is that what you want?"

Suzanne walked around beside him to observe the changes. "Yes, that's much better. Now it looks more like a custom wall unit than just plain shelves would have. Thank you."

Casey tried not to be hurt that his original drawings hadn't pleased her, but even admitting to himself that her changes were an improvement, he felt bad. He glanced around the room. The walls were painted a lovely pale apricot shade he thought too pretty to change. "I like the room this color. If you remember the name of the paint, I'll get some and paint the backs of the units to match the walls. That way the glass shelves will appear to float, and your masks will be the focus of the attention."

"What are the other options?"

"Leaving the wood unfinished, staining it to match the dark wood of your furniture, which would be overpowering, or painting it a contrasting color, none of which I'd recommend."

This time Suzanne agreed with him. "I think I still have a can of the paint out in the garage. I'll have to look for it tomorrow though."

"There's no hurry," Casey insisted. "I can have the materials delivered within a day of ordering them, so whenever you're ready will be fine."

"I really appreciate this, Casey, but there's your schedule to consider too. I'm sure you must have plans for your spare time other than to install shelves for me."

Casey stood and rolled up his drawings. "I go to the gym, visit a museum every now and then, but I can work that in around doing this for you."

He was wearing a charcoal suit and maroon print tie and looked not only handsome, but extremely efficient. While he seemed to have come around to her way of thinking, Suzanne wasn't entirely pleased with the way his impromptu visit had gone. "I'm sorry my house is so far out of your way."

Casey lived in West Los Angeles, more than twenty miles from Pasadena, but he considered Suzanne well worth the drive. "Russell's has a lot of stores, and I can visit the ones in this area whenever I please, so you'll never be out of my way."

"That's fortunate, but the traffic will be terrible this time of day."

"That's certainly true."

"Would you like to stay for dinner?"

Casey laid his sketches on the coffee table. "I'd like to stay, but not just to miss the traffic."

Suzanne wasn't certain how to reply to that suggestive comment, and so simply ignored it. "I was just going to have pasta and a green salad."

"What kind of pasta?"

Suzanne had had ample opportunity to notice the way Casey's whole face lit up whenever the subject turned to food. "You know where the kitchen is. Why don't you make supper for us?"

Casey slipped off his jacket, and loosened his tie. "No, come help me. The only trick with pasta is not to overcook it. What were you planning to use for sauce?"

"I was just going to mix the pasta with some

steamed zucchini, fresh tomatoes, and maybe a little basil."

"Sounds good."

Suzanne laughed to herself. "I usually don't give much thought to food. I'm trying to watch my weight."

"Really, why?"

"Why?" Suzanne spread her hands. "I don't enjoy looking so, well, matronly."

Casey reached for her hand and turned her around slowly. "You're a voluptuous redhead, Suz, that's a long way from being matronly. Besides, pasta and fresh vegetables make excellent diet fare. If you'd like, I can give you some great low calorie recipes."

Suzanne followed Casey into the kitchen and handed him an apron. "I can't remember the last time a man complimented my figure, so thank you. Is there anything you can't do?"

Casey frowned slightly. "Car repairs. I've tried, but I'm an absolutely terrible mechanic."

"So am I," Suzanne agreed with a regretful sigh, but as long as Casey admired her figure and knew his way around a kitchen, she was impressed.

Six

Wednesday morning, Carol was at her desk totaling sales figures when Casey came to her door. She made a final notation, and then all in one graceful gesture whisked a navy blue Evan Picone blazer off the office's extra chair, hung it on the back of the door, and welcomed him inside. "I'm afraid I don't have a coffee machine, but I can send for some."

"No, I'm fine. I was over at Suzanne's last night, and when she showed me the dress she's planning to wear to the reunion, it occurred to me I probably ought to rent a tux. I can get one for Matt, too, on Russell's discount, but with things being somewhat tangled, I wasn't sure whether to have Suzanne call him, or you."

Carol sat back in her chair. She hadn't spoken with Matt since Sunday, and she hadn't been able to get Rob's petty comments about him out of her mind. She didn't want Matt to be subjected to an entire evening of snide remarks about his choice of profession, so Casey's suggestion had a definite appeal. Surely if Matt were dressed like a successful businessman, her classmates would assume he was one without prying into just what he did.

"Tuxedoes are a great idea, but nothing's changed since I spoke with you on Monday, and as far as I'm concerned, Matt is Suzanne's date. She'll have to be the one to call him."

"I was afraid you'd say that."

"But you asked me anyway?"

"Well sure, I didn't see any harm in trying. All right, I'll go call Suzanne and have her call Matt. If he agrees, can you meet us in the men's department of the Pasadena store at five-thirty?"

"Today?"

"Yes, today. If either of us needs alterations, we have to allow time to have them done."

"Yes, of course." Carol bounced the eraser tip of her pencil on her notepad. As she saw it, she and Matt had had a terrific time on Sunday, but he hadn't called to talk with her, let alone plan another date and she was so badly disappointed she didn't know whether she wanted to see him before the reunion or not. "I really don't see why I have to be there when you and Matt will be the ones trying on the tuxedoes."

Exasperated, Casey glanced toward the heavens. "Frankly I don't care whether you're there or not either, Carol, but I'm out of excuses to see Suzanne and this is too good an opportunity to miss. If you're there with Matt, the four of us might get the spontaneous inspiration to go out to dinner, or do something else as a foursome."

"This is getting much too complicated, Casey. Why don't you just wait until after the reunion to date Suzanne?"

Casey looked down at his nails. "I know, I'm too damn anxious to please her, but I can't help it. Now will you meet us at Russell's tonight or not?"

"You're assuming Matt will agree?"

"Why wouldn't he?"

"Pride, for one thing. Maybe he owns a nice dark suit, or perhaps he's already rented a tux."

"Fine, then I'll still ask Suzanne to help me pick mine out, but if he hasn't already got one, and wants to take me up on my offer, will you be there?"

Carol stared at her friend. He was trying so hard to impress Suzanne, and Matt hadn't done anything at all to impress her. She recognized the uncomfortable tightness in her chest for the ugly emotion it was. "I'm jealous, Casey. You're showering Suzanne with attention, and Matt doesn't care enough to call and see if I'm still alive."

"Then call him."

"No, I think he'd be annoyed rather than flattered."

"He was practically drooling on you Saturday night."

Carol was certain she had been the one guilty of such open adoration. "So he likes to flirt. A lot of men do, but clearly he doesn't want to take it any further."

"How do you know? Maybe he's been up to his kneecaps in busted water mains."

Carol tossed her pencil aside. "Oh please. I can't take any more plumbing jokes."

"Does Matt tell them?"

"No, but my eldest son made it painfully clear he doesn't want his mother dating a plumber."

"I'm sorry to hear that. Of course, since you haven't heard from Matt, you aren't dating him. You're dating me."

Carol tried to smile but couldn't. "I'm sorry I got you into this mess, Casey."

"Don't apologize. Suzanne's the nicest woman I've met in a long time and I wouldn't have missed getting to know her for anything. Let me go call her, and I'll let you know what Matt says."

Casey hurried away before Carol could offer another protest, and when he called two hours later, it was to say Matt would be at the Pasadena store at five-thirty. Carol's hand was shaking as she hung up, but she was no coward; she would be there too. Then she remembered Aimee was bringing Gordon Ashbach and hurriedly called her.

"I really don't believe the men need tuxedoes," Aimee argued. "Besides, Gordon didn't sound all that enthusiastic about attending the reunion, and I doubt he'd agree to rent one. Casey and Matt can wear whatever they like, let's just leave Gordon out of it."

Carol had thought the more people gathered in the men's department the better, but when Aimee insisted she had no idea how to reach Gordon during the day had she even wanted to, which she didn't, Carol was forced to give up. Like Casey, she also visited the Russell's stores to confer with department managers and left early to reach Pasadena in time to speak with the young woman who managed executive sportswear. After having justified the visit with a productive chat about arranging the stock in more attractive displays, she crossed the floor to menswear where she found Casey pacing the aisle between the shirt counters.

"I still don't think I need to be here," she greeted him.

"Look at it this way, I've provided you with an opportunity to see Matt again. Be grateful for it."

Carol didn't feel grateful, just uneasy, as

though she had made a terrible blunder and would suffer the most painful of humiliations when it was discovered. Suzanne soon joined them but it was a quarter to six before Matt appeared. He was dressed in rust-stained white coveralls with Trenerry Plumbing embroidered across the back, and looked none too pleased about being there.

"Sorry I'm late. What is it we have to do?"

As shocked as Carol that Matt would show up in his work clothes, Casey took him aside, made a list of the sizes he would require, and handed it to the clerk. "The shirt and shoes will be no problem, but I do want you to try on the coat and pants to make certain they fit."

Matt nodded, but rather than talk with Carol and Suzanne while they waited for the clerk to produce the clothing Casey had requested, he jammed his hands in his pockets and turned away to scan the department's other merchandise. Casey gave an embarrassed shrug, but Carol just shook her head to warn him to be still. She didn't understand why Matt had chosen to be difficult. Perhaps he had just had a bad day, but she wasn't going to try and cajole him out of it when he had ignored her all week.

She found a chair and tried not to look as miserable as she felt. Had Matt still had even a flicker of interest in her, he would have left his coveralls in his truck and greeted her with a delighted smile. She began to worry about Saturday night. Casey would probably be completely enraptured with Suzanne by then. Matt might not be any better company than he was being now, and she and Aimee would be stuck with Gordon Ashbach who as a one time math whiz would undoubtedly know far more about computer programming than providing entertaining company.

The Cortéz reunion wasn't the first time Carol had volunteered to serve on a committee and seen her hopes for a fabulous evening go awry. She had a naturally optimistic outlook, but it didn't always serve her well. She had learned her lesson this time, however, and in the future, she would adopt Aimee's unconcerned attitude and avoid being so badly disappointed.

"How do I look?" Matt asked.

Startled by the sound of his voice, Carol glanced up to find Matt dressed in an elegantly tailored tuxedo. The black formal wear complimented his gray hair and blue eyes superbly, to say nothing of showing off the trim build that had been hidden beneath his baggy coveralls. He looked splendid, and she could not help but believe that he knew it.

"You don't need my opinion," she assured him as she left her chair, "when you look that good."

Matt ran his thumbs down the satin lapels. "I feel like a maitre d'."

Half a dozen more appealing images came to Carol's mind, from concert pianist to European royalty, but she wasn't in the mood to flatter him. "If you're uncomfortable, then don't wear it."

Matt caught Carol's eye with a challenging stare. "That's an odd offer. Wasn't it your idea to put us in tuxedoes?"

"No, it was Casey's." Carol turned around to look for her friend and found him studying the fit of his tuxedo in a full-length mirror. Suzanne was by his side, smiling prettily as they exchanged teasing banter. "Is that what you thought? That I'd wanted you in a tux?"

Matt squared his shoulders, but the graceful lines of his coat weren't distorted by the motion. "Yeah, when Suzanne called, it certainly didn't sound like it had been her idea."

"So you assumed it had to have been mine?"

"Fashion is your line, not hers."

Carol nodded. "I suppose that's logical, but Casey's my date, remember, not you."

Matt glanced over his shoulder at Casey and Suzanne who were still admiring his reflection. "Maybe we ought to settle this right now."

"Settle what?"

Matt reached for her hand, and guided her over to the mirror. "We seem to have a problem here, and I'd like to straighten it out before it gets any worse."

Casey shot an anxious glance toward Carol, but could make out nothing in her troubled expression. He swept Matt's attire with a critical glance, but found no cause for complaint there either. "Your tux couldn't fit you any more beautifully had it been custom made, but if it doesn't feel comfortable, I'll have the clerk bring out another in your size."

"It isn't the suit that's the problem," Matt replied. "It's the farce about who's dating whom. Now it's obvious to me you'd rather be with Suzanne than Carol, so why don't we make the trade official? I'll be Carol's escort Saturday night, and you'll be Suzanne's."

"Excuse me?" Suzanne interrupted. "Don't Carol and I have a say in this? In case you haven't noticed, this is the nineties, Matt. Men don't regard women as chattel any more and get away with it."

Surprised by her rebuke, Matt frowned slightly. "I wasn't trying to insult you, Suzanne, but it's plain to all of us that you're more interested in Casey than me so why should we pretend otherwise?"

That Matt had chosen to reorganize couples not because he liked her, but because he believed Suzanne and Casey wanted to be together made Carol feel all of two inches tall. Horribly embarrassed, she withdrew her hand from his and started to back away. "I really need to be going," she whispered.

Matt reached out to catch Carol's hand and pulled her right back beside him. "Perhaps I phrased my suggestion awkwardly, but will you and Carol agree to swapping dates?"

Suzanne was the only one to notice that Carol looked ready to cry, and she shook her head. "Just because we're attending a high school reunion doesn't mean we have to act like teenagers and pair up. When I asked you to go with me as a friend, that's all I wanted."

"Fine, so you don't want to switch?" Matt asked.

"This misunderstanding is entirely my fault," Casey explained, "and I certainly don't want to see anyone's feelings hurt."

Matt swore under his breath. "Why should anyone's feelings have to suffer? If we're all just *friends,* then what does it matter who goes with whom?"

The irritation in Matt's voice carried throughout the department and the clerk who had waited on them rushed over to silence him before the other customers were frightened away. "Is there a problem, sir?" he asked.

"There sure as hell is," Matt informed him, "but if we can't straighten it out ourselves, you'll never be able to."

"I beg your pardon?"

Casey shooed the clerk away. "I'll handle this," he promised in a hushed plea. "Regardless of how Matt made the offer, I agree with him. Rather than play musical chairs at the reunion, let's swap dates right now." He gave a courtly bow. "Will you allow me the supreme honor of escorting you, Suzanne?"

Suzanne laughed and agreed, then she looked over at Matt. "Well, Matt, aren't you going to ask Carol the same question?"

When Matt turned toward her, Carol's heart sank even lower, for there was no glint of humor in his gaze, but instead a darkly threatening defiance that sickened her clear through. "If you'd rather not go with me, just say so," she whispered. "I'd rather go alone than put you through another evening as bad as this."

"What are you talking about? Of course I want to go with you."

Fearing that was as gentlemanly a request as Matt was capable of making, Casey slapped him on the shoulder. "Great, it's settled then. I'm taking Suzanne and you're taking Carol. Now let's get out of these suits and go to dinner."

"That's a lovely idea," Suzanne said, "but I can't. I have a poetry workshop on Wednesday nights and I don't want to miss it."

"A poetry workshop?" Casey repeated numbly. "Whatever do you do there?"

"People read their poetry and we discuss it. The focus on language helps me write more colorful descriptions of the artwork I share in my classes and the occasional journal article I submit. It's really an entertaining group, and often the highlight of my week."

Disappointed his plans for dinner hadn't worked out, Casey quickly switched tactics. "Do they allow visitors?"

"Yes, of course, would you like to come with me?"

Carol listened enviously as Casey and Suzanne planned their evening. Matt was still facing her, but she found it impossible to meet his gaze. She again pulled her hand from his. "I'll see you Saturday night."

"Wait, have dinner with me."

"Tonight?"

"Yes, tonight," he answered too sharply. "Give me a minute to change my clothes, and we'll go."

Carol wasn't at all sure she wanted to, but reluctantly gave in. "Fine, I'll wait right here."

Matt reappeared before Casey, but thinking there was nothing more to discuss with her amorous colleague, Carol walked over to the parking structure with Matt. "Where would you like to go?" she asked.

Carrying his coveralls rolled up in his hand,

Matt was dressed in a blue work shirt and Levi's. "Do you know the Wild Thyme on Fair Oaks?"

"Yes."

"Good. I'll meet you there."

Carol watched him walk away, still uncertain just what she had let herself in for, but by the time she reached the charming restaurant, she was sufficiently intrigued to stay. Recently redecorated with French country charm in an exuberant mixture of aqua prints, the Wild Thyme served some of the most delicious food in the San Gabriel Valley. Butcher paper covered the white tablecloths, and containers of crayons beside the bouquets of fresh flowers kept adults, as well as children, doodling between courses.

Arriving first, Carol was shown to a booth by the windows, and ordered iced tea which was subtly flavored with passion fruit. Before she had taken more than a sip, Matt pulled up in a white van marked Trenerry and Son Plumbing. She watched him climb out, comb his curls with his fingers, and thought, as she always had, that he was absolutely gorgeous. She still felt slighted about not hearing from him since Sunday, but managed a smile as he joined her.

"I'm sorry for the misunderstanding about the tuxedoes," she offered graciously. "I assumed you owned a suit, but Casey was determined to make the most of his chance to impress Suzanne."

Matt picked up the menu. "He seems to have succeeded."

"Yes, I think so." Following his example, Carol turned her attention to the evening's specials. Saturday night, Matt had made her uncomfortable by being so damn direct, but sitting with him now, when he appeared far more interested in having dinner than talking with her, she felt twice as uneasy. Her first impulse was to apologize again, but she didn't know for what, and kept still. Unlike Casey, she didn't regard dating Matt as a campaign to be won with grand gestures, and she was at a loss for what to do.

When their waitress returned, Matt ordered blackened red snapper, and Carol chose a bowl of cream cheese soup. She folded her hands in her lap, and waited for Matt to begin the conversation, but he continued to stare out the window at the rush-hour traffic long after it was polite to do so.

She had divorced two men who had been more attentive than this, and if there was anything she could not abide, it was a distracted silence. "If there's something you'd like to say to me, I wish you'd just say it, but I'd rather not be ignored."

Matt shrugged slightly. "I'm sorry. I guess I'm

not very good company. I ought to get out more, so I don't go into shock when I do."

Carol held her breath. "Do I remind you of your late wife?"

"No, not at all. She was a tall brunette, not a petite blonde." Matt grabbed a green crayon and began to draw a palm tree on the butcher paper with short choppy strokes. "I'd much rather talk about you than Deborah. Your son, Rob, must resemble his father. Does he share the same temperament?"

"Oh yes, indeed he does. They're both perfectionists which makes them exceptionally fine dentists. But please, I'd rather not talk about my ex-husbands. It will spoil my appetite."

Matt looked up from his sketch. "They both gave you a bad time?"

He had completely disregarded her request! Carol sighed. "Let's just say they had certain expectations, and I had others, and that led to more problems than we could solve."

"What sort of expectations?"

Carol shifted uncomfortably in her seat. Matt was handing her the perfect opportunity to confide her opinions of what made for a successful marriage and to determine his, but she thought it was much too soon for such a serious discussion. Then again, what couple ever discussed important issues while there was still time to part with no hard feelings? She glanced toward the kitchen and wished the chef would hurry up with their order.

"Bob was so neat he wasn't happy unless I sterilized the utensils after each meal, and Cliff's law practice demanded so much of his time he had none for me. Now could we please talk about something else?"

Matt studied her averted gaze and while her discomfort was painful to observe, he thought she was glossing over problems he would have preferred to hear about in depth. "It takes two people to make a marriage work."

"Yes, that's true, and I'll willingly admit I'm as responsible as my ex-husbands for the failure of my marriages, but just because a couple stays together doesn't necessarily mean their marriage is a success."

"I agree."

His gaze was more curious than belligerent now, and Carol could see his memories of marriage were good, if tainted with sorrow, while sadness was all that she had. "When I was younger, I believed if two people really loved each other, then they could solve whatever problem life gave them. I'm no longer that naïve."

Matt tossed his crayon back into the container. "Neither am I."

The waitress brought their orders then, and Carol was relieved for the distraction. The soup was as flavorful and rich as she had remembered and the garlic-laced flatbread served with it was scrumptious too. She licked her fingers after having a slice and looked up to find Matt watching her with a wicked grin that brought a bright blush to her cheeks.

"What did Rob think of me?" he asked.

"Rob? Well, he really didn't speak with you long enough to form an opinion."

"Come on, I'm sure he has an opinion on every man you bring home."

Unwilling to share Rob's bigoted views, Carol shook her head. "I don't bring that many men home, and he doesn't live there so he wouldn't meet them even if I did. I'm sorry you missed my other son, Tom. He's a chiropractor, and not nearly as judgmental."

"Then Rob didn't like me."

"I didn't say that."

"You didn't have to. If Rob made judgmental remarks, it stands to reason he wasn't impressed. That's too bad. I'm sure my son would like you."

Carol hadn't meant to reveal Rob's opinion with a careless remark and hated herself for making such a stupid slip. "Please, Rob's opinions don't matter to me."

"Of course they do," Matt argued. "Parents are no more immune to their children's criticism than they are to ours."

Feeling at a horrible disadvantage, Carol took

a spoonful of soup. "This is absolutely delicious."

"Hey, don't you ever talk about anything important?"

Insulted, Carol sat back. "What an awful thing to say. Of course I do."

"Fine, then ask me an important question."

Startled, Carol tapped her spoon against the rim of her bowl. She was afraid to ask him what he thought of her, but did summon the courage to inquire about something that concerned her. "Except for when my sons were small, I've always worked. Did Deborah have a career?"

"Other than keeping me happy? No. I have a lucrative business, and there was no reason for her to work."

"I don't know what I'd do with myself just rattling around the house all day. I enjoy what I do: meeting people, having the responsibility for selecting elegant merchandise, seeing it sold. It's really a very satisfying career."

"Deborah had lots of friends, belonged to clubs, she didn't just twiddle her thumbs. Haven't you ever wanted to do anything but work for Russell's?"

Disappointed at Matt's accusing tone, Carol took a moment to compose her thoughts before describing her dream. "I'd like to own my own shop someday. My years with Russell's have taught me everything I need to know to be successful, and other than becoming a merchandise manager, or perhaps managing a branch store, there's nowhere else I can go with them. Opening my own store would be a real challenge, but I'd like to take it on someday."

"Most new businesses fail."

"Yes, I know, that's one of the reasons I'm reluctant to go out on my own, especially in a poor economy."

"You're an ambitious woman, and if you've got the skills to succeed, then you will."

"Thank you for that vote of confidence, but I'm not ready yet."

"Most new businesses are undercapitalized. Is financing a problem for you?"

Grateful they were discussing something less personal than her failed marriages, Carol became far more animated. "Not really. I own my home, so I'd be able to arrange a loan fairly easily to finance a small business. Aimee manages a bank and she'd be happy to handle the arrangements. But as I said, this just isn't the right time to go into business for myself. Several of the major department store chains have merged, or gone out of business, but as long as Russell's is holding its own I'll stay with them."

"The safest road isn't always the best in business or in life. What if Russell's management announces tomorrow that they're merging with one of their former competition. Would you be out of a job?"

"That's difficult to say. It would depend on which firm occupied the stronger position, but I'd really rather not contemplate losing my job, if you don't mind."

"There you go again. You claim not to be naïve, but you avoid even thinking about unpleasant topics. Avoidance isn't an attractive trait in an adult."

Carol was beginning to believe Matt took a vicious delight in needling her. "I had no idea plumbers were licensed to provide psychological advice."

Matt laughed as though her caustic remark had been made in jest. "A man doesn't have to be a psychologist to understand life."

Carol leaned close and lowered her voice. "You have an obnoxiously superior attitude at times, Matt, and I don't like it any better than Suzanne does."

"Yeah, and I don't like being dismissed as a fool just because I'm a plumber rather than a dentist or an attorney."

"Is that what you think I'm doing?"

"Tell me what Rob said."

Cornered, Carol looked away. "I don't think it's your trade that's the problem here. I think you're comparing me to Deborah, which isn't fair. We're two entirely different women, and no matter how hard you try to push me into her mold, I just won't fit."

Matt glared at her, then shoved his plate away. "The cheesecake is very good here, would you like some?"

Carol didn't even feel like finishing her soup, let alone having dessert. "No, thank you. Let's just go." She opened her purse, took out her wallet, and looked around for their waitress.

"I asked you to dinner and I'll pay," Matt informed her coldly. "I'm not poor. I've got so much work I'm thinking of hiring another man, and you can believe me when I tell you I'm well paid."

"This isn't about money," Carol insisted. "It's about respecting someone else's opinions."

"What opinions? You're afraid to share yours."

"I am not!" Carol saw a dozen heads turn in her direction and wished she had said something remarkably witty rather than just having spoken too loud. "I'll leave the tip," she announced and she slapped three dollars down on the table before Matt could argue with her.

She didn't wait with him as he paid their bill at the cashier's, but stood outside the front doors to tell him goodbye. At that moment, she did not care how blue his eyes were, she didn't ever want to see him again. Matt had another view, however, and upon leaving the restaurant, took her arm.

"I'll walk you to your car."

"You needn't bother. I won't get lost."

"You're already so damn lost, lady, you don't even know it."

Carol tried to pull her arm free, but Matt refused to release her. She led him straight to her car, and quickly unlocked the door. "About Saturday night—" she began.

Matt dismissed Saturday night with a single crude expletive, then pulled Carol into his arms and kissed her not as gently as he had at her place, but with a demanding, consuming passion that brought a wildly enthusiastic cheer from a teenager riding by on his skateboard. Unmindful of the stares they were drawing from the restaurant, he didn't end his lavish show of affection until he was good and ready.

"Does that convince you I'm not confusing you with my wife?" he asked in a husky whisper against her cheek.

Carol closed her eyes to shut out the sights and sounds of the traffic, but that only increased her awareness of Matt. She could feel his heat through her clothes, and caught the faint scent of Antaeus on his cheek. She raised her hand to his temple and caressed his curls all the while knowing she ought to tell him precisely what she thought of his outrageous behavior. The problem was, he felt much too good for her to summon even a faint protest, let alone any righteous anger. When he stepped back, all she could do was regard him with a befuddled stare.

"I'll pick you up at seven-thirty on Saturday," Matt told her before turning away.

Carol leaned back against her BMW, grateful for the solid comfort of chrome and steel when her legs had turned to jelly. How had she ever gotten herself into such a ridiculous situation? she agonized. It had all started with wanting a date for the reunion, but without analyzing her actions any further, she knew she had gotten a lot more than she had bargained for. Appalled as much by her own behavior as Matt's, she drove home humming the chorus of Cortéz High's fight song, and praying she would survive their next scrimmage with her heart intact.

Seven

Casey followed Suzanne home and they took his car to the community center where the poetry workshop met. Built in the 1930s, the two-story, Spanish-style building had seen a variety of uses over the years, and while still imposing in bright sun, when shadowed by twilight it became strangely forlorn. The wall along the back of the parking lot had been painted with colorful dancing figures but gang graffiti marred more than one. Accustomed to street art and its usual gang embellishment, Casey wasn't particularly worried about his car, but set the alarm on the Pontiac Trans Am all the same.

He and Suzanne followed the dirt path across the parched grass to the arched entrance of the center. On the left there was a small bookstore stocked with literary fiction and poetry, and on the right a large meeting room. The walls, floor, and ceiling of the makeshift auditorium were painted black, but it was brightly lit by overhead spotlights. A low platform shoved against the back wall served as a stage when the room was used for amateur theatrical productions, with rows of folding chairs providing seating for the audience. Tonight twenty-five of the brown metal chairs had been placed in a large circle in the center of the floor.

Casey had seldom seen a more forbidding room. "This is positively spooky. Russell's has several subbasements that are more inviting than this. Do they use this place as a funhouse on Halloween?"

They were the first to arrive, and crossing to the far side of the circle, Suzanne took a chair facing the door. "I like to think of it as a dramatic setting, rather than a depressing one."

"You've obviously got a much more vivid imagination than I have." The evening was warm, and the air in the black room uncomfortably close. Casey stepped up on the platform to raise a black window shade, and opened the window, but when it immediately began to slide closed, he grabbed the piece of a two by four lying on the ledge to prop it up. The next window also needed propping, but again, a convenient length of wood had been provided. He was pleasantly surprised when the third window stayed up on its own.

Having done all he could to improve the atmosphere of the stark facility, he took a chair beside Suzanne. "How did you hear about this group?" he asked.

"I saw a notice in the paper last year and thought it might be fun to attend. It was, so I've kept coming. I seldom write poetry, but I like listening to other people read theirs, and the discussions that follow are often spirited. There's apparently no general agreement as to what constitutes good poetry, and that makes for lively debate."

Suzanne was holding a notebook on her lap, and Casey gestured toward it. "If you've brought some poetry you've written, I'd love to hear it."

"I'm not really any good. I just feel that I ought to contribute something occasionally to earn my place in the group."

"I'd still like to hear it."

Although embarrassed, Suzanne opened her notebook. "I like writing a form of Japanese poetry called Haiku. They're just three lines and seventeen syllables and that's about as much as I can manage. What do you think of this one?

> Snail slime promises
> Iridescent in sunlight
> Vanish in the rain."

Casey asked her to read it again, and then

nodded thoughtfully. "That's not really about snails, is it?"

"No, but one of the beauties of poetry is that people often find multiple meanings in even simple verse."

"I think I've been snail slimed a time or two. In fact, I know I have. Read me another one."

"All right.

> Raindrops bathe the lawn
> Slugs glide along secret paths
> Delicate, unloved."

Again Casey was certain Suzanne had been talking about something far more personal than the poignant loneliness of garden pests. "I like that one too. Maybe you have more poetic talent than you realize, Suzanne."

"No, when I read these a couple of weeks ago, people were amused by the subject matter, but I don't confuse an ability to find unlikely topics with talent. Here's the last in that series:

> Drunk, in the gutter
> Snail sliding by on his spit
> Sunlight in his eye."

A cold shiver of dread shot down Casey's spine and he couldn't suppress a shudder. "That's quite an image. I wouldn't go so far as to say it's disgusting, but it certainly conveys a wretched circumstance."

"Yes, the group liked that one the best."

"Did they?" Casey reread the three Haiku and then shook his head. "I like the snail slime one best, but they're all good."

"They're just little exercises done for practice the way a concert musician plays scales. They're nothing special."

"Well, I disagree, I think they are. Is this an example of the lively debates that go on here?"

Suzanne closed her notebook. "You'll just have to wait and see."

They were joined then by a tall, gaunt man who looked to be about their age. Dressed in black, Casey thought he would need no more than a stovepipe hat to convincingly play Abe Lincoln. A young man wearing a white dress shirt and khaki pants entered next, stepping heavily in a bright orange pair of platform sole shoes. His blond hair had been closely cropped in the back, but sprang from the front of his head in wild corkscrew curls that dipped low to brush his eyes. Startled by the outlandish hairstyle, Casey raised his brows, but Suzanne shook her head to warn him to be still.

Two young women dressed in tank tops, jeans, boots, and black leather jackets came in together. Chewing gum, and slouching in their seats, they appeared to have ridden to the workshop on motorcycles. "What sort of poetry do they write?" Casey whispered.

"I suppose male-bashing describes it best."

"Oh good. I'll look forward to hearing it."

The next young woman to enter the circle was dressed in baggy gray sweats. Her long dark hair, parted in the center and falling straight, hid most of her face. She sat on the edge of her chair, held her notebook in both hands, and didn't look to the right or left to acknowledge her companions while she waited for the workshop to begin.

A woman with snowy white hair in an artist smock, sweat pants, and sandals came in carrying a heavy burlap sack. She slung it down on the floor as soon as she had taken a seat, and after briefly rummaging through it, produced a bottle of mineral water and took a long drink. She then began to sort through a thick folder, pausing frequently to rearrange its contents.

A bearded young man dressed in baggy print pants and a gold lamé sweater was followed by a balding man in a bright green blazer and tan slacks who sat down beside Casey. Thin and fidgeting, he crossed his legs, revealing a pair of lavender argyle socks. A stocky red-haired man sat down next to him. His T-shirt was stenciled with the name of a popular brand of beer. Jogging shorts, running shoes, and a baseball cap turned backwards completed his outfit.

Casey was already convinced this was an extremely diverse, if not downright peculiar group when a man walked in wearing a black and white knit sheath. At least he thought it was a man. The fellow sank into the seat beside the white haired woman, and crossed his legs. He had on white knee socks and black sandals, but there was nothing feminine about his pose. His hair was dyed an inky black, and getting comfortable, he adjusted the angle of his felt beret with several short jerks.

"I do believe that's the first man I've ever seen wearing acrylic fingernails," Casey confided softly.

"He is cute, isn't he?"

"An absolute dream, but I really thought transvestites had better taste in clothes."

The circle continued to fill, with men outnumbering women two to one, but none of the last arrivals would have garnered a second glance at the supermarket, let alone stood out there. At eight o'clock the workshop's leader came in from the bookstore. He was a nice-looking young man in khaki shorts and a turquoise shirt who announced the workshop's purpose was to provide critiques on work in progress and when he asked for a show of hands of those bringing poetry, most in the circle raised theirs. He immediately called on the young man with the bizarre haircut.

Casey studied the faces of those near him as the young man read. Everyone appeared to be intensely interested in the work, and nodded agreeably when he finished. While the poem had contained some pretty images, Casey hadn't thought it made much sense, but one comment swiftly led to another and it was plain the speakers understood the poet's purpose. Then like the gradual shifting of tides, the opinions grew more detailed and critical. The white-haired woman defended the poem as a quality piece, but one of the girls in black leather dismissed it as pretentious.

The oddly coiffed poet made a few half-hearted attempts to explain his intent, but soon gave up the effort and the leader called upon the Lincolnesque man to read. He supplied a brief descriptive piece on Los Angeles that was well-received, but with no dissenting opinions Casey wasn't nearly as entertained. Again hands went up as people vied for the opportunity to read.

"I've got it now," Casey leaned close to Suzanne to confide. "The discussion's the fun part, and the more controversial the poetry, the better the discussion."

"Hush!" she scolded, but her smile told him that she agreed.

The next reader delivered a poem comparing his ex-wife to a sofa and drew a torrent of criticism from the women present. In an effort to regain control of the rambunctious group, the leader chose the somber straight-haired girl, and she read a curious piece about a teenage girl and her mother that drew comparisons to Judy Blume and a stream of compliments. After her, a middle-aged man read a ponderous ode that took boredom to unexpected heights, and when the circle finally got the chance to comment they dismissed the work as pedantic drivel. Casey was embarrassed for the poor guy who had written it and relieved when the leader moved on.

By the break, Casey had had an opportunity to hear a variety of poetry, some excellent, some bad, and some downright insipid. "Can I borrow a piece of paper?" he asked Suzanne.

"Sure. Do you want to take notes?"

"No, I'm going to write a poem."

"Here? Now?"

"Sure. What's wrong with that? You go on outside and talk with everyone or whatever it is you do during the break, and I'll just sit here and work."

"You didn't tell me that you wrote poetry." Suzanne removed two sheets from her notebook and handed them to him.

"I don't, but it can't be all that different from ad copy and I write plenty of that."

"I hope you're not making fun of us."

"No, of course not. I've just gotten a sudden inspiration to write a poem and I intend to do it." Casey had no title as yet, but began work on the first line. Poetic images came easily to him, and engrossed in the task he had set himself, he did not look up as Suzanne walked away. Moving his thoughts around with ease, he played with word order and line breaks until he was satisfied he had a poem worth sharing. Giving it a title, he copied it on the second sheet of paper Suzanne had given him, and when the group reconvened, he was ready.

After brief announcements of coming events at the center, the personable leader stated he would like to hear from someone new and pointed to Casey. Now that he had the floor, Casey hoped he would not disappoint everyone, most especially Suzanne. He smiled at the people looking his way. After taking a deep breath, he read his poem in a relaxed, conversational style.

Aluminum Moons

on the floor
you'll find a scum pond of colorful linoleums
but you might find lights in reflections among
the beer drinkers
 in their folded down hats;
there's a dead stand up stove,
 metals at the windows

and the water tumult from a chain lavatory
  down the hall
but the best shimmering is in a water bowl by
  the window
where knives and forks lie,
handles sticking out like lower eyelashes in tin
  wet crescents of zinc and in
slip tight water pockets;
you might have to reach under the plates
for curled disappearances
curving steel squeaks
for scour-wire on the dark side of the bowl;
all in the rusted square iron sink

under the square window
which evacuates the necessary base metal lights
which hang
in iron wire cages
in the street.

Casey had no idea what sort of reaction to expect, but was ready to accept whatever praise or ridicule the group cared to heap on his work. When no one said anything for a long moment, he began to worry they were marshalling their harshest criticism for an outsider, but then the man seated beside him spoke.

"I like your poem," he began, gesturing with both hands in frantic dips and chops. "It has a wonderful evocative quality. I can almost smell the mildew in that dank kitchen. You have a unique ability to wring sensual elements out of inanimate objects. I especially like the line comparing the knife and fork handles to eyelashes. Very imaginative. Good work."

The white-haired woman was equally enthusiastic, and when one of the leather-clad young women said how much she liked it, Casey felt assured it was good. He had not written poetry since high school, but recalling his English teacher had praised his talent, he was sorry he had failed to pursue it.

After a brief discussion that was hugely complimentary, the leader called on the stocky red-haired man to read. Suzanne leaned close to Casey. "That was wonderful!" she exclaimed.

Embarrassed now, Casey just shrugged, but he folded his poem carefully and slipped it into his coat pocket to save. The remainder of the evening passed quickly, and when dismissed, the group dispersed in ones and twos but as they left the community center, several encouraged Casey to come back the next week.

"Thank you. You're very kind," he called in return.

"They weren't merely being kind," Suzanne insisted. "Your poem was good. I had no idea what to expect from you, but I do hope you'll write more poetry and come back again."

Her smile was very sweet as she extended the

invitation, but Casey forced himself not to leap at the chance to come with her each week. "I'll think about it," he said instead. "Let's go get something to eat."

They had reached his car and Suzanne slipped into her seat before she replied. "I'd love to have supper with you, but only if you'll promise to make me a copy of your poem."

Casey pulled it from his pocket and handed it to her. "Here, keep this one."

Suzanne held it in a reverent clasp. "I'll type up a copy so you'll have one to keep. Was this a particular place you worked, or merely from your imagination?"

"Let's just say I washed a lot of dishes when I first started working in restaurant kitchens, and those images came easily to me."

"You're being far too modest. To be able to describe a setting as well as you did is a unique gift. I do hope you'll come back next week."

Casey was glad he had impressed Suzanne. Had he had more time, he was positive he could have come up with something more romantic than a sink full of dishes, but because that had worked, he was content for the moment. "Will you come next week?"

"Yes, I plan to."

"All right, then I'll be here too." Casey pulled out of the parking lot and headed back toward her part of town. "What do you want for dinner?"

Suzanne had known Casey just a few days, but when he glanced toward her and smiled, she felt completely at ease. She named a popular rib place, and he nodded. "I'm glad I met you, Casey. It's a shame Carol hasn't appreciated you, but in a way, I'm very glad."

"Yeah, so am I."

Turning shy, Casey didn't comment again until they were seated in the restaurant. It was a place where people went to relax and have fun as much as eat. The tables were covered with red and white checkered cloths and the floor with sawdust. The lively music coming from the bar could barely be heard above the level of boisterous conversation. Suzanne ordered ribs, but Casey scanned the menu for something he could eat with less abandon. Then the irresistible urge to be as spontaneous as she overtook him, and he ordered ribs too.

"You have a delightfully uninhibited quality," he complimented sincerely.

Casey hadn't even loosened his tie at the poetry workshop and as Suzanne studied him now, he looked as carefully groomed as she was sure he had been when he arrived at his desk that morning. In one respect, his stability was comforting, but she knew Carol would describe him as rigid and controlling. Still, she was convinced he had a good heart and found it easy to smile.

"Thank you. Art was my first major in college, but I just wasn't good enough so I changed to art history, then switched to anthropology. I still share a great many characteristics common to artists. Being uninhibited, childlike if you will, spurs creativity."

"I can't even remember being a child."

Suzanne recalled his reference to a dysfunctional family, but didn't want to pry. "That's a shame. Childhood ought to be one of the happiest times of our lives."

Casey toyed with his fork rather than meet her gaze. "Well, my father was drunk more often than not, and my mother, God bless her, lacked the strength to leave him. They're both gone now, and I haven't seen my brothers or sister in years. We share the same memories, all of them bad, and getting together for holidays causes us more pain than joy so we just avoid each other."

Suzanne reached out to take his hand. "That's so sad."

Casey looked disgusted. "I shouldn't have said anything. I don't want your pity."

"There's an enormous difference between pity and understanding. When people hide things, when they aren't forthcoming, it's extremely difficult to get to know them. Everyone suffers then, not just the person who fears he won't be liked if the truth about him is known. You aren't your parents, Casey, and whatever their mistakes, you didn't make them."

Suzanne had touched a raw nerve, Casey couldn't manage more than a nod. Their waiter served their salads and relieved for an excuse not to talk, he ate his with great, gulping bites. The ribs were so delicious he soon lost his reservations about gnawing on the bones and finished them without exchanging more than a few murmured words of praise for the chef. The restaurant thoughtfully provided warm towels to clean up, but as Casey wiped the last smudge of sauce from his hands, he feared he had not been very good company.

He tried to make up for it on the ride to Suzanne's house, but the distance wasn't great enough for him to succeed. Fearing he had bored her, he was surprised when she invited him in and followed her into the kitchen. "Let me make the coffee," he offered.

Suzanne removed the can from the refrigerator. "Do you have a secret recipe for coffee too?"

"No, I just like it stronger than you usually make it."

"Well, why didn't you say so?"

"I didn't want to hurt your feelings."

Suzanne laughed softly. "We're talking about

coffee here, Casey, not something personal. Why would my feelings be hurt?"

"I just didn't want to take the risk." She was at the sink, filling the pot with water and Casey walked up behind her and slipped his arms around her waist. He rubbed his cheek against her hair and sighed softly. "You feel so good."

Suzanne was more startled than pleased, and froze. She set the pot on the counter, and put her hands over Casey's. "Thank you, but we barely know each other. Let's not get ahead of ourselves."

Disappointed by that cool response, Casey dropped his hands and stepped back. Suzanne turned to face him. She was smiling still, but not with the endearing sweetness she had displayed earlier. "You're a very desirable woman," he explained softly. "Why are you so surprised that I want you?"

"I'm very flattered, but—"

"But what? Is this just the wrong time, or am I the wrong man?"

Suzanne had seen a change in Casey the instant he described his family. He had retreated inside himself, but now he was reaching out to her and she did not want to discourage him just because she could not accept. "I like you very much. I just don't want to rush things."

"I'm not suggesting a one night stand."

Suzanne knew Casey was far too serious an

individual to engage in casual sex, and couldn't help but smile. "I know you're not, but we've each had our disappointments, and—"

Casey pulled her into his arms and silenced her softly voiced rejection with a lingering kiss. He tangled his fingers in her long curls to hold her close until he realized she wasn't objecting. He kissed her again, followed by a teasing, playful bite to her lower lip and then relaxed his grasp.

"Primitive societies intrigue you. Why not give in to primitive emotions?"

Casey was the last man Suzanne would have expected to be intent upon arousing her emotions, but his kiss had been remarkably enticing and she could not help but want more. "Take off your glasses," she urged, and when he complied, she raised her arms to encircle his neck and kissed him. He did not disappoint her by being too eager, but again kissed her in a gently adoring fashion, warming her clear through and making her crave more.

"Better remove your tie," she suggested.

Casey had it off in a second, and their next exchange of kisses left them both breathless. Suzanne helped him peel off his coat, and in another minute had his shirt unbuttoned. His belly was smooth and hard, clear evidence of the hours he spent in a gym each week. Suzanne tried to step back and think calmly, but Casey began to nibble her earlobe, coaxing forth a sparkling burst of giggles. In that instant she knew he was right. It was high time she lived with the passionate abandon of the tribes she admired for life was meant to be lived, not merely observed from a scholarly distance.

She laced her fingers in Casey's. "Did you really want some coffee?"

"Later."

Suzanne led him back through the living room to the stairs, but stopped there. She was excited, but more than a little frightened. Since her divorce, she had met so many nice men, but she had not gone this far with any others. "Do you believe in love, Casey? Do you really believe it exists?"

"Come on, I'll show you," he promised in a husky whisper.

His answer was in his smile, and Suzanne took the first step up the stairs. That Casey could write poetry had been a surprise, but as she turned toward him, she was certain he would provide a great many more. "No matter what happens, let's promise ourselves we'll have no regrets."

"Absolutely none," Casey agreed, "but if we don't get to your bedroom soon, I'll be forced to make love to you right here on the stairs."

When they reached her room, she turned on the lights, but just as quickly Casey shut them off. Lost then in an affectionate daze, Suzanne did not need anything but him to create a night well worth remembering. She started to remove her blouse, but he stopped her.

"Wait, I want to undress you."

The soft glow of the streetlight on the corner bathed them in a magical haze and Suzanne stood still as he removed first her blouse, then her skirt and slip. When he knelt to untie her sandals, she ruffled his hair. "You ought to let your hair grow longer," she coaxed.

"All right, I will." Casey stood and kissed her. "Would you like me to wear ruffled shirts so I'll look more like a poet?"

"No, I can't see you in ruffles."

"That's a relief." Casey unhooked her bra, tossed it away, and bent down to kiss the smooth softness of her breasts. "You're a very beautiful woman, Suzanne, very, very beautiful."

Again Suzanne slid her fingers through his hair to hold him close. "I think I'm very lucky to have found a man who likes voluptuous women."

"Don't all men like them?" Casey slipped his thumbs into the waistband of her panties and removed them with a quick tug. Now nude, Suzanne turned toward her bed, but Casey caught her hand and pulled her back into his arms. He thought her curvaceous figure absolutely luscious and ran his hands over the soft swells as he savored another deep kiss.

"There's no hurry," he whispered against the curve of her throat.

Suzanne disagreed, and reached for his belt buckle. "Wait, I'll find a hanger for your pants."

"I'm not that compulsively neat, Suzanne, don't bother."

He was laughing as his mouth met hers, and Suzanne ceased to worry about details. Casey was so very special, tender, and yet self-assured as he led her to the bed. As he pulled her down beside him on the down comforter his caress was light, knowing, exquisitely sensitive and when Suzanne thought she could stand no more of his delicious teasing, he followed the path of his fingertips with his lips branding her very soul with the heat of his kiss.

Suzanne had not known a man could be so exciting, and yet thoughtful, but while Casey wasn't her first lover, he taught her a great deal that night. When at last she fell asleep in his arms, she had never felt more deeply satisfied, nor loved. As for Casey, snuggled in Suzanne's embrace, he knew he had found something very precious. He made a silent vow to never let her go.

Close to midnight, Matt sat on his back steps scratching Taffy, Deborah's cocker spaniel, behind the ears. She leaned against his leg and gave a little yelp to beg for more. Matt continued to pet the dog, but his emotions were twisted in painful knots. Meeting Carol, and going out with her had been an important step for him, but even after four years of being alone, he wasn't certain he was ready to entertain women. Then again, he worried that he had waited too long, and now would never be able to recapture the joy Deborah had given him with someone new.

The first time he had kissed Carol, he had thought otherwise, but tonight, well, tonight there had been something frightening about how badly he had needed to kiss her. He wanted her still with an aching rage he feared might swiftly become an obsession. She was the wrong woman for him. He had no doubt of that, but it didn't stop him from wanting her.

Deborah had often had a smudge of flour on her cheek, or dirt on her knees after working in the garden, but Carol was a vision of feminine perfection. From her soft blond curls to her brightly lacquered nails, she was all any man would ever want, and then some, so why did he feel as though he were trespassing where he didn't belong? He hated being alone, but the thought of falling in love again, of risking his heart when there could never be any guarantees took more courage than he possessed.

He rose with a weary stretch, and went inside to open a can of dog food. He had survived Deborah's death by keeping up his routine from bringing in the paper in the morning to feeding Taffy every night, but now he ached to have something more than numbing chores to keep him going. The problem was, Carol Hagan promised to be far more than a momentary distraction. Was there enough left of him to tangle with her . . . and survive?

Eight

When Casey stopped in at Carol's office Thursday morning, he was wearing a grin wider than the Cheshire cat's. "I want to thank you again for introducing me to Suzanne. She is, well, there simply are no words to describe her."

Carol recognized Casey's silly smirk for what it was and fought back the rolling waves of envy that threatened to choke her. "You've either got a desperate case of infatuation, or you're in love," she replied. "This is awfully sudden, Casey. Please be careful. I don't want to see either of you hurt."

"How could we get hurt? Suzanne feels the same way I do."

"I'm happy for you then."

"You don't look happy."

In hopes of improving her spirits, Carol had worn a red Liz Claiborne outfit that day. She brushed a non-existent speck of lint from her skirt and crossed her legs. "I suppose happiness is relative, but this probably won't be one of the most memorable days of my life."

"Have you always been this cynical, or is your present attitude something new?" Casey took the chair beside her desk, and without conscious thought began piling the print-outs lying there in a neat stack. He then reached for the half dozen pencils thrown in a pick-up sticks pattern and dropped them into the container holding ballpoint pens. Satisfied the desk was now tidy, he sat back, and only then noted Carol's horrified expression.

"Is something wrong?" he asked.

"How could anything possibly be wrong with someone as efficient as you to pick up after me?"

Casey folded his hands in his lap. "Sorry."

"You needn't apologize to me. Just be careful not to drive Suzanne nuts."

"I suppose there's a real danger of that."

Carol nodded and picked up the order she had been working on when he came in. "If there's nothing else, I ought to get back to work."

"Sure, I didn't mean to bother you." But Casey didn't rise. "Did you go out with Matt last night?"

Carol made a face. "The less said about last night the better. Now go on, get out of here before I'm forced to call security and have them escort you up to your floor."

"You wouldn't."

"Don't tempt me."

Reluctantly, Casey got up and went to the door. "I'm sorry Carol. Matt seems like a nice guy and—"

Carol picked up her telephone. "That's it, I'm calling security right now and telling them there's a maniac loose in my office."

"I'm gone," Casey promised and he disappeared.

Carol replaced the receiver, and then sat staring at the telephone. If she had an ounce of courage, she would call Matt right now and cancel their date. He would be out the expense of renting the tux, which wasn't much with the discount, and she would be out the cost of the reunion tickets, but what did money matter when compared to self-respect?

Half a dozen times that morning she reached for the telephone, intent upon breaking their date in as courteous a manner as possible. She could blame commitments at work, or claim a sudden family emergency. She could even moan and say she had caught the flu. There had to be any number of ways to politely break a date when it was necessary and she was positive this was just such an occasion.

She would be sorry to miss the reunion, but

not nearly as sorry as she feared she would be if she went with Matt Trenerry. He would probably only communicate with grunts and coarse gestures and regardless of how handsome a man he was or how nicely he might be dressed, the evening was sure to be several hours of prolonged torture. When the telephone rang, she jumped, then afraid the way her life was going it would be bad news, she let it ring several times before answering.

"Carol Hagan."

"Carol, this is Suzanne. I want to thank you again for introducing me to Casey. He is absolutely incredible!"

Carol was convinced Suzanne's breathless enthusiasm came from the same source as Casey's. "You slept with him, right?"

Suzanne responded with throaty giggles. "Neither of us got much sleep. The man is absolutely tireless, Carol. Believe me, you missed a real treasure when you gave him to me."

"Are you telling me he doesn't get out of bed to remiter the corners every fifteen minutes?"

"You're right, he's extremely thorough, but the state of the bedclothes didn't concern him. He really made me wish I'd divorced Frank a long time ago, but I had no idea what I was missing."

Carol had only to close her eyes to recall what it had been like to make love with Bob. She could have set her watch by him he was so precise in his routine and she could not believe Casey would be all that different. "Wait until you've been with him a few times," she warned. "He might have perfected one approach to sex, and if that's the case, it will soon get tiresome."

"You don't understand, Carol. If Casey were to repeat what he did last night a thousand times, I'd never get bored. It was fantastic."

"I'm happy for you, Suzanne, but you're making me nauseous. You'll have to excuse me."

"Oh Carol, you're awful. What happened with Matt?"

Carol didn't even try to describe how he had kissed her when it had been a demanding rather than affectionate exchange. "Nothing happened with Matt, and if I'm lucky, every water heater in Pasadena will burst Saturday afternoon and he'll cancel our date."

"He's always been so nice to me."

"Well you and I are two different women. I'll see you Saturday night." Carol plunked down the receiver before Suzanne could stage the defense of Matt she had known was coming. She was positive everyone liked Matt. Why wouldn't they? The problem was, he did not like her and after such a marvelous beginning last Saturday night, she hated to think how badly things had gone awry.

"I still think he's hung up on his late wife," she mumbled to herself, and in a burst of nervous energy, she went out on the sales floor and reorganized her entire department.

When Carol got home that evening, Rob was in the kitchen sorting through her pots and pans. "What are you looking for?" she asked.

"I was sure you had an extra colander and I didn't see any reason to buy one when you had two."

"Making pasta for your latest conquest?" Carol opened the door beneath the microwave and pulled out the colanders. The battered aluminum one had been a shower gift before she married Bob. The white plastic one she had bought when they had been down at the beach on vacation. She handed him the newer one.

"Thanks. Linda's not a conquest, Mom. She's special; that's why I'm making dinner for her tonight."

"How is she different from your other girlfriends?"

Rob shrugged. "I don't know. She's as pretty as the others, but she has more depth. She's our new hygienist."

"Wonderful. What does your father say about your dating the help?"

"He doesn't know about it," Rob confessed

reluctantly. "He'd just start shouting that I'm laying myself open to a sexual harassment lawsuit, and forbid it, but what he doesn't know won't hurt him."

"He'd be right you know. It is dangerous to date a woman in your employ. Your other employees will accuse you of favoritism for one thing, and if you're the one to tire of her, Linda might be so insulted she'll make things difficult for both you and your dad."

"It's dangerous to date anyone these days, Mom, but trust me, Linda isn't the kind who'd pressure me for sex and then file a complaint."

"Rob!" Carol's outrage dissolved into giggles. While Rob was generally too serious a young man to tease her, he had his moments and she enjoyed them. "Just remember to put a few drops of olive oil in the water when you boil the pasta, then it won't stick together."

"Right, I'll remember. Say, could I borrow a bottle of olive oil?"

"No, but I'll pour some into a container for you." Carol got out a plastic margarine tub, and gave him several tablespoons of oil. "I'm eagerly looking forward to the day you finally have your apartment outfitted."

"I'm getting there." Rob dropped the plastic container into the colander. "What's the latest with the amorous plumber?"

Carol got herself a can of soda from the refrigerator, and opened it over the sink. "That's history, or at least it will be after Saturday night."

"I'm sure that's for the best, Mom. He wasn't nearly good enough for you."

Carol turned around to face him. She briefly debated explaining Matt was the one who didn't seem to think she was good enough for him, but decided there was no point in it. "I'm glad you found Linda, Rob, but the next time I meet a man I like, I hope you'll be far more generous in your opinions."

"Sure, it will be easy provided he isn't a bus-driver or shoe repairman."

"Suppose he is, what possible difference would that make to you?"

Rob picked up the colander and started toward the back door. "Come on, Mom, you belong with someone who can afford your tastes. Just because Liz Taylor married a construction worker doesn't mean you have to lower your standards."

"Ah yes, the family standards. God forbid they should be compromised for something so petty as happiness."

"Mom?" Rob paused at the door. "It's not that I don't want you to be happy. I just don't want you to have to be ashamed of the man you're seeing."

Carol just shook her head and took another

swallow of soda. The only thing shameful about Matt Trenerry was how strongly he affected her, but a purely physical attraction would have played itself out in a matter of weeks, leaving her right where she was now, cynical and alone. What a disgusting prospect, she bemoaned silently.

"Have a good time with Linda."

"Thanks, Mom. See ya'."

Carol went in to check her answering machine and found a call from Barbara Collins, one of the reunion committee members. Happy to lose herself in last minute details, she returned her call, and tried not to think how much she would have liked to have heard Matt's voice on the tape.

When Suzanne got home, Casey was sitting out on her deck. He leapt to his feet and came to meet her as she got out of her car. "It's late," he said. "I was getting worried."

Suzanne raised her hand to caress his cheek, but the gesture failed to erase his anxious frown. "I have office hours on Thursday afternoons, and today I also had a meeting with another professor. I wish you'd called to say you wanted to meet me after work, and then I could have given you my schedule."

Casey jammed his hands into his pockets and

followed her to the back door. He had had to leave in a hurry that morning to get home and dress for work, but didn't use that as an excuse. "After last night, I didn't think I'd have to call to make an appointment to see you."

Suzanne hesitated before inserting her key in the lock, then decided if they were going to get into a shouting match she would prefer to do it indoors. "Come in," she coaxed. She carried her books in to the kitchen table and then turned to face him.

"Last night was wonderful," she began, "but no matter how often we make love, we still need to respect each other's privacy. I wouldn't show up at your place unannounced, and I'd appreciate it if you'd let me know before you come here."

Casey tried to keep the bitterness out of his voice, but failed. "How many men are you seeing, Suzanne? If I don't give you ample warning that I'm on my way over, am I going to have to stand in line?"

"I ought to slap you for that." Thoroughly disgusted with him, Suzanne went into the hall to pick up her mail. She sorted through it as she walked back into the kitchen. It was the usual collection of bills and advertisements and she tossed them on the table beside her books.

"You've a great many marvelous qualities, Casey, but if you're going to be obnoxiously possessive then I'd like you to leave. We can forget the reunion, and the shelf project too. You see, I regard love as a plus, an enchanting addition to my life, not a smothering limitation. I'm not promiscuous, I wouldn't dream of seeing other men now that I've slept with you, but if you can't, or won't believe in me, then nothing I can ever do or say will reassure you and whatever we might have had together is over right now."

Casey clenched his fists at his sides. He knew he was behaving like a complete ass, but when Suzanne hadn't been there when he arrived, his imagination had supplied all sorts of lurid possibilities of where she might be, from the unmade bed of one of her students to the top of some museum curator's cluttered desk. She didn't deserve those crazy suspicions, and he knew it.

"I'm sorry," he finally admitted. "I like you so much, and I don't want to spoil it by grabbing for you, or holding on too tight. It's just difficult for me to step back and be detached."

"I don't want you to be detached, Casey, but you'll have to find the confidence to trust me. I mentioned counseling to you before. We could go together if you like."

Casey shook his head. "I don't want to dredge up the past."

"Wouldn't it be worth the pain if it saved your future?"

"Is that going to be one of your conditions, that either I get counseling or you won't see me again?"

"No, it's only a suggestion. If you can treat me respectfully without it, then fine." Suzanne wasn't certain where she had found the strength to discuss something so important in such a calm manner, but she knew it was absolutely vital that they understood each other from now on or their friendship would go no further. "Last night meant a great deal to me, but obviously we need to understand each other better, or we'll never recapture that magic."

That complimentary reference gave Casey hope and he began to smile. "It was magical, wasn't it?"

"Yes, it most certainly was."

"Could we just pretend this never happened? I'll go home, and go to the gym. I won't come back until Saturday night if you like. I won't lie and tell you it will be easy for me to stay away until then, but if that's what you want, I'll do it."

"Oh Casey, you can't ignore what you want in an attempt to please me. You'll just end up resenting me if you do. I'm flattered you want to see me. More than flattered really, delighted. All I ask is that you call me first so we can plan things together. Now since you're already here, let's fix dinner. I have a chicken in the freezer."

Enormously relieved that she hadn't thrown him out, Casey relaxed and began to loosen his tie. "Great. Do you have some honey and oranges?"

Suzanne nodded, but she wondered if it were even possible to set a man in his forties on a new course in life. She was willing to give it a try, but unlike Frank, this time she would know when the effort it took was no longer worthwhile.

Saturday afternoon, Carol planned to meet with Barbara and another of the reunion committee members at the Ritz Carlton Hotel. Located atop a knoll on the border of Pasadena and San Marino, the newly constructed hotel was a replica of the Huntington Sheraton Henry E. Huntington had built in 1906 to house the friends from the east he'd lured to Pasadena on his trains to enjoy the warm winter weather. The original hotel had stood until the late 1980s when the cost of reinforcing the structure for earthquake safety had been found to be prohibitively expensive. Torn down and rebuilt by new owners, the community landmark was an enduring monument to the glory days of the railroad barons.

Carol parked in the front lot and as she left her car, she was sufficiently intrigued by the adjacent row of boutiques to walk past them rather than head straight for the hotel. The Amadeus Spa offering a full line of beauty services and pampering occupied the end spot and Flowers by Piccolo, a florist who also carried exquisite gifts, was next door. Moving on, she paused at the window of the Pygmalion Boutique, and on an impulse, went inside to browse. A quick survey revealed the shop carried the usual selection of clothing found in hotel boutiques, ranging from designer sportswear to evening gowns and accessories.

She flipped over the tag on a white linen suit on the sale rack and was surprised by the $426 price. Knowing the manufacturer, she knew exactly what the suit had cost wholesale, and while stylish and well-made, it was marked higher than comparable apparel at Russell's. Thinking the location of the shop had a great deal to do with the price of the merchandise, Carol continued on her way. There were for-lease signs in the windows of the next two shops, and a real estate agent's telephone number. Curious as to the rent, she made a quick note of the number and slipped it in her purse.

Past the vacant stores was the Paradissimo, another clothing shop which catered to the elegant tastes of the guests at the hotel, but this time Carol was content to scan the merchandise from the walk. The corner unit was also for lease, but was serving temporarily as display space for the watercolors of two talented California artists. The last unit had a sign announcing a proposed museum which would display photographs and memorabilia from the hotel's long history, but it was not expected to open until fall.

Carol looked back along the colonnade. Domed blue awnings gave each shop an inviting entrance, but with so many units empty, she doubted any cleared much above their expenses. Shopping excursions always rekindled the hope of owning her own boutique, but she was far too cautious to rent a store in such an expensive location, fill it with an even more expensive inventory, and then pray everything sold so that she could remain in business a second month.

Shoving her dreams aside for the moment, she went on into the tile-roofed hotel. The Viennese Ballroom was off the courtyard. The high arched ceiling was painted white, but its delicate molding was liberally decorated with gold. Three magnificent crystal chandeliers and crystal wall sconces provided romantic lighting. The carpeting featured a diamond pattern in muted greens, and the walls were covered in pale green paneling and gold and green wallpaper. The first time Carol had seen the beautifully decorated room, she had been impressed by its elegance and had immediately envisioned the most marvelous of reunions.

Now she just wanted the evening over.

She approached the volunteers sorting name tags. "Barbara, Helen, how can I help you?"

"Oh Carol, this is an absolute mess," Barbara cried. A plump woman dressed in a blue denim jumpsuit, she waved a handful of name tags as she explained. "Shirley did these in calligraphy as the reservations came in so they're not in any order. Then some people just checked the space indicating they were bringing a guest but didn't state the guest's name so those are blank. We can't hand anyone a blank tag."

"Of course not," Carol sympathized. "Let's just have pens on the table and let people write their own names."

"But they won't be done in calligraphy and Shirley's are so pretty."

Carol doubted that was much of a problem. "Why don't we ask Shirley to man this table then, and she can fill in the missing names as the people arrive."

Helen and Barbara exchanged a worried glance, and then seemingly relieved, nodded. "Fine, we'll ask Shirley to come early, but I swear it's going to take us the whole day to straighten these out."

Carol circled the table. "I'll sort them if you

like. Why don't you two put the decorations on the tables?"

"You don't mind?"

"Not at all." Carol hoped the project would take the whole afternoon, but in half an hour she had the name tags laid out in alphabetical order so her classmates could easily find them. She had added Casey and Matt's name to the guest list at the first of the week, and was pleased to see there was also a name tag for Gordon Ashbach. She then caught up with Barbara and Helen who were adding small Cortéz High pennants to the floral centerpieces on each table.

"Everything looks perfect," Carol exclaimed.

"I'm worried we're going to be too crowded," Barbara said. "When everyone gets here, the room will be completely filled."

"Well better that than being strung around the walls the way we used to sit at sock hops. Do you remember those? Nobody wanted to start the dancing."

"I remember," Helen agreed with a dreamy smile.

"I still say we're going to be too crowded."

"We can move out across the corridor into the courtyard," Carol suggested. "The weather will be balmy. It will be fun to dance outside."

"People will trip on the green slate," Barbara predicted, "and fall into the pond. The hotel must be insured for mishaps like that, but what if someone were to sue the reunion committee?"

"Were you always such a worrier?" Carol asked.

"Yes, she was," Helen answered.

Three quarters of the room was set with round tables draped in white damask, topped with bouquets of white chrysanthemums and red rosebuds. A parquet dance floor had been laid at the end. "After dinner, I doubt people will want to remain at their tables," Carol said. "They'll be moving around, looking for friends, and some will always be dancing. If the hotel says this room comfortably holds two hundred, then I'm sure it will."

"We're going to be jammed in here too tight," Barbara again complained.

"Look, I'll take on the responsibility for shooing people out onto the patio," Carol declared. "There are tables out there. The people who don't want to dance might spend the whole evening seated there. People who don't like either the music or their classmates' conversation can always go sit in the bar. I bet we'll have people all over the place. Now why don't you go call Shirley so she'll know to come early, and then go on home. I'll finish up with the pennants before I leave."

"You don't mind?"

"No, I don't." As promised, Carol added the last of the red and white pennants, but then she was reluctant to leave. The stately ballroom was so beautiful, and at that hour serene as an empty cathedral. Desperately needing to cultivate some serenity of her own, she pulled out a chair and sat down simply to enjoy her surroundings before they filled to overflowing with the laughter of the classmates she had not seen in ten years.

She could imagine the questions she would receive. She was still at Russell's, and while some were sure to be impertinent enough to ask, she would not agree to buy anyone designer clothes on her employee discount. She did have good news to report on her sons' careers; after all, how many families nowadays could boast of producing both a dentist and a chiropractor? Of course, their success would be offset by the news of her second divorce.

Depressed that she would have to make that admission, as well as pretend to be having fun with an escort she feared would be sullen at best, the evening became even less appealing. Why had she gotten involved in the reunion in the first place? she wondered. That they had all attended Cortéz High was a tenuous link after thirty-five years, and she doubted many coming that night would want to come back for the next reunion. She promised herself right now that she would skip it.

Thoroughly depressed, she got up as two young men appeared carrying an amplifier. They debated briefly where to place it and then went out to bring in the rest of the band's equipment. The brief period of tranquillity over, Carol walked to the door. She lingered there, then thinking the setting would be perfect that evening, even if nothing else was likely to be, she went home to dress.

Aimee had had her hair trimmed, and bought a new pair of red satin shoes, but it wasn't until she ran her bath that she decided to add perfumed salts and make the evening really special. She soaked a long while, leafing through the stack of women's wear catalogs that had come that week rather than risk dropping a book in the tub. She had allowed herself plenty of time, and once out of the bath, painted her nails and toenails as bright a red as her dress.

She watched the early news as her nails dried, and then finished dressing. She was ready more than half an hour early and reviewed her last yearbook in a final attempt to recall more about Gordon Ashbach. If he had participated in class, she didn't remember him being particularly clever. In fact, other than being a vague presence in the back of the room, she had no impression of him at all.

Determined to make the best of her mystery date, she reread the front page of the *Times* to have current events well in mind should they not find anything else in common to discuss. Restless, she went back upstairs to her bedroom to check her appearance in the full-length mirror and while she was pleased she looked damn good for fifty-two, she certainly hoped Gordon wasn't disappointed. She turned and glanced over her shoulder, but even from that view she presented a polished picture of a successful woman.

She turned off the lights and went downstairs to wait for her date, but as the time neared, she couldn't help but feel foolish. This was almost as bad as a blind date, which everyone knew never turned out well. What if she had known Gordon in high school? Thirty-five years was a long time and while she certainly hoped he had led a happy and productive life, she supposed there was a real possibility he had become a troll-like eccentric who existed solely to serve his aged mother's every beck and call.

When the doorbell rang, she took a deep breath, and doing her best to smile, opened the front door. "Gordon?" she gasped, for the man standing on her stoop wasn't what she had expected at all.

No one would have called him a nerd. He was just over six feet tall, with curly auburn hair and green eyes lit with a dancing sparkle. His tuxedo showed off his broad shoulders and narrow hips, but it was his charming smile that completely dazzled Aimee.

"I'm sorry, I don't mean to stare," she blurted out, "but I was expecting Gordon Ashbach."

"Then I'm at the right house. That's who I am. I like your hair that color, Aimee, does it have a fancy name like silver mist?"

Aimee managed to take a step backwards without stumbling so Gordon could come in. "I'm so sorry I didn't recognize you. I guess we've both changed since high school."

"In my case, it could only have been an improvement. I've grown a couple of inches, gained twenty-five pounds, got the braces off my teeth, and traded my glasses for contact lenses, but you, well, other than the difference in your hair, I would have known you anywhere." He handed her a clear plastic box containing an orchid corsage.

"I didn't have the nerve to ask you to the prom, but I would have liked to. I wanted to bring you a corsage, even if it is thirty-five years late."

Aimee held the florist's box in trembling hands. "That's very sweet of you. Thank you.

I have a mirror in the dining room. Come with me while I put it on."

Gordon followed her, then stood behind her as she pinned it to her beaded dress. "I still can't believe that you called me. It was like a fantasy come true."

Aimee was more embarrassed than flattered by that declaration. "Why Gordon, did you fantasize about me?"

"Oh yes, but then the whole math club did. Would you like me to describe my fantasy? I'm sure I could still do it in delicious detail."

Aimee could see his smile in the mirror but reversed she couldn't tell if it had turned teasing, or become a suggestive leer. It was unnerving to think she was alone in the house with a stranger who might have kinky tastes she did not even want to imagine let alone hear about in detail. All she wanted to do was leave.

"I don't think I'll need a jacket tonight," she said as she plucked a beaded handbag from the dining room table. "Shall we go?"

Again, Gordon followed her at a respectful distance. He didn't seem threatening, but she was sorry she hadn't insisted upon his meeting her at the hotel. She pulled her front door closed, and locked it. "Where's your car?" she asked.

"Right in front."

There was a pale gold Mercedes 450SL

parked at the end of her walk; Aimee hurried toward it.

Gordon lengthened his stride to overtake her. "Are we late?"

"No, the party doesn't start until eight."

Gordon helped her into her seat, and then walked around to get in on the driver's side. He buckled his seatbelt and waited for Aimee to fasten hers. "Are you as nervous as I am?" he asked.

"Probably more."

"Well, don't be. Fantasies are better left to teenage boys. I won't try and make mine come true." He winked at her then. "At least not tonight, anyway."

That promise wasn't in the least bit reassuring and as Gordon drew away from the curb, Aimee wished she still had a pair of pom-poms to wedge firmly between them.

Nine

For the reunion, Carol had planned to wear a swirling white chiffon skirt with a sequined top patterned to resemble woven ribbon. In a bright rainbow of hues, it was exquisite but as she stared at her reflection, she saw not a pretty blonde in a gorgeous outfit, but a miserably unhappy woman. Her hair was perfectly coiffed. Her nails were polished a bright red-orange to match one of her top's many colors. With an extra brush of mascara, her eyelashes were so long and thick they made her eyes appear enormous, but no amount of lipstick could make a smile remain on her lips.

She went to her closet, and briefly debated wearing something less festive, but knowing the bleakness of her mood really had nothing to do with her clothes, she chose not to change them. As she slipped on a sparkling pair of silver heels, she could not help but think of Cinderella. Her story had a tragic difference, however, for she was going to the ball with the prince, but most definitely would not be living happily ever after.

"Might as well wear pumpkins on my feet," she complained to herself. "Matt would never notice."

She had considered calling him as late as an hour ago, to feign some dreadful illness, but now as she waited the last few minutes for him to arrive, she really was beginning to feel ill. She hadn't felt like eating all day, which was undoubtedly a contributing factor, but it wasn't hunger pangs that made her heart ache. She reminded herself the committee was relying on her to pass out the door prizes that evening, but that chore wasn't sufficient motivation to attend.

"If only I'd left well enough alone," she moaned, for now going with Aimee and Suzanne seemed like a wonderfully practical, rather than pathetic idea. Of course, if she had not invited Casey, then he and Suzanne wouldn't have gotten together, so that was at least some consolation. As for Aimee and Gordon Ashbach, she did not hold out much hope there, but perhaps something good might come of their last-minute date.

When the doorbell rang, she straightened her shoulders. Determined to give the performance of a lifetime and convince everyone at the reunion that she was enjoying herself thoroughly, she went to answer. She pasted a smile on her face as she opened the door, but one would have lit her expression naturally once she had seen Matt's.

"You look," he paused as his gaze swept over her in a sensuous arc, "delicious. Are you ready?"

Matt looked even better in his tuxedo than he had on Wednesday night, and now scented with Antaeus, he was definitely on the delicious side too. "Thank you. You look incredibly good yourself. You have the build for formal wear. It's a shame your work doesn't require it."

"I think that's chimney sweeps, rather than plumbers."

"You're right," Carol agreed, and thinking the evening hadn't gotten off to too bad a start, she picked up her purse and after pulling her front door closed, started down her walk.

Then she saw the white van marked Trenerry and Son parked at the curb. Thinking Matt was playing some kind of tasteless joke, she turned back to face him, but his expression was one of relaxed innocence. "Let's take my car," she suggested. "I had it washed today, so not only will it get us there, it will look good on the way."

Matt shook his head. "No way. The escort provides the transportation, and while my van may not be all that pretty to look at, it will also get us there and the valets won't have any trouble finding it after the party."

Carol stared at him, certain he was deliberately pushing her into an argument. Perhaps he had decided he would rather not take her to the reunion, but like her, had also lacked the courage to call and break the date. *Coward!* she fumed silently. She had a clear choice now, to refuse to ride in the lumbering van, which would be tantamount to a refusal to go with him, or to ignore the fact he had arrived with a totally inappropriate means of transportation for a formal party. Livid, she stubbornly chose the latter.

She continued on down the walk with a jaunty step and climbed up into the van without a worry as to whether there might be grease on the passenger seat that would ruin her pretty clothes. What did a little grease matter, when plumbers probably preferred it to perfume! There was a cardboard box filled with an odd assortment of elbow joints occupying the space where her feet would naturally be, but she adjusted her pose and swung sideways to avoid it.

Matt got in and fastened his seat belt, started up the van, and then reached for the knob to turn on the radio. Dwight Yokum was singing one of his favorite songs and tonight unmindful of Carol's tastes, he turned it up a bit and began to hum along. Filled with equipment, the van rattled and swayed as they left Carol's neighborhood and headed out onto Huntington Drive.

Carol concentrated on the passing scene rather than her attractive, but maddeningly contrary companion. At more than one stoplight she noticed passengers in adjacent cars gaping at them, and lifted her hand to wave. After all it wasn't every night a plumber and his date could be seen wearing formal clothes while they rode in his van. Not amused to be part of the curious spectacle she hoped every last one of her classmates got to the Ritz Carlton before them so that only the valets would see her climbing out of a plumber's truck.

She held onto the door as the van rumbled up Oak Knoll toward the hotel, but her heart fell when they turned into the entrance and she sighted the line of cars waiting for valet service. She was embarrassed clear through.

Clustered in front of the hotel, old friends were greeting each other with excited whoops, but Carol prayed no one would recognize her until they got inside. As they left the van, she saw more than one couple pointing toward them, and raising hands to cover their laughter, but she was no longer a teenager who could be so mortified by her classmates' giggles. No, she was concerned more with Matt, and what his insistence upon coming in his van said about his respect, or lack of it, for her. She checked her watch, and hoped he would not prove to be difficult the entire evening.

"Carol Powers! Is that you?"

Carol turned to the woman approaching. She vaguely remembered standing beside her in chorus, but she could not recall her name. Inside they would all have the benefit of name tags, but out here, she was simply at a loss. She smiled, and tried to look pleased. "How nice to see you," she said. "How have you been?"

The woman hooked her arm through her husband's. A chubby pair, they resembled each other closely enough to have posed for a set of salt and pepper shakers. She was dressed in red, and he was wearing a tuxedo with a red tie and cummerbund. "We've been very well, thank you, well, that's not exactly true. I fell while out riding one of our horses last fall and broke my wrist, but the doctor said I was fortunate not to have shattered my shoulder."

"Oh yes, fortunate indeed," Carol repeated. She tried to remember a reference to anyone owning horses, but if she had heard one at any of the committee meetings she had forgotten it.

"Well," the woman urged, "aren't you going to introduce us to your husband?"

At a loss for a way to go about it when she could not recall their names, Carol turned toward Matt, and while her gesture was graceful, her expression was one of complete panic. A painful second went by, and then another.

"I'm Matt Trenerry." Matt immediately extended his hand to the man. "Glad to meet you."

"Rick Betts," the man replied, "and this is my wife, Cecilia. I didn't go to Cortéz High myself, but after attending all the reunions over the years, I feel as though I did."

"Let me give you my card," Matt offered, and quickly produced one from his jacket pocket. "Whatever your plumbing problem, I'm sure my son and I can handle it."

Rick studied the card, and then glanced toward Matt's van. "Well now, I'll certainly keep you in mind. Come on, dear, we want to get places at a good table before it gets too crowded."

Carol breathed a sigh of relief as the Betts hurried away. "Thank you, I couldn't think of their names. They're the kind who always make a point of speaking to everyone so I really should have remembered them."

Matt looked far from pleased. "I thought it was my name you'd forgotten."

"Yours? Of course not."

"Well, you might have pointed out their error when they mistook me for your husband."

Carol swallowed hard. It was plain he had been insulted by the Betts' assumption, and that hurt. "You're absolutely right. I'm sorry for that too. I won't let it happen again."

One of the black-coated valets reached them then and handed Matt a ticket. "We can't be responsible for what's in your van, sir."

"I doubt any of this crowd will steal a toilet," Matt assured him. "It will be fine."

It hadn't occurred to Carol that Matt would be taking a risk other than drawing ridicule, in driving his van. "What about your tools? Aren't they valuable?"

"They're in locked compartments. You needn't worry about them."

Matt took her arm, and drawing in a deep breath, Carol walked with him into the hotel. They stepped over the brilliant blue mat with the Ritz Carlton crest emblazoned in white then across the cream-colored marble and followed the signs pointing the way to the Viennese Room. Decorated in beige, peach, and pale green, the hotel exuded a tranquil air, but the sound of excited laughter carried down the hall. Warmed by it, Carol patted Matt's arm and hoped that from now on everything would go right.

After picking up their name tags, they joined the line at the bar. Carol smiled and nodded to people who looked as vaguely familiar as Cecilia Betts, but was greatly relieved when no one else approached them. At the twenty-fifth reunion, she had been surprised at the difference in appearance between her male and female classmates. Many of the men were balding and overweight, while the majority of the women were slim and attractive. Like Carol, many had been married more than once, and some who had married right out of high school had begun careers when their children were grown. As a group, they were far more vital in their outlook than the men they had had crushes on as teenagers.

After ten more years, the difference she had noticed then was even more pronounced. More of the men were balding while their waistlines had spread several additional inches. The women, however, obviously took far better care of their health and figures. Some who had been rather plain during their days at Cortéz High had actually blossomed into extremely attractive women.

Carol felt Matt watching her and turned toward him. "I was just looking around, trying to remember everyone and trying not to be too surprised by how some of them have turned out. Do you see the tall man near the door?"

"The one with the goofy haircut?"

"Can you call attempting to wind three long hairs all around your head a haircut?"

"I was trying to be polite. Yes, I see him."

"His name is Jack Shank. He was captain of

the football team, and Homecoming King. He had several scholarships, but dropped out of college and went to work selling insurance. The little redhead is his wife. She didn't attend Cortéz so I don't know anything about her, but I couldn't help but feel sorry for her at the last reunion. Jack had too much to drink, got really loud, and wouldn't listen to her when she begged him to leave."

"Every reunion must have its share of obnoxious drunks."

"I suppose, but I still felt sorry for her. I hope he doesn't do it again tonight."

When they reached the bar, both Matt and Carol ordered mineral water. As they moved off to the side, he whispered a question. "Were you the homecoming queen?"

Pleased that he would ask, Carol shook her head. "Aimee was the queen the year Jack was king, but he was quite handsome then and everyone envied her."

"I'll bet."

Carol wasn't sure how he meant that, but before she could ask, two more of her former classmates came up to them. Grateful they were wearing name tags, she greeted the two women easily and introduced Matt. To her dismay, Matt again handed them his business cards. The pair looked somewhat nonplussed, but Matt wasn't deterred.

"Whatever your plumbing problem, I'm sure my son and I can handle it. We do quite a bit of consulting as well as redecorating. One of our regular customers is hosting a wedding reception at her home tonight and I suggested she rent at least three portable toilets, but do you think she would listen to me? I can guarantee she'll be calling later when every toilet in her house has backed up, but I'm off for the evening so it will be just too bad. It will be a shame to see her party ruined, but I warned her. Don't let the same thing happen to you."

At the mention of portable toilets, both women had begun to back away, and by the time Matt finished his pitch, they rushed off into the crowd lined up at the bar. Carol couldn't believe he had really wanted to discuss such a subject. "Was that an attempt at humor, or were you deliberately trying to disgust my friends?"

Matt shrugged as if he had no idea what she meant. "That was good advice. If you ever have a big party at your home, rent portable toilets and you'll be glad you did."

"This is no time to discuss toilets!" Carol hissed.

"I'm a plumber, what else could possibly be on my mind?"

Matt looked gorgeous. Trim, tanned, fit, he was easily the most attractive man in the room, but Carol couldn't abide his superior smirk.

"Let's go out on the courtyard for a minute," she suggested between clenched teeth and she led the way across the corridor outdoors. As she had predicted, the tables were already filled with graduates of Cortéz High who preferred the cool night air to the warmth of the ballroom. Remembering Barbara's warning, she took care not to trip over the rough green slate, or to get too close to the edge of the pond.

"If I've somehow given you the mistaken impression that I'm bothered by your profession, then I am sincerely sorry, but I don't appreciate your belligerent attitude. We're both adults. Let's make the best of the evening and then if we never see each other again, I doubt either of us will mind."

"I'd mind," Matt argued. "You've got a big house. I'll bet you need to call a plumber at least once a year and I'd hate to lose your business."

"You have already lost it!" Carol replied.

"Lost what?" Suzanne asked as she and Casey joined them. She was dressed in an aqua gown with a scarf hem that flattered her vivid coloring as well as her ample figure. She had caught her hair atop her crown with a rhinestone barrette that sent her red curls cascading over her shoulders. While she was pleased with her appearance that night, it was Casey's company that kept her smiling.

"A mere figure of speech," Matt assured her. "Should we be worried about saving places so we can have dinner together?"

"We've already reserved six seats at one of the front tables," Suzanne explained. "Have you seen Aimee? I understand she's coming with Gordon Ashbach and I'm dying to meet him."

"Ashbach?" Matt asked. "Is he with the Jet Propulsion Lab?"

"He was a math whiz, so he might be with JPL. Why, do you know him?" Carol asked.

Matt started to laugh. "I'd like to say that I hang out with rocket scientists, but I don't. I remodeled the kitchen for a man named Ashbach, so if he's Aimee's date, that's how I met him. You see, Carol, eventually everyone needs a good plumber, even brilliant scientists."

Carol tried counting to ten, and then twenty, but it failed to ease her growing distress. Dinner wouldn't be served for an hour yet and she knew without any doubt that Matt was going to mention portable toilets to everyone they met. Her only question was: why?

As soon as they had picked up their name tags, Aimee began looking for Carol and Suzanne, but didn't see them. Thinking they must have arrived first, she tried to be patient. "Would you like to check the reservations list? I'd hate for you to spend the entire evening looking for your buddies from the math club if none are here."

Gordon frowned slightly. "I came to be with you. I don't give a damn who else is here."

Uncomfortable with what she assumed was a heavy dose of flattery, Aimee tried not to let it show. "That's sweet, but I'm sure you'd at least like to know what's become of them."

"Not really. Would you like something to drink?"

"Yes, thank you." A naturally friendly person, as they walked toward the bar Aimee responded to greetings from her former classmates. Some she could still greet by name, others, she had to take a quick peek at their name tag to recognize. Unlike Gordon, most of the men had not changed for the better.

"They always give prizes for the person who's come the greatest distance, or has the most children. They'll probably have a grandchild category this year. If they were to have a prize for the person who's changed the most, I bet you'd win."

"I'm sure you mean that as a compliment, but it hurts to think how much of a nerd I was in high school."

Horrified that she had inadvertently insulted him, Aimee hastened to reassure him. "Teenagers are far too clannish," she insisted. "That you and your friends were interested in something more serious than football and girls was admirable. You shouldn't think of yourself as a nerd."

A faint smile played across Gordon's lips. "I thought a great deal about girls, or rather one particular girl."

That brought a blush to Aimee's cheeks—a blush that she feared wasn't at all becoming. She asked for a glass of *chablis,* but resisted the impulse to toss it down her throat in a single gulp. She had almost no tolerance for alcohol, and a single glass of wine was her limit. Liquor did not make her more sociable nor obnoxious as it did some people. It merely made her sleepy and the possibility she might fall asleep face down in the entrée in the middle of dinner was enough to prevent her from ever overindulging.

As they moved away from the crowded bar, a fellow nearly as tall as Gordon, but almost painfully thin, adjusted his thick horn-rimmed glasses and came uncomfortably close to peer at their name tags. "I don't believe it," he gasped before thrusting out his hand. "Lee Whitson. How have you been doing, buddy?"

"Lee?" Gordon appeared startled, then quickly recovered. "I would have known you anywhere. You remember Aimee Stewart."

"The cheerleader, of course." Lee also gave

her hand an enthusiastic shake. "Finally got a date with her, huh?" Lee poked Gordon in the ribs. "They say all things come to he who waits and I guess this proves it. Where are you working?"

"JPL," Gordon replied. "How about you?"

"Hughes Aircraft. Here, let me give you my card. We really ought to get together soon." Lee reached into his jacket for a card, but before he could produce one, his wife appeared at his elbow. She was also tall and slim, with short tightly permed hair and thick glasses. Lee gave her a hug and introduced her. "Denise is also with Hughes. The guys used to tease me about falling for the first woman I met who carried a slide rule in her purse, and I did."

Denise beamed, and while Aimee thought she must have heard that same story a thousand times, clearly she still enjoyed it. "It's only natural that people are drawn to others with similar tastes," she agreed.

"Not always," Gordon argued. "I've never found a woman who's into theoretical physics all that exciting."

"Theoretical physics?" Aimee mumbled, unsure what that was. "Is that your field?"

"Yes, but it's not my only interest," he promised. "Just as I'm sure banking isn't your whole life."

"That's true," Aimee replied, but she feared

he was mistaken for now that her daughters were grown, her career *was* her life's major focus. There was no emotional risk involved, and the time she devoted to it always paid off. She listened attentively as Lee and Denise summarized their current projects, but she was at a loss to understand engineering terminology and when they asked Gordon about his work, she was completely lost. Trying not to look bored, she scanned the crowd for Suzanne and Carol until the Whitsons went on their way.

"I'm sorry," Gordon apologized. "I'm sure they bored you witless. That's why I'm not that interested in looking up the crowd from the math club."

"I wasn't bored," Aimee quickly denied. "Lost perhaps, but certainly not bored. I think it's wonderful Lee and Denise found each other. They probably have wonderfully bright children."

"Yes, I'll bet they do, but they'll undoubtedly be tall and skinny with poor eyesight."

"Come on, you fit in that category at one time."

Gordon laughed at that reminder and winked at her again. "I'm just a late bloomer. There are a lot us over at JPL. What sort of work did your husband do?"

Startled by that abrupt change in topic, Aimee needed a moment to find a reply. "Steve was with the Edison Company, but he managed industrial accounts, he didn't climb power poles."

"I'm sorry, I guess I shouldn't have mentioned him."

"No, it's all right. Let's see if we can find Carol and Suzanne before time to find a table for dinner. I'd like to sit with them, and I want to make certain they're not counting on us to save places for them."

"Of course. I'll look for a redhead."

He took her hand as they made their way around the edge of the ballroom and Aimee had to admit the gesture was rather nice—innocent, and yet conveying a concern she had not felt in a long while. Gordon might not be what she had expected, but after having spent a half hour in his company, she wasn't at all disappointed.

After a few minutes conversation with Carol and Matt, Suzanne and Casey went on to speak with some of Suzanne's other classmates. She introduced Casey proudly, and he was charming to everyone. When they found themselves alone for a moment, he pulled her aside.

"Let's rent a room," he suggested.

Suzanne couldn't see any need of that. "My house isn't more than two miles from here and neither of us is likely to have so much to drink we can't get there safely."

"I'm not worried about a DWI arrest," he assured her. "If we had a room, we could spend the time before dinner far more productively than just catching up with your old friends."

Flattered at first by what she assumed was affectionate teasing, Suzanne soon realized Casey was serious. "You aren't kidding, are you?"

"No, I'm not. Sleeping with you the last three nights hasn't dimmed my appetite one bit. You look good enough to eat, and I'm real hungry." He leaned down to growl in her ear.

"Casey O'Neil, you stop that this instant!" Suzanne looked around to make certain no one had overheard him. "Passion is wonderful, but not all the time."

"I'm not talking about all the time, only about now."

"I doubt you could get a closet here for less than a hundred dollars."

Casey took her hand to lead her out of the courtyard. "Thanks for the idea. Let's go find a linen closet. It will be full of pillows and—"

Suzanne drew him to an abrupt halt with an angry jerk. "I realize this is a high school reunion, but you're being positively adolescent and I want you to stop it right now."

Casey's smile widened as he shook his head.

"Does it embarrass you that you turn me on so easily? You ought to feel proud."

"Proud? I'm close to being insulted. No, make that frightened. I won't be pushed, wheedled, or coaxed into something I don't want to do. Not tonight, or any other night."

"What about high noon?"

"Casey, you're being impossible!"

"I like to think of it as romantic. Why don't we go speak with the desk clerk? If I tell him you're suffering from a migraine, he'll probably give us the use of a room for free. After all, the reunion must be bringing in several thousand dollars so they can afford to be generous."

"Not on your life. I came to enjoy the reunion and that's all I plan to do."

"Spoil sport. Why not make this reunion really memorable?"

"Suzanne?"

Relieved beyond words for an excuse to end what she considered a totally ridiculous argument, Suzanne turned to find Cecilia and Rick Betts at her elbow. A quick peek at their name tags allowed her to introduce them to Casey. "Cecilia and I had several art classes together. Tell us what you've been doing the last ten years."

Annoyed that Suzanne found Cecilia more interesting than she did him, Casey began to rub her back in small, seductive circles. When she took a step away, he moved with her but this time took her hand, and rubbed her palm with his thumb. Suzanne was the most delightfully affectionate woman he had ever met, and he wasn't ashamed by how much he wanted her.

Far from immune to Casey's appeal, Suzanne pulled her hand from his. "Maybe we ought to go back to the ballroom. It's almost time for dinner, and I don't want anyone to take our seats."

"I think we're at your table," Rick said. "Aren't we, hon?"

"Yes, we saw you had six places saved, but that left four and we took two. I hope you hadn't asked someone else to join you."

"No, we hadn't," Suzanne assured her. "Come on, Casey, I'm still anxious to meet Gordon Ashbach, and maybe he and Aimee have already found our table."

Casey followed along willingly, but as they neared the ballroom door, he leaned down to whisper, "What about after dinner?"

Suzanne looked over her shoulder and glared at him. "After dinner I want to dance. I missed most of the dances in high school, and I'm not going to miss a minute of the dancing tonight."

Casey moaned.

"You do like to dance, don't you?"

Suzanne looked as though she might cry if he said no, and Casey quickly assured her that he did. "Say, is that Gordon Ashbach?" he asked.

Suzanne followed his glance and saw Aimee talking with a tall, good-looking man whose face wasn't even vaguely familiar. "I've no idea who that is, but come on, let's go meet him."

"I'd still rather go look for a linen closet," Casey whispered, but he followed closely.

Aimee had located the table where Suzanne had written their names on place cards, but when she found Jack Shank and his wife Megan also intended to sit at their table, she gagged. She moved to the adjacent table, hoping to find names of a couple she could switch, but before she managed it, Jack and Megan reached their table.

"There's my queen!" he greeted her, and not content merely to give her a boisterous hug, he planted a sloppy kiss on her cheek.

Aimee cringed all the way to the toes of her red satin slippers, and placing her palms on Jack's chest, pushed him away. "How nice to see you, Jack, and I remember your wife from our last reunion."

Rather than looking pleased, Megan simply pulled out her chair and sat down. She had flaming red hair and freckles, but none of the impish charm that might have been expected to go along with her vivid coloring. She was dressed in navy blue, and looked tired, rather than excited about the evening.

Gordon reached out to shake Jack's hand. "Gordon Ashbach," he reminded him. "We had a couple of classes together. Spanish I think it was."

"Really?" Not at all interested in Aimee's date, Jack pulled out her chair and helped her get seated before sitting down beside her.

Suzanne and Casey joined them, but Jack greeted them from his chair. Suzanne sat down beside Gordon and sent a knowing smile Aimee's way. "I'm so happy to see you again," she told him. "I want to hear everything you've done since leaving Cortéz High."

"And risk putting everyone to sleep?" Gordon replied. "I've been with JPL since graduating from Cal Tech, and that's all you really need to know." Gordon saw Matt approaching and rose to shake his hand. "Matt, I didn't expect to see you here tonight."

"Nor I you," Matt responded. He introduced Carol, and then helped her into her seat before taking his own beside her. He looked around and saw the Betts barreling toward their table. "This looks like it will be a great evening, doesn't it?"

Carol tried to smile. Suzanne brushed Casey's hand off her knee, and Aimee scooted her chair closer to Gordon's to put more distance between herself and Jack Shank. When the Betts joined them, she was grateful for the enthusiastic pair's company. She hoped Jack Shank wouldn't make a bigger ass of himself than he already had.

Ten

A sandy-haired young man in a tweed sportcoat and maroon bow tie began to weave his way through the tables as people took their seats. "I'm Keith Baumgarner, your reunion photographer. I'll be available all evening. You'll want plenty of photos, so don't wait too long."

"How can we wait too long if you'll be available all evening?" Jack Shank asked in a blustering tone.

The photographer laid order forms on the table. "At midnight, all the people who've waited for photos will come rushing over to my corner and be disappointed when they have to wait in a long line. Avoid the rush," he advised. "Have your photos taken now."

Jack leaned toward Aimee. "Come on, sweetheart, let's have our picture taken together again."

Aimee glanced toward Megan. Her mouth was

a malevolent line. "Have your picture taken with your wife, Jack. She's your date tonight."

Jack took a drink of his scotch and soda. "I have dozens of photographs of Megan. I want a new one of you and me."

"Take one of the whole table," Matt suggested. "Then we'll all be in it."

"Excellent suggestion, sir." Keith moved back, raised his camera and then looking over it, gestured for the Betts to move over slightly. "Yes, just squeeze in there a little and I'll be able to fit you all in. Now say striptease!"

Everyone but Megan managed a charming smile, but apparently not noticing her frown, the photographer marked a number on their order forms, then moved on to the next table. Blinded by the flash, Jack blinked several times. He gulped down the last of his drink, then rose unsteadily.

"I'm going to the bar. Can I bring you something, Aimee?"

"No, thank you, but perhaps someone else would like something?" She glanced at her tablemates, but all shook their heads and Jack went stumbling off.

When no one else offered a topic for conversation, Cecilia Betts rushed to fill the awkward silence. "Let's see, we have six graduates of Cortéz High seated here. Do you suppose that's the most of any table?"

"It might be," Carol agreed. "It's not a category we've had before though, and there isn't a prize for it."

"What sort of prizes do you have?" Matt asked.

"I didn't collect the prizes myself, but I believe there are the usual gifts from stores in the area, complimentary services from beauty salons, tickets from theaters, and dinners from restaurants. That sort of thing."

"Why didn't you ask me? I would have been happy to donate a free service call and it could save someone a lot of money. Just ask Suzanne what I charged to replace a washer last week."

There was a taunting gleam in Matt's eye, but Carol wasn't about to give him the opportunity to launch into another pitch for portable toilets. "I'm sorry I didn't think of it."

"Well, it's not too late. I can state the value of the prize on the back of one of my business cards and you can still give it away."

Seeing no way to politely refuse his insistent offer, Carol nodded. "That's very kind of you. I'm giving away the prizes between dinner and dessert. You can wait until then to give me the card."

Matt polled the others at the table. "Does anyone else have a service they could volunteer to the cause of dear old Cortéz High?"

Cecilia Betts giggled. "I'm a checker at Von's

Market. We have gift certificates, but only the manager can authorize a donation of those."

Her husband shrugged. "I'm a foreign-car mechanic, and like Cecilia, my manager would have had to donate a gift certificate. Sorry."

Megan squirmed uncomfortably as the attention shifted to her. "I'm just a housewife. What about you, Aimee? I'll bet you could have provided an expensive prize."

Megan's comment had been laced with venom, but Aimee responded graciously. "I manage a bank, and they're understandably reluctant to give out samples."

Her sly comment drew laughter, and when it became his turn, Gordon offered a novel prize. "I could volunteer to provide math tutoring for someone's son or daughter, but that's the kind of prize only a small percentage of those present could use and usually door prizes can be used by anyone."

"That's true, but it's still a wonderful idea," Suzanne told him. "I could have donated a nice philodendron. I'm ashamed that I didn't think of it sooner."

"We should have had this discussion last Saturday night," Casey said. "I could have donated a toaster oven or a gift certificate from Russell's."

"I donated a gift certificate," Carol said. "So Russell's is covered."

Jack returned to the table then, and after

barely missing a collision with a waiter carrying a tray of salads, lurched into his chair. "Did I miss any good gossip?" he asked. "Come on, tell me what happened while I was gone."

"We were just talking about the fact we could have donated more items for door prizes," Matt assured him. "Did you donate something?"

"Sure did," Jack boasted. "I brought enough ballpoint pens with my insurance firm's name for everyone. They'll be given out later."

Carol thanked him. "That was very generous of you."

Jack shrugged. "Not really. We buy them by the gross."

"How appropriate," Matt muttered under his breath.

Jack stared at him. "What did you say?"

"How considerate," Matt stated in a louder tone. "Everyone can always use another pen."

"Damn right they can." Jack again turned to Aimee. "Where are you working now, sweetheart?"

Aimee named her bank and branch. Gordon reached under the table to give her hand an affectionate squeeze, and she returned the sympathetic gesture. If only they had reached the table a few minutes earlier, she could have seen that Jack and Megan were seated elsewhere and saved them all from what she feared was fast becoming a terribly embarrassing evening.

"I'll come and talk to you on Monday," Jack promised. "I'm not at all happy with the service my bank provides and I know you'd give me real special treatment, wouldn't you?"

"We provide all our customers with excellent service," Aimee insisted.

"Well sure, your bank makes that claim in its television ads, but you know what I mean." Jack winked at her.

Gordon had winked at her earlier, but Jack's gesture was lewd rather than teasing. "I haven't the slightest idea what you mean," Aimee replied. "We pride ourselves on providing outstanding customer service, but no one receives favors they don't deserve."

Taken aback by the firmness of her tone, Jack's expression grew sullen. He was about to reply when a waiter arrived with their salads. A colorful concoction of mixed greens, tomatoes, avocados, bell pepper, and carrot curls, it drew ecstatic sighs from the Betts. Cecilia was nearest the dressings and after heaping a spoonful of thousand island on her salad, she passed the three-bowled container on to her husband.

When the dressings reached Jack, he held them in a precarious grasp as he took a dollop of blue cheese dressing. Then changing his mind, he scraped it off his salad, slapped it back into its bowl and took a spoonful of French dressing instead. When he looked like he might be about to change his mind a second time, Aimee quickly took the dressings out of his hand and set them down between her and Gordon while she served herself.

Carol leaned close to Matt. "After dinner, I hope you'll take Jack into a corner and explain the workings of portable toilets in minute detail. He deserves it."

Matt laughed at her suggestion and again Jack turned toward him. "What's so funny?" he asked. "I don't hear anyone else laughing."

"A private joke," Matt insisted. He added dressing to his salad and took a bite. "Good salad."

"Croutons would have been nice," Casey said.

"Oh I wish you hadn't said that," Cecilia moaned. "Now I absolutely have to have some croutons." She nudged her husband. "Honey, ask the waiter to bring us some croutons."

Rick blushed with embarrassment, but looked around for their waiter. "If I ask for croutons, then everybody else will want them too. What if they cost extra?"

"How much can a bowl of croutons cost?" Cecilia asked.

"Croutons!" Jack shouted. "We want some croutons!"

"God help us," Carol sighed.

A waiter rushed to Jack's side. "Is there something wrong, sir?"

"Yeah, we didn't get any croutons."

The waiter smiled nervously, and scanned the faces of the others at the table, hoping they would not all be as demanding. "The banquet menu was selected several weeks ago, sir, and croutons were not included. There is a basket of rolls on your table. May I suggest you have a roll with your salad?"

Megan leaned out of her chair to reach for the basket of rolls and nearly flung it at her husband. "Here. Have a roll."

Jack glared at the waiter, then at his wife, but outnumbered, he meekly reached into the basket for a roll. "We should have had croutons," he muttered under his breath.

"I'm sorry I mentioned them," Casey swore.

Suzanne gave his knee a playful squeeze. "Just be more careful with the next course," she urged.

Casey nodded. "You're right, Matt. This is an exceptionally good salad. Everything's fresh, and that's what makes the difference."

"What are you?" Jack asked, "the food critic for the *Times?*"

"No, I'm a chef," Casey responded. He caught himself then, but rather than put the title in the past tense, he let it stand.

"What kind of a sissy job is that for a man?" Jack bleated out.

Casey stared at Jack, and reminded of his father's drunken taunts, he lost his temper. "It's never wise to insult a man who works with a meat cleaver," he warned.

"Are you threatening me?" Jack bellowed.

Casey looked him straight in the eye. "No, I'm providing advice you'd be wise to take."

"Damn sissy job," Jack repeated.

"Jack!" Megan begged. "Hush."

The whole table waited, forks poised above their salads, but Jack stopped mumbling about Casey's occupation and began to eat. He stabbed at the lettuce, then poked great gobs of it at his mouth. When the bits that didn't fit fell in his lap, he seemed not to notice.

"I am really sorry," Carol whispered to Matt.

"Don't be. You're not responsible for him. He's only embarrassing himself."

"That's a nice way to look at it."

"Believe me, it's the only way."

Suzanne touched Casey's arm. "Let's go have our photographs taken now. There's no line, and I'm sure we'll have plenty of time to finish our salads when we come back."

Obviously still provoked with Jack, Casey resisted the idea, but after a long hesitation, he rose and walked with Suzanne back to the far corner where Keith Baumgarner had set up a romantic, cloud-filled backdrop. "You better take our pictures now," he proposed, "before we get any more angry with the loud-mouthed jerk at our table."

The photographer came close. "I work reunions all the time and Cortéz will be lucky if there aren't half a dozen here just like him or worse. If I were on the committee for the next reunion, I wouldn't send the clown an invitation."

"My what a charming idea," Suzanne exclaimed. "We could always insist it must have gotten lost in the mail if he found out about it anyway." She took Casey's hand and after stepping up to the line the photographer had made with masking tape on the rug, began to smile.

"You're a handsome couple," Keith called as he focused his camera. "Say antifreeze!"

Casey found it easy to smile with Suzanne so near and was positively beaming when the photographer snapped the picture. "I think I'll order several dozen of those and include them with all my Christmas cards."

Thinking Casey was serious, Keith complimented him on the idea. "Why not have photo cards made," he suggested. "Then you'll save the expense of buying additional cards."

"I'll think about it," Casey promised.

Suzanne thought it was much too soon for him to order Christmas cards with her picture.

It was presumptuous, and she did not enjoy being taken for granted. "Why don't we wait until we see how the photo turns out? Maybe we'll look so ghastly we won't want anyone to see it, let alone all your friends."

"No one ever looks ghastly in my photos," Keith claimed, "but if you like, I'll take another pose so you'll have a choice."

"Yes, take another one, please," Casey agreed.

"I really don't think we need two," Suzanne argued.

"This was your idea!"

Suzanne had forgotten that. "Yes, I suppose you're right." She tried to stand up a little straighter for the second shot. Hoping to look slimmer, she turned at more of an angle.

"Say Diogenes!" Keith urged. He handed them more order forms with the number of their photos already stamped on them. "If you aren't satisfied with these, then just come by my studio and I'll take replacements free."

"Thank you."

"Thank you. I'll suggest that everyone use tonight's photos on their Christmas cards. I should have thought of it myself."

Rather than head straight back for their table, Casey led Suzanne out into the corridor. The carpeting here was a magical garden of entwined vines on a beige background. He pulled her into his arms and nuzzled her throat. "I'm sorry if I embarrassed you with what I said to Jack, but his behavior is way out of line."

"It certainly is, but if he doesn't move to sit elsewhere after dinner, we will. There's no point in letting him ruin the whole night."

"I don't suppose there's any chance we can get him to move now?"

Suzanne laced her fingers in his as they walked up to the front entrance of the ballroom. "None at all, but life is filled with lop-eared weasels and when you don't see them coming, it's difficult to avoid them."

"Lop-eared weasels," Casey savored the term. "I like that. Have you ever used it in a poem?"

"No, but I should."

"Yeah, you really should."

They rejoined their table and found everyone finishing up the salad. Jack was playing with a roll, and for the moment seemed content to mind his own business. Relieved, Casey picked up his fork, but he paused when their waiter returned with two bottles of *Beaujolais*. He placed one on the table, and opened the other.

"I think we're going to be in real trouble," Casey whispered under his breath.

"There are ten of us," Suzanne reminded him. "No one should get all that much." She nodded as the waiter began at her place, and he filled her wine glass and then Casey's.

Neither Carol nor Matt took wine, but the Betts both did. Megan Shank shook her head, but as expected, her husband accepted a glass of the fruity Burgundy. Aimee had already had her wine for the evening, but Gordon wanted a glass. The waiter had come full circle, and Jack gestured for him to refill his glass before he left them. That finished the first bottle, but the waiter opened the second and left it for them to serve themselves.

"We should have a toast," Rick Betts announced. "Long live Cortéz High!"

Those with wine raised their glasses, while the others joined in with water. "A long life for the graduates of Cortéz High!" Gordon then added and they all drank to that toast too. Saving their wine to drink with dinner, most took only a sip, but Jack finished his second glass.

"Pass the wine," he ordered.

The bottle was in front of Suzanne, but she pretended not to hear him and continued eating her salad. It wasn't until he called her by name that she was forced to look up. "I'm sorry, did you say something to me, Jack?"

"I sure did. Pass me the wine."

Reluctantly, Suzanne did. Jack filled his glass but the instant he had replaced the wine bottle on the table, his wife passed it on to the Betts. "Hey, wait a minute, I might want more."

"The wine is for everyone, Jack," she reminded him.

"Well, if we run out we'll buy more," he scolded. "Now send that back here, Butts."

"It's Betts," Rick corrected.

"Whatever," Jack grumbled.

Carol had eaten only half of her salad, but with Jack ruining what little appetite she had after an anxious day, she laid her fork across her plate.

"Not hungry?" Matt asked. He had eaten every bit of his salad and eyed what was left of hers longingly.

Not noticing the direction of his gaze, Carol leaned back in her chair. "I was just wondering where the last thirty-five years have gone. They went by much too fast."

"Oh please don't start that," Cecilia Betts wailed. "I'll cry for sure if you do."

"Yeah, and so will I," Matt agreed. "Come on. Let's go have our pictures taken."

Carol shrank back. "You don't really want to do that," she chided.

"Oh yes I do, now come on." Matt rose and taking her hand, coaxed Carol out of her chair. "You look adorable. Why wouldn't I want to have my picture taken with you?"

Once he had her on her feet, he wrapped his arm around her waist and propelled her toward the rear of the room. She held her breath as

Keith posed them. Matt stood behind her, his hand resting lightly on her hip, but his touch generated a seductive heat that radiated clear through her, and she began to tremble.

"Relax," he whispered in her ear. "This isn't a mug shot."

Keith moved back to his camera. "Say anchovies!"

Carol began to laugh and Keith took their picture. "You're a very attractive couple. How long have you been married?"

"We're not," Carol was almost too quick to deny.

"That's probably why you look so happy," Keith laughed. He handed them order forms. "You save a dollar on the prints if you order them together rather than separately."

"Thanks, I try and save money wherever I can."

Carol waited for Matt to hand the photographer his card, but he simply took her hand for the walk back to their table. She hoped she had heard the last of Trenerry and Son Plumbing for the evening.

Busboys had begun clearing the tables. The clatter of dishes made conversation difficult, but apparently unmindful of the noise, Jack chose that minute to question Rick Betts about his work.

"I'm a foreign-car mechanic," he cried out over the din.

"People ought to buy American cars!" Jack snapped.

"A great many do," Rick assured him, "but those who don't need good mechanics too."

"Wouldn't drive a damn foreign car myself," Jack swore. "It's not simply unpatriotic; it's downright subversive."

"I own a Mercedes," Gordon interjected coolly. He had been drawing a lazy filigree on the tablecloth with the handle of his spoon, but looked up to speak to Jack.

Jack swung his gaze toward Gordon and recognizing his comment for the clear challenge it was, he squinted slightly. "Are you positive you went to Cortéz? I sure don't remember you and I thought I knew everyone."

Fearing Jack would get increasingly obnoxious, Aimee tried to distract him. "I remember Gordon," she remarked. "We were in the same senior English class."

"Yeah?" Jack asked. "So you can place him at Cortéz, but just what did he do? I mean did he do anything significant, like pitch for the baseball team?"

"Sports aren't as important to everyone as they are to you, Jack," Aimee replied. "Gordon was active with the math club."

"Math club? Oh please!" Jack began to laugh

so hard he had to use his napkin to wipe the tears from his eyes. "First a chef, and now somebody from the math club. We sat at the wrong table."

"Why don't you move?" Gordon suggested. "If the rest of the football players are seated together, they're probably looking for you."

Jack continued to laugh. "No, you can't get rid of me that easily. I wanted to sit with Aimee and that's why we're here."

Aimee was not even tempted to thank Jack for that exquisite honor. She glanced around the table, and found her companions' expressions as disgusted as her own. Then she noticed Megan Shank was regarding her husband with a look of such utter contempt it was frightening. After all, the eight of them would only have to put up with Jack for the evening; she would be going home with him.

Cecilia Betts's expression turned to ecstatic bliss when she was served first. Delighted with the slice of rare prime rib, rice pilaf, and steamed broccoli smothered in cheese sauce, she cooed excitedly until everyone had been served and she could finally take a bite. "Oh look," she exclaimed. "I can cut my meat with a fork it's so tender."

"Well, Mr. Food Critic," Jack ordered, "how would you rate this meal?"

Affecting a serious concern for the question,

Casey sampled everything on his plate before he pronounced the dinner superb. "Cooking for a banquet this size is never easy," he added, "which makes the spectacular results all the more impressive. I'd hold the next reunion here if I were a graduate of Cortéz."

"Are you a graduate of anything?" Jack asked,

"Why don't we discuss our professional degrees later," Casey offered. "Our dinners are getting cold."

Jack responded by cutting off a chunk of prime rib he chewed with only one savage bite before attempting to gulp it down. He began to choke and cough in wheezing gasps, but no one leapt to their feet to attempt the Heimlich maneuver. His face turned red, and he grabbed up his napkin and began to gag into it, but unable to dislodge the meat, he continued to choke. Finally his wife balled up her fist and socked him between the shoulder blades. He winced at the blow, but was finally able to cough up the piece of meat into his napkin.

"You're awfully flushed," Megan said between bites. "Why don't you go to the restroom and wash your face?"

Jack coughed another time, then after jamming his napkin into his pocket, he left the table and with a slow, weaving gait left the room. Megan smiled at everyone. "Jack eats like a pig and chokes fairly often. One day he'll be alone and that will be the end of him." Obviously unfazed by that evening's incident or the threat of widowhood, she took another bite of her prime rib and proceeded to enjoy her dinner.

Cecilia Betts stifled a sob. "I'm not sure I can eat now."

Her husband put his arm around her plump shoulders and gave her a comforting hug. "There, there, honey, everything's all right. Have a taste of your wine and you'll be fine."

While she looked unconvinced, after a couple of sips of wine Cecilia had regained sufficient composure to eat the tempting meal. "This is so good," she said. "What do you suppose they'll serve for dessert?"

Shaken, Carol found it difficult to hang on to her fork. "Was it just my imagination," she whispered to Matt, "or were we all going to sit here and watch Jack choke to death?"

Matt could see that she was really disturbed by the prospect and did not joke about it. "You may not have noticed, but two waiters were on their way to our table when Jack caught his breath. They would have helped him had none of us gotten to him in time."

"None of us even moved!"

"Yes, I know, but sometimes people do get what they deserve. That may have been a disgusting spectacle, but Jack was never in any real danger. Don't fret about it. Have a bite of broccoli, if you can't begin with the prime rib."

Carol nodded, and after a drink of water scooped up a cheese-laden forkful of broccoli. It was as delicious as it looked. She tried the rice, then cut a tiny bite of meat, and after eating it without mishap, relaxed enough to enjoy her meal.

In hopes of being able to duplicate the savory prime rib, Suzanne quizzed Casey on meat preparation while Gordon did his best to distract Aimee. "Thank you for standing up for me, even though I doubt you remember me all that well."

Unable to prove that she did by citing amusing events involving him, Aimee had to rely on a disarming smile. "At the last reunion it was plain that a great many of the men who had been star athletes in high school hadn't enjoyed the same success as those who had had more serious pursuits. Football games are fun, and most coaches swear sports build character, but there's far more to life than just playing on a winning team."

"I happen to agree, but that might just be because your theory fits my case," Gordon said. "What about cheerleaders? How many were there? Could you make any assessment of their success?"

Aimee had no difficulty answering his question. "Originally, there were five of us. One died in her twenties. Another went back East for college, married someone there, and hasn't kept in touch with anyone. That leaves three of us and I believe we're all here tonight. One is a teacher. The other owns her own escrow firm, and if a bank manager can be considered a success, then we've all been successful. I really think the personality traits that attract girls to cheerleading—friendliness, a gregarious nature—help them deal with the public and be successful in any profession."

"I'm sure you're right. I wonder if anyone brought an old annual," Gordon mused aloud. "We could try getting some of the old groups back together again for photographs. While I really don't care all that much about the members of the math club after all these years, it might be fun to take another group photo just to see how we turned out."

"Yes, that's a wonderful idea."

Gordon lowered his voice slightly. "I don't want to leave without having our picture taken. While I hope this isn't our only opportunity to have our photograph taken together, it's the first, and I don't want to miss it."

Gordon's smile was so wonderfully genuine, Aimee found it easy to comply with his request. "Let's go back to the photographer right after dinner. Do you like to dance?"

"That all depends on the music, and the partner."

"Yes, of course, that's understood."

"Good, the answer's yes. I definitely want to dance with you."

Suzanne could overhear just bits and pieces of Gordon and Aimee's conversation but she was thrilled it was going so well. She leaned forward, caught Aimee's eye and smiled to encourage her interest in Gordon. With Jack absent, the conversation became an easy exchange of thoughts that drifted around the table in sparkling waves frequently punctuated with laughter.

"Do you think someone ought to go and check on Jack?" Carol finally asked Matt.

Megan was still eating her dinner, and, without her husband's constant interruptions, conversing easily with the Betts. "His wife doesn't seem worried about him."

"I know, but—"

Matt put his arm on the back of her chair to whisper in her ear. "If I go and look for him, you can be certain he won't be coming back."

Her thoughts clouded with the haunting scent of Antaeus, Carol turned to look at him. He cocked a brow, silently asking if she understood. "You wouldn't."

Matt nodded. "Oh yes, I would. Now finish your dinner, and I'll help you with the door prizes. We can get an envelope at the desk so my donation doesn't look quite as spontaneous as it was."

Several committee members had already volunteered to help pass out the door prizes, but not one to refuse Matt's company since the evening was going so well, Carol reached out and touched his sleeve. "Thank you. I'm glad you could be here tonight."

Matt responded with a ready grin. "How often do you have reunions, every ten years?"

"Yes," Carol held her breath, hoping he would not tell her to call him when the next one came around.

"Then we ought to make it memorable. Now finish your dinner. You're much too thin."

Carol didn't consider herself thin by any means, but she appreciated his teasing compliment all the same. She watched Megan for a moment, and while it was true the woman showed absolutely no sign of distress over her husband's absence, she thought it was a terrible shame. Then she silently berated herself for still holding such an idolized view of marriage when she had failed twice herself. Still, had either Bob or Cliff choked on his supper, she would been out of her chair in an instant to assist him.

Megan had not displayed much in the way of loyalty, but Carol doubted Jack gave her any reason to. She glanced at Matt, and in an instant knew *he* would be loyal. But would his loyalty to his first wife ever end?

Eleven

The committee members in charge of door prizes had worked so zealously, there was a startling array of prizes for Carol to award. With Matt holding a glass bowl containing the names of everyone present, she drew winners for gift certificates for car detailing, pet grooming, video rentals, and Dodger tickets. Squeals of delight echoed through the ballroom each time a name was read, and applause greeted every winner.

There were bags of gourmet popcorn, exotic cookbooks, bottles of imported wine, and a mini-espresso machine complete with Amaretto-flavored coffee beans. There were silver picture frames, and Nintendo games. By the time dessert had been distributed to every table, Carol was not even half the way down the list of prizes.

She turned to Matt. "Shall we just keep on going?"

"Sure, nobody will eat our dessert."

Carol glanced toward their table where Rick Betts was already spooning up the last bite of his French vanilla ice cream. Served in a bittersweet chocolate shell and topped with raspberry liqueur, it looked absolutely divine. "I don't know, that looks awfully good."

This was her party rather than his, and Matt was flexible. Behind them the musicians were already in place, and ready to play. "Let's eat dessert then, and finish giving away the prizes whenever the band takes a break."

"I'll give out just one more then." Carol reached into the bowl, and as she had each time, prayed she would not draw Jack Shank's name. Again another of her classmates was the winner and this time she handed out the envelope containing Matt's card donating a free service call. The recipient was as thrilled to have won a prize as all the others and the applause enthusiastic. Relieved to have that out of the way, Carol announced she would give away more prizes later, and with Matt still holding onto the bowl of names, she returned with him to their table.

"Wait until you try this," Suzanne said. "It's the best dessert I've ever eaten."

Before Carol could sample hers and comment, Jack Shank reappeared. His dinner was still at his place, but he pushed it away. The wine bottle was within reach, and he poured the last of the *Beaujolais* into his glass.

Concerned about him, Rick Betts leaned forward. "Are you all right, Jack?"

While he appeared to have some difficulty focusing his eyes on Rick, Jack finally replied in his usual belligerent tone. "What's it to you, Butts?"

"The name is Betts!"

Jack made no apology or correction, but instead called to Carol. "That can't be all the prizes. I didn't win one. Did you get one, Aimee?"

As she had tried to do all evening, Aimee included everyone in her response. "We haven't had any winners at our table yet. Maybe we'll all be lucky later."

The band began with an enthusiastic version of Chuck Berry's "Hail, Hail Rock and Roll," and anything Jack might have wanted to add was lost in a thunderous hum of electric guitars loudly backed by an aggressive drummer. Dressed in pink shirts and pegged black pants, the group appeared to have been transported right out of the fifties.

At first Aimee thought the music was much too loud, then relieved she would not have to listen to any more of Jack's inane comments, she decided it was precisely the right volume. Her more energetic classmates soon filled the dance floor, but she was content just to watch. Then as happened so often, the present blurred in her mind and rather than a reunion, it was as though she was watching a dance she had attended while still in her teens.

Steve had been a wonderful dancer, and thoughts of him stirred feelings of indescribable longing. Not wanting to sink down into them, Aimee looked away from the dancers to break the heartbreaking link, and focusing firmly on the present continued to eat the luscious dessert. She had been looking forward to dancing with Gordon, but she had not realized how strongly the exuberant tunes of the fifties would remind her of her lost love. Now she wasn't certain she could dance at all.

The Betts went to the dance floor immediately, but the rest of the table was content merely to observe for the moment. Busboys cleared the dessert plates, people felt free to move around again, and soon the room was alive with dancing and animated conversation. The reunion was a success, and classmates returned to the bar, ordered drinks, and toasted each other.

Gordon waited until Aimee had finished eating. "The photographs, remember?"

"Yes, of course." As she left her chair, Jack reached out to catch her wrist. She recoiled at his touch, but he did not release her.

"You owe me a dance," he bellowed.

"Later," Aimee promised him, then pulling free she grabbed for Gordon's hand.

As they walked to Keith Baumgarner's corner, Gordon leaned down so she would be sure to hear him. "You needn't dance with anyone but me if you don't want to. Don't let Jack bully you into dancing with him. I'm sure you could put those three or four minutes of your life to much better use."

There was a line waiting for Keith, and as they joined it, Aimee agreed with him. "You're absolutely right. I'm so used to going out of my way to please customers at the bank, that I'd forgotten he's no one I need ever see again. I wonder where he was all that time."

"Probably in the bar."

"I hadn't thought of that. I really feel sorry for his wife. It was plain she was miserably unhappy when the evening started and I hate to think she's jealous of me when I can barely tolerate her husband."

"I didn't think you liked him even that well."

Gordon had a very charming smile and Aimee found it easy to return it. The band was playing, "Earth Angel," and more couples had moved onto the dance floor. The lighting had been dimmed after dinner, and the mood in the ballroom was a romantic one. Think only of tonight, she urged herself. Just be here with Gordon and let the past stay where it belongs.

When it came their turn, they stepped up in front of the cloud backdrop and when Gordon laced his hands around Aimee's waist, she found it easy to relax against him. Their pose was both natural and attractive.

"Say Pekingese!" Keith called again, prompting amused smiles. "Think about using this photo on your Christmas cards," he suggested as he handed them order forms. "Then you won't have to rush out and have photographs taken in November."

"Thank you," Aimee replied, but she blushed slightly as they turned away. She supposed she and Gordon did make a handsome couple, but for Keith to assume they actually were one, was disconcerting.

"Let's go out on the courtyard for a minute," Gordon suggested. The music could be heard clearly enough that they could have danced around the pond, but the slate was too uneven a surface. Gordon kept hold of Aimee's hand as they wandered toward a shadowed corner.

"I didn't go to any of the dances while I was at Cortéz, but I bet you went to them all, didn't you?"

"I think I missed one my freshman year, but other than that, I was usually there. Only the prom was as elegant as this though. Most of the dances were held in the gym, and even decorated with miles of crepe paper, the place always smelled like dirty sweat socks."

Gordon laughed with her. "I hadn't thought of that. I just imagined you dancing with your current boyfriend, and as I recall you had quite a few."

"Not simultaneously!"

"Well, no, that's true, but I was never one of them."

He pulled her around to face him then, and Aimee knew he was going to kiss her. It was a romantic spot on a lovely starlit evening, but at the very last second she turned away. "I'm sorry. I don't mean to disappoint you, but—"

Gordon's voice was soft, as enticing as it had been on the telephone. "You don't disappoint me, Aimee. You never could. Besides, it's charming to find a woman who regards a kiss as something special nowadays."

Intrigued, Aimee wondered aloud. "Even if you've never married, I'll bet you've been involved with lovely women and come close."

"Several times," Gordon admitted, "but I've never regretted remaining single. I've dated a great many nice women, but none I ever liked as much as you."

Stunned by that admission, Aimee couldn't believe he was serious. "Gordon, you didn't really know me. Even if we did have a class together, you couldn't have known nearly enough about me to be that impressed."

"Perhaps not, but I was. Besides, I'd noticed you long before we had English together our senior year, so even if we never met, I felt as though I knew you."

"Then I'm sure I'm going to disappoint you terribly tonight."

Gordon brought her hand to his lips and kissed her palm. "No, the evening will be as perfect as you are."

Aimee didn't feel at all perfect at that moment. She felt hopelessly shattered and panicked under his adoring gaze. "Excuse me, will you please? I'd like to go to the restroom."

"Of course. I'll meet you back at our table."

Ashamed he must think her distracted, if not far worse, Aimee checked her watch to make certain she did not stay away too long.

"Let's dance." Matt took Carol's hand to urge her from her chair without waiting for a reply.

Carol wasn't at all certain she could dance with him without fainting, but as the band began, "Just The Way You Look Tonight," she ceased to worry. He pulled her close, but held her with a light touch. He moved to the music with an easy masculine grace, and wishing the song would never end, she closed her eyes.

Their bodies fit together seamlessly, and she could not help but wonder what it would be like to make love to him. She had not thought she would have the chance, but dancing to the romantic tune made her hope that she would.

When the music ended, Matt didn't leave the dance floor, but waited to see what the next number would be. When it was another slow tune, the Everly Brothers' hit, "All I Have To Do Is Dream," he pulled Carol back into his arms. People who had won prizes waved as they danced by and he nodded and smiled as though they were his friends as well as hers.

Suzanne and Casey were dancing just as close, only he was nuzzling her ear. "If you won't go for the closet, what about sneaking out to the car and making love in the backseat?"

"Casey, you stop that," Suzanne hissed.

"It would be fun."

Suzanne leaned back slightly. "Have you ever done it in a backseat?"

Casey's grin widened. "Try me."

"Maybe some night when the car is safely parked in my garage, but not here. Besides, the valets have the keys, and we don't know where they parked it."

"A minor problem," Casey assured her. "I'm sure we can find a car that's unlocked."

"Just anyone's car?"

"Yeah, why not?"

"You want to get us arrested?"

"For what?"

"Car theft if nothing else."

"That would be a difficult charge to prove with us both in the backseat."

Suzanne shook her head. "No, now cut it out. Let's just dance. I can't remember the last time I danced with someone as nice as you."

Content for the moment, Casey held her more tightly, and when the next number was the poignant "Mr. Blue," he thought it remarkable how much his life had changed in the week he had known Suzanne. He had longed to meet someone special, but she was so delightfully unique, he could never have envisioned a woman like her. The next tune was "La Bamba," and the romantic spell broken, they returned to their table along with Matt and Carol.

Gordon was already there. He stood as Aimee approached, but Jack Shank lurched from his chair to meet her. "I want that dance," he exclaimed.

Unable to decide if it would be better to just get the ordeal over with on a fast number, where she wouldn't have to get all that close to him, Aimee hesitated to say no, but she was also extremely reluctant to agree. She looked at Gordon, and wished she had asked him just how to refuse Jack's invitation without creating a scene.

"I'll tell you what, Jack—" she finally began.

"Can't you see that she doesn't want to dance with you?" Megan gave an insistent tug on her husband's coattail. "Sit down and leave her alone."

Jack turned to swat her hand away. "You stay out of this, Meg," he ordered gruffly. "I'll dance with whomever I please."

Matt gave Carol a little push toward her seat to send her out of harm's way before he stepped up to Jack. "I can only assume you wouldn't speak to your wife that rudely unless you'd had too much to drink. I think it's time you went home."

Jack peered at Matt, as if trying to identify him. Slowly recognition dawned in his bloodshot eyes. "And I think it's time you started minding your own business. Come on, Aimee, let's dance."

He reached for Aimee, but Matt brought the heel of his hand down on Jack's forearm with a bruising blow. "You bastard!" Jack screamed, and he swung his fist at Matt, who easily dodged to the right to escape the clumsy blow.

That might have been the end of it had four of Jack's former football buddies not been on the dance floor. Seeing him throw a punch at a stranger, they all left their astonished partners to come to his defense. One grabbed Matt by the shoulder to turn him around, but not about to allow Matt to take a beating, Casey rushed forward to block the newcomer's punch.

Gordon had been too thin to take on any of the football players while he was in high school, but he was far more athletic and fit than any of them now. He tore into the group converging on Matt, and slammed his right fist into a bulging stomach, and his left into a gray-bearded chin.

The bearded man fell backwards, crashing heavily into the next table and overturning it. Anyone who had failed to notice a fight had broken out before that point, saw it now. The band continued with their spirited rendition of "La Bamba," while dancers either fled toward the safety of the back of the ballroom, or abandoning their women, joined in the fray.

Carol grabbed for the glass bowl containing the names for the prizes before one of Jack's friends could use it as a club. She screamed to Matt to watch out, but he was doing quite well on his own. His tie was gone, and the right sleeve of his jacket ripped at the shoulder seam, but he landed three punches for every blow aimed at him. With Casey on his right, and Gordon on his left, he forged a wide swath through what was left of Cortéz High's former line.

Suzanne grabbed both Carol and Aimee to pull them back toward the wall. "Jack deserved a punch in the nose, but my God, this is a brawl!"

Fearing their instruments might suffer damage, the guitarists ceased playing and ran for the exit while the drummer positioned himself in front of his kit and with windmilling arms struggled to protect it. A pair of cymbals went crashing as the scuffle spread out over the dance floor, but the drummer fought back with strategically placed kicks to maintain his line of defense. At that point, the original intent of the fight was impossible to discern. Men who hadn't been in a fistfight since grade school socked, gouged, and tore each other's hair. A toupee went flying, and landed amid the drums, but its owner did not even notice its loss.

Cecilia Betts had a firm hold on Rick, but he was content to watch the fight rather than join in. "Jack deserved it," he shouted.

"Oh hush," Cecilia wailed. "This is just awful!" A man's black loafer came sailing by, and she had to duck quickly to avoid being hit. "Come on, let's get out of here!"

The Betts brushed by them, but Carol, Aimee, and Suzanne stayed put. Their eyes wide, they followed the brutish exchange of blows with rapt fascination, wincing and crying out each time their dates got hit. That the party was ruined did not concern them; they just wanted their men to survive.

The bartenders in the rear had called security when the fight began, but not understanding the seriousness of the problem, only one guard came to investigate. Horrified to find a riot tearing up the ballroom, he quickly called for the Pasadena Police. They arrived with sirens blaring. Wrenched from his quarters, the hotel manager met them at the entrance. He marched with them down the hall, but by that time, most of the men attending the reunion had either leapt or been dragged into the fight. In their expensive dresses, the women formed a colorful line around the edge, but none had thrown a punch herself.

Using a bullhorn, the police sergeant demanded order. When his first call met with no response whatsoever, he motioned for the men with him to move forward. "I didn't think we'd need riot gear at the Ritz Carlton!" he exclaimed. "I want order now, or I'll book you all for resisting arrest," he announced.

The uniformed patrolmen had only to brandish their nightsticks to subdue most of the combatants, but others too incensed to notice the policemen's arrival kept on battering whomever they could. A full five minutes passed before order was finally restored. At the center of the brawl, three unconscious men were found lying in a heap. They were carried off to the side, and paramedics called to revive them. Those left standing were scraped and bloody, but not in need of immediate medical care.

The women pressed close, some livid with their husbands for behaving so stupidly. Others, elated by the whole ghastly spectacle, were shouting encouraging cheers. The police sergeant had to threaten them with arrest as well before he finally got the silence he demanded. He walked around, surveying the overturned tables, torn tablecloths and smashed glassware.

"I'm Sergeant Vasquez. This must have been some party," he remarked with a low whistle. "Someone want to tell me how it turned nasty?"

Jack Shank was holding a handkerchief to his broken nose. The long hairs he had taken such care to swirl around his crown were now hanging lank down his neck, revealing a large bald spot atop his head. He pointed to Matt. "That bastard hit me for no reason at all. I wasn't about to take it, and my friends backed me up."

Matt's right eye was nearly swollen shut, the studs gone from his shirt, but all in all, he was still in better shape than many of the others. Without an opponent to lean against, some men had had to sit down rather than risk a fall. Casey had a gash in his lower lip that had bled all over his shirt, and with a long cut on his cheek, Gordon's shirt was equally gory. The three men stood together while members of the once proud Cortéz High football team clustered around Jack.

Sergeant Vasquez was a wiry little man with an intense gaze. He studied Jack and his friends a long moment, and then turned to Matt. "Well, what do you have to say for yourself?"

"He's right in that I hit him," Matt agreed, "but I had a damn good reason."

The sergeant put his hands on his hips. "And what was that?"

"He insulted a woman, his wife."

The sergeant scanned the disheveled men. A couple he recognized as prominent Pasadena businessmen, and he shook his head in disgust. "Are you telling me this hellacious mess was all over a matter of honor?"

"Yes, sir, it was."

The sergeant pointed to a man using a handkerchief to mop blood from a cut in his brow. "Is that your understanding of what happened?"

The fellow shrugged. "All I know is that my brother-in-law was getting beat up, so I jumped in to help him."

"Well, where is he?"

A pudgy red-haired man stepped forward. "I didn't even go to Cortéz," he swore, "and I couldn't name the man who hit me."

"Can you pick him out of these prime specimens of Pasadena manhood?"

The redhead took a quick look at the men surrounding him and shook his head. "No, sir."

"With so many wearing tuxedoes, they all look alike, is that it?"

"Must be."

The sergeant took another slow walk around his prisoners. He clucked his tongue and shook his head. "The jail's going to be mighty crowded tonight." He came to a stop in front of Matt. "You a graduate of Cortéz?"

"No, sir. I'm just a guest."

"My, my." He looked toward the rows of women. "Is one of you willing to claim this man?"

Carol came forward immediately. "He's with me, and his story's correct. Jack was loud, rude, and obnoxious all evening. When he insulted his wife, Matt asked him to leave. He refused, and got abusive. His friends have no more sense than he has and they're the ones who turned the incident into a brawl."

"Wait a minute," Aimee interjected. "Where is Jack's wife?"

His curiosity piqued, the sergeant nodded. "Yes, where is the little woman who prompted this wild defense of her honor?"

Most of the people in the room didn't know Megan Shank and looked as puzzled as the sergeant. It appeared she might have gone, but finally Suzanne found her huddled beneath their table. Megan wasn't making a sound, and had the tablecloth not been pulled to one side, Suzanne would never have noticed her. She bent down and extending her hand, coaxed her out.

"I've found her, sergeant." Suzanne kept her arm around Megan's shoulders. "Poor thing, she's scared to death. You seem chilled; did you have a jacket, Megan?"

Megan shook her head. Matt started to remove his jacket, but the sergeant stopped him and gestured for Jack to offer his. "She's your wife," he reminded him.

Jack sloughed off his jacket, but tossed it rather than draped it over Megan's shoulders. "You just wait until we get home," he murmured under his breath.

"I heard that," the sergeant cried. "If you'd rather not go home with him, I'll see that a relative comes for you, or if you'd rather, you can go home with a friend. I think I have a pretty clear picture of what went on here." He sucked in his breath. "It's a real sorry state of affairs when a nice reunion party ends up like this." He noticed Keith Baumgarner, holding his camera, standing with the women.

"Did you get any photographs of what went on here?"

"No, sir, I didn't. It's never wise to get too close to a brawl with an expensive camera."

"My God, a man with sound judgment. I didn't think we had one in this room." He glanced over toward the men being treated by the paramedics. Two were already sitting up, and the third, while still lying down, was talking with them. "I've a good mind to take every last one of you down to the station."

"That really wouldn't be fair," Carol argued.

"All right," Sergeant Vasquez agreed. "I'll

just take your date, and this man who has a complaint against him. Would you like that better?"

"No, that doesn't make any sense at all."

"Carol," Matt urged. "Stay out of this."

Jack started to laugh, but clipped it short when he caused himself an agonizing burst of pain. "Wait until he starts calling her names," he said. "He's no better than I am."

"Every man in this room is a damn sight better than you are, Jack!" Carol yelled.

Afraid he was about to witness the start of another fight, Vasquez raised his hand. "That's enough. Now I want you men to line up in two rows. We'll take everyone's name right here. Any of you who weren't involved can get busy straightening up the room, or I can guarantee you the manager is going to send Cortéz High one hell of a bill for damages."

"Are you all right?" Carol called to Matt.

"Sure." Matt moved into line with Casey and Gordon.

Suzanne led Megan to a chair. "What do you want to do?" she asked.

Megan sniffed loudly. "Jack's not all that bad. He's just loud sometimes but he never hits me or the kids."

Suzanne looked up at Aimee and Carol. She hadn't seen Megan dive under the table, but it didn't seem like something a woman who wasn't terrified of being hit would do. After all, none

of the other women in the room had ducked for cover. "Are you sure? It's not your fault if he's abusive, but you can stop it now."

Megan just shook her head.

"How old are your children?"

"The boys are in their twenties, grown and gone. Only our daughter is still at home. She's 16."

Aimee moved closer to Carol. "Do you think Megan's telling the truth?"

"Probably not, but we can't force her to leave Jack against her will. I'll bet Vasquez will talk with her again. If he doesn't, Suzanne is sure to suggest counseling. Come help me straighten up. It will be a nightmare if we have to bill everyone for damages."

"Oh Carol, this was supposed to be such a wonderful party." Aimee glanced over her shoulder at Gordon, who waved at her. "I should have just danced with Jack, and then none of this would have happened."

Carol couldn't believe her ears. "Jack made everyone uncomfortable from the moment he sat down at our table. Don't blame yourself for his rude behavior. Besides, why should you have to dance with a man you don't like? Women aren't love slaves who were placed on Earth for men's amusement."

Aimee certainly didn't feel like a love slave.

"I know, but I can't help but feel guilty. Looks like the party's over," Aimee murmured.

"Not entirely, there are still prizes to give out." She looked toward the microphone. The musicians had returned and were dismantling their equipment. "How long did the band play, about half an hour?"

"If that."

"Oh well. Matt, Casey, and Gordon were wonderfully brave, weren't they? Just seeing them fight was almost worth what we paid to come tonight."

Still heavily burdened by guilt, Aimee couldn't agree. "I really wish it hadn't happened." They moved on to another table. "What do you think of Gordon?"

Carol studied her friend's hopeful expression before responding. "I don't remember him, but he's certainly gorgeous now, almost as good-looking as Matt. He seems to be really interested in you too."

"He claims I was his fantasy."

Carol had an instant image as to why. "He must have seen too many X-rated films starring naked cheerleaders."

"Perhaps, but it's difficult to live up to such high expectations."

"Believe me, those girls aren't much in the way of competition. Too much makeup for one thing, and every last one of them has had silicone implants."

Aimee rolled up a tablecloth into a ball. "Will you just try and be serious for a minute?"

Carol straightened her shoulders and saluted. "I'll do my best, but as I recall you didn't have a nice male friend to ask to the reunion, so I hope you'll make the most of your chance to get to know Gordon."

"I'm not sure that I want to."

"Now you're the one who's not being serious!" Carol grabbed up the next tablecloth. "They must have one of those linen carts we could use. You know the kind the inmates always hide in in prison movies? Now give me one good reason why you wouldn't want to continue seeing Gordon."

Aimee sighed softly. "He has me on a very tall pedestal, and I feel insecure."

"You really do, don't you?" Carol came forward and gave her a hug. "Just take things slowly. Let them evolve naturally and you may surprise yourself."

"That's just what I'm afraid of," Aimee admitted with a shudder. "After being married to Bill, I don't want any more surprises."

"Gordon isn't anything like Bill," Carol insisted, "but if you're really worried, hire a detective and check him out. Now come on, that's it for the tablecloths, let's see what we have to do to spring the men from Sergeant Vasquez's custody."

They walked back up to the front of the room where the uniformed policemen were still taking names. After having stood, or sat together, most of the men were talking amongst themselves in a good-natured fashion. Clearly who had punched whom had already been forgotten. Only Jack, who was standing off by himself with Sergeant Vasquez, still looked angry. He was standing in a dejected slump, his lower lip thrust out in an angry pout.

After speaking with Jack, the sergeant conferred briefly with the hotel manager. "Other than a couple of broken glasses, the manager assures me there's been no damage to the room and that your group won't have to pay any additional charges. By taking names and addresses, I've assured myself that despite evidence to the contrary, this is a responsible group who's unlikely to go out and disturb the peace any further. Just to make certain that doesn't happen, I'm going to release you ten at a time. The first group may go."

"Is that ten couples, or ten individuals?" someone asked.

"Make it couples," Vasquez answered with a wave.

"Could we wait just a minute?" Carol asked. "I still have several very nice door prizes to give out, dinner at the Chronicle for one. I'm sure everyone wants a chance to win that."

The sergeant looked amazed, but polled the now orderly crowd. "Do you really want the chance to win door prizes?"

The response was a resounding yes, and Vasquez told Carol to go ahead. Aimee held the bowl of names for her this time, and while the applause was now more subdued than enthusiastic, they awarded the last of the prizes to appreciative classmates. Then it was time to wait for their turn to go.

Suzanne was still talking with Megan. Aimee had no more doubts to confide, and Carol was left to wonder what else could possibly go wrong. She had had such high hopes, and while this was definitely a reunion no one would ever forget, she thought she would be exceedingly lucky if Matt felt well enough to kiss her good night. If he did, she just hoped it would not also be goodbye.

Twelve

Suzanne and Casey were among the first to leave. She gave Megan Shank's frail shoulder a final squeeze, and hoped her advice to seek counseling would be taken. She held Casey's hand, but as soon as they reached the more brightly lit corridor outside the ballroom, she pulled him to a stop.

"I think we ought to take you straight over to the emergency room at the Huntington Hospital. Your lip needs stitches."

Casey sagged back against the wall. "God, that sounds painful."

"I'm sure they'd give you a shot to numb your lip first."

Casey closed his eyes. As long as he had been standing with Matt and Gordon, he had felt fine. More than fine actually, like a veteran of some wildly exciting campaign. Now he was beginning to feel terrible. "I'm afraid I'm going to be sick," he moaned.

"Oh Casey," Suzanne slipped her arm around his waist. "You poor baby, come on let's get out of here before you faint and I have to call an ambulance."

"Was that supposed to make me feel better?" Casey pushed himself away from the wall and tried to make it out front, but got so dizzy he had to stop off at a chair in the lobby. "I was fine until you mentioned stitches."

"Just stay here. Where's the ticket for the valet?"

Casey slid his hand into his pocket and produced a wrinkled stub. "No stitches," he begged.

Suzanne touched his tousled hair. The wire frames of his glasses were bent, giving him a thoroughly pathetic look, but somehow it was remarkably endearing. She bent down to kiss his cheek. "I'll hurry," she promised.

Casey looked around for a potted plant in case he couldn't make it to the restroom. There was a large palm handy, and he relaxed slightly. The heroes always swaggered off after fistfights in films, but he felt sore all over. Film fights weren't real, he reminded himself, but still, they gave the wrong impression of what men could endure and remain standing. Of course most leading men weren't forty-six years old, and if they were, they had stunt doubles to fake their blows.

Suzanne returned sooner than he had expected, and Casey struggled to his feet to meet her. "I was just wishing I were Jean-Claude Van Damme," he admitted rather sheepishly.

"Now there's a thought," Suzanne replied. "I'm glad you're not, or you wouldn't be here with me."

When they reached the curb, Casey didn't even pretend he felt well enough to drive. "Can you drive us back to your place?" he asked.

"Sure, come on." Suzanne glanced his way frequently on the short trip home. "Maybe stitches aren't necessary, but it wouldn't hurt to stop by Huntington's emergency room."

"No thanks, just let me sleep on your floor."

"The floor? I most certainly will not. You'll sleep in my bed like you always do."

"Always?" Casey managed a lopsided grin. "I like the sound of that, but it's only been three nights."

Suzanne had lost count. She chided herself silently for making the type of presumptuous comment she did not appreciate coming from him. "All right, so this will only be number four, but who's counting?"

When Suzanne pulled into her driveway, Casey opened his door and would have climbed out on his own had she not rushed around the car to help him. The prospect of being babied all weekend by the woman he adored was so appealing he eagerly accepted her help. "I sure hope I can make it to work on Monday," he murmured.

"With a hot bath, a couple of aspirin, and a good night's sleep, you'll be much improved by tomorrow."

"I sure hope so," Casey replied, but he did not plan to recover nearly that quickly and he had to force himself not to grin so widely it hurt.

Aimee and Gordon were in the next group to leave, but while his face had also been cut, he didn't feel nearly as bad as Casey. He drove to Aimee's house, and then checked his watch. "It's still early. Let's find an oldies station on the radio and have that dance you promised me."

Gordon couldn't see the gash in his cheek, but Aimee certainly could. "Let's take care of your face first."

"Is it that bad?"

"I'll let you judge for yourself." As soon as they entered her home, Aimee led the way through the den to the downstairs bathroom. Papered in a wild yellow print with exotic birds in deep blue and rose, it was a bright and cheerful room. She waited at the door as Gordon stepped up to the mirror.

"Better take off your shirt. I'll soak it in cold water or you'll never get out the bloodstains."

Gordon reached for a navy blue washcloth and after wetting it, held it to his cheek. "You needn't bother."

"It's no bother, really. I talked you into attending the reunion. And if I'd gotten to our table in time to seat Jack and his wife elsewhere, or had sense enough to dance with him without arguing, there wouldn't have been a brawl and you'd not have gotten hurt. So the least I can do is wash your shirt."

Gordon turned to regard her with an astonished gaze. "Can you possibly repeat that? No, don't bother. I absolutely refuse to allow you to take the responsibility for everything that happened tonight. I went to the reunion because I wanted to, and Jack started the mayhem all by himself. The man's a real—" Gordon had to search for a word that wasn't too obscene to use with Aimee, "creep. I'll bet he gets thrown out of every party he goes to."

Aimee inhaled deeply and exhaled in a poignant sigh. "I wish I could believe that."

Gordon rinsed out the washcloth and after again wiping his cheek was satisfied he had cleaned the long cut as best he could. "I think somebody got me with his ring."

"I have some Bactine upstairs. Take off your shirt while I get it."

"Aimee—" Gordon started to argue, but she left without listening. His tie was already in his pocket, and after removing his studs and cuff-links he peeled off his jacket and then his blood-stained shirt. He heard Aimee coming down the stairs and hurriedly put his jacket back on.

"Bring your shirt and come into the kitchen with me," she called. She got out the blue plastic tub she used to soak lingerie, filled it with cold water, and when he joined her, tossed in his shirt. "Sit down at the table, and I'll put some Bactine on your cut."

"Yes, Mother."

Amused, Aimee was smiling when she approached him. "Do I sound that bad?"

"There's nothing wrong about wanting to take care of me. I think it's cute." Gordon stifled the impulse to reach out and hug her and instead sat still as she dabbed the antiseptic on his cheek.

"Speaking of mothers," Aimee began in what she hoped was not blatant prying. "I was surprised to find you still at your old number. Are you living with your family?"

"Still, you mean?"

It had sounded like prying, Aimee agonized. "I'm sorry if that was too personal a question."

"Don't panic, it wasn't. When my parents

moved to Sedona, Arizona ten years ago, I sold my house and bought theirs to add to their retirement fund. Matt Trenerry remodeled the kitchen a couple of years ago. I'm sure you know how it is with these older houses; there's always something that needs remodeling, or replacing, or repairing."

"Do I ever. I had to replace the waterheater, garbage disposal, and furnace this past year. I'm just holding my breath about the washer and dryer, and the garage roof leaks something awful."

"Ah yes, the joys of home ownership."

"Exactly." Aimee stepped back and set the Bactine on the counter. The slash crossing his cheekbone was long, but not deep. "I hope it doesn't leave a scar," she worried aloud.

"There aren't many men who have the chance to get scarred up in a brawl at fifty-two. It will make a hell of a good story." No longer able to resist holding her, he reached out to grab her hands and pulled her down on his knee.

"Gordon!"

"My friends call me Ash." He nuzzled her throat with a playful nibble. "You still look gorgeous in red."

For an instant, Aimee wasn't sure where to put her hands, but then looped an arm around his neck. "I'm afraid tonight was more of a nightmare than a fantasy come true. I'm really sorry."

"Will you stop apologizing?" Gordon gave her an enthusiastic hug. "Besides, the night isn't over. Do you have a stereo, or will we have to dance to music on your kitchen radio?"

"I did have a stereo once, but my older daughter, Karen, talked me out of it when she moved into her studio. It's just another of the things I need to replace."

Gordon watched her curl her hair behind her ear. "You used to do that when we were in high school."

"Do what?"

"Comb your hair behind your ear like that. You haven't changed at all, lady, but I am so glad that I have."

His chest was covered with auburn curls, and while tempted to slide her fingers through them, Aimee resisted the impulse. "You're wrong, Gordon, Ash, we've both changed." When he leaned close this time, she didn't pull away and his kiss was light, yet deeply stirring. Immediately she slid off his lap. "I think we better dance."

Gordon rose and followed her over to the radio on the counter. "I know a good oldies station," he offered. He turned the dial, and in a moment had the Platters singing, "Smoke Gets In Your Eyes." He took her hand and led her back into the dining room where they had room to dance in front of the mirror where she had pinned on her corsage. The lovely white flower was in the way now that he wanted to hold her close.

"Maybe you ought to put the orchid in the refrigerator."

Aimee set it on the dining room table instead and stepped into his arms. He was taller than Steve had been, but after that fleeting comparison, she ceased to think of her first husband. He held her close, but so gently she didn't feel confined. There was a dimmer switch on the overhead light, and she reached out to turn it down.

"There, that's much more romantic."

Pleased beyond words that she wanted to set the scene, Gordon kept moving slowly to the music. "The Great Pretender" was next, and he laughed to himself as he thought of how many times over the years he had dreamed of dancing with Aimee Stewart. He had waited a lifetime to hold her in his arms, and it had been worth it.

"I wish I'd known you were alone a long time ago," he whispered. "I would have knocked on your door the very next day."

Aimee tilted her head to look up at him and this time welcomed his kiss. She had met men whose kisses were so possessive she could not abide them, but Gordon's was perfect. Tempting, barely brushing her lips at first and then deepening to a long, slow caress. She missed a beat and stepped on his toe.

"Oh, I'm sorry."

Gordon drew a chair away from the dining table and again pulled her down across his lap. "Hush, I'd rather kiss you than dance anyway."

Her shyness falling away, Aimee slipped her hand inside his jacket. His skin was warm, and the wiry curls spread over his chest were a delight to comb. Then she had her hands in his hair, and tangled her fingers in the thick curls. Kissing him felt so good, so right, that when he pulled away slightly, she couldn't hide her disappointment.

Gordon clucked her chin with his knuckles to banish her frown. "Another couple of minutes, and I'm not going to be able to stop. Do you want me to stay the night?"

Surprised by his question, Aimee rested her forehead against his. Yes, she did want him to stay, and badly, but the last time she had followed her heart it had led her into a disastrous marriage to a con artist. She swallowed hard. "I definitely want you to stay, but I'm going to ask you to go."

"Is that some kind of strange feminine logic?" he whispered against her ear.

Aimee leaned against him. "I won't pretend

that I don't want you, but I don't want to be sorry tomorrow."

"I won't give you any reason to be sorry," Gordon promised in a seductive whisper.

"I don't really know you."

That she would want to argue with him while still seated on his lap gave Gordon hope that eventually he would prevail. "You've known me for thirty-five years."

"No, that's not true. We were in a class together thirty-five years ago." Aimee leaned back to study his face. "Your resemblance is still close enough to your senior photo in the last Cortéz album to be certain you're no imposter, some friend of Gordon's who's come in his place, but—"

"What?" Gordon was absolutely astonished by that outlandish bit of speculation. "Where did you ever get such a bizarre idea?" he asked. "Do you honestly think anyone would try and pull such a goofy stunt? I suppose after thirty-five years some men might actually prefer to send a better-looking double to their reunion, but I doubt anyone has ever done it."

Aimee knew just how badly she had upset him when he offered no resistance as she moved off his knee. "I'm sorry, I didn't mean to insult you. I don't date much and perhaps I phrased my remark poorly, but—"

Gordon rose to face her. "Well, I date quite

a lot and I've heard women say no in a dozen different ways, but no one has ever accused me of not being who I am. That's a real novel approach, how does it usually work?"

Infuriated by a taunt she was positive she did not deserve, Aimee raised her hand, but caught herself before she slapped him. "You see, we don't know each other well enough to sleep together, and it would have been a mistake if we had." She turned around and walked to the front door.

Gordon walked out without even saying goodbye and she closed and locked the door behind him. He had provided the perfect ending to an absolutely wretched evening and it wasn't until she returned to the kitchen to turn off the radio that she noticed his shirt was still soaking in the sink.

"Oh damn." She ran back to the front window and looked out, but Gordon had already driven away. She would have to launder the shirt as promised and return it to him. She decided to mail it. It might be cowardly, but it was better than giving him the opportunity to laugh at her again.

Sergeant Vasquez kept Matt and Carol waiting until everyone else had gone. He then adopted his most persuasive tone. "I have a last word of advice for you, Sir Galahad. The next time you overhear a man insult his wife, or any woman for that matter, ask him to step outside to teach him some manners because if I ever find you at another scene like the one you caused here tonight, I'll arrest you before you can offer the first word of an explanation. Do we understand each other?"

"Yes, sir, completely."

Carol surveyed the room with a sorrowful glance; it had been so lovely that afternoon. The paramedics were gone, and only a couple of policemen were waiting by the door. The tables were now bare, the linens all collected by the busboys, and the floral centerpieces taken home by the committee members and their friends. One of the housekeeping staff was running a vacuum cleaner in the back. No telltale reminders of the evening marred the stately scene. The Viennese Ballroom could be shown off the very next day to members of a committee searching for a banquet site. Carol doubted the people who had attended the reunion felt as untouched as the well-appointed room.

"What about Mrs. Shank?" she asked. "Are you going to follow up on her?"

The sergeant frowned slightly. "She refused to file a complaint against her husband, but I'll make a point of keeping in touch. I can't abide seeing a woman abused either, Mr. Trenerry."

Matt nodded. "Are we free to go?"

The sergeant made a sweeping gesture toward the door and Matt took Carol's hand and walked out. "I'm sorry," he began when they reached the corridor, but Carol promptly interrupted him.

"For what? You gave Jack exactly what he deserved. It's a shame the party ended so soon, but I'm real proud of you, and as far as I'm concerned, you needn't apologize to me or anyone else for tonight."

Matt could see by the tilt of her chin that she was sincere. "Thank you, but I was afraid you were going to have to bail me out of jail and that wouldn't have been any way to end the evening."

"I raised two sons," Carol reminded him. "I've made more than one trip to police stations on a Saturday night. Didn't you ever have to go get Dan?"

Matt stopped to stare at her. He couldn't see all that much out of his right eye, but again, she looked serious. "You are teasing me?"

"No, of course not."

"Well, when he first started driving Dan got a couple of traffic tickets he should have been smart enough to avoid, but I never had to bail him out of jail, or even pick him up at a police station. Just what did your kids do?"

Carol was certain she had probably forgotten

more than she remembered, but did her best to downplay their escapades. "Nothing major. Stupid stuff really, like drinking beer on the front lawn of an elementary school. The police take a dim view of that."

"Typical teenage pranks?"

"Yes, exactly, but they're a dentist and chiropractor now, so obviously they turned out all right."

Matt would have heard the pride in her voice had he not been able to make out her smile. She had such an effervescent personality sometimes he wasn't sure when she was teasing and when she was being serious, but it was plain she adored her sons. They were professional men like their father, while his son had followed in his footsteps and become a plumber. It was a jarring thought that their sons, while near the same age, probably shared nothing in common.

"Come on, it's time I got you home."

As predicted, the valets had no trouble locating Matt's van. The peculiar conveyance no longer troubled Carol and she climbed in without a blush. "I should have offered to drive. Can you make it?"

Matt managed to fasten his seat belt without groaning aloud, but twisting to the side had hurt. "Just keep an eye out on our right. My vision isn't all that good on that side."

Carol grabbed his arm. "Wait. If you really

can't see, let me drive you to the hospital. You might have a detached retina or some other serious vision problem."

Matt had had ample opportunity to note Carol tended to be melodramatic at times. "Look, I may be squinting like Popeye, but the only reason I can't see is because the lid is swollen, not because my eyeball is squished."

"I wish you hadn't said that." Carol grimaced. "I hadn't noticed the resemblance to Popeye until you mentioned it, but please, if you're hurt, let's stop by the Huntington emergency room."

"Right. It's Saturday night. The floor will probably be slippery with blood gushing out of all the guys cut up in knife fights, to say nothing of shootings. They'd just keep me waiting a couple hours; then charge me several hundred dollars to tell me to go home and put a steak on my eye. No way." Exercising caution, Matt turned right onto Oak Knoll.

"Why is it men go out of their way to neglect their health?"

Matt replied with a derisive snort. "Plenty of women do it too."

Carol was about to argue when she realized he might be referring to his late wife. Perhaps Deborah could have been saved had she sought medical treatment sooner. It wasn't a subject she wished to pursue that night. Leaning forward, she scanned the intersection at the bottom of the hill. "It's all clear."

"Thanks."

Carol kept a close watch all the way to her house. The traffic had been light, and the signals green all the way, but she had worried they would inadvertently plow into someone the whole time they were on the road. Relieved to reach her home safely, she could not bear to send Matt off alone. "Come on in. I picked up a couple of steaks this morning and I'll readily sacrifice one for your eye. Then I'll drive you home in my car. This was a scary trip even with me riding shotgun. I won't let you risk driving home alone. Your son can help you come get the van tomorrow."

Matt had not enjoyed the trip to Arcadia any more than Carol had, but he was reluctant to agree to her offer. "This van's as heavy as a tank. If someone runs into me, it won't even scratch the paint."

"That may very well be true, but what if you were to hit some sweet little family on their way home from grandma's in some low-priced import?"

With that image, Matt could actually hear the sound made when he stomped an aluminum can flat and in a collision with his van, it wouldn't just be soda spraying out of the other vehicle's wreckage. He winced. "You have an excellent point there. Okay, let's give the steak a try and then I'll take you up on the ride."

Carol had to hide her smile as she drew him through her front door. "Stretch out on the sofa. I'll get the steak." She had bought a couple of filets to slice up for stir-fry and she was grateful she had not had time to slice and freeze them because she could imagine how difficult it would be to talk Matt into letting her pile thinly sliced frozen beef on his face.

"Here we are." He had kicked off his shoes before lying down and looked not only comfortable, but completely at home on her couch. She definitely liked seeing him there too. She sat down beside him and between them, they lowered the cold filet into place.

"How long is this supposed to take?" he asked.

"I've no idea, but since you're the patient, just leave it on until your eye feels better."

"Does this really work, or is this just an old wives' tale?"

Carol shrugged, but knowing if she voiced any doubts as to the efficacy of the remedy he would probably ask to go home, she responded with a reassuring smile. "Steak has always been expensive, so it must work, otherwise no one would recommend it."

"Now we're right back where we started. Just

who is it that recommends slapping a steak on a black eye?"

"Beats me, prize fighters' trainers, perhaps?" She got up to turn on the stereo. It was tuned to an oldies station and she walked back to the sofa to the sound of the steel guitar instrumental, "Sleep Walk," and kicked off her heels. "I've been listening to this music all week to get in the mood for the reunion."

"That's Santo and Johnny, right?"

"Yes, I'm sure it is."

"You needn't apologize for your taste in music if you don't criticize mine."

"Fair deal." Carol sat down beside him again. "If the steak's getting warm, flip it over."

"No, it's still cool." He fumbled for her hand. "I'm really sorry the reunion ended so badly. Thanks for not calling me a jackass, or worse."

Carol grasped his hand between both of hers. "I meant what I said, Matt. I'm real proud of you. Rather than stick up for the person being abused, too many people turn away when faced with an unpleasant situation like the one between Jack and Megan. You just leapt right in."

"With both feet, I'm afraid."

His knuckles were scraped, and Carol brought them to her lips. He had very handsome hands with long tapering fingers and neatly trimmed nails. She had always noticed men's hands and he had precisely the type she liked.

The minute her tongue caressed his torn skin Matt knew he was lost. He should never have come in the house. He sat up, tossed the steak on the wrapper on the coffee table, and pulled Carol into his arms. He needed her kisses too badly to allow her to waste them on his hands. He moved over to make room for her, but the sofa wasn't nearly wide enough for what he wanted to do.

Carol's taste was delicious, distracting him so completely it wasn't until their passionate need for each other made slipping off on the rug a dangerous possibility that he stopped to catch his breath. "Let's go take a shower," he suggested in a hushed command.

Disappointed, Carol sat up slightly. "I don't want to cool off."

"Neither do I," Matt assured her. "I just want to be clean enough to make love to you."

"Oh, that kind of a shower. What marvelous fun." Carol rose, and pulled him to his feet. "Oh, just a minute, let me put the steak back in the fridge."

"You're still going to eat it?"

Carol wrapped it up carefully. "I think the injured party is probably the one who ought to eat it, but we can worry about that later. My bedroom is the last on the right, and the bathroom's off it. I'll meet you there." Then with what she feared was unladylike haste, Carol dashed for the refrigerator before Matt changed his mind. She paused long enough to get a drink of water, then hurried down the hall.

Matt had already stripped off his shirt, slid back the glass door on the tub, and was running the shower. "You ought to have one of the newer showerheads to conserve water," he advised as she came in.

Carol laughed and raked the tips of her nails over his belly. "Give me the plumbing tips later. All I want now is you."

After savoring that vow with an appreciative kiss, Matt turned her around and undid the single button at the neckline of her top. "Rainbows become you," he whispered as he peeled it off over her head. She stepped out of her skirt, hung it on the back of the door with her sequined top, and hurriedly removed her rhinestone earrings.

"You're so very pretty." She had on such delicate lingerie Matt was afraid of tearing it, but the ivory-colored silken garments fell away as easily as rose petals. She was wearing thigh-high stockings with lace edging at the tops and he laughed as he rolled them down to her ankles. "You have such tiny feet." Her toenails were painted the same vivid red-orange as her nails. "Go on, hop in the shower. We're wasting water."

As the warm spray hit her face, Carol thought it remarkable that she had just let Matt undress her without a single worry about the firmness of her muscle tone. She did exercise regularly, and believed in keeping fit, but she had never expected the effort to pay off so handsomely. When he stepped into the tub behind her she relaxed against him. He had the soap in his hands, and began to spread lather over her shoulders. His touch, while new, was wonderfully familiar, as if they had showered together for years.

She turned to face him. The hair covering his chest was as dark as his lashes and brows, and made a fine mat to work up lather. She had had plenty of evidence that night that Matt was in excellent shape, and he was certainly no disappointment nude. With showering together as the perfect excuse to slide slippery hands all over each other, they were soon in as great a danger of falling as they had been on the sofa.

The bathroom was decorated in soft shades of pink, and once they had rinsed away the soap bubbles, Carol turned off the water, and handed Matt a pink towel which he draped around his hips. She wrapped herself in another, and used a third to dry his hair.

"Stand still," she complained. "I don't want to hurt your eye." Not only was the lid badly swollen, it was deep blue with streaks of purple. "As black eyes go, this is a beaut."

"The only kind to have." Matt teased her nipples playfully through her plush velour towel. He stood quietly for another minute, then caught the towel she was using and flung it on the counter. "You don't have to worry about my getting the pillowcase wet. I'm not going to sleep for hours yet."

"I just didn't want you to catch cold."

"I don't plan on catching anything," Matt assured her.

"You won't. I've a drawer full of condoms and I expect you to use them."

Matt swatted her bottom as they entered her bedroom. Decorated in lush shades of rose and moss green, the room was as attractive as its stylish owner. While Carol pulled the shams off the pillows, Matt rolled back the rose and green paisley comforter.

"A whole drawerful in a single night?" he gasped in mock horror. "That's quite a challenge, lady."

"You're quite a man." Carol let the damp towel fall to the floor and climbed into bed. Matt joined her in an instant, and now freed of the worry of rolling off the sofa or slipping in the tub, he became far more athletic. Already excited, Carol slid her fingers through his damp curls and returned his eager kisses with a devouring passion all her own.

Between them, there was none of the hesitancy that makes new lovers blush. Instead, there was only the mastery that comes with years of practice with the same partner. As though coming together after a long separation, they explored each other's bodies with enticing caresses and deeply satisfying kisses until, nearly faint from desire, Matt yanked open the drawer in the nightstand and spilled condoms all over the floor.

There were not just the standard variety either, but ribbed ones, and colored ones, and even some guaranteed to glow in the dark. Matt started to laugh, then grabbed one and got up to turn off the lights. "My God," he whispered a moment later. "The damn thing really is florescent!"

Carol had to slap her hand over her mouth to stifle her giggles, but managed to recover nicely. "It sure is, and I hope you don't plan to waste it."

Matt grabbed her and pushed her down into the feather pillows and with a slow, teasing seduction, proved that he didn't. Imaginative and yet tender, he was a lover of extraordinary skill, and in every way, Carol was his equal. The pink glow of dawn had begun to light the room before they fell asleep in each other's arms. Thoroughly sated with the most exquisite of pleasures, neither could have asked for more.

Thirteen

Karen had already dragged her laundry basket onto the service porch before she saw Gordon's shirt hanging over the sink. She had spoken with her mother at the end of the week and knew Aimee was going to the reunion with a former classmate, but the sight of the man's formal dress shirt was still a shock. Thinking he must have spent the night, she was about to tiptoe out, then decided she ought to at least leave her mother a note saying she would call later and come over to do her wash when it was more convenient.

She peered around the door, and finding no one in the kitchen came in to get a piece of paper and pencil. When she saw her mother seated outside on the patio, alone, she tried to remember if she had seen a car parked in front of the house, and certain she had not, she decided her gentleman friend must have left for home.

"How did it go last night?" she asked as she came through the screen door.

Ashamed that Karen had caught her crying, Aimee hurriedly wiped away her tears. "I'm afraid nothing went as it should."

"Have you been crying?" Karen pulled out a chair and sat down at the glass-topped table.

Aimee was seated in one chair and had her feet propped on another. The massive Sunday edition of the *Los Angeles Times* lay unread on the table, and a cup of cinnamon tea sat beside it cooling in the sun. "Believe me, I have good reason."

Karen encouraged her mother to talk and nodded thoughtfully as Aimee described what had to have been one of the most memorable parties ever given at the Ritz Carlton. "You're not just exaggerating," she gasped. "There was a real brawl?"

"I thought the police were going to take us all away in paddy wagons."

Karen grabbed the table's fourth chair for her own feet. "If you'd called, I'd have come right down to the station to bail you out, but I'm not even sure how to go about it."

"Neither am I, but just wait, it gets worse." The sound of the back door opening and closing alerted Aimee to another arrival and in the next moment, her daughter, JoAnne, joined them. "Hi, honey."

"How was the reunion?"

Karen gave up the extra chair for her sister. "It was great until the riot started, but just sit down and listen. Mom was just getting to the good part."

"What riot? Mom, what's she talking about?"

Both girls resembled their father, but JoAnne had not inherited Steve's curls. She wore her long hair knotted atop her head for work, but left it flowing over her shoulders when she was off-duty. Dressed in jeans and a knit top like Karen, were it not for the difference in their hair, they could easily have been mistaken for identical twins.

Aimee summarized what she had told Karen, and then paused. "I don't think I ought to tell you anymore. None of the experts advises parents to confide the details of their personal lives to their children."

JoAnne moaned. "We're adults now, Mother, you needn't consult Dr. Spock anymore. You're not going to tarnish our image of you, nor inspire promiscuous behavior in us no matter what you've been up to. Karen said this was the 'good part,' so don't think you can get away without providing all the details."

Aimee took a sip of her stone-cold tea. Unfortunately, she needed more in the way of tranquillity than a mere cup of tea could provide.

She glanced toward her daughters. They were lovely young women whom she felt sure knew far more about men than she did. "You're right," she finally agreed. "I can use your advice."

She told them about her confrontation with Gordon, but omitted the more delicious details about his hairy chest and marvelous kisses. "I told him we didn't know each other nearly well enough to sleep together. He still looked enough like his photograph in the annual for me to recognize him, but after all, it's been thirty-five years since I last saw him. Somehow he got the mistaken impression I was accusing him of being an imposter, and he stormed out."

"No," JoAnne argued. "He walked out because you refused to sleep with him. It must have been a severe wound to his masculine pride and men simply can't take that kind of rejection."

Karen sat forward. "No, wait a minute. That's just a little too pat. Let's assume he was reacting solely to the imposter comment. Maybe he didn't misunderstand you at all. Maybe you hit real close to home, and even if he was the person he was supposed to be, something else might be fishy about him. Where does he live?"

"In his family home in Pasadena. I'm not sure just where."

"That puzzle's easily solved." Karen went inside and returned with the telephone book. "What's his name?"

"Gordon Ashbach."

JoAnne made a face. "Sounds like one of the Muppets."

Karen kicked her chair leg. "Shut up. Let's see, Ashbach, yes, it's right here. He lives on Hillcrest Avenue. Wow. Is there anything up there worth less than a million?"

Her curiosity piqued, JoAnne's expression softened. "What kind of a car does he drive?"

"Mercedes, 450SL."

Karen whistled. "What sort of work does he do?"

"He said he was a theoretical physicist with JPL."

"There you go. That's an occupation he could have been certain you'd not know enough about to question, but it will be easy to check," JoAnne assured her mother. "Just call in the morning and ask for him."

Aimee shuddered at the thought. "I've nothing to say to him."

"You don't have to speak with him," JoAnne stressed. "Just ask for him and see if they put you through to his secretary. If they do, hang up, but if the operator says they've never heard of him, you'll know his story wasn't straight."

"Wait a minute," Karen said. "What about his shirt? Aren't you going to return it?"

"Yes. While you have the directory open, make a note of his address for me, please, and I'll mail it to him."

Karen went inside for a paper and pen, but after copying down Gordon's address, she had another concern. "I know we're all touchy about this after your experience with Bill Dunham, but isn't it just possible that this guy is as nice as you thought at first and that this was just a silly misunderstanding?"

"He didn't misunderstand," JoAnne argued again. "She said no and he split. It's as simple as that. You've probably never turned a guy down, but—"

Karen reached out to give her sister a playful jab. "Stop calling me a slut. I've said no plenty of times and yes, I've met guys who'll pick a fight so they can stomp out with their dignity intact. It's a childish stunt, but this guy is your age, isn't he, Mom?"

"Yes, but so was Bill, so age doesn't necessarily equate with wisdom, or honesty."

"If he's a physicist, he can't be stupid."

"If he's really a physicist," JoAnne cautioned. "No, I'd say the guy's behavior was inexcusable. I think you caught him in some kind of a lie, Mom, and he ran out rather than risk your discovering what it was."

"You're being paranoid," Karen argued.

"With damn good reason," JoAnne insisted. "Mom's lonely and she's an easy mark. I don't want husband number three to be anything like number two. That was the perfect number for Bill."

Aimee wasn't surprised by her daughters' argument. Despite the similarity in their looks, they had never seen eye to eye on anything. Karen was a free spirit, all laughter and fun, while JoAnne was far more cautious. She had read the firstborn child was usually the more serious individual, and the second the social, outgoing one, but her daughters' temperaments were just the reverse.

Of course, JoAnne had only been a year old when Steve was killed, and the happy laughter that had lit Karen's first three years had not been there for her. Had it not been for her daughters, Aimee doubted she would have survived her husband's death, but she knew JoAnne had suffered for having a grief-stricken mother, while Karen had done all a bright three-year-old could do to entertain her baby sister.

Karen closed the telephone book. "What did your instincts tell you, Mom?"

Aimee chewed her lower lip thoughtfully. "He made me nervous at first because he came right out and admitted to having had a crush on me. He kept making that same point all evening. Apparently I was his 'dream date' and I really didn't remember much about him at all."

"Well, you're still a fox, Mom," Karen exclaimed. "It's no wonder he was so impressed. Your red dress is gorgeous. Will you let me borrow it sometime?"

"And where is Roger going to take you that you'll need it?" JoAnne asked with a wry laugh.

"Roger is history," Karen assured her. "I've decided to follow your example and date only doctors from now on. Only I'm going to limit myself to unmarried ones."

"Karen!" Aimee scolded, but as the color drained from JoAnne's face, Aimee feared Karen hadn't just been speaking in jest. "Have you been seeing a married man, JoAnne?"

JoAnne's eyes filled with a misty hint of tears, but she shook her head. "No, but I was sure tempted. The only mistake I made was in telling Karen about it."

Aimee turned to Karen. "I thought you knew better than to violate your sister's trust."

"I do!" Karen swore. "It was just a joke and I apologize for not having more sense. I never would have said anything if JoAnne had really been seeing the guy. It's difficult enough to find a man who's interesting, but we're both smart enough to know married men are poison. If they'd cheat on their wives to see us, then they'd cheat on us just as fast with other women and neither of us needs that kind of grief."

"Your sister's right, JoAnne."

JoAnne nodded. "I know, especially since his story was a cliché. According to him, his wife had put him through medical school, but hadn't kept up with him intellectually. She bored him witless, but he felt he had to stay with her out of loyalty. We just talked. I wouldn't even let him kiss me.

"I won't pretend I wasn't flattered, but I told him to give me a call when he got a divorce. From what I've heard, he's still with his wife and dating another of the nurses. It makes me mad. Women ought to stick together. If none of us would sleep with a married man, a lot more men would have to really face their marital problems."

"You're damn right," Karen agreed. "Women ought not to betray each other, but if I ever catch you with Roger, you better watch out."

"I thought you said he was 'history'?"

"Yeah, I did."

Anxious for the next installment in Roger's continuing saga, Aimee rose to her feet. "Come on inside. Let's make some pancakes and then you can tell us what's happened with Roger since last week."

Karen carried the telephone book, and JoAnne

brought the *Times*. "Honestly, Mom, the guy has been such an ass lately."

"Well, what man isn't?" JoAnne asked.

"Ladies, ladies, please," Aimee cautioned. "Some men are as terrific as we are."

Before making the pancakes, Aimee put Gordon's address on her desk in the den. It might take a little bit of doing, but if her preliminary investigations proved him to be exactly what he said he was, she would gather her courage, and return his shirt in person.

Suzanne awoke wrapped in Casey's arms. She tried to adjust her pose slightly, but he responded by holding her all the more tightly. "Casey?" she whispered, but he continued to sleep soundly. Thinking he must still be worn out, she waited for him to move of his own accord so that she could get out of bed without disturbing him.

Last night she had drawn a bath for him, and filled it with foaming crystals to make soaking more fragrant, as well as fun, but left him on his own while she brewed a pot of herbal tea. She had insisted he drink a cup, and take some aspirin before climbing into bed, but her biggest challenge had been to assure him she did not mind at all that he did not feel well enough to make love. Just snuggling with him had been so nice, and waking up with him was too.

Jack had been an early riser and despite a long marriage, she doubted she had awakened in his arms on more than a half-dozen occasions. She had felt bad about it at the time, for it had been just one more rejection along with all his others. She raised a hand to sift Casey's hair through her fingers. He was the type of man who not only invited petting, but enjoyed it as much as she did. Unlike Jack, he would never brush her hand away when she reached out to caress him.

She glanced over at the clock on the nightstand and was surprised it was nearly noon. She was wide awake and yet filled with a lazy warmth that made getting up not at all appealing. She closed her eyes, and savored Casey's embrace. He was such a dear, sweet man, and she did so hope he would feel like his old self when he awoke.

The sound of a car horn blaring down the street awoke Casey a few minutes later. He opened one eye, recognized the bright colors of Suzanne's bedroom, and then the lush softness of her breast beneath his cheek. He sighed contentedly. His whole body ached from the pummeling he had received, but mere physical pain failed to wipe the joyous expression from his face.

"Casey?"

"Hmm?"

"Let me go, sweetie, so I can get up."

"Stay."

Suzanne gave him a loving hug. "I want to make us some breakfast. Do you think you could eat a waffle?"

"I'd rather eat you."

Suzanne laughed along with him. "Yes, that's a delectable idea, but I think you better wait until your lip is healed."

Casey ran his tongue over his lower lip and winced at the swollen glob surrounding the cut. I probably did need stitches, he thought, but he would never admit it. "You're right. Give me a rain check?"

"Written on what, a pair of lace panties?"

"That would be appropriate."

Suzanne might have continued to snuggle with Casey but his stomach growled noisily, prompting her to renew her request. "Let me go."

Reluctantly, Casey released her. After a lazy stretch to test the extent of his discomfort, which was still considerable, he propped his head on his elbow. "I like waking up here with you."

Suzanne had on a sheer floral nightgown and reached for her robe. "It is nice waking up together, isn't it?"

Suzanne's curls were in wild disarray, but Casey thought she looked absolutely captivating. "If we put our minds to it, I'll bet we could figure out a way to do it all the time."

Suzanne knotted the belt on her robe. "What do you mean?"

"If we lived together, we could do it every morning. It's a fairly common practice nowadays, or so I've heard." Now that he had broached the subject, Casey grew positively inspired. "I'd invite you to move in with me, but you have more stuff than we could ever fit into my condo. I'm sure I could lease my place for enough to cover the payments plus pay my share of the expenses here. What do you say?"

Even all beat up, Casey was appealing, but Suzanne shook her head. "I love waking up with you too, Casey, but statistically, living together increases rather than lessens a couple's chances for divorce if they later marry and I don't intend to ever go through the trauma of another divorce. Thank you, but no thanks. Now did you say yes to the waffle?"

That such a delightfully feminine woman could be so analytical was a jolt. Casey tried to remember she was also a respected professor, but that didn't help him much. "I know you're an anthropologist, so I'm not surprised you can quote statistics, but don't feelings matter more to you than percentages in some survey?"

Suzanne paused in the doorway. "I was talking about my feelings when I said I wouldn't put myself through the horror of another divorce. Now excuse me please, I want to fix our breakfast."

Casey was absolutely dumbfounded. Since his divorce, he had dated several women, most for far longer than he had dated Suzanne, but he had never wanted to live with any of them. Suzanne hadn't even thanked him for the compliment, nor said she was flattered! He threw back the covers and tried to leave the bed with the same grace Suzanne had shown but strained muscles in his arms and legs put up too painful a protest. He sat back down on the side of the bed, and struggled to catch his breath.

"Damn it, Suzanne," he complained, although he knew she was too far away to hear. She had taken his shirt to soak, but he put on his pants and jacket, and went into the bathroom. The first night he had stayed there, Suzanne had produced a new toothbrush and package of Bic razors for him. He had thought it such a thoughtful gesture, but now he realized she must have had them ready for whomever turned up. Maybe she didn't consider him special at all.

Brushing his teeth was a real challenge with his lower lip swollen into a grotesque flap and when he began to shave, he discovered bruises he had not even known he had had. Slowed by caution and the gnawing suspicion Suzanne wasn't as crazy about him as he was about her, it took him a while, but by the time he finished his grooming he felt he looked the best he possibly could under the circumstances. He had an extra pair of glasses in the glove compartment of his car, but lacked the energy to go out and get them. Afraid he looked like a clown in the bent pair, he left them in the bedroom.

"I planned to bring you breakfast in bed," Suzanne told him when he joined her in the kitchen.

"That's very kind of you, but I think I'll be better off if I stay ambulatory." But rather than remain on his feet, he slid into what he now considered his place at her kitchen table. "Can't we at least discuss this, Suzanne?"

Suzanne had caught her hair at her nape with a rubber band to keep it out of her way while cooking, but she was still in her nightgown and robe. "You're not talking about the waffles, are you?"

Afraid he was drooling, Casey picked up a napkin to wipe his mouth. "You know I'm not. I realize we've only known each other a week, but damn it all the attraction is either there from the beginning or it's not. I know, or at least you've given me every reason to believe, you're as strongly attracted to me as I am to you."

Suzanne poured the batter into the waffle iron and lowered the lid. Casey's swollen lip gave his words a rakish slur, but she understood him clearly. "I'm fifty-two, Casey. That's too damn old to play house."

"Christ! You're not old! With all that gorgeous red hair, you don't look a day over forty."

"That's just because you're not wearing your glasses." Suzanne didn't want to take her eye off the waffle. She always burned the first one, every time. Her eyes filled with tears, but she shook her head. "The answer's no."

"Is that it then? Do you want me to go?"

"No, of course not." She pried open the lid of the waffle iron to peek at the edge of the waffle but it was still creamy white rather than golden brown.

"Well, I suppose I should be grateful I'm still welcome to stay for breakfast."

"Don't pout. That's a real unattractive habit in a man."

Brought up short by that unexpected rebuke, Casey put his head in his hands. He was going to lose Suzanne, if he hadn't already. "I'm so sorry," he mumbled. "I didn't mean to rush you."

"I beg your pardon? Oh damn!"

Casey looked up. "What's wrong?"

"I let the waffle burn, which I always do." She chucked it into the sink and poured more batter onto the steaming iron. "I always have to throw the first one away, and then the rest are all perfect."

"It's not you. That's a poorly designed iron. I'll bring you another one. Suzanne, if you don't even want to talk about living together, what are your thoughts on marriage?"

"As an institution, you mean?"

"No, just as it relates to you and me. I'm trying to ask you to marry me."

Suzanne turned around slowly. "You don't mean that."

Casey tried to reassure her with a smile that he sure did, but succeeded only in splitting his torn lip. He raised the napkin to his mouth, and it came away covered with blood. "Oh God."

Suzanne ripped the waffle iron's cord from the wall. "Just sit still. I'm going to throw on some clothes and take you to the emergency room before you bleed to death."

"Is that a no?"

Suzanne handed him a clean terry cloth hand towel. "Here, use this. This is no time to talk about marriage, or anything else." Suzanne planted a kiss on the top of his head, and ran from the room.

That, Casey thought, was a definite maybe,

and it was enough to keep him from fainting at what now seemed to be the certainty of stitches.

Carol reached out for Matt, felt only the coolness of the sheets and sat up slowly. When she found him seated on the floor, leaning back against the foot of the bed, she crawled over the rumpled comforter to reach him. He had put on his pants, and was hugging his pillow across his lap as though it were a giant teddy bear. She planted a kiss on his bare shoulder and ruffled his soft silver curls. Touching him brought a burst of pleasure, just as she had known it would.

"Good morning."

"It's afternoon."

Carol yawned sleepily. "Really? Well, I'm not surprised. Can I fix you some brunch?"

"No, we need to talk."

He continued to stare out the French doors at the backyard, and alarmed that he hadn't turned to face her, Carol scrambled off the side of the bed. "Wait a minute. I didn't take off my make-up last night and I'm not discussing anything looking like a raccoon."

"How do you think I look?"

He turned slightly and Carol winced. "I don't think we left the steak on your eye nearly long enough." She grabbed a ruffled, pink silk robe, and went on into the bathroom. The seriousness of Matt's mood frightened her, and she hurriedly removed what was left of her smudged mascara, washed her face, and brushed her hair. She then quickly applied the subtle hint of blusher, lip gloss, and mascara that she hoped would pass for 'natural' beauty.

She came back into the bedroom and sat down on the floor beside Matt. Curling her legs beneath her gracefully, she felt ready to face him. "After last night," she began with a smile, "I can't imagine what you have left to say."

Matt had been awake long enough to have rehearsed, but Carol's sweet prettiness was an awful distraction. "I owe you an apology for picking you up in the van, for one thing. I was deliberately being obnoxious, and my comments about portable toilets were uncalled for too."

Thinking that was all he wished to get off his chest, Carol was enormously relieved. "I'll admit to being obnoxious myself at times, but as I said, after last night, I thought everything was definitely forgiven."

Matt closed his eyes a moment, and hugged the pillow even more tightly. "Last night was, well, I suppose a poet could describe it accurately, but I don't have the words. All I know for sure is how I feel now." He looked up at her. "This is a beautiful house, Carol, and you've got it looking like an Ethan Allen showroom. Everything is as perfect in color and design as you are."

"Well, thank you."

"Please, don't interrupt me, just let me finish."

Not at all pleased by his curt rebuke, Carol tried not to let her hurt feelings show. He had paid her a compliment and she had thanked him. That scarcely counted as an interruption in her view.

"You're a beautiful woman, with expensive tastes, the kind who ought to be dressed in sequins and wined and dined every Saturday night by a man who owns his own tuxedo and limousine. Last night was the first time I've had an occasion to wear a tuxedo since my son's wedding and I know I wasn't at all gracious about wearing it either. I can't help but feel you'd like me to be someone I'm not, someone super respectable, with a prestigious career. A heart surgeon, or classical composer, hell, it's difficult to think of a job with any less prestige than a plumber's."

There had been a time when the fact Matt was a plumber had bothered Carol, but it was long over. "Matt—"

He raised his hand. "Please, just let me finish. That we're so great in bed together is something I'll never forget, but I don't want to try and push whatever we have going for us physically into anything more. I'd like to just kiss you goodbye and leave before either of us becomes disillusioned and bitter because we're such an odd mix."

Carol stared at him for a long moment. "No way, Mr. Trenerry. You're not walking out of here like some noble self-sacrificing peasant who knows he and the princess are too different to live happily ever after. I want a say in this too and I think you're hiding behind your damn portable toilet. Tell me how you feel about me, not why you think we're not a viable couple when last night proved we are."

"That was only sex, Carol," Matt reminded her softly. "Don't try and make it anything more."

Carol pushed herself to her feet. "Liar. I won't let you dismiss what was easily the best night of my entire life, one you just admitted only a poet could describe, as merely 'sex.' It was one hell of a lot more and that's what scares you, isn't it? The fact I might have a flair for interior design, or wear designer clothes, that I buy at a discount by the way, doesn't have a damn thing to do with it!"

Matt tossed the pillow up on the bed and rose to face her. "I didn't want this to be ugly."

"That's another damn lie," Carol shot right back at him. "You have a clear choice, to try for something extraordinary with me, or to slip back into the miserable abyss from which you came. I thought you had far more courage. You sure did last night. What's happened to you today?"

Matt picked up his shirt, and jacket, jammed his socks into his pocket, and slipped his bare feet into his rented shoes. Torn by the most painful emotional conflict of his life, he walked out without saying a word. He still couldn't see worth a damn out of his right eye, but there was such little traffic on the roads on a Sunday afternoon he wasn't worried about running into anyone on the way home. What he would do when he got there was as impossible for him to foresee as it was for him to share his torment with Carol.

Carol didn't walk him to the door, nor hurl stinging epithets at his back. She just sat down on the bed and sobbed for the joyous life they could have had, if only Matt had wanted it too. "How could he not have wanted it?" she sobbed, but even a flood of tears could not wash away her painful sense of loss.

The nurse insisted Suzanne remain in the emergency room's waiting area when Casey's name was called. She fidgeted in the uncomfortable plastic seat and wished she had remembered to bring something to read, because she certainly needed a distraction. Believing the hospital would have a gift shop which carried magazines, she made a hurried trip to pick up a couple and becoming engrossed in the current issue of *Newsweek,* she shut out all thought of Casey's impromptu proposal.

It wasn't until that afternoon when she took him back home and sent him straight to bed to sleep off the lingering nausea having a dozen stitches in his lower lip had caused that she finally had to face the fact his question could not simply be ignored. She went outside to work in her yard. Pulling weeds had always helped her to focus on solutions to problems and she knew she had better find a way to gracefully decline Casey's proposal without crushing his feelings so badly he would never want to see her again.

When pulling up three buckets full of dandelions hadn't helped ease her conscience nor inspire an appropriate reply, she went inside and called Carol. "Can you find an excuse to come to San Marino tomorrow and meet me for lunch at Julienne? I'll call Aimee, too, if you can. I really need your advice, Carol. Casey's asked me to marry him, and I don't know what to say."

That Casey would propose to Suzanne, while Matt had walked out on her, was almost more than Carol could stand, but she and Suzanne had been friends for too many years for her to desert her now. "I'd planned to take a vacation day tomorrow," she replied. "How's eleven forty-five?"

"Great. I'll call Aimee. See you tomorrow."

"Yeah, *ciao.*" When the telephone rang Carol had foolishly hoped Matt had changed his mind and called to beg for her forgiveness. "Fat chance," she whispered. He was gone for good, and she would never understand how he had expected her to let him go with no more than a grateful wave.

Fourteen

Julienne *Boulangerie* and *Patisserie* was a French cafe which catered to the women who patronized the exclusive hair salons and expensive boutiques along the two-block Mission Street shopping area in San Marino, one of southern California's most affluent communities. The marble-topped tables placed along the sidewalk were crowded with friends who had stolen an hour from shopping and working on charity fund raisers to conduct their own special brand of networking. Among the sprinkling of career women who occasionally managed to eat there, Suzanne was shown to the table she had reserved and ordered the sweetly spiced iced tea. Carol arrived next, closely followed by Aimee.

Suzanne had apprised both her friends of her problem when she had asked them to meet her for lunch, but facing them now, she feared her dilemma might sound absurd. "Poor Casey's still at my house. I had to call in sick for him this morning. With his lip looking like the hem of a patchwork quilt, he didn't think he'd be of much use at Russell's. Luckily for me, it's difficult for him to talk, so I've given him a notebook and pencil for basic communication and told him we won't have any serious discussions of any kind until next week. I'm just stalling him, and he knows it as well as I do, but what else can I do?"

To hide her tear-swollen eyes, Carol had worn the darkest pair of sunglasses she owned, and did not remove them as she perused the menu. "Let's order first and then see if we can't come up with a solution. The chicken tarragon salad sandwich on the rosemary raisin bread is always good."

Thinking Carol awfully subdued, Aimee touched her arm. "Are you all right?" she asked.

Carol shook her head. "No, but it's Suzanne who needs the help today."

"Oh Lord." Suzanne quickly apologized. "I shouldn't have been so lost in my problems that I failed to notice you're hurting. Did you have trouble with Matt?"

"Later," Carol promised. The waiter appeared at her elbow, and she ordered the chicken sandwich.

"I'll have the marinated lamb sandwich,

please," Aimee said. With caramelized onions, avocado, tomatoes, and basil on a French *baguette,* it was more than she usually ate for lunch, but whenever she visited Julienne she felt justified in splurging.

Suzanne scanned the scrumptious possibilities. "Just reading the menu here is enough to excite a feeding frenzy." She usually ordered the chicken tarragon sandwich, but wanting something new, chose the grilled eggplant with peppers, zucchini, red onion, mozzarella, and fresh basil. The adjacent tables were close, but with each group intensely involved in its own private conversation she wasn't worried about being overheard. "I'd love to remarry," she readily admitted, "but not to someone I've known only a week."

"It's been a week and two days now," Carol reminded her.

"True, but we're not in the midst of a war. His haste to propose makes me question his judgment. Granted, I am a terrific person and all, and he seems to be a real treasure, but what kind of a man proposes to a woman he's only known nine days?"

"One who's in love?" Aimee suggested. "You know Casey best, Carol. What do you think of his character?"

"Is this a character issue?" Carol asked.

Suzanne nodded. "Yes, I think it is. I can't

help but wonder if a man who would rush into marriage wouldn't be just as anxious to flee the bonds of matrimony soon afterward."

"Is that your real worry?" Carol inquired. "That Casey's ardor will quickly cool and he'll want to move on?"

"Yes, and I'd like to grow old with the next man I marry," Suzanne explained wistfully. "Casey's attractive and fun, incredibly loving, but underneath, he has a strain of almost pathetic neediness that frightens me. He was devastated when his first wife left him, and the helpfulness he displayed at your party, and I've seen since, can be interpreted as an excuse to involve himself in our lives, to cling."

Carol had also ordered the delicious spiced tea, and took a refreshing sip. She had again worn red to lift her mood, but her version of color therapy wasn't working any better than the last time she had tried it. "I like Casey, I really do, but the party at my house was the first time I'd seen him away from Russell's and our personalities just clashed. That's probably more my fault than his, but there's a very thin line between the person who's wonderfully helpful, and the one who's never satisfied with the way others do things. My experience with Bob makes me afraid Casey's the latter type."

Suzanne leaned back as the waiter brought their lunches. The sandwiches were served with fresh fruit on a colorful ruffled-edged ornamental cabbage leaf. Her sandwich looked absolutely delicious, but she doubted she would really enjoy it. "Casey isn't critical though. What I mean is, he volunteers his suggestions without deriding my efforts. I really think he's too good-natured to harbor the type of hostility you got from Bob. He's begging for love, not trying to put anyone down."

Aimee had to finish a bite of her sandwich, which was incredibly good, before she could comment. "They say a camel is a horse designed by a committee, and I have the feeling this isn't a question that would benefit from a group effort either. We could discuss Casey, and I barely know the man, up one side and down the other but the real question is whether or not you love him, Suzanne, or think you could. You mustn't allow our feelings to influence you in such an important matter. After all, we're not the ones who'll be living with him."

"Ah yes, feelings," Carol agreed. "Unfortunately, feelings change, sometimes overnight."

Suzanne and Aimee exchanged a perplexed glance. "Is there something you want to tell us?" Suzanne prompted.

"There's nothing to tell," Carol lied, and because this was the first time she had ever held out on her dearest friends she felt a sharp twinge of guilt. This was too personal though, and much too painful to share fully. She offered instead only a vague hint of her argument with Matt, and nothing at all about his remarkable prowess in bed.

"Matt thinks we're too different to make a go of it, and that's that."

Carol was staring down at her sandwich rather than looking toward them, and neither Aimee nor Suzanne was fooled. "It sounds as though you disagreed with him," Aimee said.

"Violently, but Matt's incredibly stubborn. It's just a shame he had to look so damn good." She wiped her mouth, and deciding to take the rest of her lunch home with her, pushed her plate aside. "Now tell us how the evening ended with Gordon, and then we'll get back to Suzanne's problem."

"No," Aimee argued. "We need to help Suzanne first. Frankly, after marrying Bill Dunham, I don't feel qualified to give anyone matrimonial advice. That was one of the worst mistakes of the century."

"It scarcely compares to the wreck of the Exxon Valdes," Carol argued with a touch of her old humor. "Besides, you caught on to him before any real damage was done, except to your pride, of course."

"And my confidence," Aimee mused aloud. She again turned to Suzanne. "Have you talked to Patricia about Casey?"

Suzanne had just taken a bite of sandwich and at the mention of her daughter, nearly choked. "Oh my God," she replied when she was able. "I haven't had time to even think of her, let alone call and talk with her. I suppose I should call her when I get home, but what could I possibly say that would make any sense?"

Aimee blotted her lips. "You could simply tell her you've met a man you're considering marrying. He's bright, attractive, has a responsible job. He can handle himself with his fists fairly well too."

"That last point ought to impress her," Suzanne sighed. "Why couldn't it have been Jack Shank who needed a dozen stitches rather than Casey? Poor Casey didn't deserve that misery."

Carol reached out to touch Suzanne's arm. "That's the second time you've called him that, and I've begun to think of Casey as, 'poor Casey' too. I don't believe that's an attractive feature in a husband."

Suzanne immediately agreed. "No, it isn't. I'm afraid love and pity might be mutually exclusive emotions." Her appetite gone, she pushed her plate aside too. "Thanks, you've really helped me to see my choices more clearly."

"We have?" Aimee asked.

"Yes, definitely. Casey's wonderful in so

many ways, but that pitiful streak is a real turn-off."

"You've only known the man nine days," Aimee reminded her. "And he got beaten up so badly he ended up in the emergency room. Give him time to recover. Anyone would be pitiful after what he's been through." Then with sudden insight, she offered a suggestion. "You quoted us a statistic on living together."

"Yes, it's not a good predictor of success in marriage, so I'm against it. I told Casey that. I think that's what inspired him to propose."

"Fine, why don't you make up another statistic to prove people who know each other a minimal length of time before marrying have a high rate of divorce. Insist you want to know him six months, or a year, or whatever figure you care to use, before you consider marriage and because you're basing your opinion on statistics, rather than mere whim, he won't feel insulted."

Suzanne frowned slightly. "That's a creative solution, but as a scientist I'm opposed to making up statistics on ethical grounds, but I just might be able to find a study on length of engagement and how it relates to duration of marriage. That ought to be enough to impress him."

Carol thought back to the conversation she had Sunday with Matt. She had had the suspicion then that he was withholding something vital, and she couldn't go along with Aimee's plan. "The truth is always best, Suz. Tell Casey he's been marvelous so far, but you'd like to know him a whole lot better before you consider marriage. From what I've seen of Casey, he doesn't discourage easily."

"What if Matt had proposed to you? What would you have said?"

"Our situation's a bit different," Carol reminded her. "I met him the same time you met Casey, but saw him only briefly on Wednesday night and then again on Saturday. You've spent a lot more time with Casey."

"You're hedging the question," Suzanne scolded. "You've said he's gorgeous, so how would you have responded if he had fallen madly in love with you on Saturday night and proposed?"

Carol would not allow herself to even imagine such a remote, although wildly exciting, possibility. "I doubt plumbers are ever that impulsive. As things stand now, I'll win ten million in the lottery before I'll see him again. It's your turn, Aimee. Tell us what happened with Gordon"

Frustrated by Carol's evasiveness, Suzanne sat back in her chair while Aimee began to squirm in hers. "We had, how shall I describe it, either a ridiculous misunderstanding, or a brilliant epiphany. As yet, it's too soon for me to be sure which it was."

"Now there's an intriguing dichotomy," Carol remarked. "Our reunion tally appears to be one definite strike out, one proposal, which has to be counted as a grand slam, and one what, scoreless inning? Love is such a fascinating game, isn't it? It's a damn shame no one has ever been able to devise a satisfactory book of rules."

Carol's sarcasm wasn't lost on Suzanne and Aimee, but each was too concerned about her own problems with men to realize just how heartbroken she truly was.

Dan Trenerry unwrapped his sandwich. Tuna salad, he discovered with a smile; one of his favorites. His wife made the best tuna salad he had ever eaten. She always used whole wheat bread, and alfalfa sprouts rather than celery. He opened a cold can of soda.

"Aren't you going to stop for lunch?" he called to his father.

Matt was busy restocking the van and just shook his head.

Dan sat down in the sun on the loading dock at the back of their shop. He ate half the sandwich, then made an effort to draw his father into conversation. "Even if you aren't hungry, the least you could do is keep me company. You told me how you got the black eye, but not how you did with Carol. When are you going to see her again?"

"Never!"

"As good as you looked on Saturday night? She's got to want to see you again."

Matt gestured with a wrench. "What Carol wants doesn't matter. It's what I want that counts and I called it off."

Dan had his father's once dark curls, and his mother's brown eyes. In the last four years, he had done everything he could think of, short of hiring an escort and plunking her down on his father's doorstep, to get him interested in women again. When he had first heard about the reunion, he had been more excited than his father, and he was not about to let the matter drop.

"It's been four years, Dad. Mom wouldn't want to see you moping around like you do. You said Carol was pretty. If she's a buyer for Russell's, she's got to be smart. What more do you want?"

"A little peace and quiet."

Dan ignored that hint, and kept right on prodding. "No, that's just the problem. You've spent too damn much time alone since Mom died." Then a truly horrible thought occurred to him and he had to set the rest of his sandwich aside. His dad had given him the old birds and bees talk when he had been nine. They had not talked about sex again until he was in his teens and then the subject had been responsibility, not mechanics.

Rather than those awkward talks, the loving way his father had always treated his mother had taught him what it meant to be a man. His parents had been such an affectionate pair, Dan could think of only one reason why his father wouldn't want to become involved with another woman, and while it would be embarrassing as hell to discuss, he felt he had to do it.

He got up, walked over to the van, and lowered his voice to a confidential whisper. "Dad, I know older men sometimes have trouble. I'm not sure how to put this delicately, maybe that's impossible, but sometimes they have trouble performing. You must know what I mean. If that's the case, doctors have all kinds of things they can do now. Why don't you make an appointment, and get some help."

Annoyed rather than pleased by his son's sudden interest in his health, Matt stepped back. "Just what the hell are you talking about?"

Dan looked around to make certain they had the back parking lot to themselves. "Getting it up," he replied.

Shocked at first that Dan would want to give him advice on impotence, when that was the very least of his problems, Matt couldn't help but laugh. He laughed so hard he had to sit down on the loading dock to catch his breath. "There's not a damn thing wrong with my personal plumbing, Dan. Christ, I'm only fifty-four." He began to chuckle again as he recalled the night he had spent with Carol. Probably had set some kind of record for his age group, but he had been too busy to keep a count, and so had she.

Matt's expression had been glum all morning, but as Dan watched him now, his face took on the faint smile of a deeply contented man. Amazed then to think there must have been a great deal more going on than his father cared to admit, he adjusted his view of the situation. "If that smile means what I think it does, you'd be a fool to call it off and I know you're no fool."

Unable to take that advice, Matt's expression darkened as he got to his feet. "It doesn't bother you that I've been with a woman other than your mother?" he asked.

"Hell, no!" Dan slapped him on the back. "Congratulations! It's about time is all I'll say, and Mom would too. She would never want you living like some pious monk who refuses to taint his flesh by mixing with women."

"Yeah, I know," Matt replied. "Carol's the wrong woman though."

"Why?"

"I sent for a photograph from the reunion. Wait until you see her. She's petite, but as perfect as a Barbie Doll. Everything about her is *perfect.* She's a real classy lady. Drives a BMW, and I own a truck."

Dan went back to pick up his sandwich. "You're really working hard to talk yourself out of this, aren't you? I didn't realize you had a prejudice against good-looking women who drive BMW's. The business is doing real well, Dad. I'm sure you could afford her no matter how expensive her tastes are, but I doubt she's interested in you for your money."

Matt kicked a pebble with his toe. "No, she doesn't know I have any."

"I think we're just talking ourselves all the way around this, Dad. You and Mom were lucky. You had a lot of good years together before she got sick. Don't you want that same happiness again?"

"Sure I want it, but—" his voice dropped to a whisper, "your Mom's dead."

Dan stared at him. "Is that what's stopping you? Do you feel guilty because you're alive and enjoying yourself and she's not able to do the same?" When his father turned away, again retreating behind the wall of silence he built around himself so often, Dan was tempted to kick him in the seat. "You deserve a swift kick in the butt!" he yelled instead. "Why didn't you just jump in the grave with Mom?"

Matt looked over his shoulder. "We had her cremated, Dan."

"Oh hell, I know there was no grave!" Dan yelled. "That wasn't the point!" He jammed the last of his sandwich in his mouth and chewed it with ferocious chomps as he watched his father walk away. They were the same size, could borrow each other's clothes if they wanted, but that's where the similarity between them ended.

Dan understood grief. He still missed his mother too, and always would, but he would be damned if he would let his father retreat into tomb-cold loneliness. Maybe Carol hadn't been the right woman to lure him out of his self-imposed solitary confinement, but there had to be another woman who could.

"I'll just have to see he keeps on looking," he promised himself, but he hoped the reunion photograph arrived soon because he was real curious about Carol, and he could not understand how such a "perfect" woman could have failed to make a big dent in the armor his father had clamped over his heart.

Suzanne found Casey seated out on the deck. She had loaned him a pair of bright yellow sweatpants and bare-chested, he had been sunning himself and reading through some of her magazines. When she bent down to brush his cheek with a light kiss, he handed her a postcard from Perfect Match. He had drawn a question mark across it, and from the accusing look in his eyes, it was plain he was not simply curious, but jealous.

The railing around the deck was wide enough to serve as a bench, and Suzanne sat down across from him and tried not to shriek so loudly any of her neighbors who happened to be at home would hear. "Do you make a habit of reading your girlfriends' mail?"

Casey shook his head, then drew another question mark in the notebook he had been forced to use to talk with her.

In a continuing attempt to hold on to her temper, Suzanne looked away. She supposed Casey had heard the mailman slip her mail through the slot in the door, and being the wonderfully helpful soul that he was, he had gathered it up, and carried it into the kitchen table for her. In the process, he could have noticed the postcard. The fact he had seen it did not have to mean he had searched her mail for correspondence from other men. Still, he had been very quick to hand it to her.

It was difficult to believe she had just spent the last hour discussing the advisability of marrying a man when she knew so little about him she did not really know whether or not he might read her mail. Of course, this was only a printed postcard advising her someone wished to meet her, rather than a torrid love letter he had steamed open, but still, she was uneasy.

What if their situations had been reversed? she asked herself, and she had come across a postcard from Perfect Match addressed to Casey. She glanced back toward him. He had been using the bent pair of glasses to read, but had removed them when she had appeared. His eyes were a bright, clear blue, but she didn't think he could see her all that well without his glasses. Well, his eyesight wasn't really the issue here; her privacy was.

"I joined Perfect Match a few months ago because I was interested in meeting someone as special as you. I've met some nice men too, but no one I've dated more than a couple of times. Now I've no idea who this particular gentleman might be, but when I get a chance, I'll turn down his request and put my membership on hold." She flipped the card toward the pile of magazines beside his chair.

"Did you honestly believe I'd want to date someone else?"

Casey wrote: Hope not.

Suzanne came forward and knelt beside him. "Do you feel well enough to drive home?"

Casey scrawled a reply: Are you mad at me?

Suzanne ran her hand up his arm. "Yes, I sure am and for two reasons. First, I can understand how you might have noticed the postcard while picking up the mail, but you really had no right to question me about it. I'd not sort through your mail, nor ever read it, and you simply must respect my privacy too. Is that understood?"

Casey nodded.

"Good. Now for point two. Your experience with your first wife has left you terribly insecure, but that's your problem and I refuse to make it mine."

Casey hung his head a moment, and then wrote: If I go home, I won't be able to talk with you.

Casey's responses were so predictable Suzanne wasn't at all surprised, but he was dangerously dependent and not only for her own peace of mind, but also for his, she would not do anything to encourage it. "Yes, I know. I'll miss you terribly too, but we'll get along just fine on our own for a few days. Now do you feel up to driving, or will I have to take you?"

Casey drew a sad face and wrote beneath it: You'd throw out an invalid?

"You're no invalid, Casey O'Neil. You're a strong, resourceful man and you're fully capable of taking care of yourself."

When? Casey wrote.

Suzanne gave his arm an affectionate squeeze. "Why don't you come for dinner Saturday night?"

Casey turned a page and wrote in big block letters: SATURDAY! I'll die of neglect!

Suzanne stood up, and put her hands on her hips. "You've lived forty-six years without me, Casey. You'll survive four days on your own."

It's five days until Saturday, Casey wrote.

"You can't count either today or Saturday," Suzanne argued. "Now stop quibbling."

Casey could see he was getting absolutely nowhere and wished he possessed more in the way of artistic talent so his notes would have more impact. He used the side of his pencil lead to make wider strokes: Don't you feel just a little bit sorry for me?

"No, you were wonderfully brave to defend Matt without a thought of your own safety. I'm too proud of you to think you're pitiful. Now go on home, or I'll start charging you rent."

Casey drew a smiling face, and wrote: I'll pay!

"Go on, git!" Suzanne moved out of his way, but as soon as he stood, he grabbed her in a boisterous hug. She wrapped her arms around him and ran her hands over his bare back. Closing her eyes, she decided he definitely felt right which was a terrific plus in his favor, and she savored his warmth before stepping out of his arms.

"I'll see you Saturday night," she told him. "Call me before then if it's not too difficult for you to speak. Better yet, write me a letter."

Casey raised his brows.

"Yes! In fact, make it a love letter. I haven't gotten one in thirty years."

Casey frowned slightly, conveying the impression he considered her comment a real shame. He nodded, then turning to a new page, he drew a big heart, put their initials inside, tore out the page, and handed it to her.

"Yes, I knew you could do it." Suzanne gave his cheek a last kiss and then went into the kitchen to look over the rest of her mail while he got ready to leave. She walked with him out to his car, and waved goodbye but he had not been gone more than fifteen minutes before she began to miss him. She had not expected that sweet sadness.

"Maybe I should have asked him to come for dinner on Friday night," she wondered aloud, and then decided being apart until Saturday would do them both good. She was smart enough not to try and cook for him though. Instead, she would order honey walnut shrimp from the Panda Inn and maybe a few of their other specialties too. Yes, she would serve such a delicious meal that no matter how she told him it was much too soon to discuss marriage, he would readily agree.

* * *

When Aimee got back to the bank after lunch, she had several calls to return, then in an attempt to continue working in the same efficient, businesslike manner, she dialed the Jet Propulsion Laboratory. "May I please speak with Gordon Ashbach?" she asked. She held her breath, expecting a confused request for a repeat of the name, or the ready response that JPL had no such employee. Instead her call went right through.

"Dr. Ashbach's office, Ms. Rainey."

The prompt reply forced Aimee to the stunning realization of just how little faith she had had in Gordon to be there. Ashamed of herself, she offered an apology. "I'm sorry, Ms. Rainey, I have another call. I'll have to catch Gordon later."

"He's right here."

"Thank you, no, there isn't time." Aimee replaced the receiver and feeling exceedingly foolish, got up and walked to the window. Her branch had been redecorated recently in shades of cool blue accented with touches of terracotta. The decor was wonderfully soothing, but for now she preferred to focus on the lively jumble of colors out on the street.

The probability that a man who lived on Hillcrest Avenue and worked at the Jet Propulsion

Laboratory might be a fraud were extremely remote. In that case, she and Gordon had simply misunderstood each other Saturday night, and believing it was more her fault than his, she felt she had to take it upon herself to set things straight. Then she began to wonder if Ms. Rainey was as young and attractive as she sounded.

"He's right here," she repeated softly. Well, she had Gordon's shirt in her car and would drop it off on the way home, along with a brief written apology. She turned back to her desk, and continued reviewing loan applications, but her glance strayed all too often to the clock.

Hillcrest Avenue branched off Oak Knoll just above the Ritz Carlton Hotel. The street swelled to the east in a graceful curve, and then looped back again to Oak Knoll. Just over the San Marino border into Pasadena, it was the site of a great many lovely homes. Driving along with Gordon's address in her hand, Aimee was very curious as to which his might be, but she was still stunned when she reached it.

In the years before World War I, Charles and Henry Green, brothers who were extraordinarily gifted architects, built a number of their masterpieces of the Arts and Crafts movement in Pasadena. When Aimee found one at Gordon's address, she nearly ran her car right up over the curb. Beautifully landscaped, the superbly designed shingle bungalow had front doors of Tiffany glass, and she assumed every detail of the magnificent custom home would be as fine.

Fascinated by the remarkable dwelling, she hesitated to get out of her car, and before she could make up her mind whether to drop off the shirt, or simply go, Gordon drove up behind her. He immediately got out of his Mercedes and came toward her, and she was desperately afraid he was still too angry with her to listen no matter how tactfully she phrased her apology.

Fifteen

With fear knotting her stomach, Aimee slowly rolled down her window.

Gordon was in his shirtsleeves, and loosened his tie as he leaned down. "You don't know how glad I am to see you," he exclaimed. "I know I came on too strong Saturday night and I've been trying to think of a way to make it up to you ever since. Come on in."

He opened her car door, and took the shirt she handed him, but he looked badly embarrassed. "I didn't mean for you to do my laundry."

Bill had sent his shirts out, so it had been twenty-five years since she had washed and ironed a man's shirt. Gordon's had been sprinkled with her tears. "It was the least I could do." She tossed the note she had meant to leave with the shirt aside, left her car, and leaned back against the door.

"I came to apologize to you. There was a reason I made what you accurately described as a 'bizarre' reference to an imposter, but you had no way of knowing that. There's so much you don't know about me, nor I about you, and it's bound to cause us problems if we pretend a gap of thirty-five years in our acquaintance doesn't matter."

Gordon was so damn happy to see her, he would have agreed with anything she said, but it just so happened that he did see the truth in her comment. "Yes, you're right. Now come on in," he coaxed again, unwilling to let her get away, "and we can get better acquainted."

After a slight hesitation, Aimee took his hand and they started up the walk. "I didn't expect you to have such a remarkable house. Oh, that didn't sound right, did it? There's no reason why you shouldn't have a lovely home, I just meant—"

"Relax, Aimee, I'm not going to run out on you again. I live here. Besides I know what you mean." At the front doors, he reached into his pocket for his keys. Up close, the doors were even more impressive than they had been from the street. The pattern in the stained glass was an elegant tangle of pale white lilies on writhing green stems.

"The house was in sad shape when my parents bought it in the forties. Fortunately, they did a magnificent job of restoration, but it's always been rather like living in a national monument. I'd never sell it, but it's more of a museum than a home. Especially with just me rattling around here all alone. I have a housekeeper who comes in to clean, and a gardener to care for the grounds, but that's not like having a family.

"Come into the kitchen with me and I'll get us something to drink. I'll give you the tour later." He led the way through the wide entry hall and to the left into the kitchen.

Everywhere Aimee looked she saw the evidence of the superb craftsmanship which makes a Green and Green home so special. Not a single detail had been left to chance. All the lighting fixtures were Tiffany glass, and the teak and mahogany paneling throughout glowed with a luxurious sheen. The kitchen was small for such an impressive residence, but Matt Trenerry had modernized it without destroying its original charming character.

"Everything is so beautiful. This must be like living inside a jewel box," she complimented sincerely.

Gordon opened the refrigerator. "Or an emperor's prison. I've got diet and regular Coke and orange Crush. Or maybe you'd rather have a beer?"

"No, the orange Crush would be fine, thank

you." She waited while Gordon went into the adjacent pantry for a glass. When he filled it with ice and handed it to her, she smiled. "Your cheek looks good. As though it were no more than a scratch."

Gordon grabbed a can of Coke for himself. "Yeah, it was difficult to make the brawl sound as brutal as it seemed at the time when I didn't have more gruesome evidence."

Astonished, Aimee gasped. "You told people about it?"

"Sure, didn't you?"

Aimee shook her head. "Just my daughters."

"Did you hear from Jack this morning?"

Shuddering at the mention of the offensive man's name, Aimee was enormously relieved that the day had passed without a call from him. "No, thank God, and doubt I ever will."

"I hope you don't either. Come on, let's go out on the terrace. It's through the living room."

As she walked along with him, Aimee marveled at the complexity of the house. The open beams and wood detailing often inspired comparisons to Japanese architecture, but the Green brothers' designs had been intended to meet the demands of California's terrain and climate. Facing west, the tiled veranda was pleasantly warm, but shaded by the timbers of the bedroom upstairs.

"What a charming spot." Aimee looked out

over the softly rolling hillside. "Oh, you have a lily pond. How perfect."

"Yes, in addition to the front doors, there's a lily theme throughout." He gestured toward a comfortable wicker chair whose bright green print cushion was splashed with white lilies. "Please, have a seat."

As soon as she was seated, he pulled a matching chair into place opposite her. "I don't have any plans for the evening. Do you?" When Aimee shook her head, he was delighted. "Good. Then you can take your time telling me about yourself."

Because that wasn't an appealing prospect, Aimee stalled with a long drink, then forced herself to face up to the situation. "I really feel very foolish."

She was dressed in a short-sleeved black sheath trimmed with white piping and big white buttons and looked every bit as pretty as she had Saturday night. She had crossed her legs, and pale stockings and black patent leather flats accented their shapely length. Gordon tried to imagine how he would have felt had she not still been slim and attractive. Badly disappointed he supposed, because the Aimee he had loved would have been forever lost. Fortunately, she was right here with him.

"Please don't. We're old friends, remember? Say, did you try and call me today?"

Bill had told so many lies Aimee refused to resort to one. "Yes, I'm sorry if I bothered you. I just wanted to know if you were there."

Gordon looked puzzled. "What do you mean? Were you worried I'd left town, or were you verifying my employment?"

Finding it difficult to admit her motive, Aimee glanced toward the lily pond. "The latter I'm afraid, and it was a stupid thing to do. I'm sorry."

Gordon took a drink of his Coke then leaned back and tried to get more comfortable. "I don't think a woman's ever done that. I'll try and be flattered by your interest."

"You ought to be horribly insulted, infuriated with me."

"I'll be the one to decide how I feel," he chided.

There was a faint breeze, and thinking the setting perfect, while her story was tawdry in the extreme, Aimee sighed softly. "I told you I'd been widowed in my twenties, and raised my daughters alone, but I didn't want to admit that I've also been divorced. Five years ago a man came into the bank where I was working and asked to open a commercial account. He wasn't what anyone would describe as handsome, but he was well-dressed, neatly groomed, and wonderfully charming.

"He made several more stops by the bank in

the next week or so, and he was always so warm and friendly that I looked forward to seeing him. He'd introduced himself as a developer from Phoenix who'd come to California seeking investors for Sunrise Mesa, a new resort and retirement complex, which he intended to build south of Phoenix. We do a great deal of commercial real-estate business, and nothing about him, or his comments gave me any reason to suspect he was anyone other than an honest businessman."

Gordon could already see where her story was heading. "But he wasn't, was he?"

"No, unfortunately, he was anything but." While Aimee felt there really was no justification for the mistake she had made, she tried to at least provide the circumstances. "My daughters had finished college, had their own apartments, and were beginning their careers, so they required very little of my time. I had an occasional date, but I wasn't romantically involved with anyone. I'll readily admit to being lonely, and perhaps that colored my perceptions. When Bill invited me out for dinner, I was flattered, and soon we began dating regularly. He had a wonderful sense of humor, and told such entertaining stories. But he didn't just make me laugh, he made me feel loved in a way I hadn't felt since Steve had died." Tears began to fill her eyes. "I'm sorry, I didn't want to cry."

Gordon handed her a linen handkerchief, and waited patiently for her to compose herself. They had lived within a few miles of each other for so many years and that he had not known, or even tried to find her caused him such profound regret it was difficult for him not to weep too. Positive tears would not impress her, he took a sip of soda and had to force it over the painful lump in his throat.

Struggling to complete her wretched confession, Aimee wadded his handkerchief into a tight ball. "Bill made frequent trips to Phoenix, but because of my responsibilities at the bank, I was never free in the middle of the week to go with him. He spent the weekends with me though, and the fact he was away so often made the time we had together all the more precious. When he asked me to marry him, I said yes without taking any time to consider it. He had been so sweet to my daughters that they loved him too, and we married right away.

"Almost immediately things started to unravel. Bill suddenly reported problems with the contractor he had hired to build his project and straightening them out required more and more of his time. Rather than merely being away for a few days, he'd be gone a week or more at a time. He called me every day, sent flowers, lovely presents, and sounded as though he missed me as terribly as I missed him. It never even occurred to me to question the truth of his story. I just accepted it all as fact. Then one evening, a young woman named Cheryl called to alert me to the fact she had been living with Bill before our marriage and still was."

"My God, what did you do?"

"I hung up on her, of course. I thought her story was ridiculous, that she was just some jealous ex-girlfriend hoping to cause Bill trouble; but the more I thought about it, the more upset I became. After all, my job had prevented me from joining Bill on any of his Phoenix trips, and I'd never met any of his friends. We'd had a small private wedding with just my daughters and dearest friends. He'd said his friends were all business associates, rather than close, and that he didn't care to include them. Like everything else he had ever told me, it sounded plausible at the time. It was only later, when I grew suspicious, that the lies became pathetically obvious.

"Then I began to wonder about Sunrise Mesa. All I'd ever seen of the project was the architect's renderings and promotional brochures which featured the same illustrations. Bill had a professionally produced video tape of the acreage where it was to be built, taken at sunrise to capitalize on the spectacular desert scenery, but it was his description of the facility, and the fun it would be to live, or vacation there, that attracted investors."

Aimee looked utterly defeated. "Had Bill requested a loan from the bank, I would have run an immediate credit check on him. Stupidly, I married him without taking such a precaution."

Alarmed by the darkness of her mood, Gordon reached out to touch her knee. "Aimee, you mustn't beat yourself up over this. What did you do?"

Aimee shrugged. "I called TRW the next morning and they supplied a routine credit report that showed an absolute nightmare of indebtedness and bankruptcies. I promptly hired a detective in Phoenix who had a report within hours. Bill was not a developer and never had been. He had worked as a real estate salesman at one time but his license had been revoked and he was currently under investigation for possible fraud in connection with Sunrise Mesa. The problems he had reported to me were definitely real, but they were legal in nature rather than having anything to do with construction.

"He'd been running a typical real estate scam. He had the architect's drawings, and the video tape I'd seen, and when in Phoenix was happy to drive anyone out to see the open land where construction was supposed to begin any day. He didn't own the land, however, and no matter how much money had been invested in Sunrise Mesa, it would never have actually been built."

Aimee gestured helplessly. "And he was living with Cheryl. Everything she had said was true. The detective got pictures of them together. She was a thirty-two-year-old former Las Vegas showgirl who definitely knew how to show prospective investors a good time."

"Your typical bimbo."

Aimee nodded. "When Bill arrived home, I told him what I'd discovered about him, and said I'd seen an attorney and intended to divorce him. Rather than protest his innocence, which I had really expected him to do, he just shrugged, and made some crack about not being able to use my connections with the bank anyway, so it was no real loss. He also made some rather graphic comparisons between Cheryl and me. I had already packed what few belongings he had at my house and told him to get out. I never saw him again. Thank God. I did learn the state of Arizona tried to prosecute him for land fraud, but somehow he managed to avoid a conviction.

"I'm too embarrassed to tell that story unless I'm absolutely forced to. Nothing about Bill was as it seemed, but when I mentioned an imposter Saturday night, you had no way of knowing about my disastrous second marriage and it was no wonder you were insulted."

Gordon wanted to hold her in his arms and reassure her he would never lose his temper with her ever again, but he didn't want to repeat the mistake of being too forward. "You shouldn't be embarrassed."

"Hey, if you're entitled to your feelings, then I'm entitled to mine."

"Yes, that's true, but it's Bill who ought to be mortified by the lies he told, not you."

His expression was so kind, Aimee longed to believe him. "My friends know the truth, but the time or two I've tried to tell others about Bill I've been scolded for not showing better judgment. Apparently people are supposed to have an innate ability to recognize who's honest and who isn't. I simply don't have that talent. Apparently I suffer from terminal gullibility."

Gordon was angry, but not with Aimee, only with the idiots who had increased her doubts about herself. "I've met people who claim they can spot a phony within the first half hour of knowing him, and all I have to say is that it takes one to know one. You'd not be managing a bank if you lacked sound judgment. Honest people don't expect to be lied to, and love, well, anyone is vulnerable when they're in love."

Aimee wiped her eyes. "Thank you for being so understanding, but when I discovered Bill had deceived me, about everything really, whatever I'd felt for him dissolved in an instant. The warm loving man I'd adored hadn't really existed. I'd been in love with a dream, and woke up too late."

Panicked by that depressing comment, Gordon leaned forward. "What do you mean, 'too late'?"

Surprised by his desperate frown, Aimee tried to make herself understood. "Well, I wish that I hadn't rushed into marrying him, that's all."

"Oh, thank God," Gordon sighed. "I was afraid you were going to say you're HIV positive because of him."

From somewhere, Aimee found a small laugh. "No, I'm not, but that was the first thing I worried about when I found out about Cheryl. Both Bill and I had tested negative before our marriage, and I tested negative twice afterward. That would have been the final blow, wouldn't it? At least I escaped that horror."

Gordon rose to his feet and again extended his hand. "Let's go down to the lily pond."

Aimee set her soda aside and went with him. From the terrace, a path curved down the hillside to a lovely pond that appeared to be a natural part of the landscape rather than a charming addition. The late afternoon sunlight played across the water, and she couldn't help but wonder how the delightful pond might look bathed in moonlight.

Gordon pulled a dime from his pocket. "Here, make a wish and toss it in. Good luck is guaranteed."

Aimee held the dime a long moment, and then wished she would soon have the opportunity to come here again on a wonderfully romantic evening. She looked up at Gordon as she tossed the coin, but when he leaned down to kiss her, she was afraid to even hope her wish might come true.

Matt had avoided Dan for the remainder of the afternoon, but he hadn't been able to stop replaying their conversation in his mind. He knew he ought to get on with his life as well as Dan did, but he couldn't help the way he felt. Restless, he didn't want to go home to the house he had shared with Deborah. It was so empty without her that his footsteps echoed with the sound of her name.

He didn't enjoy his own cooking and often stopped for take-out food, but none of his favorite meals appealed to him that night. Pasadena was full of fine restaurants, as well as coffee shops with counters where a single man could eat without drawing any attention to himself. There were places where the "regulars," who gathered there each evening, treated each other like family, but he wasn't comfortable in any of them.

He hadn't eaten a dinner alone until Deborah died and the first time he had sat down in a restaurant alone, he had had to get up and walk right out again for fear he would miss her so badly he would make a fool of himself by breaking down in tears. He had a beeper on his belt and had told the startled waitress he had just gotten an emergency call, but he had not put himself through the same painful embarrassment ever again. Now he stood in take-out lines where no one had to know he would be eating his dinner all by himself.

Now with nowhere to go and nothing to do, he found himself driving through south Pasadena. The charming community had changed so little in the last fifty years that Hollywood studios frequently shot films requiring a thirties or forties atmosphere there. The residential streets were wide, and lined with massive oak trees.

Last summer he had done some remodeling there on a Victorian home for a man named Carl Hendricks, who had bought the house hoping to turn a handsome profit on a quick resale. Carl hadn't foreseen the continuing slump in the real-estate market, however, and even with drastic reductions in the price, the house hadn't sold. Carl had telephoned a couple of times hoping to interest him in buying it, but while Matt thought it was a lovely home, he certainly hadn't needed it.

Until that evening. He rounded the corner where the house sat, and not surprisingly found a for sale sign still in the yard. He parked his truck and got out. Even in the fading light it was a magnificent place, a relic of far more graceful times, but Carl had spared no expense in modernizing it. He had even jacked it up and poured a new foundation beneath it. It had all new plumbing, which Matt was sure was good because he had done it, and it had brand new wiring too.

The oak floors and paneling had been refinished, the three bathrooms and kitchen completely remodeled and retiled. Matt had been in enough houses to recognize each had its own distinct personality separate from the people who lived there and this one had remarkable warmth and charm. It was a dream home, with high ceilings and bright sunlit rooms and as Matt stood out in front, he knew he was sadly in need of a dream.

Not everyone appreciated the charm of Victorian houses, but he certainly did. Vacant, the house looked as lonely as he felt, and thinking he ought to give Carl a call, Matt finally had a reason to go home. He was beginning to get hungry too, and stopped off for a pizza on the way.

Buying a five-bedroom house might seem like a damn fool thing for a widower to do, but at the moment, Matt could not think of a single reason why not. He had spent too many years building up his business in the Pasadena area to move away, but he desperately needed a change. All too often he felt as though he was suffocating, and he had to do something to escape the horrible, guilt-ridden panic which had shaken him to the core on Sunday morning because he did not want to ever feel that bad again. A new house would give him not merely a new address, but a whole new outlook on life, and he was going to take it.

Gordon took Aimee to the Rose City Diner in Pasadena's Old Town where they had cheeseburgers, french fries, and chocolate milkshakes for dinner. A jukebox filled with fifties tunes provided such raucous background music, there was little need for conversation and just as Gordon had intended, the light-hearted atmosphere of the popular cafe had a favorable affect on Aimee's mood and her smiles became increasingly frequent. It had been the sweetness of her smile which had first drawn him to her, and he was so glad to see her smiling again.

When they got back to his place, he still had not had nearly enough of her company. "Please stay with me a while longer."

Aimee curled her hair behind her ear. "I'm really tired." But when disappointment darkened Gordon's expression, she checked her watch. "It's still early though, isn't it?"

"Yes, if you don't count the thirty-five years we lost."

"Oh Ash, please don't say that. It makes me unbearably sad, and I don't want to cry again. I'm sure that's why I feel so drained."

Gordon put his hand on her waist to guide her up the walk. "I feel like I ought to say something profound about the healing value of tears, but I'd much rather do this!" With a ecstatic whoop, he bent down, picked her up in his arms, and then gave her a playful toss.

Literally swept off her feet, Aimee squealed, then began to laugh with him, all threat of tears forgotten. He had to juggle her a bit to free a hand to unlock the front doors, but managed to carry her inside and didn't release her until they reached the living room sofa. Even then, he couldn't bear to let her go and quickly pulled her down on his lap.

Delighted by his affectionate play, Aimee slid her arms around his neck and kissed him. "I like the way you kiss," she revealed before kissing him again.

"Oh Aimee," Gordon rested his forehead against hers. She was a dream come true, but he did not want to appear so desperately eager to make love to her again that she would be frightened away. Then, with a sparkling flash of insight, he saw the reason for her lingering sorrow over her second marriage. He leaned back slightly.

"It's not really me you don't trust yet, is it?" he asked. "It's your own instincts which frighten you."

Aimee left her hand on his nape, but looked away. "Just thinking about what you're referring to as instincts frightens me. Give me a minute to think about your question."

Gordon touched her chin lightly to turn her head. "Can't you kiss me and think at the same time?"

"No, I don't think so."

"Let's see." Gordon pulled her close and their next kiss melted into half a dozen others and he was right back where he had been Saturday night when a thousand kisses wouldn't have been nearly enough, but one more would have been one too many. He had to stop and catch his breath. "I can think and kiss you at the same time," he bragged, "but I'm sure you know precisely what I'm thinking."

"I'm afraid I'll disappoint you," Aimee murmured softly.

"What?" Gordon was about to accuse her of continually having bizarre ideas, but fortunately caught himself in time. "You're a real woman, Aimee, not an ethereal fantasy lover, and you've already exceeded my wildest dreams. You could never disappoint me. Unless, of course, you fell asleep while I was making love to you."

Aimee smiled at his attempt at humor, but she still felt horribly insecure. "You told me you've dated a lot. Nowadays women are much freer than I was raised to be. You're bound to compare me unfavorably to others."

She looked so forlorn Gordon knew she sincerely believed she was inadequate in some vital way and it broke his heart. "Aimee, look at me." He waited until she did. "I know this is going to sound absolutely nuts but I don't care. I fell in love with you when I was eighteen years old, and you've been a part of me all these years. When you called to ask me to the reunion, and said you'd been widowed in your twenties, my first thought was to thank God you were free, but as soon as we'd hung up, I was furious with myself for not having kept track of you. I just let you walk out of my life at graduation, and I'll never forgive myself for that.

"Now that we've met again, I feel as though we were meant to be together all along but that fate played some monstrous joke on us and kept us apart. Now if it takes you a week or month, or God forbid a year to come to the same conclusion, then I'll try and be patient, but please don't keep me waiting long."

A kiss would mean something far different, and being cautious, Aimee hugged him tightly. He sounded so wonderfully sincere, but so had Bill. When Bill had spoken of his joy in finding her, in loving her, she had believed his every word. She longed to find love again, but she doubted she would survive should Gordon's sweet promises prove to be lies. A lifelong bachelor, who apparently had enjoyed considerable success with women, without ever marrying one, he could be expected to have perfected his line.

Ashamed of herself for allowing her thoughts to sink to such disgusting depths, she pushed herself off his lap. "I like you too much to rush things. Maybe that doesn't make any sense. I know people sleep with one another purely for the momentary pleasure, but I want something more."

"Just name it," Gordon urged.

"No, it's much too soon."

Gordon got to his feet and had to jam his hands into his back pockets to keep from touching her. "I've only been involved with women I cared about, if perhaps not enough to marry. I never hung out at the Playboy mansion, Aimee. From my experience, when people find someone they like, which isn't easy, they want to date that person exclusively. Then if the attraction grows, and they fall in love, they become engaged, and eventually marry. That's the same sequence people followed when we were in our teens. I don't expect anything different. Do you?"

"No," Aimee agreed, "but having been widowed, and so badly deceived, I don't have much faith, if any, in the living happily ever after part. That's what truly frightens me, Ash. What if we're deliriously happy together now, and then something awful happens and it ends?"

Gordon took a deep breath. "Other than one of us dying suddenly, which I realize has happened to you once, I really don't see what could go wrong. If we go slowly, you'll have a chance to get used to the fact I won't go away. Is that what you really need, time to trust fate will not be cruel a third time?"

"It sounds rather silly, doesn't it?"

Gordon put his arms around her shoulders and walked her out to her car. "No, not at all, but let's see how things go for the next few weeks. If you're still scared to death I'm going to be struck by lightning, or otherwise abandon you, we'll find a counselor and get help. It won't just be your problem, Aimee, but ours."

"Oh Ash, you're just too good to be true."

"Would you come by my office and tell Ms.

Rainey that? She has an entirely different opinion of me."

"Is she pretty?"

Gordon looked away a moment, obviously searching for the proper term. "She is, well, efficient, but no one would ever hire her for her looks."

Aimee reached up to kiss him good night. "You don't know how glad I am to hear that."

"Hey, wait a minute. When can I see you again?"

"When would you like?"

"Tomorrow night? I'll pick you up for dinner again and there's bound to be a movie we'd both like to see."

"I'd like that." They agreed upon a time, but as Aimee left for home she started to shake. It hadn't helped to put a name on her fears. They were still there.

Sixteen

Monday night, Suzanne finished the rest of the eggplant sandwich she had brought home from Julienne and then felt sufficiently fortified to telephone her daughter. Patricia had gone to college in Oregon, and made so many wonderful friends she had decided she wanted to live there after graduation. She taught first grade in a charming elementary school in a suburb of Portland, and while infrequent, her cards and calls were filled with enthusiasm for her profession. Because a love of teaching was one of the few things they shared, Suzanne first asked about her daughter's class before revealing the real reason she had called.

"They were all angels in September," Patricia replied, "but their halos are definitely tarnished by this time of the year. They're all looking forward to second grade, but I'm counting the days until summer. How about you, Mom? What's up at Cal State?"

Suzanne gave a quick recap of the latest cuts due to California's budget crisis, and then adopted a more personal tone. "I called to tell you about a man I met, honey. He's very nice, and this is the first time I've let myself believe things might develop into something serious."

After a pause, Patricia asked, "Has Daddy met him?"

"Your father and I are divorced, baby. I don't ask his opinion on the men I date." Patricia and her father had always been close, and Suzanne knew her daughter blamed her for the divorce. While Suzanne didn't feel blame was the right word, she had been responsible for initiating a divorce when she finally realized Frank was never going to be the warm, loving, supportive man she deserved.

Patricia didn't hide her annoyance with that reminder. "I know you're divorced, Mother. I just thought if this man was so special you would have introduced him to Daddy is all."

Suzanne feared despite her best intentions, she was handling her side of the conversation poorly. Like many adult children, Patricia had been deeply hurt by their divorce, and Suzanne had never succeeded in reassuring her that it was the best thing that could ever have happened to her parents. "No, your Dad and I don't double date, so he hasn't met Casey and probably won't unless I marry him."

"You're actually thinking of marrying this Casey person?"

Patricia sounded absolutely appalled, and Suzanne doubted anything she said about Casey would change her opinion. "We had our pictures taken Saturday night at the Cortéz reunion. I'll send you a copy. He's not only a very nice man, he's very attractive too."

"Does he have a job?"

"Of course he has a job," Suzanne was becoming annoyed. "He's a buyer for Russell's department store. He was a chef at one time, and he's a sensational cook."

"Oh great, that's just what you need."

Patricia had her mother's golden-red hair, but was slender like her father's side of the family. Hurt that she would make such a pointed comment about her weight, Suzanne had had enough. "I'll write you a letter about him, honey. I've got to go now. Good night."

Suzanne hung up the receiver, and wondered if there wasn't a way she could have handled the call better, but came to the sad conclusion that Patricia wanted her parents back together, and nothing else would ever satisfy her. It was a shame, and thoroughly depressed, Suzanne began to review her notes for her Tuesday classes. She was tempted to call Casey, even if he could only mumble his responses, but because she had sent him home, she dared not call and give him the chance to offer to come back. No, she had insisted he stay away until Saturday, and she wouldn't do anything to make it any more difficult for him than it already would be.

When Carol walked into her office Tuesday morning, she found the usual stack of messages from sportswear department managers throughout the chain, and requests for appointments from sales reps. At Russell's it was business as usual, but she did not feel much like conducting it. She always made it a point to return her managers' calls as promptly as possible, and did so, but set the reps' numbers aside. After contacting the managers and promising to supply the stock they needed, she was too restless to remain in her cluttered office, and went out on the sales floor. Pleased with the executive sportswear displays, she wandered through the rest of the fashion departments housed on the third floor.

With summer just approaching, the merchandise was already geared toward fall. Carol had fought, without success, the traditional rushing of seasons. There had been a time when women had to look ahead and order, or begin sewing their own clothes to have them ready at the appropriate time, but those days were long past. Now when a woman went shopping, it was most likely for something she could wear to work the very next day, or on a date that weekend.

"If I had my own shop," Carol mused thoughtfully, "it would be stocked with spring and summer clothes now, not heavier things designed for fall." It was an opinion she frequently shared with her managers, but that day she suddenly saw her preference for fashions which matched the season as the key to a successful operation. She returned to her office with a renewed sense of purpose, and began making a list of everything her experience had taught her about women's fashions. It was four o'clock when she looked up, and she was shocked by how quickly the day had gone by.

Having missed lunch, she went up to the fifth floor to have a cup of coffee with Casey, but as soon as she left the service elevator, one of the stock boys called to her.

"Mr. O'Neil didn't come in today, Ms. Hagan. He was out sick yesterday too."

"Thanks." Carol knew Casey wasn't ill, merely too beat-up to come in to work. Sorry the reunion had left him so battered, she wrote a cheerful note and asked him to come by her office when he could. She had always enjoyed discussing business with him and she wanted to get his opinion on her chances of being successful on her own.

Back at her office, she searched through her handbag for the telephone number of the real-estate agent handling the shops for lease at the Ritz Carlton. She dialed the number, but after expressing mild interest in the costs of a lease, had to stifle a shriek when she heard them. She thanked the woman and tossed her number in the wastebasket.

"It's no wonder the clothes are overpriced there," she grumbled, for the rents could only be described as exorbitant. "Which I knew they would be." She was an experienced buyer of expensive fashions which appealed to women who could afford them. If she opened her own shop, it would have to be in a location frequented by those women, but she wouldn't allow the rent to bankrupt her.

Taking out a sheet of plain paper, she quickly sketched a map of the Pasadena area. The slow economy had caused a great many shops to close, so it wouldn't be difficult to find a vacant store in a good location. The only question would be, could she afford one, or provide such appealing merchandise in a less desirable location that the women she wished to attract would go out of their way to find her?

"That's quite a challenge." For the briefest

of instants, she recalled the Wednesday night conversation with Matt. He had struck her as having good business sense, but she knew better than to call him on the pretext of discussing her dream to own her own boutique. No, Matt was not a man who believed in dreams, and she wouldn't give him another chance to share hers.

By Saturday, Aimee had been out with Gordon two more times. Had he not had a meeting Wednesday night and she one on Thursday, they would have seen each other every night. They would be together again that evening, and looking forward to it, she washed her hair, and sat outside on the patio to read while it dried in the sun.

When JoAnne came through the back gate, she was surprised to see her, but very glad. "Hi, honey, how you doing?" she called.

JoAnne grabbed a chair and sat down. "I'm not sure how to answer that."

Alarmed, Aimee quickly marked her place and set her book aside. "Is something wrong?"

"Not exactly." Unable to get comfortable, Joanne fidgeted nervously. "I have an idea I'd like to talk over with you."

"I'm flattered you want my advice. What is it?"

Obviously troubled, JoAnne needed a moment to get started. "Since I was a little girl, all I've ever wanted to be is a nurse. Well, I've been one for five years now, and it's just not enough. I'd like to go to medical school. Does that sound absurd to you?"

Aimee could tell from the seriousness of JoAnne's expression that she had given medical school a great deal of thought. "Well, naturally I'm surprised, but no, it's not an absurd idea at all. I think it's wonderful. Do you know where you want to go?"

"I'd like to stay in California, so I'll go wherever they'll take me. Thank you for not trying to talk me out of it."

"Who's tried to do that?"

"A couple of my friends at the hospital. Nurses aren't supposed to be that ambitious. We're supposed to know our place."

"Good Lord, it sounds as though you need some new friends. There was a time when all the bank tellers were men, and the possibility a woman might actually successfully manage a bank certainly didn't occur to anyone. There's no longer any reason, and perhaps there never was one, to listen to what a woman should, or should not do, and I'm real proud of you, honey. If you want to become a doctor, then I'll do whatever I can to help you realize your dream."

"Thanks, Mom, I knew I could count on you,

but medical schools are expensive, and I know you've already spent whatever you had set aside for my education."

"We'll manage somehow," Aimee assured her. "Let's look into government loans. I know you wouldn't refuse to pay it back with service on an Indian reservation, or whatever is required."

"No, I wouldn't. I'd really like to go where I'm needed. I'm not looking to set up a lucrative practice in plastic surgery in Beverly Hills."

"It's going to take a lot of work, sweetheart, but if it's what you want, I know you'll make it."

JoAnne nodded. "I just don't want to let another year go by wishing for something that will never happen unless I make it happen. Maybe I'll flunk out, but at least I'll have the satisfaction of knowing I tried."

As Aimee continued to encourage her daughter, she could not help but think of her own life. She had been equally courageous at one time, but life had a way of relentlessly chipping away at the starry-eyed confidence of youth. While she admired JoAnne's determination to change her life, she doubted her own ability to do the same.

"What happened to the guy who left his shirt here?" JoAnne asked. "Did you find out if he was on the level?"

Her doubts forgotten, Aimee began to smile. "Yes, very much so. You should see his house. It's a Green and Green, a perfect wooden palace complete with a lily pond in the backyard. If you can call the gardens of such a pretty estate the backyard."

"Do you think he might want to adopt me and put me through medical school?"

JoAnne was teasing, but Aimee knew all she would have to do was ask, and Gordon would do whatever he could for her and her daughters. "Yes, he probably would, but let's see if we can't handle this on our own. Let's go get some ice cream to celebrate. After all, it's not everyday that you decide to apply to medical school."

"Yeah, let's do it. Baskin Robbins has a new fat-free ice cream that I've been wanting to try. Do you believe it? It's like sinless ice cream."

"Sounds delicious, let's go." Aimee went inside to comb hair and grab her purse. She still kept a photograph of herself and Steve with their girls on her dresser and she reached out to caress the frame as she went by. He had missed so much of their lives and as always she wished that wherever he was, he could see them and share her pride.

By Saturday afternoon, Suzanne had received four letters from Casey. They weren't simply cute, as she had expected, they were adorable, filled with affectionate poems, clever jokes, and even included delicious recipes. He had poured so much of himself into the marvelous letters that she was at a loss for a way to return the attention. He hadn't felt up to going to the poetry group with her Wednesday night, and while he had only gone with her once, she missed having him with her, and badly.

Looking forward to spending the evening with him, she was understandably nonplussed when a blue Super Shuttle pulled up in front of her house at four o'clock, and Patricia got out. She gave her daughter an enthusiastic hug, and then stepped back to have a better look at her. They had last seen each other at Christmas, and as always, she was delighted with how pretty and self-assured Patricia was.

"Why didn't you call and tell me you were coming home?"

"It was a spur of the moment decision," Patricia confessed. "I decided if you hadn't asked Daddy for an opinion on Mr. Wonderful, I better come home and give you mine."

Astonished that Patricia would think such an effort necessary, Suzanne stared at her daughter. "How thoughtful of you," she finally replied. "I'm sure Casey will be glad to meet you too. He's coming for dinner tonight, and that will give the three of us a chance to get acquainted." It certainly wouldn't be the romantic evening Suzanne had planned though, and she had to struggle not to let her disappointment show.

"I can hardly wait." Patricia had brought only a single bag, and started up the stairs with it. "I got a special rate by booking my return flight on Monday. I hope I won't be in your way."

"This is your home," Suzanne exclaimed. "How could you possibly be in the way?" But as Patricia turned away, Suzanne saw the mischievous look in her eyes and knew that was precisely what she intended to be.

When Casey knocked on Suzanne's door at six, he could smell a delectable combination of aromas and wondered what she had cooking. He had brought along a bouquet of red roses and a bottle of white wine. Just in case she was preparing red meat, he had another bottle of red wine stashed in the car. This had been the longest week of his life, and when the door opened, he was surprised not to be greeted by Suzanne, but instead by a beautiful red-haired girl who had to be her daughter.

"Hi, I'm Casey. Are you Patricia?"

"Sure am. Come on in." Patricia was wearing a short, skin-tight black sheath and a pair of high heeled black boots that made her Casey's equal in height. While she didn't usually wear much makeup, she had smeared on deep purple eyeshadow, and applied fourteen coats of mascara. Her lips and long false nails were a glaring fire engine red. She reached out to take his gifts.

"I'll get a vase for the flowers, and put the wine in the fridge. Mom," she called loudly, "Casey's finally here."

As Patricia passed Suzanne on the way to the kitchen, she whispered, "He's too short."

Suzanne pretended not to hear, and came forward to give Casey a hug. "The roses are beautiful and I'm sure the wine will be perfect with our meal. Your lip looks fine; is it all right to kiss you?"

"Am I late? I thought you told me to be here at six."

"Yes, I did." Disappointed both in her daughter's behavior, and Casey's apparent reluctance to kiss her, Suzanne stepped back.

She had been smiling when she had left the kitchen, and her slight frown made Casey fear he had made a serious mistake in not kissing her first, and asking about the time second. "Hey, I've waited a week to kiss you. Let's give it a try." Casey pulled her into his arms and kissed her soundly. It hurt, but he managed not to wince as he let her go. "You see, I'm fine. Your daughter is, well, charming."

"Isn't she though?" Somewhat reassured, Suzanne glanced over her shoulder to make certain Patricia was busy in the kitchen. She lowered her voice so only Casey would hear. "She decided to come for the weekend after I told her about you, so nothing she does will surprise me. Even if you were Jean-Claude Van Damme, she wouldn't be impressed."

"I don't think he's all that tall either."

"You heard that?" Suzanne asked in an anguished whisper. "I'm so sorry."

"If I stand up real straight I'm 5'10," and that's considered average, not short. She's just tall."

"Please, let's not make an issue of anything she does or says tonight. You're not her father, so she's already decided not to like you. It's childish, and unforgivably rude, but please, try not to be insulted."

Suzanne was obviously upset and Casey couldn't bear that. He gave her another kiss, and then whispered in her ear. "I came to see you. I wouldn't care if Godzilla were here. I'd still have a wonderful time."

Suzanne wasn't sure she liked having her daughter compared to Godzilla, but understanding Casey was trying to comfort her, she managed a smile. "I have dinner ready; are you hungry?"

"Very. I haven't been able to eat that much this week and now I can make up for it."

Patricia had put the roses in a crystal vase, and carried them into the dining room to use as the centerpiece. Suzanne had already set the table with her best crystal and china. "Have you been ill?"

"No, didn't you tell her about the reunion, Suz?"

Suzanne shrugged. "No, but it will certainly make for interesting dinner conversation." She made no pretense of having prepared the meal, but credited the Panda Inn as she served the war won ton. The savory soup was filled with stuffed won ton, steamed vegetables, and sliced pork. They all enjoyed it so thoroughly that the effort to talk didn't begin until Suzanne brought platters of honey walnut shrimp, scallops in mango sauce, barbecued ribs, and steamed rice to the table.

Casey then provided a brief overview of the reunion, stressing the fun it had been until Jack Shank had begun calling his wife names. "I hadn't been in a fight in years," he readily confessed, "but that one was worth it. I had to get stitches in my lip though, and that's why I haven't been eating much."

Patricia had listened to Casey's account with rapt attention, and now turned to her mother.

"What were you doing while all this was going on?"

"Trying to stay out of the way, while Jack's wife, the poor dear, crawled under our table."

Patricia took another heaping serving of shrimp. "Bet that didn't make the society page of the *Times*. How about the *Pasadena Star News?*"

"Frankly, I didn't even look for it," Suzanne stressed. "Now could we please talk about something else?"

"Sure," Patricia agreed. "Casey O'Neil has got to be an Irish name. Are you Catholic?"

Somewhat surprised by her choice of topic, Casey ate a scallop before replying. "My grandparents came from Ireland, but the only time I think of myself as being Irish is on St. Patrick's Day, and no, I'm not Catholic."

Patricia glanced toward her mother. "Do I sense a bit of reticence there, Casey? You're not a defrocked priest by any chance, are you?"

Casey laughed. "No. I've always been much too fond of women to consider going into the priesthood."

"Ah, so you were a Catholic at one time?" Patricia paused, her fork midway to her mouth. She looked as pleased as a detective who's just turned up a damning clue.

"Yes, but not after I was about twelve years

old. Do you have some prejudice against Catholics?"

Patricia chewed the bite of shrimp, then speared another. "No, not at all, but Mom used to volunteer at the Planned Parenthood Clinic and it would be terrible if you two got into arguments over the pro-life, pro-choice issue."

Suzanne did not like the direction of the conversation and said so. "Patricia, I really feel that's an inappropriate topic for the dinner table."

Patricia feigned surprise. "Really? Why? Don't you think you ought to know each other's position on such a vital issue?"

Suzanne laid her fork across her plate. "Casey is entitled to his opinion, no matter what it is and I have no intention of debating it with him tonight, or any other time."

Patricia shrugged. "You know what they say, if two people always agree, then only one is thinking."

"Your mother and I have had several rather heated disagreements," Casey was quick to point out, "ranging from the design of the shelves I'm going to build for her, to whether or not we ought to make love in the backseat of a stranger's car. It might please you to know your mother has won on everything, so far."

Suzanne didn't know which was worse, Patricia baiting Casey, or his responding with personal details she would rather he did not share. Their verbal sparring continued when Pat began to needle him about being a chef and Suzanne could see Casey was enjoying himself as much as Patricia. She had envisioned a delightfully romantic evening with Casey, and modified her hopes when Patricia had arrived, but now, it appeared Casey was having a lot more fun with Patricia than he would have had with her.

She picked up a honey-dipped walnut and while it was absolutely delicious, she had to wash it down with wine. She peeked at her watch, and wondered how long they would carry on their playful banter before they noticed she wasn't participating. Feeling completely left out, the laughter in their voices hit her like painful waves.

Seventeen minutes passed before Casey glanced her way. "Patricia is a lot like you, Suz. She knows herself. That's what I admire in you."

"Is it really?" Suzanne replied absently. She encouraged them to finish up the ribs, shrimp, and scallops, but there was more than they could eat. For dessert, she offered fortune cookies. Wrapped with colorful foil, they were dipped in chocolate, but held the expected message.

"Mine says: Love is sure to find you," Patricia exclaimed.

Casey broke his cookie in half, and read, "Your future is full of promise. That's nice to know. What do you have, Suzanne?"

Suzanne looked at hers, and then passed it to him. "Dark clouds on the horizon. What do you suppose that means?"

Casey frowned slightly. "What kind of a fortune is that? I thought they were all supposed to be good."

"Apparently the people down at the fortune cookie factory know something I don't." Suzanne got up and began clearing the table while Casey and Patricia continued to discuss the dreary nature of her fortune. She replaced what was left of the succulent meal in the restaurant's white cartons, and stacked them in the refrigerator. As she put the dishes in the dishwasher, Casey and Patricia began laughing, and she tried not to believe they were making light of her lousy prospects for the future, but their levity still hurt.

Rather than rejoin them, she stepped outside. The night was cool and clear, but the evening had gone so poorly she would have been happier had it been pouring rain. Her chest ached with disappointment, and she was on the verge of tears.

"Suz?" Casey called. "What are you doing out here?"

"Thought I'd better keep an eye out for those 'dark clouds'."

The porch light provided sufficient illumination for Casey to see her expression, and he wasn't fooled. "What's wrong?"

"Not a thing," Suzanne replied flippantly. "What could possibly be wrong?"

"I've no idea, that's why I asked you. I like Patricia. She's bright and pretty, just like you."

"Yes, she is. She's also a lot younger."

"Well, she's your daughter, so of course she'd be younger. Am I missing something here?"

Suzanne turned to face him. "Yeah, you're missing a lot, or you will be if you stay with me. I'm not jealous of Patricia, so please don't accuse me of it. It's just that watching you together, and listening to you laugh made me realize how much more a younger woman would have to offer you. You said you didn't want children, but with me, you're giving up that option, and you might one day regret it bitterly."

Casey reached out to caress her cheek. "I'd hoped my letters had made it plain how much I wanted you."

"Yes, they were such beautiful letters and I'll treasure them, but—"

"Mom?" Patricia came to the door. "I've decided to stay over at Dad's tonight. He's on his way over to get me."

Suzanne looked at Casey, hoping he would understand Patricia was trying to force him to meet her father. "If you'd rather leave now, I won't blame you," she whispered.

"I'm not leaving," Casey insisted. "I'll have to meet him sooner or later and it might as well be tonight."

"And I thought last Saturday night was bad."

"Suzanne." Casey kissed her, very slowly and deeply. It hurt like hell and he didn't even care. She was the woman he wanted and he did not care what he had to do to convince her of it, he would gladly do it.

Frank Marsh lived only fifteen minutes away and was soon knocking at the door. Patricia hurried to let him in. He surveyed the boxes stacked along the walls and shook his head. "Your mother turns every house she owns into a warehouse for her junk. I don't know why she even bothers with a house. She ought to just rent space at the Stor-Mor and sleep in her car."

Overhearing him, Casey took Suzanne's hand. "Want me to punch him out?" he asked.

"Yes, but you better not." Suzanne and Casey joined her ex-husband and daughter in the living room. "Evening, Frank," she greeted him coolly. She introduced Casey, who stepped forward to shake Frank's hand.

Casey had not known what to expect from Frank, but he was somewhat surprised to find him a tall, slender man with graying hair. He had the type of chiseled features politicians would die for, but there wasn't the slightest bit of warmth in his gaze, or handshake. Casey had been prepared to dislike him simply on principle, but he found it easy to crank up an outright hatred for this cold-hearted man.

As soon as Frank and Patricia had gone, he closed the door behind them, and let out a grateful sigh. "Where were we?" he asked.

Suzanne felt sick to her stomach, sat down on the sofa, and rested her head on her hand. "Nowhere, as I remember. I meant what I said, Casey. Seeing you with Patricia forced me to realize how much you'd have to give up with me, and I can't let you do it."

Casey knelt at her feet and pulled off her shoes. They were purple and pink flats that matched the colors in her dress. "These don't look like a little old lady's shoes." He tossed them over his shoulder and began to rub her foot. "You're tied in knots, Suz, and your blood just isn't getting to your brain."

Suzanne tried to pull her foot away but he refused to let go. "Stop it, you're tickling me."

"Yes, I know." Casey massaged the other foot too. Then he slid his hand under her skirt, and leaned over to kiss her knee. "I love the freckles on your knees. Did I ever say that?"

Suzanne reached out to ruffle his hair. "Casey."

He rubbed his cheek against her thigh. "Hmm?"

"You've missed your calling. You could sell a ton of shoes with that technique."

Casey sat up slightly. "Yeah, I have missed my calling but it isn't selling shoes. Carol's thinking of opening her own shop. Has she mentioned it to you?"

"It's been a goal of hers for years."

"We talked about it when I finally got to work on Thursday, and the whole time I kept asking myself what I was doing at Russell's when I'd much rather be a chef."

Suzanne found it difficult to concentrate on his remarks with him kneeling between her legs. She patted the cushion beside her. "Come here."

Casey moved up beside her, then leaned over to kiss her. "You were right, you know. I left a career I loved so I'd be better able to please a woman I'd not even met. That I've been successful doesn't make it any the less stupid." He laced his fingers in hers. "You wanted more time, but it looks as though I'm the one who needs it. Can you be patient with me?"

"Oh Casey, of course, that's all I wanted, just more time to really get to know each other."

She leaned over to kiss him, but took care to do it gently. "If you want to be a chef again, then go for it. I'll just schedule my fall classes for late afternoons and evenings so we can spend the days together."

"You'd do that?"

"Of course."

"You're a remarkable woman, Suz."

Suzanne leaned forward and whispered seductively. "There's just one thing I want to know, Casey."

She'd steamed up his glasses and he had to remove them and slip them into his pocket. "What?"

"When are you going to build my shelves?" Suzanne started to laugh. She reached out to tickle his ribs and they ended up in a wild tangle of arms and legs, hilarious giggles, and passionate kisses that turned into another night of such delicious loving that neither of them remembered the shelves until late Sunday afternoon.

The telephone rang as they were eating an omelet Casey had made. Reluctantly, Suzanne answered. "It's Patricia," she mouthed. She listened, agreed with everything her daughter said, and then broke into a delighted smile when she hung up. "Patricia says you're okay."

"Great. Should I be relieved?"

Suzanne leaned over to pinch his cheek. "You already know that I like you, and that's all that really matters. Oh yes, one other thing, she's spending the night with her best friend from high school, and she has a ride to the airport in the morning."

"Which means I can stay tonight too?"

He looked ecstatic, but Suzanne hesitated before agreeing. "Yes, just as long as you know you're not moving in here."

"No, of course not. I wouldn't dream of it." But the width of his smile gave him away.

Seventeen

After dining out together for most of the week, Aimee invited Gordon to her house for dinner Sunday night. Wanting a special, if more casual evening, she set the table in the dining room using apricot place mats which matched the soft shade of the room and cut white camellias for a pretty arrangement for the centerpiece. It had been awhile since she had cooked any of her favorite recipes, but inspired by the opportunity to entertain a man she truly liked, she prepared a delicious chicken dish, rice, steamed broccoli, a green salad, and carrot cake for dessert.

Running late, she had only forty-five minutes to bathe and dress and had to rush to be ready by the time Gordon was due to arrive. The day had been warm, and she put on a coral sundress, and tan sandals. She was still upstairs when he rang the bell, and came running down to meet him. "Hello, Ash. I'm so glad you could be here with me tonight."

Gordon noted her flushed cheeks and gave her a quick kiss. "I hope that breathless note in your voice is because of me, rather than merely a dash for the door."

He had been a perfect gentleman all week. Warm and attentive, he hadn't pressured her once for more than a good-night kiss, although neither of them had ever settled for just one. Now, as she looked up at him, her excitement was real. "Yes," she replied with unusual candor, "I am excited to see you. I hope you're hungry. I'd forgotten how long it takes to get everything ready, and I'm sure I've made too much."

Gordon followed her into the kitchen. He liked her dress. She usually wore tailored clothes but this outfit was far more softly feminine. "That dress looks very pretty on you. You belong in bright, cheerful colors." He was wearing Levi's and a pale blue shirt that gave his green eyes an aqua tint. "Although the black dress you were wearing last Monday looked awfully good too."

Unused to such open admiration, Aimee was embarrassed by his praise. "Thank you, but I've begun to suspect you're prejudiced."

Gordon spread his hands in a gesture of complete innocence. "Prejudiced? I'm surprised at you, Aimee. Why would I be prejudiced when it comes to you?"

"Thirty-five years of wishful thinking might do it." She lifted the lid on the chicken and stirred it one last time. "I think everything's ready."

"I hope that tastes just half as good as it smells."

"It should. It's just chicken baked in onion soup with stewed tomatoes and topped with mozzarella cheese but it always has a marvelous flavor."

Gordon stepped out of her way as she removed the salad from the refrigerator. He had played out the same domestic scene countless times with other women, but not with Aimee and being with her made all the difference in the world.

"I can actually prepare passable meals myself," he said. "I'll cook for you next time."

"I'd like that. A man's never cooked for me, unless you can count barbecued hamburgers, which I don't."

Gordon looked stricken. "Maybe I spoke too soon."

Aimee was sure he was teasing. "If all you can do is barbecue, that will be fine. It will still be a treat."

"Why?" Gordon coaxed.

Aimee was about to serve the plates, but

paused. "Why? I just told you; I've never been invited to a man's home for dinner."

"Damn, I thought you were referring to being with me."

She could see he was teasing her still, but she thought there was some truth behind his jest. His lifelong affection for her had taken a bit of getting used to, but now she felt perfectly at ease having him in her kitchen. In fact, she felt something much better than mere relaxation. Just seeing his smile when she had greeted him at the door had filled her with a delicious warmth and wanting to share it, she set her pot-holder aside and came close to slip her arms around his waist.

"It's always a treat being with you, Ash. It really is." He responded with a kiss as she had known he would, but as she relaxed against him, the doorbell rang.

"Were you expecting someone else?" Gordon asked. "You only have two places set for dinner."

"It's probably just a neighbor with a petition to save something or other, I'll be right back." But as she left the kitchen, she felt him follow her, and turned back to blow him a kiss. When she opened the front door, she found Karen's friend, Roger. Tall and blond, he was dressed in frayed Levi's and a tank top that showed off his deep tan and muscular build. He looked more like a model than an artist.

"I'm sorry to bother you, Mrs. Reis, but have you seen Karen? She isn't home and she hasn't answered my calls. I'm real worried about her."

He did look as sincerely worried as any man who so closely resembles a Greek god can, and Aimee felt an unexpected twinge of sympathy for him. "I didn't think you two were seeing each other anymore, Roger, so I'm surprised to hear you're concerned about her whereabouts."

Roger jammed his hands in his hip pockets. "Well, that was last week," he admitted sheepishly. "I'm just afraid something's happened to her. It's not like her to be away from home the whole weekend."

He looked so distraught Aimee took pity on him. "Karen went up to Ojai with a friend who's into ceramics. I've forgotten her name."

"Cindy Tanaka?"

"Yes, I believe so. Why don't you give her a call tomorrow?"

Enormously relieved, Roger started to back away. "Thanks, Mrs. Reis, but I'm still going to try and reach her tonight."

"Well, of course, if it's important."

"It is, you could say the whole future of the universe is at stake." He waved as he started down the walk. Aimee closed the door and turned to find Gordon leaning against the arched doorway between the dining room and hall. "That was Roger, Karen's sometime boyfriend. I would have introduced you, but Karen says it's definitely over and I didn't want to give him false hopes."

"I caught a glimpse of him. He looks like a surfer."

"He is, among other things. He's also an artist, and while that gives them a common bond, Karen says it also causes them too many problems."

"Professional jealousy?" Gordon again followed Aimee into the kitchen. He would have liked to have continued where they left off, but she immediately began serving their plates and distracted by the delicious aroma of the stewed chicken, he had to put his amorous thoughts on hold. He helped her carry everything into the dining room.

The late afternoon sunlight gave the apricot walls a soft golden tint that he found wonderfully romantic. The setting was superb, his companion perfect, and everything she had prepared was so good, he had to make an effort to talk and eat at the same time. First he complimented her on the delectable meal, and then he attempted to learn more about her daughters.

"I've heard so many horror stories of the trials of raising children from my friends at work that I've never missed having them, but you seem to get along real well with your girls."

"We've had our moments," Aimee admitted readily, "but Steve's death naturally made us close and the closeness got us through the difficult times. Still—"

She was frowning slightly, and Gordon urged her to continue. "Yes, go on."

"Both girls resemble their father, and I know they suffered for not having grown up with him. Being an artist, Karen naturally meets artistic types like Roger and while they're often charming, they aren't always the most stable men. JoAnne's the more serious of the two, and now that she's decided to go to medical school, I can't help but wonder if she hasn't been thinking about it for some time. She's had several very nice boyfriends, but as soon as they got serious, she broke up with them and it might have been because marriage didn't fit into her plans."

"Maybe she'll meet someone special in medical school."

"I hope so. I'd like for both her and Karen to have a chance at having it all: a husband, family, and a career."

"I've met some women who believe that's an impossible desire."

Aimee had served iced tea with their meal and paused to take a long sip. "Why should it be impossible for women when men have never been asked to choose between having a family or a career? Except for some religious orders which demand celibacy, men are free to do as they please."

"Uh oh, am I treading on dangerous ground here? Are you an ardent feminist?"

"Any woman who's raised two daughters alone is bound to have become a feminist real fast. My girls are self-reliant which is as it should be, but that doesn't mean they don't like men, because they do."

A subtle smile played across Gordon's lips. "What about you?"

Aimee pretended not to understand his question. "Yes, I pride myself on being self-reliant too."

"No," Gordon prompted. "I was asking for your feelings about men. Some feminists aren't all that fond of us."

"Yes, I know and that's unfortunate because it isn't men who are the enemy, but ignorance, and prejudice. I've met a great many men who are wonderfully supportive of the women in their lives."

Gordon felt certain she had also met some men who weren't. "What if a man were to say, Aimee, I have a comfortable home, an excellent job, plenty of money in the bank so you don't need to work. Stay home and look after the house and me. What would you say to him?"

Aimee wasn't certain how much of Gordon's question was hypothetical in nature. After all, a lifelong bachelor might want a woman who would stay home and dote on him. Still, she had to tell him her feelings, not what she believed he might want to hear. "Is this just some fellow taking a survey on the street corner, or someone I love?"

"Let's say he's the love of your life." Gordon winked before taking another bite of chicken.

"Hmm." Aimee pretended to need time to think. "Well, I'd certainly not want to break his heart, but I'd have to tell him I'd worked very hard to get where I am in my career and that I enjoy my work far too much to quit."

"What if he were the stuffy, traditional sort who would not hear of his wife working outside the home?"

"A barbarian, you mean? I'd probably not have dated him once, let alone fallen in love with him, Ash, so the question just wouldn't arise."

Gordon contented himself with enjoying his meal for a few minutes, but when he looked up, he was smiling. "I really admire you, Aimee. In many respects I've led a charmed life and never really had to struggle to accomplish a goal. I can hear the pride in your voice when you talk about your daughters, and your work. Your daughters must have inherited your spirit. It isn't easy to succeed as an artist, and attending medical school will undoubtedly be hard, but your girls just go right on and do it, don't they? No wonder you aren't interested in 'barbarians.' They'd never be able to keep up with you."

"Thank you. I've been afraid you still thought of me as a cheerleader with nothing more important on my mind than the big game."

Gordon was disappointed to hear that. "Really? I guess I laid on the fantasy part rather thick, didn't I?"

Aimee nodded. "Yes, you did, but it was rather sweet, and certainly flattering." She reached out to take his hand. "I've had such a good time with you this last week. It's nice to have a second chance to know you."

"Thank you, but I'd still like to make up for the times we lost as teenagers. Let's go up to my place after dinner and watch old movies. I've got Steve McQueen's version of *The Blob*. We could pretend we're at the drive-in."

"The Blob?" Aimee remembered that one well. "Do you have *Casablanca* too?"

"Yes, would you rather see it?"

"Let's watch them both." They laughed easily together for the rest of the meal, and Gordon volunteered to help with the dishes without being asked. They took the carrot cake with them to his house, and ate it during the opening scenes of *The Blob*. Gordon had a big screen TV in the downstairs bedroom he used as a den and it made the ravenous red slime all the more frightening.

"Thank God I know how this ends," Aimee murmured between bites.

"It would be great if life worked that way, wouldn't it?"

Aimee considered his comment a moment, and then disagreed. "No, it would be awful to know what tragedies lay ahead."

The film forgotten, Gordon ate the last bite of his cake and set his plate aside. "Are you still worried I'm going to slip in the bathtub and break my neck?"

Aimee feared now that she had confided too much. Each time she had seen him her fears had faded a bit and if she had only kept them to herself, she would have spared him the anguish of sharing them. She scolded herself silently then, for she knew every secret she kept would make it more difficult for them to know and trust each other. Trust was definitely a problem for her after being betrayed by Bill, but it was terribly unfair to make Gordon pay for Bill's crimes.

"No," she revealed softly. "I was thinking only of life in general, not about you."

Gordon howled. "I'm crushed."

Aimee set her plate aside too, and catching his more lighthearted mood, grabbed him in an affectionate hug. She wouldn't deny that she still lacked faith in the future to be good, but she had more than enough confidence in him to make it the best he could. His response was immediate, and so passionate that he soon had to lean back and smooth her soft silver hair away from her face.

"I can't take much more of this, Aimee. Please come up to my bedroom with me."

Aimee appeared to give the matter deep thought. "I don't know," she replied hesitantly. "Could we put *The Blob* on pause?"

Gordon's expression mirrored his dismay until the bright sparkle in her eyes gave away her teasing intent. Charmed, he pulled her back into his arms and laughed with her. "I love to hear you laugh. It's such a happy sound and I want you always to be happy."

"You did promise me a tour," Aimee reminded him. Unwinding from his embrace, she rose and offered him her hand. "Your bedroom will be one of the stops, won't it?"

"There are five bedrooms upstairs, and we can stop in every one if you like." Gordon pulled his shirt out of his Levi's and began to unbutton it as they started for the stairs. "We could work our way through the entire house, a room at a time."

Standing on the bottom step, Aimee was his equal in height. She looped her arms around his neck, and kissed him with a lazy delight. "What about the garden?" she asked in a seductive whisper. "I'll bet the lily pond is wonderfully romantic at night."

Gordon nuzzled her throat. "Yes, it would be if we were frogs, but we're not. There's a balcony off my bedroom where we'll have a clear view of the pond without any fear of making the neighbors jealous."

"Ribet, ribet."

"Aimee!"

Aimee had found teasing Gordon to be such wonderful fun she doubted she would ever want to stop. Giggling like the teenager he had loved, she took his hand as they climbed the stairs. When they reached the top, he flipped on the lights, and led her into his room. It was painted an off-white to accent the honey-toned paneling, the king-size bed was covered with a deep green comforter, and the custom-designed rug was of the same verdant green with an entwined lily border.

"Oh Ash," she exclaimed. "We have the pond right here."

Gordon unzipped her dress and whistled as she stepped out of it. She was wearing a bra and half-slip in a muted floral pattern that were as pretty as her dress. He bent down to untie her sandals, and then tossed them aside. "Have you always admired lily ponds, or is mine something new?"

As Aimee watched him peel off his shirt, she remembered JoAnne's determination to not let another year go by wishing for something that would never happen unless she made it happen. Her daughter was right, but she had not been wishing for love. She had given up on it entirely until Gordon had entered, or returned, to her life.

"It's you," she assured him. "You've brought back feelings that I'd lost all hope of ever having again. That's so sad, isn't it? It's much better to have a fantasy, to have hopes, than to merely exist without them."

Gordon silenced her musings with a kiss, and then wanting to feel every inch of her bare skin next to his he helped her off with her lingerie before discarding the last of his clothes. He was so nervous he was shaking, and she kissed his fingertips, silently assuring him that he was all she needed to be happy. He had made love to her a thousand times in his mind, but it had never been as incredibly good as really having her in his bed.

The comforter's padded depths enfolded them as they stretched out across it, and Gordon kissed Aimee's eyelids, earlobes, and lips before lapping gently at her breasts. He wanted to taste all of her delectable sweetness, but terrified she was going to retreat into herself once again, he moved very slowly, treating her with an awe-laced adoration that made him dizzy with desire.

Aimee ran her hands down his back and through his hair, gracefully encouraging the affection he was doling out in such delicious bits. Gordon was deliberate in his approach till she felt as though she might faint from desire before he ever got past his tender wanderings. Trying to consider herself fortunate he was such a considerate lover, she called his name in a husky sigh, but the rapid beat of her heart cried out for something far more urgent.

Gordon knew he had pleased other women, but he was so afraid of disappointing Aimee he let his mind set his pace rather than the longings of his heart. When she suddenly pushed him aside and moved astride him, he could not believe he was with the same woman who had had so many doubts only the week before. She was wearing a wicked smile now that both delighted and terrified him. "Tell me what you want," he gasped.

"I want to be treated like a real woman rather than a porcelain statue in a shrine. My God, Gordon, we've four other bedrooms to visit and if you don't hurry up, we'll be in here all night." She moved over him then with a serpentine grace, spreading an exotic trail of kisses down his flat stomach swiftly convincing him she was no fragile fantasy but a woman whose passions matched his own. He grabbed her arms, pulled her up beside him, and made love to her with an equally aggressive passion until he had absolutely no doubt that she was satisfied.

And he had never felt so completely fulfilled.

Their tour never got any further than the edge of their dreams, but after a lifetime apart, they snuggled together in a sleepy tangle, too deeply content to leave each other's arms for a mere change in decor.

The reunion photographs Matt had ordered arrived at the first of the week and just as he had anticipated, Dan was so impressed with Carol's petite prettiness he gave Matt a renewed burst of enthusiastic encouragement to see her again. While Matt could handle being needled incessantly, he had not foreseen that Dan would recognize Carol on the street. They had just repaired a leaking pipe in a dentist's office on Huntington Drive in San Marino and were about to call it a day when Dan grabbed his arm.

"Isn't that Carol?" he asked.

Matt followed Dan's excited gesture and sure enough, there was Carol standing in front of a vacant shop across the drive. She was holding a notebook and apparently jotting down her impressions. "Yeah, that's her."

"Well, go on," Dan urged. "Don't let her get away without talking to her."

"I haven't a thing to say, Dan."

"Oh hell, you've got a lot to say to her if you'd just let yourself. Tell her you got the reunion pictures and how cute she looks. Tell her how good she looks today. Tell her you're an idiot for not calling her. Tell her—"

"Give it up, Dan. I'm going home."

Dan looked ready to spit. "All right, fine. You just slither off but I'm going to go over there and introduce myself." Intending to do just that, he stepped out past the van and waited for a break in traffic.

"Dan, butt out, this is my life, and I don't need your advice on how to run it."

"The hell you don't!" Dan started to shout and wave. "Hey, Carol!"

When Carol turned and saw them, Matt felt trapped. He knew if he didn't go and talk with her, Dan would and imagining what embarrassing stuff Dan would unload on her, he had no choice about talking with her himself. With all the enthusiasm of a doomed man, he crossed the street.

"Hi, how are you?" he asked. He could tell from the pretty blush in her cheeks she was pleased to see him and that made him feel all the worse. That she was such a lovely creature only added to his pain, but he was still determined his only choice was to avoid her.

Carol had seen Matt in a variety of moods, but she could not identify this one. He looked annoyed more than anything and she could not imagine why he would approach her after the way they had parted if he did not really want to speak with her. Hoping he had just had a lousy day, she closed her notebook, and tried to make the best of what she feared might be an extremely awkward exchange.

"I'm fine, thank you. And you?"

"Never better," Matt lied, for it took him hours to fall asleep each night and then he would awaken long before dawn and have to face another day alone. He glanced back at Dan who was leaning against their van, his arms folded across his chest, and looking very pleased with himself.

"My son recognized you from the reunion pictures. They were very good."

Heartbreaking was the way Carol would have described them. She had also ordered both the picture of them seated at the table, and the one of them individually but she had put them away rather than leave them out as a continual reminder of a love story that had barely begun before it had come to what she thought of as a tragic end.

"Yes, Mr. Baumgarner is a wonderful photographer." She gestured toward the shop she had been checking out. "I'm seriously considering opening my own boutique, and if I do, I'll have him come take photographs of the opening."

Grateful for a neutral topic, Matt turned his attention to the two-story brick building. There was an interior designer in the corner unit, next a stationers with colorful displays in the window, two vacant units, then a jeweler, and an academy offering computer lessons for children. The second story was given over to medical and dental office space.

"How many locations have you looked at?"

"Half a dozen so far. This is a good spot, and the rent is reasonable, but I'm worried about the fact two of the units are vacant. The building is new so no one has been here long, but I don't want to open a shop here if there's a high turnover rate because I won't be able to attract customers and I'll need all the foot traffic I can get."

"When you mentioned owning your own shop I didn't realize you were so close to doing it."

Carol found it difficult to recall that conversation when even in wrinkled work clothes Matt looked so good. That had always been the problem, she told herself. His looks were incredibly appealing while his abrasive personality left a great deal to be desired.

"Well none of us is getting any younger, and I decided if I'm ever going to leave Russell's and go out on my own, I ought to do it now. It's true the economy has depressed sales, but women who are used to wearing expensive clothing still are. They're just buying less, but if enough of them buy it from me, I'll do fine. I've talked it over with Casey. He's in the same position really. He'd like to be a chef again, but with more restaurants closing than thriving now, it may be difficult for him to find a position."

"How serious is he about making a change?"

Carol couldn't really believe Matt had all that much interest in Casey. The traffic was building on Huntington Drive as people began the commute home, and she had to take a step closer to him to make certain they could hear each other over the cars' steady hum. "Casey's fallen in love with Suzanne, and that's prompted him to reevaluate his life. I'd say he's very serious about being a chef again. It's what he loves, and Suzanne is encouraging him to do it."

Matt gestured for her to follow him as he approached the vacant units. They weren't all that wide, but they were deep. "Has Casey considered opening a place of his own?" he asked. "This end of town could use an elegant cafe that catered to the lunch crowd. If you were next door to each other, women would shop at your place and eat at his, and vice versa."

Carol regarded Matt with a thoughtful gaze and saw in an instant that not only was he serious, his observation was extremely astute. "How much work would have to be done to convert the back of one of these shops into a kitchen capable of supporting a restaurant?"

While Matt had been sincere in his suggestion, he hadn't realized where it would lead. In spite of himself he began to smile. "The place would probably have to be rewired, and then it would be up to Casey as to how much he wants to invest in equipment. I remodel kitchens, and starting from scratch isn't all that different. There are a lot of places vacant now and I imagine the owner of the building would be willing to stand the cost of remodeling to suit a tenant who's likely to stay for a good many years, and successful restaurants don't move."

The two units were bare now, but the building itself had a great deal of charm and Carol could quite easily envision an elegant boutique and a classy cafe side by side. She took a deep breath and let it out slowly. "Frankly, this scares me to death."

"With good reason. More new businesses fail

than succeed. Still, you know what you're doing, and from what I've seen of Casey's passion for cooking, he does too. This might be the ideal location for you both, but you've said you've looked at others."

"Yes, and some have had two units available, but not adjacent to each other. I don't know Matt, this looks awfully good."

Matt could see how much she wanted her own shop from the longing in her expression. It was close enough to the way she had looked at him when they had been in the shower for both his conscience and heart to feel a sharp stab of pain. "Have you talked to Aimee about financing?"

"Yes, my home is worth enough for me to qualify for a sizable loan, so money won't be a problem initially. The problems will be horrendous if I don't quickly show a profit though."

Matt moved over to where he would have solid brick at his back and leaned back against it. He crossed his arms over his chest, and after a thoughtful moment, urged her to consider all her alternatives. "Let's say you and Casey go ahead, open a boutique and cafe and only one of you is a success."

"Oh Lord."

"Exactly, but he's not in love with you so whatever hard feelings or resentments there are won't destroy your personal relationship."

"Matt, really—"

"Now wait a minute, just listen. I hope you'll both be a tremendous success, but you ought to consider all the possibilities. If Casey can't make a go of it, he could still find work as a chef somewhere. It might not be at Chasen's, but I'm sure a man with his culinary talents can find work. What about you? If you leave Russell's to go out on your own, and fail, what will you do? I doubt Russell's will take you back, but would The Broadway, or May Company offer you a position as a buyer?"

Carol listened as Matt painted a disturbingly dark picture of her future should her solo venture fail. According to him, most businesses were cutting back, not hiring staff, and when it came to people at her level, the situation was even more bleak. He was right, of course, she would not be able to go back to Russell's, but that did not mean there wouldn't be opportunities for her elsewhere. She knew all the clothing manufacturers in Los Angeles, and she was positive an ambitious woman could earn more as a sales rep for one of them than she had as a buyer. That wasn't really the point, however.

"Look, Mr. Trenerry," she informed him with a jab of a crimson-coated fingernail. "If I open my own shop, it will be a success because I don't quit on anything I begin. Now I appreciate your suggestions and I'll discuss them with

Casey, but I won't for an instant entertain the possibility that we'll fail. We're not losers, and it isn't in *our* natures to start something we can't finish."

With that pointed reference, Carol turned on her heel and walked to her car. Matt straightened up, but didn't follow. He waited for the light at the corner to create a break in the traffic and returned to his van. Dan had watched their conversation, but he was grateful his son hadn't been able to hear a word.

"What did she say?"

Matt gave him a dirty look. "She told me to go to hell, again. Now I don't want to hear another word about her, understand?"

"Oh Dad—"

"Shut up!" Matt shouted.

Startled by the harshness of his father's tone, Dan gave up on Carol for now, but he had seen how she had leaned toward his father as they had talked, and the dramatic swirl of her skirt as she had turned away. If that was the way the woman said, "Go to hell," then his father had definitely mistaken her message. Dan hadn't though, and thinking the situation still showed promise, he had to turn away so Matt wouldn't see his smile.

Eighteen

The next afternoon, Carol went up to the fifth floor to see Casey. She had a cup of coffee with him and listened patiently, balancing a dangling shoe on her toe, as he described the shelves he was building for Suzanne. His continued ecstatic praise for Suzanne was touching, but Carol doubted she had ever inspired the same depth of devotion in a man, and most especially not in Matt Trenerry, and that failing caused a constant nagging ache in her heart. When Casey finally ran out of effusive compliments for Suzanne, Carol slid her foot in her shoe, sat up, and promptly changed the subject.

"I was out scouting locations for a shop yesterday and found a good one on Huntington Drive in San Marino. Matt Trenerry happened by and when I mentioned your interest in working as a chef again, he suggested you rent the unit next door to mine and open your own cafe."

"Open a cafe," Casey repeated numbly. "I almost had the money to open my own place once, but my ex-wife got it all in the divorce settlement. It's a terrific idea, Carol, but I just can't afford to do it now."

"You own a condo. You could get a home equity loan like I am."

Casey got up to refill his coffee mug. "I've also got the woman of my dreams, and this is no time to screw it up with a business venture that would require all the time I'd much rather spend with Suzanne."

Carol waited for him to sit down. "Fine, so you build shelves for her, and then what are you going to use as an excuse to go over to her house everyday?"

Casey broke into a wide grin. "I really don't need an excuse. While it might be a surprise to you, I do have other talents."

The cause of his silly smirk was unmistakable. "Believe me, Suz has nothing but praise for what you're referring to as 'talent,' but you can't keep her in bed all the time. She's a successful anthropologist with a great many interests and like most women, she admires success and determination in a man. The stronger and more independent you are, the more you're going to appeal to her."

Well aware of his flaws, Casey's smile faded. "Yes, I know I'm far from perfect, but I'm working to overcoming my faults with a psychologist."

"Good for you, but in the meantime consider how exciting this venture would be. A cafe in that location would do a tremendous luncheon business. You might even consider being open a couple of evenings a week for intimate suppers. You could cater private parties on the weekends. Suzanne has free time between her classes and on weekends and she can make fruit kabobs just as easily as anyone else."

Casey looked overwhelmed for a moment, and then an appreciation for Carol's plan lit his eyes with a radiant glow. "She'd be eager to help me, wouldn't she? There would be no danger of her growing bored with my company if we had a thriving new business to run."

He found the possibility of realizing the dream of owning his own restaurant while at the same time tacitly encouraging Suzanne to pursue him almost diabolically sweet. "I've worried there's a danger Suzanne is going to tire of me being constantly underfoot, but if I were to open a cafe, I know she'd be there to help. She'd come to me."

Carol sipped her coffee as Casey mulled over the tantalizing prospect of not merely achieving one dream but two, and envied him his enormous capacity for love. "You're a good man, Casey, and Suzanne knows it. Why don't we make an appointment to meet with the owner of the building I'm interested in and see if he'll remodel both units to suit our specifications? Matt seemed to think there is a good chance he will. Having two vacant units has got to be a drain on his profits, and that ought to incline him to be cooperative. Aimee can arrange your loan as well as mine. We can do this, Casey, all it takes is the guts to try."

"Doesn't this scare you at all?" Casey asked. "We'd be leaving reasonably secure jobs with Russell's to go out on our own, and we can't overlook the chance we might fail."

Carol leaned forward to tap his knee. "I've already sworn to Matt that I won't fail. I know beautiful clothes, and you know fine food. Neither of us is afraid of long hours or hard work and it will surely take both. The only way to do this is to go full out, and if we pour our hearts and souls into it, we're bound to succeed."

Casey sat back in his chair. "My God, Carol, you ought to be doing motivational tapes. Give me the address of the place, and I'll take Suzanne over to look at it tonight. I'll let you know in the morning what we decide. If for any reason I can't do it now, I'll still help you in every way I can."

Satisfied she had done her best to set him

ablaze with the fire of her enthusiasm, Carol rose to her feet. "Thanks, Casey, I knew I could count on you." She returned to her office in high spirits. Having Casey next door would make opening her own place a lot easier, but she sure wished she had Matt to count on, the way Casey could count on Suzanne.

That evening, Casey took Suzanne over to see the building on Huntington Drive. Built of used brick with white trim, it was attractive even at night. Lit for security, the vacant units cried out for ambitious tenants. Casey leaned back against his car. "Well, what do you think?"

They had walked the length of the building, peeked through the window at the lovely furnishings in the interior designer's shop, noted the stationers' display, the jeweler's empty satin pillows where they could only assume spectacular gems were displayed during the day, and sent a hasty glance toward the computer academy.

"I think we're going to be late for poetry," Suzanne replied.

Disappointed by her lack of interest, Casey straightened up. "Of course, how thoughtless of me. What's a major career decision compared with arriving late for a poetry workshop? Hop in, let's go."

Suzanne cast a final glance at the empty

units, and then slipped into the car on the passenger side. When Casey had mentioned he wanted to stop by the building, she had not known what to expect, but she didn't like being pressured for an opinion on a subject about which she had absolutely no expertise. The decision was his, and she did not feel comfortable sharing in it.

"If you want to open a cafe, then do it," she exclaimed. "You know the restaurant business, while all I know is that I enjoy eating out. I feel totally unqualified to offer advice on something this important to you."

Casey started the engine, but didn't pull out of the parking space. "I didn't expect you to offer business advice, Suz. I know you're not a CPA. I just wanted your reaction to my interest in opening my own place here."

Suzanne knew she had let him down, but she did not know how to tactfully make him understand her reticence to share in the decision. He was so special to her, but their love was very new, and she could not take on the responsibility for his future. "I don't have any psychic abilities, Casey, so I've no way of knowing whether or not you'll succeed."

She looked so anguished by their discussion that while he was dismayed by her attitude, Casey let the matter drop. They drove to the workshop, and the evening promised to be as entertaining as the first one he had attended. He recognized several people: the Lincolnesque man, the nervous fellow who was again wearing lavender argyle socks, the white-haired woman, and the leather-clad girls. The transvestite wasn't there, nor was the young man with the platform shoes and corkscrew curls, but there were some fascinating newcomers.

One man had a marvelous voice and claimed to do voice-overs for commercials, but his poem bordered on pornography and drew derogatory comments from the women. Several men, however, described the piece as very strong. "Did you like that?" Casey whispered.

Suzanne shook her head. She hadn't brought anything to read, and she made only a few comments, and those were all complimentary. Casey watched a smile tickle on her lips as an older gentleman read a poem entirely composed of nonsense syllables. Childlike and charming, everyone enjoyed it, and the leader thought it a good time to take a break.

Casey stood up to stretch. "If I open a cafe," he confided. "I could host poetry readings. Wouldn't that be fun?"

Suzanne stood and leaned close to reply. "It would all depend on whom you invited to read."

Knowing exactly what she meant, Casey took her hand as they walked outside. "I promise, no X-rated stuff. Poetry readings are a good idea though. There's also the chance to serve as a mini-art gallery. Lots of restaurants decorate with artwork by local artists. The artists have the opportunity to have their work displayed; they might sell some, and the restaurants benefit from the artists' publicity and attract new customers. Plus they have attractive art on their walls. Didn't Aimee say one of her daughters is an artist? She might like to have a show at my cafe."

Suzanne looked up at the stars. It was a bit disconcerting to have Casey channel the enthusiasm he had previously shown her into plans for a cafe, but in another respect, it was a relief not to feel as though he had made her the center of his life. "Yes, Karen does big colorful paintings that would add to any decor."

She turned toward him, and tried to be more honest. "I'm sorry I wasn't more enthusiastic earlier. I guess I was just worried that if things didn't work out for you, you might blame me, and that would spoil everything between us."

Casey framed her face with his hands and kissed her soundly. "I know what makes a restaurant succeed, Suz, and it's a rare combination of setting, cuisine, and service. I don't know anything about the costs yet, and they may stop me cold, but if I can swing this, then I'm going to do it, and I will succeed. Unless of course, California really does get hit with the 'Big One' and the state ends up a pile of rubble, but only a terrible earthquake could stop me."

The excitement in Casey's voice was infectious, and when the workshop leader blinked the lights in the community center's bookstore to signal the start of the second half of the poetry group, she was reluctant to return. "We could leave now if you like, Casey. I'm sure you'd much rather discuss your plans than listen to more amateur poetry."

Casey pulled her toward the door. "No, you're wrong. Poetry is something you love, and I wouldn't dream of leaving early. Say, maybe I'll call my place Aluminum Moons. How does that sound?"

"Intriguing," Suzanne agreed, "most definitely intriguing. We could print your poem on the front of the menu."

She had said 'we,' and thrilled to find her as supportive as he had hoped, he gave her a boisterous hug, and smiled all the way through the rest of the evening.

When she arrived at Russell's Thursday morning, Carol found Casey pacing what little room there was in her office. He had left his jacket in his office, and with his sleeves rolled up, looked ready to get to work. "Well, what did you decide?" she asked.

Casey took the precaution of closing her door before he replied in a hushed voice. "I'm in if Aimee can get me a loan, but because money will be tight, I'd like to hang on to my job here for as long as I can so any planning we do has to be done on our lunch hour away from the store, or at night."

Carol opened the bottom drawer of her desk and dropped in her purse. "I'd planned to give my notice as soon as I sign a lease. This is a full-time job, and so is setting up a boutique, or at least it will be for me. You do whatever you think is best."

"I wasn't going to attempt doing both jobs either," Casey swore, "but there's a chance the owner of the building won't want the bother of remodeling for a restaurant, and I'd rather not broadcast the fact I'm thinking of leaving, until I know I actually can."

"I understand how awkward that would be. Gossip travels fast here, and there's no point in our running the risk of being dismissed before we can resign."

"Exactly, but people must have already noticed how much time we've spent together lately, and I'll bet the rumors are already circulating."

"I won't be embarrassed if people believe we're sleeping together. Actually, it's quite flattering." The fact she slept alone, except for one recent spectacular exception, certainly wasn't a source of pride. She smiled as though she were teasing, but she wasn't.

"Well, thank you," Casey responded, but to him, Carol didn't really look flattered. She had always been guarded with her feelings, but studying her expression now, he felt torn. He wanted to reach out and touch her, to hug her close, but he could sense she wouldn't welcome any such spontaneous display of affection from him.

"I'm not sure how to ask this," he hedged.

Carol leaned back against her desk. "Just spit it out, Casey. If we're going to be next door neighbors, we ought not to have secrets."

"This isn't a secret," Casey explained. "I was just thinking that when we speak with the owner of the building, it might be wise to take someone along who'll know what type of remodeling we'll require. Because Matt's the one who suggested you include me, and he does the kind of work involved, I'd hate to cut him out of the chance to do it."

Casey was right of course, but the thought of having to work with Matt, when he wore his disinterest in her as proudly as a cowboy wore his Stetson, made Carol feel sick to her stomach. She pulled out her chair and sat down. What she needed was a carpenter to build dressing rooms. It was Casey who needed a complete kitchen installed, and he was the one who had every right to hire whomever he wished to do the work. She tried to project a calm she didn't feel as she looked up at him.

"I liked Matt a lot," she confessed, "but he didn't care for me, so that was the end of that story. I'm not one to hold a grudge though, and if you want him there when we meet with the owner, he's a physician, Dr. Strauss is his name, then fine. I'm sure he'll be an asset."

Casey swept Carol with an appraising glance. As always she was beautifully groomed and dressed, and there was a sparkle about her he had always admired. While it was true she didn't flirt, or play up to a man's vanity, she was definitely an extremely desirable woman. "How could he not like you?"

Carol shrugged. "Not every man goes for petite blondes, Casey, some actually prefer voluptuous redheads."

"Yeah," Casey agreed with a charming grin. "Still—"

"Let's not get sidetracked talking about our love lives," she cautioned, "when we ought to be concentrating on business. What are you going to call your cafe?"

Casey moved to the door, but did not open it. "Aluminum Moons. It's odd, but people will remember it. How about you; have you chosen a name?"

"How does Crimson Luxury grab you?"

"Crimson Luxury." Casey closed his eyes and found it easy to visualize an elegant shop with that name. "Perfect," he assured her. "I got Aimee's work number from Suzanne. I'll give her a call this morning, and get back to you." He held out his hand. "Can you see how I'm shaking? I think I'd sooner take up skydiving than risk failing, but I keep telling myself we're not going to fail."

"No, we're not." Carol agreed emphatically. "Talk to you later."

After Casey left, Carol looked around her office. Despite the clutter, she knew where everything was, but if she were going to be leaving soon, she wanted to go out with a flourish rather than a mess, and spent the morning putting everything in its proper place. With methodical diligence she made a real dent in the chaos, but with every order she stored away in the file cabinet, and every swatch she tossed in the trash, she wished the frayed ends of her personal life were as easy to repair.

Carol had expected Dr. Arthur Strauss to be an older gentleman, probably retired, who dabbled in real estate. When he turned out to be not yet forty, she began to fear the persuasive argument she had carefully scripted in her mind might not run nearly as smoothly as she had hoped. The doctor definitely exuded the confidence she had anticipated, and his appearance was nearly dazzling. He was dressed in a navy-blue blazer, white flannel slacks, gray loafers, a monogrammed tattersall shirt, and a maroon and navy striped tie.

She couldn't decide if he looked as though he had just stepped off the cover of GQ, or like his mother had dressed him for church. Handsome with a slight resemblance to Richard Gere, he looked so damn perfect that in her mind he made their task all the more difficult. After all, it was one thing to discuss a lease with a businessman, and quite another to talk with a man who looked better than most movie stars.

Wanting to present a professional image, she had worn a stylish pearl-gray suit. Casey was also well-dressed in dark blue, but Matt had shown up in his usual Levi's and blue workshirt. It was Saturday, and she had had since Thursday to get used to the idea of him being there, but it still didn't make it any easier to be near him again. She had managed a cool hello, and he had responded with a distracted nod, which she took as a warning not to expect anything more.

They had met at the vacant units, and Matt

walked around both, checked their small bathrooms and then stood back to listen while Dr. Strauss interviewed her and Casey at length. The physician was interested not simply in their plans, but in their employment and personal histories as well, but as Carol had with both Casey and Matt, she stressed their wealth of valuable experience as the prime indicators of how well they would do.

After more than an hour of discussion, Dr. Strauss shook his head. "The dress shop presents no problems, but I just can't get excited about putting a restaurant in here. Most fail, and then I'll be left with gigantic stoves and sinks to haul away, and two inches of grease to scrape off the walls before I can rent the unit to anyone else."

Casey was so insulted he did not know how to respond, but Matt did. "Mr. O'Neil won't be frying hamburgers in here, but preparing gourmet meals. The stoves will be well-vented, so there's no danger of grease splattering the walls even if he used some, which I doubt. Should the need ever arise, used restaurant equipment commands a high price, and you'd have people standing in line to buy it rather than having to pay someone to haul it away. Frankly, I don't see how you can afford not to rent to these two. The boutique and cafe will be unique attractions, and draw customers for the other shops located in your building.

"It's a lot easier to collect rent from thriving businesses than ones that are barely getting by, or in this case, vacant space which isn't earning you a dime. There are already too many empty stores in the area, and not everyone is looking for two units, if they are even out looking for one. You impress me as a man of vision, Dr. Strauss. You must be or you wouldn't have put up this building in the first place.

"Now if you're sincerely worried about Casey's chance to succeed, why don't you have him prepare supper for you and your family tonight? I swear one bite is all you'll need to know you'll kick yourself all the way to San Diego if you force him to open up down the street and miss out on the business he'll bring in here."

Strauss eyed Carol and Casey with a curious glance. They had introduced Matt as a plumbing contractor, but he appeared to be much more than that. "Is this guy your business manager?"

"No," Casey assured him, "but he knows what he's talking about."

Still undecided, the physician pulled a small brass case from his pocket, removed a business card, and wrote his home address on the back. "I'll think about this. Bring one of your fabulous suppers for four to my house tonight at seven, along with a breakdown of what it will cost to bring in restaurant equipment, and I'll give you my decision after we've had dessert. Agreed?"

"Agreed." Casey took the card and offered his hand. The four of them left the building together, and Dr. Strauss drove away in a burgundy Jaguar. "The man's a gynecologist," Casey read from the card, "and he lives out on Lombardy Road. Is that a good address?"

"The best," Matt said. "I hope you didn't have other plans for the evening, but I thought if he tasted your cooking, he'd be sure to accept you as a tenant."

"I have no other plans," Casey insisted, "and I hope neither of you do either because I'm going to need all the help I can get."

Carol started to back away. "Suzanne is a better cook than I am."

Matt reached out to catch her hand. "Oh no you don't. If I'm going to peel potatoes, or shuck corn, then you are too."

Carol looked down at his hand. Deeply tanned, his skin contrasted sharply with hers but it was the heat of his touch that seared her heart as well as her skin. So much for detachment she thought. If the man was within sight, she could feel it, and he still felt so damn good she had to force herself to pull away.

"All right, fine. I'll knead bread or whatever else you want me to do, but I'll have to go home and change my clothes first."

Casey checked his watch. "I'm going back to Suzanne's. I need to plan a menu, and shop. With the Saturday crowd that's going to take me some time so why don't you two meet me there at two? And don't worry, I'll prepare enough for the four of us to have dinner too."

"Casey," Carol called when he turned away. "I won't rent space here if Strauss refuses to take you."

Casey came back. "Wait a minute, Carol, if this is the best place you found, then take it."

"No, being together is too good an idea to throw away. If we can't do it here, then we'll find another place where we can, but I intend to be next door to Aluminum Moons and that's all there is to it."

Matt felt as though he were eavesdropping, and yet he hesitated to leave. He knew Casey and Suzanne had something good going, but as he listened to him talk with Carol now, he wondered if he might not switch his affections back to Carol if they went into business together. He told himself that was no concern of his, but it didn't ease the painful jealousy rising in his chest. After walking out on Carol, he could scarcely provide romantic advice, but he was worried all the same.

"Save that threat for a trump card," Matt suggested. "I think the doctor will rent the place to Casey tonight, but if he's still hesitant, then you can tell him it's the two of you, or nothing. Losing the rent on two units ought to be enough to convince even a wealthy man he's making a mistake. See you at two. Do I need to bring an apron?"

"No, just a good appetite." Casey waited until Matt had gotten into his truck. "You can tolerate his company just for tonight, can't you?" he asked.

Carol was about to assure him that she could, when she noticed the sparkle in his eyes was just a little too bright. "Are you trying to play cupid? Is that what you're doing? You ought to be ashamed, Casey O'Neil. I'll find my own men, thank you."

"As I recall, you asked me to the reunion because you couldn't find one on your own."

He had her there, but Carol made a face at him rather than admit it, and walked away.

"We're going to do what?" Suzanne shrieked.

"We're going to prepare dinner for Dr. Strauss, and if he likes it, then perhaps, but it's a rather vague perhaps, he'll rent me one of his vacant units. We've been cooking together all week, Suz, this won't be any more difficult."

Suzanne collapsed into a chair at the kitchen table. He was right; they had cooked together but it hadn't been anything more complicated than spaghetti, or baked chicken, and the mood had been relaxed and easy then. There had been no pressure to impress anyone, but now the future of his cafe depended on what they could turn out from her kitchen and she couldn't stifle a moan.

"You don't understand, Casey. I can't bear to cook for company. That's why I ordered food from the Panda Inn for you. There's just too much pressure involved, and I'm so afraid I'll burn the meat, or serve it half-cooked and make everyone ill. I really can't do this."

She was shaking with fright, but rather than scold her for being silly, Casey attempted to allay her fears. "I'll be the one doing the cooking, Suz, not you, and Carol and Matt have promised to come and help. Our worst problem will be staying out of each other's way." Casey sat down with her and began making out a shopping list. "Trust me, Suz, I'm sure you can give sensational lectures on the Indians of the Northwest Coast without your notes, and I can prepare dinner for a hundred without batting an eye."

"I think I'm going to be sick." Suzanne put her head down on her arms.

Casey reached out to ruffle her curls. "Go

outside and work in your garden, or go upstairs and take a nap until I get back. Then I promise you won't have to do anything more strenuous than slice the bread for croutons."

"Croutons?" Suz opened one eye and looked up at him.

"You intend to make your own croutons?"

"Of course, Suz." Casey bent down to kiss her goodbye before leaving for the market, but Suzanne wasn't at all reassured.

Matt got home and had to step around the boxes he had been packing before going to meet Carol and Casey. Carl Hendricks had nearly cried he had been so grateful Matt wanted to buy the Victorian house, but moving meant he had to do something about the one he already owned, and everything it contained. After Deborah's death, a couple of her close friends had come in and taken her clothes to donate to one of the charity thrift shops. He couldn't have done it on his own, and he was relieved there was nothing of hers left to get rid of now.

He made himself a ham sandwich, and as he sat down to eat it he hoped he would not regret offering to help Casey. It was tough being around Carol, but he liked Casey and wanted him to have a chance at owning his own cafe. That was what he enjoyed about remodeling jobs, not that people weren't grateful when he fixed a leaky pipe, but they were far more appreciative when he turned a dreary bathroom or outdated kitchen into a room they were proud to own. He was looking forward to working on a restaurant set up. The only drawback was that Carol Hagan would be right next door.

It was a such a nice day that he went out to sit on the back porch when he finished eating. Taffy came over and sat down beside him, expecting attention and he stroked her honey-colored coat with a lazy caress. Taffy didn't get nearly as much affection from him as she had from Deborah, and she had a way of looking up at him with her big, sad eyes that made him feel negligent in the extreme.

"Good girl." He rubbed her ears and wondered how she would adjust to their new home. He broke out in a sweat every time he thought about moving but he was going through with it. The yard was fenced like this one, and he hoped Taffy would appreciate a change in scene. "That's exactly what we need, girl, a place where we can make new memories, and cut loose the old ones."

Taffy yawned.

Matt laughed in spite of himself. "All right, so my plans don't sound all that exciting to you, but they are to me and you're just the dog here, remember? You're supposed to do as I say."

Again Taffy looked unimpressed.

Matt checked his watch but he had plenty of time left before he had to leave for Suzanne's. Savoring the sweet smell of the spring grass, he recalled the size of Suzanne's kitchen and knew they wouldn't have much in the way of room. He would probably bump into Carol no matter how carefully he tried to avoid it.

She sure had smelled good that morning. Her gray suit had been rather severe, but he understood she wanted to look as though she were already successful to impress Dr. Strauss. Of course, she was successful, and that was probably the type of clothes she wore to work every day.

"Little Ms. Success," he mumbled to himself. The pair of Levi's he was wearing was beginning to rip at the knee, but that was the way most people wore them nowadays so he had no intention of throwing them away.

"I met this woman, Taffy, but we're the worst mismatch of all time. She sure is pretty though."

This time Taffy licked his hand, and encouraged, Matt continued to tell her all the wonderful things he dared not admit to Carol.

Nineteen

Casey was not only a superb chef, he was also a master of organization. Suzanne's kitchen was woefully inadequate when it came to space, but she had an excellent gas range, and a microwave oven so once he got a dish prepared, he had a place to bake it. When Carol and Matt arrived at two o'clock, he set Suzanne to work, slicing one-inch cubes of French bread at the kitchen table, put Carol at the sink washing lettuce and vegetables for the salad, and gave Matt the list of ingredients to mix for the salad dressing.

He had written out the recipes for everything he intended to make, and checked them off point by point as they worked through them. They tuned a radio to an oldies station, and with Casey in such a relaxed yet energetic mood, they were all soon humming along with their favorite songs and joining in on the chorus. Matt had a good voice, and he and Casey harmonized on the Everly Brothers song, "Let It Be Me."

Suzanne applauded when they finished. "This is more fun than the reunion, and I doubt there's any chance of a brawl."

"I just hope you haven't spoken too soon," Carol warned.

Matt scoffed at her fears. "Dr. Strauss might know how to dress, but he didn't look like he could fight his way out of a Cub Scout meeting, let alone tangle with us."

Carol had to step around him to get another bowl. "Oh yeah? Well, that's precisely the type who has a black belt in karate. Besides, if we get into a fight with him, he'll never rent both units to us, so let's not even think about it."

"I was only joking," Suzanne said. "I didn't expect you to take it so seriously."

"I know," Carol replied, "but disasters have a way of befalling us and I'd like to avoid another. Can we talk about color schemes instead? With the name Crimson Luxury, I'd like to have pearl gray walls, and a crimson carpet and crimson accents. While I know you'll not want to carpet your cafe, it would be great if we could have a unified, or at least a harmonious, color scheme."

"Gray and red?" Matt looked skeptical. "Why does a battleship come to mind?"

"Not battleship gray," Carol corrected, "a

delicate pearl gray and crimson, which is a deep, purplish red, warm and yet refined."

"Refined," Matt muttered under his breath, obviously unimpressed.

"I thought your specialty was plumbing, not color coordination."

Casey turned to Suzanne and rolled his eyes. There was a sharpness to Carol's voice that wasn't at all conciliatory and as for Matt, it was clear he was deliberately giving her a hard time. If Casey had ever had any hopes of playing cupid, he abandoned them now.

"My contractor's license covers both plumbing and heating; but color coordination is such a small part of the business the state doesn't bother handing out certificates for it."

That sarcastic claim irritated Carol all the more and she continued to rip up a head of red leaf lettuce with savage strokes. "I happen to think color is too vital an element to be left to a plumber's taste, but you were the one I was talking to, Casey. What do you think of crimson and gray?"

Not really wanting to be drawn into their argument, Casey still felt compelled to respond. "I could use them too. There are too many places with a Southwest blend of peach and aqua so a striking new contrast would be most welcome. I like the idea of having original art on display and neutral walls would be best to showcase it. If we use the same colors, we might want to print both names on the matches, bags, receipts, whatever, and we'll have to have an awning because I'd like to put tables out on the sidewalk. Crimson with gray lettering would be handsome as well as eyecatching."

Carol glanced over at Matt who was attempting to measure dry mustard into a teaspoon without spilling any. He had completely unnerved her at their first meeting, grated on her terribly at their second, been absolutely fantastic for most of the reunion night, and then broken her heart by slamming the door on her hopes for a future. At least he was speaking to her again, which was an improvement over the way he had left her house after making love to her all night, but that wasn't nearly enough to please her.

Her eyes began to sting with the threat of tears, and determined not to cry in front of Matt and her friends, she bit down on her lip and stubbornly forced them away. She and Matt might be able to create a passable salad under Casey's direction, but she was not going to let herself hope for anything more. Who would want anything more from a man with such erratic behavior? she asked herself. She had a bell pepper to chop and whacked it up into tiny bits, all the while wishing their parting had left wounds as deep in Matt as they had in her.

The violence of Carol's actions wasn't lost on Matt, and he was careful to stay out of her way whenever she had a knife in her hand. He could understand her anger, and admit he deserved it, but that did not mean he wanted it to continue. As he saw it, they were adults, and ought to accept things as they were rather than beat each other up over them.

Under Casey's able direction, the preparations went smoothly and when they had the meal well underway, he suggested they take a break, have something to drink, and go out on the deck. Suzanne opened a diet soda, and went outside immediately, but both Matt and Carol hung back. "Keep working if you like," Casey called as he went out the back door.

Carol was dipping strawberries in melted chocolate and picked up another. She gave it a languid twirl in the thick, creamy mixture, then laid it on a sheet of waxed paper to set. As she reached for the next one, Matt caught her hand. She looked up at him with the meanest gaze she could muster. "Did you want to do this?" she asked.

"No," Matt confided softly. "The strawberries aren't the problem. This has been the most uncomfortable afternoon of my life. I know I handled things badly, and I apologize for it. Now can we please declare a truce so we can concentrate on impressing Dr. Strauss rather than taking out our frustrations on each other?"

When Carol tugged on her hand, Matt released her and she continued dipping strawberries with a methodical precision. "You didn't just handle things badly," she began, "you behaved despicably, and it's not frustration I feel around you, it's absolute rage." The last traces of his black eye were faint. She doubted Dr. Strauss had noticed the lingering hint of lavender and green in the crease of his lid, but she knew he was lucky he didn't look a hell of a lot worse.

"You better go outside and sit with Casey and Suzanne because the compulsion to push your face into this chocolate is almost more than I can control. I agreed with Casey that you're the most obvious choice to do the remodeling for him, but that doesn't mean you and I have to spend another minute together after tonight. Trust me, I want your company even less than you want mine."

The blush in her cheeks and fire in her eyes convinced Matt that Carol wasn't exaggerating her anger. She was furious with him and he knew she had a good reason. That did not make him any less anxious to square things with her, but he knew a hopeless cause when he saw it. "I am sorry," he repeated, but convinced words wouldn't sway her, he cautiously strode out of the back door rather than risk being smothered in chocolate.

As the door closed behind Matt, Carol felt as though she might simply explode in a thousand jagged fragments. Her disastrous affair with Matt had served to confirm her suspicions that she was meant to spend the rest of her life alone, and that added a painful dimension to her existence. She hated being alone and having nothing but work to fill her nights as well as her days, but that was just the way things were and she knew the sooner she accepted her solitary status, the better off she would be. It was just so terribly hard to accept though.

Suzanne came in, counted the dipped strawberries, and finding plenty, sampled one. "These are delicious. Have you tried one?"

"I'm sure they're good, but I doubt I could swallow another thing this afternoon."

"What do you mean? We've not been nibbling." Suzanne licked her fingers, then noticed the belligerent set of Carol's features. Certain Matt had to be the cause, she lowered her voice. "Casey thought he would be doing you and Matt a favor by providing an excuse to be together. Looks like he was wrong."

"Very, but I know he meant well." Carol dipped the last of the berries, and set it with the others. "I'd like to go home and try and forget I ever met Matt, but I'll stick it out. I'm too curious about what Strauss will say to miss the dinner party we're throwing for him."

"I wish I'd met him."

"I'm sure you will, if not tonight, then sometime soon, if he okays our being tenants."

"You look tired. Why don't you go on up to my room and take a nap? The three of us can handle the rest of the preparations, and I'll wake you in plenty of time to get ready to go."

"And miss getting my share of the credit? No, I'll stay. I can sleep in tomorrow." Carol opened a soft drink, but remained in the kitchen to drink it. By the time Casey and Matt came back inside, she again had her feelings under firm control. Matt had merely been a very bumpy detour on the already none too smooth road of her life, but she refused to allow him to sidetrack her again.

The estates located along Lombardy Road were larger than the fraternity and sorority houses at most universities. There were Spanish-style residences with red tile roofs and gracefully arched doorways, timbered English Tudor homes, lovely French Provincial chateaus, and Colonial mansions with columned verandas. Beautifully landscaped, many with circular drives, several had both swimming pools and tennis courts in addition to extensive gardens. Discreet signs stating deliveries were to be made in the rear were posted at nearly every house but as Casey pulled into the driveway of the Strauss home, he needed no directions and headed for the kitchen door.

Because there had been no other way to transport their feuding companions, Matt had ridden with Casey, while Suzanne had followed in Carol's car. The women parked out on the street, and walked down the driveway to help carry everything inside. A Spanish-style home, the Strauss residence was painted a pale terracotta with white trim, and the wrought iron balconies were a deep blue. The man apparently took as beautiful care of his home as his person, for the house was magnificent in every respect.

"Nice to see how the top half lives, isn't it?" Carol whispered.

"Several years ago you could buy a house up here for a million dollars; now they're closer to three."

"What would the monthly payments be on that?"

"I think it's like a yacht," Suzanne replied in a burst of giggles. "If you have to ask, then you can't afford it."

"It must cost a fortune just to heat this place."

Matt overheard that remark as Carol came through the back door. He raised his finger to his lips. "Be careful. Mrs. Strauss let us in. She was very friendly and asked us to call her Donna. She's gone to get her husband and kids."

"What's she like?" Suzanne asked.

"Just what you'd expect," Matt replied, "gorgeous."

Despite Carol's resolve to exclude Matt from her life, hearing him describe another woman in such glowing terms hurt badly. She pretended an interest in the kitchen. Like many of its neighbors, the house had been built in the 1920s but the kitchen had been extensively remodeled with colorful Spanish tile and the latest in modern appliances. Well lit and roomy, a dozen cooks could have whipped up a dinner without bumping into each other there. "I wish we could have done the cooking here," she whispered.

"Me too," Casey replied, "but don't worry, if this dinner doesn't impress them then they just can't be impressed." He had prepared a crisp green salad filled with delectable chopped vegetables and garnished with delicately seasoned croutons, fresh baked rolls, Norwegian salmon with an exquisite saffron sauce, breast of duck in an orange and honey sauce with wild rice and asparagus, and a beautiful cheesecake adorned with chocolate-covered strawberries. Leaving nothing to chance, he had brought the wine for each course, chocolate milk for the kids, and freshly ground beans to brew a full-bodied coffee.

Donna Strauss opened the kitchen door and called to him. "We're all ready, Mr. O'Neil. I gave our staff the night off, but it looks as though you've brought plenty of help. Just let me know if you need an extra spoon or anything and I'll try and find it."

Wondering just what sort of woman Matt would describe as gorgeous, Carol tried not to stare, but she was saddened to find Donna was her complete opposite. She was tall and slender, a tanned athletic beauty who probably played tennis several mornings a week with friends who were equally trim and fit. She wore her dark brown hair in a classic pageboy, and was dressed in the same type of expensive separates Carol was accustomed to buying for Russell's. Thinking if Donna were Matt's type it was no wonder he had grown bored with her so quickly, Carol's spirits sank even lower.

When Donna Strauss returned to the adjacent dining room, Casey took the precaution of looking in to make certain someone had set the table, and was relieved to see they had. He had brought along four place settings of Suzanne's best china, and a tray to carry each course to the table but he had not wanted to make the mistake of serving the first course to people who had neither napkins nor forks. He considered the fact Mrs. Strauss was so friendly a good sign, and hoped the evening would go as well as they hoped.

Casey had already insisted he would be the one to serve the meal since he knew how, and no one had argued with him. Suzanne and Carol helped to serve the plates, while Matt sat at the kitchen table reviewing the figures he had made on the cost of remodeling one of Strauss's units for a cafe. He was as nervous as the rest of them, although his stake in the new businesses was small compared to Carol and Casey's.

"They're all smiling," Casey reported after serving the main course, "but I still don't like the wait."

"I should have brought along a deck of cards," Matt responded. "What do the servants do in a case like this?"

"They probably do play cards," Carol replied before realizing she hadn't meant to speak to Matt ever again. They could hear Dr. and Mrs. Strauss talking softly to their sons, whose high voices frequently rang with boisterous laughter. "Lovely little family," she whispered. She could remember when her own sons were small. Those years, like all the rest, had passed much too quickly. Joining Matt at the table, she massaged her temples and hoped the effort to reach Dr. Strauss through his stomach paid off.

She looked very small and afraid, and Matt longed to reach out to her, to offer a word of encouragement, but when his suggested truce had met with such a bitter rejection he decided he would be better off keeping still. From everything he had seen, Carol was a woman with unlimited energy, but she was sitting very still, as though all the life had been drained out of her and knowing only too well how that felt, he made a silent vow to do whatever it took to convince Dr. Strauss to rent her the shop she wanted.

By the time Casey served coffee and dessert, the tension in the kitchen was nearly unbearable. Unable to cope with it another minute, Suzanne went outside to sit on the porch. Matt began filling a blank piece of paper with obscure diagrams, and Carol rinsed the dishes and set them back in the laundry basket they had used to bring them. They would run them through the dishwasher back at Suzanne's, but Carol was trembling so badly she feared she might not get them there.

Finally Dr. Strauss came to the door. "Would you all come in here please?"

"We'll be right there," Casey assured him, and he hurried to bring Suzanne back inside.

His family had left the table, and Dr. Strauss looked ready to do business. Matt handed him the folder containing the estimate he had prepared, and stepped back. "You can put the job out for bids if you like, but mine will be the lowest."

The doctor perused the costs at such length the silence in the room had grown exceedingly awkward by the time he finally laid the folder aside. He looked up at Casey, then glanced toward Carol. "All right. You've sold me. The dinner was superb. You're a hell of a chef, but it was the chocolate milk that convinced me you'd pay the proper attention to detail. I admire that. I'll have my attorney prepare the leases and give you a call when they're ready to sign. As soon as they're out of the way, request the necessary permits from the city. Then you can begin the remodeling, but be careful not to disturb my present tenants."

"We'll start early each day," Matt assured him, "and have most of our work done before they open for business."

"Good." He rose and shook hands with them all. "Thank you again for the delicious dinner. We'll be sure to dine at your cafe often."

"I'll look forward to seeing you there," Casey assured him, but it wasn't until they had packed everything in his car and returned to Suzanne's that he really felt able to celebrate.

"I'm afraid I'm too excited to eat," Carol told him as she helped carry everything inside. "If you'll excuse me, I'd rather just go on home."

"No, I won't excuse you," Casey exclaimed. He put his hands on her shoulders and steered her into the dining room. "I want your opinion on the meal."

"I tasted everything while we were cooking," Carol argued.

"That's scarcely enough to qualify for a serious comment. Now you worked all afternoon and I promised you dinner. Sit down and make yourself comfortable and I'll serve it in just a minute."

Carol opened her mouth to argue, but Suzanne shook her head. She knew Casey was elated they had gotten the leases, and she could understand how much he wanted to celebrate, but she just felt numb. For both Casey and Suzanne's sake she remained seated, and made a try at being sociable, but she just couldn't do it. Casey and Matt talked about the remodeling. Casey knew exactly what he wanted which made Matt's job an easier one, but Carol couldn't get interested in the size of ovens, or the capacity of a commercial dishwasher.

"I'm sorry," she said. "This is all so good, but I have to go home, I really do." She got up, grabbed her purse and went out the front door before any of her companions could swallow and argue.

Casey watched Matt's expression darken as Carol fled the meal he had hoped she would enjoy and he came to a quick conclusion. "Carol's a good friend of mine, and I don't know what you did, but you obviously hurt her very badly. You're a lot stronger than I am, so I can't take you out back and whip you for it, but I saw you step in to keep Jack Shank from abusing his wife and I just can't imagine why you'd deliberately hurt Carol."

"I didn't," Matt was quick to deny, but both Casey and Suzanne looked unconvinced. "Hurt her deliberately, that is. Look Casey, you and Carol didn't hit it off, so you know from experience not every relationship works out. Ours just didn't, that's all. I'm sorry as can be, but there's nothing I can do about it."

Suzanne shook her head. "That was the lamest excuse I ever heard. Do you lie to yourself like that?"

Shocked that she would speak to Matt in such an insulting tone, Casey reached out to take Suzanne's hand. "Suz, honey—"

Suzanne pulled her hand away. "I'm sorry, but Carol's one of my best friends and seeing her so unhappy hurts me too. I've a good idea what you did, Matt, and you ought to be ashamed of yourself. You're a grown man, not some college kid with a love 'em and leave 'em attitude. Excuse me, I've lost my appetite too." She got up and carried her plate into the kitchen.

"Well, at least no one's complained about the food," Casey remarked, "but I sure wish this evening had ended differently." He took another bite of duck, and modestly decided it was the best he had ever prepared, or tasted.

Matt felt as though several burly bikers were standing on his chest in hobnailed boots and he had to struggle to draw a breath. While he wanted to leave too, he waited until Casey had finished eating. "Call me as soon as you've signed the lease and I'll get the permits and start work. I'm sure Carol will stay out of my way and I have every intention of staying out of hers, so you won't have to sit through another awkward dinner."

Casey got up to walk him to the door. "Carol only seems tough," he warned him. "She isn't really; she's just trying to protect herself is all. I think you're the same way."

Not appreciating that insightful observation, Matt just walked away. He had accomplished what he had come for, which was to get Casey the lease, but it hadn't left him with any sense of pride. He drove to the Victorian house rather than home, got out of his truck and sat on the front step. The neighborhood was quiet, peaceful, but the silence failed to sooth the tumult in his heart.

He had known he had disappointed Carol, but he had not really understood how deeply he had hurt her until that night. From her standpoint, he could be accused of offering something precious, and then snatching it away as soon as she had reached for it. What he had done was a hell of a lot worse. He had given her a glimpse of love, and then overcome with guilt he had turned his back on her. She hadn't deserved that. He could think of only one way to make everything right, if only he could find the courage to try.

Suzanne hadn't said a word as they had done the dishes, and as Casey rinsed out the sink he feared her thoughts were a million miles away. "I'd like to stay, but if you'd rather I go on home, I will."

Casey's voice startled her from her melancholy reverie and the sorrow in his expression touched her as always. "No, I want you to stay. I wish Matt were more like you, Casey. I wish all men were. What Matt did to Carol was absolutely rotten."

Casey leaned back against the counter. "Just what is it you think he did?"

"Isn't it plain he started something he can't, or won't finish? I don't understand why men behave that way. Why do they offer affection, and then just turn it off as if it were nothing? Don't they regard women as real?"

"Look, I won't even try to defend Matt, much less men in general when there are plenty of women who play men for all they can get and then move on without so much as a thank you. Men aren't the only ones who break hearts, Suz. It's just that women complain much louder to their friends when it happens to them."

"Complain?" Suzanne repeated. "If a man treats a woman badly she has every right to complain. You make it sound as though a broken heart is no more painful than a stubbed toe. You really don't give a damn what happens between Carol and Matt, do you?"

"Of course I care, but what am I going to do about it? I thought if they had a chance to be together this afternoon they might have such a good time they'd want to go on seeing each other. I was wrong. Now I'm not going to meddle in their affairs, and that's no pun, any further. Don't we have enough trouble understanding each other without worrying about someone else?"

"Is that all I am to you, 'trouble'?"

"No! That's not what I meant at all." Casey reached out to draw her into his arms. She resisted a moment, and then relaxed against him. He closed his eyes savoring the sweet softness of her for a long moment. "All of us have our battle scars, Suz. It's plain Frank disappointed you badly, and my wife sure as hell disappointed me. Let's not get caught up in Carol and Matt's misery when what we have together is so good."

"Maybe it's just a matter of time, Casey, maybe all there is is disappointment."

Saddened by that dreary thought, Casey stepped back to meet her gaze. "It can't be. People would be leaping from windows all over the place if it were."

"Some people won't leap though. They just walk around with so much pain in their eyes I'm surprised they can see. I'm really worried about Carol, Casey. Will you keep an eye on her?"

"Sure, but I'm not the one she wants."

"Thank goodness!"

Casey wrapped her in an enthusiastic hug. His psychologist had warned him not to become involved in other people's problems, but he thought he could make an exception in Carol's case. He just wished he knew what to do.

After Carol got home, Tom came by to pick up his tennis racquet. "Sharon doesn't have much time to play, but with summer coming, I'm hoping we'll have a few chances. How are the plans for the boutique going?"

Carol sat down at the kitchen table, and Tom moved around behind her and began massaging her neck and shoulders. "You're all tied in knots, Mom. What's wrong?"

"I got the lease on the location I want. Now all I have to do is pull everything together."

Tom concentrated on her left shoulder for a moment, his motions steady and sure. "You feel more frightened than excited."

"Yeah, I suppose I am. I've dreamed of having my own place for so long that it's scary to think I'm finally going to do it."

Tom moved to her right shoulder and continued working the stress out of her muscles. "What's happened with the plumber?"

"That went down the drain," Carol responded flippantly, "and I sure hope it's not a bad omen."

"When you own your own business, you'll probably be asked to join the Rotary Club, and who knows what else. You'll soon have more men after you than you can fend off."

He was such a dear soul, and Carol reached up to pat his hand. "That feels wonderful, Tom. You don't happen to know an amorous chiropractor my age, do you?"

"No, but I'll ask around. Maybe one of Sharon's professors would appeal to you."

Carol tried to imagine what he would be like. He would definitely have great hands, but would he have an equally charming personality, and if so, wouldn't he already have a wife?

"Yeah, but would I appeal to him? That's the real question."

"Oh, Mom, what's not to love about you?"

"This may be difficult for you to believe, but there are men who prefer willowly brunettes."

"No!"

"Believe me, it's true."

"Astounding." He worked a little more on her neck. "I'm sure it's no coincidence that Sharon is little and blonde, but I suppose everyone has a type they go for."

Carol didn't lament the fact that while Matt was most definitely her type, she obviously wasn't his. That seemed like such a superficial thing though. There had to be millions of couples who would have been successful together but had passed each other right by because they were the wrong height, or their eyes weren't blue. Disgusted by self-pity, she caught herself.

"I'm hoping to cultivate a passion for short, balding men who laugh too loud."

"Is that some kind of a joke?"

"No, it's just that there are so many of them, my odds of success have got to be good."

A perceptive young man, Tom could hear the pain beneath her teasing and came around to face her. "You don't really enjoy living alone, do you?"

Carol shook her head. "No, but that doesn't mean I want you and Sharon living here with me. Now you better get going. It's Saturday night, and I'm sure she doesn't want to spend all her time studying."

"I certainly hope not." Tom kissed her goodbye, and left swinging his tennis racquet.

Carol could remember being his age, and filled with optimism, but now she had been hammered into the ground one too many times. "Crimson Luxury will be a tremendous success though," she swore as she started down the hall to her bedroom. She was determined to create something marvelous and good from it, even if she couldn't spark a flicker of hope for herself.

Twenty

At his first opportunity, Dan Trenerry went through the back door marked Crimson Luxury. A carpenter had finished converting the rear into a stockroom and had built three spacious dressing rooms. Their louvered doors stood open and he caught a glimpse of himself in the full-length mirrors and quickly combed his curls with his fingers before going on. A crew of painters was working in the front, and the whole place smelled of the fresh coat of pearl gray paint they were applying.

Disappointed not to find Carol supervising them, he turned to go, then met her at the rear door. She was even prettier up close than she had appeared in the reunion photographs and he was glad he had made the effort to speak with her. She looked startled though, and he smiled and introduced himself.

"Good morning, Ms. Hagan. I'm Dan Trenerry, and since we're working next door, I just wanted to come in and say hello."

He was a handsome young man, and resembled his father so closely Carol would have known him even without an introduction. Only their coloring was different, and she assumed he must have inherited his mother's brown eyes.

"Good morning," she called brightly as she hurried by him. "I'm sorry, but I've got at least a million errands to run this morning and I've no time to stop and chat."

"Another time then." Dan peeked out in the alley, and not seeing his father anywhere around, he felt free to offer a bit of advice. "My dad might not know much about impressing women, but he has a good heart. Don't give up on him."

"Dan, really, I don't think—"

Dan shook his head to warn her to be still and ducked back into Casey's cafe. The Trenerry van had been parked in the alley for several days, but unwilling to risk seeing Matt, Carol had used the front door of her shop until the painters had blocked it with their ladders. She appreciated Dan's devotion to his father, but thought the young man badly misguided if he believed Matt's problem was merely a lack of social skills. His advice was also too late. She had not only given up on Matt Trenerry, she refused to waste another minute brooding over him.

She hurried to the front and taking care to keep out of the painters' way, admired their work. The pearl gray had a luminous glow that remained even after it dried and she was delighted with how pretty it looked. "The color's absolutely perfect."

"We're glad you're pleased, ma'am," the foreman replied. "We painted a store three times last month when the owner couldn't make up his mind."

Carol took care not to tread on the paint splattered dropcloth. "I can understand how that might happen, not everyone is able to imagine how a whole room will look from a tiny paint swatch."

"Almost like a first date, isn't it?" the painter chuckled. "Initially someone might look awfully good, but after a whole evening, we've often had more than enough of their company."

The painter was a tall man whose barrel chest filled out his overalls. He had thick gray hair and a beard, and while certainly not handsome, he possessed a jovial nature that made Carol smile each time she spoke with him. "What an interesting metaphor. I don't believe I've heard anyone compare paint to first dates, but you're right. There are both colors and people that rapidly lose their appeal."

"We're all looking for paint, as well as people, that look better to us each time we see them, but that fellow I mentioned was just plain confused. He started with a pale yellow, then had us paint the place light blue, and when he wasn't happy with that, we did it again in mint green."

"Was he satisfied then?"

"No, but he was out of money."

"Poor soul," Carol replied sympathetically. Dr. Strauss was covering the cost of the work in her shop, but she knew it wasn't cheap. Of course, neither was his rent, and he would recover his investment in the remodeling in a few months time. She wished the friendly painter a good day and excused herself. She walked back to the dressing rooms, shut the doors, and went on out to her car. She was on her way to the printers, but as she put her key into the ignition, Matt came out of Casey's cafe to get something from his van.

She hadn't seen him for a couple weeks, and in that time she had done everything she could to forget him. She had once had a terrible weakness for chocolate cake which she had cured by deliberately associating the delicious dessert with cockroaches. Now she could walk right by the pastry display in restaurants without so much as a tiny flicker of craving.

The cockroach trick hadn't worked with Matt

though. She had tried visualizing him as a grotesque sewer-dwelling mutant, but as she watched him walk back into the cafe, she knew her ploy had failed miserably because he still looked too damn good. "A worm-eaten molding mummy, a toxic waste spewing reptile, a lizard-skinned demon," she chanted, but while those images all conjured up thoroughly disgusting individuals, her imagination refused to superimpose Matt's face on any of them. The man had really gotten to her and he adamantly refused to let go.

The crimson carpet had been laid, the fixtures were delivered, and each day Carol was more delighted with the progress she had made. She had taken pictures of the place the morning they had signed the leases when there had been nothing but bare walls and now she saw the stamp of her dream everywhere she looked.

She and Casey had been running ads in both the *Pasadena Star News* and the *San Marino Tribune* announcing the coming opening of their businesses. She frequently saw people peeking in the front windows so she was certain they would attract a crowd when they opened. Keeping the customers would be the challenge, but she intended to offer not only expertise but also personal service other clothing shops couldn't match. She had had a rolled-top desk delivered, and was seated at it simply enjoying the fun of being the boss for a change when she heard a knock at the back door. She wasn't expecting a delivery, but hurried to answer.

Matt was standing there holding a dish of chocolate frozen yogurt sprinkled with chopped almonds. "Dan just came back with sundaes for all of us, and he must have miscounted because there's an extra one. I thought you might like to have it."

He held it out, and Carol had to admit it looked very tempting. She tried to focus on the creamy confection's soft swirls rather than his smile. "Is it nonfat yogurt?"

"You bet."

"Let me get my purse; I want to pay you for it."

Matt followed her into the shop. "No, you needn't do that. Think of it as a poor orphan sundae that will just melt into a sad puddle if you don't adopt it."

Carol plucked her purse off the desk. "Don't you have Casey's freezers hooked up by now?"

Matt hadn't expected her to see through his story so easily. He attempted a befuddled look. "I didn't even think of that."

Carol didn't bother to call him a liar, but she sure thought he was one. As she took the sundae, their fingertips touched and she felt the same jolt of magical energy that had previously been her undoing. She had to make a desperate grab so as not to drop the dish, then pretending to merely be clumsy she picked up the plastic spoon and took a bite. The yogurt was cool, smooth, and absolutely delicious.

She had continued to park out front and use the front door to avoid him, and she was astonished he had come looking for her, especially with such a feeble excuse. "You must have a very guilty conscience," she mused aloud.

"You don't know the half of it," Matt muttered under his breath. "It's just a spare sundae, not a bouquet of long-stemmed red roses."

"My mistake. This is awfully good. Would you like a bite?"

"No thanks, I've already had mine. That desk is a beauty." He ran his hand over the top, then walked toward the front of the shop, looked around and then came back to her side. "The pearl gray is a pretty color. I'm sorry I didn't sound more enthusiastic when you first mentioned it."

"You been sniffing some kind of toxic fumes, Matt? You just don't seem like yourself this afternoon. Maybe you ought to call the gas company and have them come out and check for leaks. I'd sure hate for the building to blow up after all the work we've put into it."

She was licking the frozen yogurt off the spoon with a provocative sweep that reminded him all too vividly of how warm her mouth had felt on him. He had to clear his throat to get his thoughts back where he wanted them. "You've got a real wicked sense of humor."

"Maybe it comes with being petite, a defense mechanism, you know? My fists aren't big enough to give a guy taller than a midget a black eye."

Matt watched her slide another spoonful of yogurt into her mouth and nearly choking on desire, had to turn away. "When does your stock arrive?"

"Not until right before the opening. I still have to hire a couple of salesclerks, and find someone to do alterations. I've made a list of everything that has to be done, and I'm counting my way down through it. What about you? Are you finished next door?"

"Just about."

Carol couldn't help but feel the yogurt was merely an excuse and that Matt had come over for a far more serious reason. He certainly looked uneasy, as though he were struggling for the words to convey something more meaningful than mere small talk about her boutique. Deliberately not making it easy for him, she continued to silently savor the refreshing coolness of the frozen yogurt.

"I enjoy doing remodeling," Matt remarked suddenly. "Home prices are so high most people can't afford to move and we're getting a lot of work on kitchens and baths."

Certainly remodeling couldn't possibly be what he had come to discuss either, Carol had a difficult time keeping the sarcasm out of her voice. "That's got to be a lot more exciting than a stopped-up toilet."

Matt knew he deserved that dig, but kept right on talking. "Yes, it most certainly is. I worked with a man last year who remodeled a Victorian house in South Pasadena hoping for a quick resale at a big profit. Unfortunately, he couldn't find a buyer even at a greatly reduced price, and so I finally bought it from him. Maybe you'd like to see it sometime."

"Sometime?" Carol had learned long ago that invitations that vague weren't worth the breath expended to extend them. "I suppose it's something of an architectural masterpiece?"

"Yeah, you could say that."

Carol stared at him a long moment. He kept shuffling his feet and taking his hands in and out of his hip pockets. He was usually such a confident person she was amazed to see him fidgeting as though his skin were itching from a bad sunburn. "Are you trying to ask me out on a date?"

"Well, not a date exactly," Matt rushed to explain. "I did the bathrooms and kitchen on the house and they're very attractive, but the rest of the place is empty. Your house is so pretty, I thought maybe you could give me some advice on how to decorate my new place."

Carol set the dish of yogurt down on her desk rather than hang it on his nose. "As I recall, you criticized my home for being too perfect, for looking like an Ethan Allen showroom, I believe you said."

"Well, let's just say I've come to appreciate home furnishings a lot more since I bought a new house. I'd really like you to see it."

Carol could hear a workman hammering next door, but the noise did not compare with the fierce pounding that had begun in her head. "First of all, I'm busy trying to open a boutique, so I have absolutely no time to do consulting work in interior design. Second, even if I had so much free time I were looking for volunteer work, I wouldn't help you decorate an outhouse. Now get out of my shop and don't come back."

"Maybe I phrased my request poorly."

Carol pointed toward the rear door. "*Au contraire,* Mr. Trenerry, no matter how beautifully you might have stated it, the answer would still have been no. I don't want anything to do with you. I don't even want to be around you. Having you next door has sickened me thoroughly and if you ever dare step in here after I've opened,

I'll call the police and have you arrested for shoplifting."

Matt walked out the door before Carol could continue.

Dan was waiting just outside. "Well, how did it go?"

"She threatened to have me arrested if I set foot in her shop again. Does that give you some idea of how fond she is of me?"

Dan had seen his father angry on several occasions, and he knew enough to stay well out of his way for the rest of the afternoon. He had really hoped a thoughtful gesture like a dish of frozen yogurt would provide his father with an opening. He had heard of women playing hard to get, but he feared Carol Hagan was taking it to ridiculous extremes.

Matt's temper remained on a slow burn for hours. He had completely lost patience with Carol, but the trouble was, he had no one to blame but himself for her present low opinion of him. His work for Casey was nearly finished, and he would be back to installing water heaters and making routine repairs, but the work that had once filled his days with activity, if not meaning, no longer presented a challenge or held any appeal.

He had tried to tell Carol he hoped to increase the time he spent on remodeling, but somehow he had failed to make his point. If she hadn't had a mouthful of yogurt, she probably would have spit on him. His talk with her had been about as successful as an attorney's questioning of a hostile witness but he had been a stupid fool to hope for anything better.

"I should have known," he moaned.

He went by the Victorian house on the way home. All he had moved in so far was a brass bed. He had splurged on Laura Ashley linens, but he had not slept there yet. He had not been able to shake the absurd notion the beautiful bed ought to be initiated with someone special. Someone like Carol.

He flopped back across the bed and lay still. He had not been able to forget Deborah when he had been with Carol, and now that Carol wanted no part of his life, he couldn't stop thinking about her. She definitely had spirit. It was part of her charm, but it was also damn intimidating. He stared up at the light fixture in the ceiling. It was functional, but not particularly attractive and he wanted his bedroom to be perfect.

"A fan!" he cried. What the bedroom needed was a Casablanca fan with glass tulip shades on the lights, and a rug, a beautiful Oriental carpet with the same blues and pinks as the floral linens. He checked his watch and cursed. It was too late in the day to go shopping now, but tomorrow, he would make a point of buying a ceiling fan and rug, then all he would need was a way to lure Carol back into bed.

Dan Trenerry waited until what looked like the last of the applicants for the salesclerk positions Carol had advertised had left before he stepped in the back door of her shop. "Excuse me, Ms. Hagan, I don't mean to bother you."

Carol was seated at her desk and swung her chair around to face him. "If you've come to offer more advice about your father, please leave before you embarrass us both."

Breaking into a disarming grin, Dan came on in. "No, actually this has nothing to do with him. My wife used to work at the Russell's in Pasadena and now that our son goes to preschool in the mornings, she's been thinking about looking for a part-time job. She's pretty and smart and I'd know you'd like her. Shall I tell her to come over for an interview?"

Carol had a pencil in her hand and placed it on the desk rather than snap it in two. "I think the less involvement your family has with mine, the better, Dan. I'm sure your wife is a lovely person, perhaps Russell's will hire her again."

"Russell's isn't hiring," Dan replied before realizing how insulting that would sound.

"What I mean is, she would rather work for a smaller place where she could learn more about the operation of the business. Dad's told her about you, and she admires what you've done on your own."

"I can't imagine your father having anything good to say about me."

"Well, that's where you're wrong," Dan insisted. "My mother's death hit him awfully hard. Maybe he wasn't quite ready to meet you when he did, and made some mistakes, but I wish you'd give him another chance."

Carol swallowed hard and pushed herself up out of her chair. "This isn't about chances. Your father walked out on me; it wasn't the other way around. You know how every time football season comes around Lucy holds the football for Charlie Brown, and he always falls for the same old trick and lands flat on his back when she jerks it away just as he kicks it? Now Charlie Brown is just a cartoon character, and that's a running gag in the strip, but I've learned the hard way that a man who'll abandon me once will do it again and again and again.

"There's no revolving door on my heart, Dan, and I won't go around and around when the result is so damn predictable. Now if your wife wants to apply for a position here, she's free to do so, but I sure wouldn't recommend it."

Badly disappointed, Dan's expression reflected his dismay. "I guess maybe you've never made any mistakes. That must be a real source of pride for you."

"No, it's precisely because I have made so damn many mistakes, and one of them was definitely with your father, that I know just how futile your suggestions are. Now would you please excuse me? I have more interviews scheduled for this afternoon and I'd rather not have anyone arrive while we're in the midst of an argument."

Carol Hagan was so little and cute Dan was tempted to just pick her up and carry her next door where she would have to face his father, but he had gotten to know her well enough to be certain that would only make her so angry she would never be civil to him. "You're exactly like my father," he said instead. "You're both so damn stubborn that it's amazing you ever got to know each other in the first place. Good luck with your business and your life, Ms. Hagan, you're going to need it."

Carol returned to her desk rather than hurl the bitter insult she thought he deserved. She wasn't stubborn, she was principled, but obviously he did not know the difference.

About an hour later, Casey came into Carol's shop. "How are your interviews going?"

Carol picked up the folder holding the applications she had received so far. "I should put out a pamphlet on tips for interviews, and not chewing gum would be right up there at the top. I don't think coming in a spandex outfit right after leaving an aerobics class is all that impressive either. Then there are the women who think it would be such fun to work in a place like this one day a week, but expect me to sell them clothes at a fifty percent discount. There were others who claimed they couldn't carry anything heavier than a single garment on a hanger, let alone work in a stockroom. What about you? Got your waiters and busboys all lined up?"

Casey shook his head. "I wouldn't complain if I were you. It sounds to me as though you've been getting the cream of the crop when it comes to prospective employees. I've hired a couple of men, and one woman who look like they'll be good workers, but I need more. I think we should have begun our hiring interviews much sooner."

"That's what worries me, Casey. We've put a lot of thought into everything we've done, and still we're making mistakes. It's the problems we can't anticipate that are going to kill us."

"Let's hope the consequences aren't that dire. Have you talked to Aimee yet? She wants to invite us for dinner this week to celebrate. It will be up at Gordon's place, which is apparently worth seeing."

"Oh yes, that's what I've heard. That would be fun, I could use a break from my own cooking." They were interrupted then by an attractive brunette who was neatly dressed, and not chewing gum. "Looks like things are looking up," Casey told Carol as he turned to go. "I'll talk to you later."

"Ms. Hagan? I hope it's all right for me to just stop by. If you have other appointments scheduled, I'll be happy to wait."

Impressed by the young woman's polite charm, Carol gestured toward the chair Casey had just left. "No, please come and sit down. Quite a few people have called and then not shown up so I have plenty of leeway." She handed her a clipboard with an application and a pen. "If you'll just fill this out first, then we'll talk."

Carol watched her write her first name and was relieved to find her printing legible. She had been handed other applications that were so impossible to read they did not even appear to be in English. It was a standard application form requiring personal information as well as references. She had already told several women who could not supply a single reference that she would be unable to hire them, and hoped this woman did not have that problem.

She had things to do at her desk and didn't look up until the young woman had completed the application and handed her back the clipboard. Her name was Janet Trenerry, and appalled she had not asked her name first, Carol was uncertain just how to respond. "Dan told me you thought you might be interested in working for me."

"Yes, I am. I used to love working in the executive sportswear department at Russell's. That was the one you bought for, wasn't it?"

Janet was tall and slender, and Carol couldn't help but think Dan and Matt must share the same taste in women. "Yes, I did, and that's the same type of merchandise I'll carry here." Carol worked her way through the questions she had asked the others and Janet supplied all the right answers. She was not only enthusiastic, but knowledgeable. Easily the best applicant she had interviewed, Carol knew she would be foolish not to hire her because of her father-in-law.

"I'm very impressed with your experience, and your charm, Janet. We're having a party at Casey's this Friday night, and then we'll be open for business on Saturday. Now Dan mentioned you'd be available when your son is in preschool, but what about Saturdays? Will they be a problem for you?"

"No, Dan is home then, and if there are any

emergencies, his father, or one of his other men can handle them."

"Other men?"

"Yes, Dan and his father have several other plumbers working for them."

"I didn't realize it was such a vast enterprise."

Thinking Carol was teasing, Janet laughed. "Hardly vast, but certainly very profitable. I want a part-time job, but I don't have to have one to help support us. There are doctors and attorneys who don't make what Matt and Dan do. But, they're always the ones who are invited to join the country clubs, aren't they?"

"Does that bother you?"

"No, not at all."

"Good." Carol pulled a card from one of the slots in her desk. "Here's an invitation to Friday night's party. Bring Dan along with you. It'll be informal. There will be others your age there, and I'm sure you'll enjoy it. I will check your references, but I expect them to be good so I'll need you here at nine on Saturday morning."

"Thank you, Ms. Hagan. I won't disappoint you."

As Carol told Janet goodbye, she couldn't help but wonder how much Dan had told her, then decided it really didn't matter. Matt was a part of the past, and she intended to have a great future. Before she could return to her desk, a young man came in.

"Ms. Hagan, I'm Wayne Stowbridge. I spoke with you earlier. Your shop is divine, absolutely divine and I can't wait to go to work for you."

Wayne's spiked hair was dyed a deep burgundy shade that contrasted sharply with what had to be aqua contact lenses. He had three gold earrings in his left ear, and was wearing a purple silk shirt, and zebra-striped pants. Had she not worked in downtown Los Angeles where such flamboyant individuals were commonplace she might have thought his appearance odd, but she had seen plenty of men with such unusual taste in apparel and did not even bat an eye.

"Would you mind unpacking boxes, Wayne, or steaming out wrinkles in dozens of garments, or changing window displays?"

"No, I would love it, especially the window displays. That's my real forte. I hope someday to work for one of the big chains. I can't imagine anything more rewarding than walking into a store in Pasadena or San Diego and finding the decor I had devised throughout. What a thrill!"

"Just fill out this application, Wayne, and I'll see what I can do for you." Her merchandise was due to begin arriving the next day and Carol knew she could put an ambitious young man like Wayne to good use, and then she would send him off to Russell's with a recommendation to the manager of the display department, and hope he found work where he belonged.

Carol was as impressed with Gordon's beautiful home as Aimee had been. At his urging she wandered the downstairs taking note of every exquisite detail. There wasn't an inch of the magnificent house that wasn't superbly done, and she wished she could achieve that same level of artistry in her shop. She heard Suzanne teasing Casey as he helped Aimee and Gordon in the kitchen and feeling very alone, followed the path down to the lily pond.

It was a place of such tranquil beauty, she could not help but envy Gordon's good fortune in owning it. Spotting a penny on the path, she closed her eyes to make a wish, hoped for success, and tossed it in. It made a tiny splash, and the ripples traveled across the water, scattering the moonglade but in a matter of seconds, the dark pool was again calm.

If I were a pond, she thought to herself, I'd be one with a Jacuzzi, and the water would be in a constant state of turbulence. Fearing she was being rude to stray off on her own, she turned back toward the house, but hesitated when she saw a man coming her way. At first thinking it was Casey, she waited for him, and too late she recognized Matt.

"I didn't realize you'd been invited."

"It's very rude to ask your hostess for the guest list before agreeing to attend a party," he replied. "Why wouldn't I be invited? I've been a part of this group longer than Gordon."

"If this is a 'group,' then it's one of people who care about one another, and you and I don't belong."

The moonlight lent her blond curls a silvery sheen and Matt wished the romantic nature of the spot would affect her as strongly as it did him. "I stopped by a bookstore today to look for something to help me have better relationships."

"My God, I'm astounded. You must be the first man ever to venture into that section. Did the clerks faint?"

Matt tried to view her sarcasm as pain, and held his temper. "No, none did, but there were so damn many books on the shelves I couldn't decide which one to buy. It really looked to me as though the so-called experts have no idea what they're talking about. I guess love has always been a mystery."

They were outdoors on a balmy evening so Carol couldn't accuse him of sniffing funny fumes again, but he certainly didn't sound like himself. "Yeah, it's a mystery all right, with too many red herrings and dead bodies for my tastes. I think we ought to go on up to the house. Supper was almost ready when I left."

Matt shook his head. "Not yet. They'll wait for us."

Carol tried to think of cockroaches, mutants, and demons as he lowered his mouth to hers but the warmth of his lips felt too good. Thoroughly distracted, she slid her hands across his chest, and felt his heart beating as rapidly as her own. Now she could smell the fragrance of his cologne, and combined with his delicious taste and touch, she might have been content to remain in his arms for hours, but something soft and wet hopped across her instep and she leapt back, barely able to stifle a scream.

"What's wrong?"

Terrified, Carol backed away. She kept looking around and trying to find the creature. "Some slimy swamp thing just slithered across my foot."

Matt bent down and swished his hand through the water. "I don't see any swamp things. What an imagination you have."

"No, you're the one with the imagination. Just who do you think you are coming down here and kissing me like, like—"

Slowly, Matt rose and stretched to his full height. "Like what?"

Several brutal epithets came to Carol's mind, but she swallowed them all. "Like a man who doesn't know what he wants from one day to the next. Now come on, let's go back to the house."

Matt moved across the path to block her way. "No, not until you promise to come home with me. I want to show you my new house."

"I haven't the slightest desire to see it."

"Then we'll just stand out here all night." He folded his arms across his chest.

"Bully."

"Yes, I am. It's the house I want you to see, Carol. Hell, I haven't got anything left to show you."

Carol could see four figures silhouetted against the living room lights. "They're all watching us."

"So what? We're not doing anything particularly interesting, let alone lewd. If you don't count looking for swamp things."

Thoroughly exasperated with him, Carol put her hands on her hips. "If I agree to visit your house, I'm going to go in my own car, and I'm not staying a minute longer than it takes to walk through the rooms."

"Fair enough." Matt moved aside and gestured toward the path with a deep bow. "After you, my dear."

Infuriated more with her weakness for him than with him, Carol just wished he weren't too big to flush.

Twenty-one

Matt swatted Carol's fanny as she slipped by him. She turned, and while he could not see her expression clearly in the shadows, he knew she had to be livid. In one of the books he had perused, he had come across the statement that indifference was the opposite of love, not anger. That had been such an encouraging thought he savored it still. Carol's attitude could be described in many colorful ways, but indifference certainly wasn't among them.

"Isn't the pond lovely?" Aimee asked as Carol and Matt returned to the house. "In the daytime you can see frogs sunning themselves on the lilypads. It's as perfect a scene as the illustrations in children's classics."

"Frogs," Matt repeated with a wicked grin. "Carol was sure she was being attacked by swamp things."

"Then it's lucky you were there to protect

her," Casey offered with a teasing poke to Matt's ribs. They had become good friends in the time Matt had worked on Casey's cafe.

"Yes, indeed." Matt winked at Carol, but she did not look in the least bit amused.

"Wasn't *Swamp Thing* a film?" Suzanne asked.

"Yes," Gordon answered. "It was about a scientist who, due to a botched experiment, was more plant than man but as I recall he was quite fond of Adrienne Barbeau."

Carol listened as her friends continued to discuss monster movies as they moved into the dining room. They seemed to be totally unaware of her discomfort and with all of them enjoying themselves she wasn't about to point out how truly frightened she had been. Because the brief scare had gotten her out of Matt's arms, when the wine had been poured, she immediately raised her glass. "To swamp things everywhere."

Once they had all drunk to that peculiar toast, Gordon proposed another. "To Aluminum Moons and Crimson Luxury. May you both have unlimited success and enduring happiness."

Touched, Carol took a second sip, but not wanting the evening to end in a wine-drenched haze, she only pretended to drink to all the others. Gordon and Aimee had prepared spinach-stuffed chicken breasts baked in orange juice, which were superb. Casey exclaimed how good the dish was at length. Although hungry, Carol had to concentrate on chewing and swallowing, and all the while she felt the heat of Matt's body beside her.

It's only chemistry, she tried to convince herself, merely a bizarre happenstance which did not have be to indulged. What she was looking for was a short, balding gentleman who laughed too loud, and while she was positive he would not excite her clear to her toes, she was equally sure he would never treat her like a one night stand.

"Karen says her paintings look spectacular in your cafe, Casey," Aimee said. "She's had several shows, but I don't believe she's ever been as excited as she is about this one."

"Her work is what's spectacular," Casey exclaimed. "I'm delighted she was able to participate in the opening. Several of her friends have come to see me in hopes I'll invite them to display their work after Karen's so I'll be able to continue having original art for some time. I hope indefinitely."

He raised his wine glass in another salute. "I owe this all to you, Matt. If you hadn't told Carol how smart we'd be to open our own businesses together, I wouldn't have had the courage to begin now."

Matt couldn't accept his praise. "You've

turned a mere suggestion into reality, so the credit rightfully belongs to you and Carol."

Aimee added a toast of her own. "I'd like to thank Carol for a different reason. If she hadn't been so adamant about us having dates for the reunion, none us would be here tonight."

As they raised their glasses, Suzanne leaned over to kiss Casey and Gordon gave Aimee a hug. Carol could feel Matt watching her, but she felt none of the other two couples' elation. "Let's regard it as serendipity," she suggested. "After all, all I wanted was for us to have partners for the dancing. I didn't envision any lasting romantic liaisons or business ventures."

"You're being far too modest," Matt argued. "Who knows, maybe the reunion was merely the beginning of a whole chain of remarkable relationships and events."

"Yes," Suzanne cried, "and we've only seen the first couple of links."

"Please," Carol begged, "I'm not usually superstitious, but I'd rather not begin celebrating before the first month's receipts are all in." She pushed a bit of chicken around her plate. "Whenever things are too good to be true, you know they're not going to stay that way long."

Gordon smiled at Aimee. "Has Carol always been such a pessimist?"

Aimee considered his question, and provided a thoughtful response. "I think most of us lose a bit of our youthful optimism over the years. Life has a way of handing us all disappointments, and tragedies. It's difficult not to fear the sorrows won't repeat themselves."

Knowing she was referring to her husband's death, Gordon was sorry he had asked. "Well, I'm optimistic, and I'm looking forward to tomorrow night. Now is everyone ready for dessert? Aimee made the peach cobbler and it's awfully good."

The cobbler was as delicious as promised, but even with a cup of coffee Carol felt tired. When she attempted unsuccessfully to cover a yawn, her friends all laughed at her. "I'm sorry. Will you excuse me please? I got up early this morning, and I've got to get up early again tomorrow. I'll see you all tomorrow night."

Matt rose with her. "I've got an early job tomorrow too so I'll walk you to your car." He thanked both Aimee and Gordon, wished Suzanne and Casey a good night, and then had to hurry to catch up with Carol. "Wait," he called as she preceded him down the walk. "You need my address."

"What I need is a good night's sleep."

"A promise is a promise," Matt insisted. He pulled a business card from his wallet and wrote the address of his new house on the back before providing simple directions. "I know you won't get lost, but why don't you follow me?"

Feeling trapped, Carol took the card. "I can't stay more than a few minutes."

"That's all I ask." Matt started to back away. "See you there."

Resigned to visiting the house, Carol got into her BMW and followed Matt. They turned south on Oak Knoll, and west on Monterey Road until they reached his street in south Pasadena and turned north. Matt had left lights burning inside the lovely Victorian home and as she parked in front, Carol could not help but be both impressed and intrigued.

"Isn't this place a bit large for you?" she asked as Matt opened her door.

"It has five bedrooms," Matt replied, "but I like having lots of room. Come on in." He took her hand as they went up the walk, but didn't attempt to touch her again after he had unlocked the front door. "The floors and paneling are all oak. The previous owner tore out about half a mile of wall-to-wall carpeting, and I intend to buy rugs to show off the floors."

"Yes, you should." Even bare, the living room held an inviting warmth. There was a fireplace framed with marble, and she could easily imagine the long mantel spread with Christmas greens. The room had a fresh coat of white paint, as did the dining room. "You might want to experiment with more color."

"Thank you, yes, I don't like everything

white either." He led her through the den, and downstairs bath which was painted in a soft rose, with rose tile.

"You did all the work in here?" Carol asked.

"I can't take all the credit. Another firm did the custom shower doors, and the man I usually work with on remodels did the tile."

The bathroom looked brand new, and impressed by the expert craftsmanship, Carol managed a slight smile. "This is as beautiful as the work Russell's design department does. Let's see the kitchen." She followed Matt down the hall into the spacious kitchen and breakfast room. Pale blue and white, it was not only charming, but well planned to provide the optimum use of space and the latest in appliances. "I understand you must have had to hire subcontractors, but you do extraordinary work, Matt. I'm really impressed."

Matt had not been hoping for praise for his work, and embarrassed, just shrugged. There was an intercom system that could pipe music throughout the house and he switched it on to what had become his favorite station. Smokey Robinson's poignant, "Tears of A Clown," was playing. It struck him as all too close to the truth and he turned the volume down low.

"I want you to see the upstairs." The wide staircase had a handsomely carved oak banister and railing, but their steps echoed with a hollow ring as they climbed to the second floor. "Let's start down at the end," he suggested, and with sparing comments, he directed his informal tour so that it ended at the master bedroom.

After walking through a succession of empty rooms, Carol was delighted by the lovely decor. The walls were a pale mauve, nearly matching her bedroom. The brass bed's undulating curves were appealing, the Laura Ashley comforter inviting, the lace curtains at the windows draped perfection, the floral-patterned carpet a gentle cushion for her step, and the overhead lights and fan a delight.

"If you did this room yourself, then you don't need any help, Matt. It's lovely. Just trust your instincts and I'm sure you'll have an attractively decorated home."

Matt had remained at the door, subtly blocking her exit. "Thank you, but there's a big difference between putting a single bedroom together and decorating an entire house. Sit down a minute. I need to talk with you."

Carol turned to look for a chair, but the only place to sit was the magnificent bed. "Oh no, you don't. I think I better stand. Better yet, let's do this another time."

Doubting he would have both the nerve and opportunity to speak with her there any time soon, Matt shook his head. "No, this won't take long. You always look as though you're wound too tight, Carol. Just try and relax for a minute if you can." Taking his own advice, he folded his arms across his chest to get comfortable, and leaned against the doorjamb.

"My wife died just before our twenty-fifth wedding anniversary. She'd been sick for a couple of years, and despite having the best doctors and treatment available, she didn't make it. I had really believed that she would though. I kept thinking the next round of chemotherapy, or radiation would zap the last of the cancer and we'd be together to not only celebrate our twenty-fifth anniversary, but probably our fiftieth as well.

"The last time she went into the hospital, her doctor tried to tell me she wouldn't be coming out, but I refused to believe him. Deborah knew though, and she didn't fight it. She just let go. I knew it was a blessing that she'd been freed from her pain, but still I was angry to have been left alone, and even worse, I felt guilty that I'd never had a sick day in my life and she'd suffered so horribly."

When Matt paused to wipe his eyes, Carol wanted to say something, anything to let him know she understood, but fearing he would simply criticize her for interrupting him, she kept still. She gripped the edge of the bed, wadding the luxurious comforter in her fists. She knew his confession would be therapeutic for him, but as long as his memories of his late wife were so intense, she doubted he could ever care for her, and that impossibility hurt very badly.

"The last four years have been a blur because all I've done is work. One day was exactly like the next until I met you at the barbecue at your place. The instant our eyes met I remembered exactly what it felt like to be attracted to a woman."

With the subject no longer as sensitive, Carol felt obliged to speak. "But I'm not your type, Matt. I'm not tall, or brunette, and my tennis game is lousy."

Matt appeared to be puzzled. "What makes you think I only go for tall, brunette, tennis champions?"

Carol sighed softly. "You described Donna Strauss as gorgeous, and we couldn't be more dissimilar."

Matt walked over to the bed, sat down beside her, and took her hand. "You see what I mean about being wound too tight? You're like one of those little wind-up plastic frogs hip-hopping all around without any idea where you're going. Donna is attractive, but I was being flippant because her husband looked so damn perfect I was sure he wore starched pajamas. I didn't realize you'd think I was seriously attracted to her or I'd have kept my mouth shut."

"Strauss would wear silk pajamas if he wears any, but I see what you mean."

"Good, I'm making progress then." Matt had rehearsed the next part endlessly but still wasn't satisfied he would make any sense. "I swear I'll never forget the night of the reunion, but when I woke up the next morning–"

Carol opened her mouth and knowing she was going to tell him to stop, Matt gave her a quick kiss to silence her. "Please be patient with me for just a little while longer," he begged. "When I woke up, you were all snuggled against me, all warm and sweet, and for an instant I felt as though the world was perfect again, and then I was overwhelmed with guilt for enjoying being with you so much when Deborah was gone and would never make love again.

"In a split second I was right back where I was the night she died. The anger, the rage, the guilt, they were exactly the same and I didn't want to ever feel that bad again, so I sat on the floor just trying to hang on to my sanity until you woke up and I could tell you making love had been a mistake. That you saw right through me didn't surprise me, but I was afraid you'd think I was nuts if I told you being as happy as you'd made me caused me such terrible guilt."

Dan had encouraged her to be patient with Matt, but Carol doubted she would live long enough for him to get over his wife's loss. She gave his fingers a fond squeeze. "And it's guilt that's prompted you to speak to me now, isn't it? You know you've hurt me, and you're ashamed. What do you want me to say, that I forgive you?"

"No, I want you to say that you love me, and the future is all that matters now."

Dumbfounded, Carol was certain she could not possibly have heard him correctly. "Excuse me?"

When she opened her eyes that wide, her lashes nearly swept her brows, and Matt thought her astonishment wonderfully endearing. "I bought this house not simply to escape the past, but to put it behind me. Deborah and I had something very special, but that doesn't mean that I can't love you, or that we can't have something even better together. You sure haven't given me much in the way of encouragement, but if you'll just forgive me for getting so lost in my own misery that I couldn't see how terrific our life together could be, I'll never make you sorry."

When Carol just continued to stare at him, Matt took another tact. "Look at it this way, this house is a lot closer to Crimson Luxury, so if you move in here, you'll not only save time on the commute, you'll save quite a bit on your gasoline bills too."

That prosaic comment was enough to jar

Carol out of her shocked silence. She didn't want to live with him. He had married the last woman he had loved, and she wouldn't settle for anything less. He had said that he loved her though, and that was at least a place to start. "I wish you'd been honest with me that afternoon at my house."

"I couldn't; it hurt too much."

"But not too much to lie? No, Matt, if we're ever going to have anything more than that one night together, you have to promise to always be honest with me. Love can't survive in a climate of lies."

"I know." But rather than offer the promise she required, he drew her into his arms and kissed her. Not wanting to frighten her away, he was very gentle until he was sure of her response, then feeling free to give way to his passion for her, he pulled her down onto the bed with him. "I love everything about you," he whispered between kisses, "even your sharp tongue."

Flattered, breathless, aroused, Carol answered each of his tender kisses with an ever more demanding ardor. He unzipped her dress. She unbuttoned his shirt, and then with clothes only in the way they had to leave the bed to shake them off. Matt had installed a dimmer switch on the lights, and turned them down before returning to the bed. The strains of, "A

Summer Place," were floating softly in the background and he moved up over her, nuzzling her creamy skin the whole way.

"I wish I had some yogurt," he whispered, "so you could lick it off me the way you licked it off that spoon."

Carol knew what he wanted and readily supplied it with sweet kisses, teasing nibbles, and languid licks. He was so easy to love when the warmth of his skin drew her close. His taste was delicious, his scent intoxicating and she knew making love with him would always be an adventure. His caress grew insistent, his kisses deep and she lured him on, wanting still more of his thrilling affection.

She wondered ever so briefly how many other couples had found the same bliss in the pretty room, and hoped it had been a great many. She knew she had been set up when Matt reached into the nightstand for a condom, but was in no mood to complain that he had lured her there under false pretenses. He had brought her here for this, for love, and she wanted all he could give.

Hungry for him, she writhed beneath him, meeting his thrusts in an ageless dance that fused their very souls before bringing them to a stunning climax. Matt's soft moan of surrender matched her own, and thinking they were as perfect a pair as any who had ever found each other, she held him in her arms until he fell asleep. She slid her hand over his hip and up his back, trapped by his weight and yet loving it. She knew he was right about her usually being far too tense, but at that moment, she felt at perfect peace, and wished the night did not have to end so soon.

But Matt wasn't asleep. He was simply savoring how good it felt to hold a woman in his arms. It had been too long, but pressed against Carol, he knew she wasn't just a woman who shared his need for affection, but the perfect woman for him. He raised up slightly. "Am I crushing you?"

"No, you feel good." Carol looped her arms around his waist.

She was resting easily beneath him, all trace of her earlier anxiety gone. He brushed her lips with an adoring kiss. "Do you feel as peaceful as you look?"

"Hmm." He nuzzled her throat, and she raised her hands to ruffle his curls. "You have such great hair."

"Thanks, but what if I go bald?"

Carol frowned slightly, pretending to be imagining him without his gorgeous silver curls. "I'd have to cultivate a passion for bald men, but I don't believe that would be much of a challenge when you have so many other fine qualities."

"Really? Like what?"

"You needn't fish for compliments. I'm sure a great many come your way."

"I hadn't noticed," he denied with teasing modesty.

Carol raised up to kiss him. "I've got to get home. Let me up."

"You're going home?"

He was obviously astonished, but Carol tried not to offend him. "Yes. I told you I couldn't stay long, and I meant it."

The firmness of her tone left no doubt as to her determination to leave, and Matt rolled over. He sat up on the side of the bed. "I just thought you'd want to stay."

Carol reached out to caress his back. "I do, but I have a shop to open this Saturday. If I lie in bed all night with you, I'll be too tired tomorrow to get any work done and I won't be ready when my first customers arrive."

Elvis' recording of, "You Were Always On My Mind," was playing and as he listened to the guilt-laced song, he was firmly convinced she was making the wrong choice. He also knew if he said so, he would probably lose her for good. An icy chill shot up his spine. Go slow, he told himself. He looked around for his pants, got up and yanked them on. He pulled on his shirt, but left it unbuttoned.

"I'll walk you out to your car."

"Thanks, but I'll need a few minutes. She carried her clothes into the adjacent bathroom to dress. It was papered in a pretty print with bunches of violets on a lacy white background. The tile was white, with lavender accents and she thought it a beautiful compliment to the bedroom. She opened the door a crack and called out, "This room is perfectly lovely!"

Right then, compliments on the decor weren't what Matt wanted, but he tried not to sound as disappointed as he felt. "Thanks."

Once dressed, Carol grabbed a tissue to wipe the smudges of mascara from beneath her eyes. She had a brush in her purse and fluffed out her curls before putting on lipstick. She looked presentable enough to drive home, but she didn't really want to leave. She longed to stay with Matt, but couldn't, and torn, she found it difficult to smile as she joined him.

She would have offered another apology, but Matt took her arm and escorted her down the stairs and out to her car before she could get out a single word. He had described Deborah as a homemaker who had had many friends and interests, and from the way he was behaving it seemed obvious he would prefer her to be the same. Well, she doubted she was anything like Deborah and she did not even want to be.

She paused before getting into her car. "The party's tomorrow night. Are you coming?"

"I wouldn't miss it," Matt swore. "But what about tomorrow? If you've got so much to do, I'll be glad to help."

"Thank you, but Wayne and I can handle everything."

That she might have another man who had already volunteered to work in the shop and her life was more than Matt could accept calmly. "Who the hell is Wayne?"

Matt looked flabbergasted, and Carol couldn't help but laugh. "He's a stockboy with hopes of becoming a display artist, all of twenty-two years old, and absolutely no threat to you. Really, Matt, did you think I'd scheduled several lovers to help me on different days?"

Feeling very foolish, Matt opened her car door for her. "Frankly, I'm not all that sure just what you might do, but I'm looking forward to finding out."

Carol gave him a last kiss, then got into her car, and drove away. It was one of the most difficult things she had ever had to do, and knowing how badly she had disappointed Matt, she hoped she could make things up to him soon.

After Carol and Matt had left, Suzanne and Casey had stayed with Aimee and Gordon for more than an hour, and despite their divergent careers, the men got along well with one another. The conversation flowed easily, and they parted looking forward to seeing each other again on Friday night. Aimee and Gordon waved goodbye from the front porch, and she hugged him as soon as they went back inside.

"I think Casey and Carol have a good chance for success, don't you?"

"Yes, I do. We can eat at Aluminum Moons as often as you like, but you'll have to be the one to patronize Carol's shop."

"Not necessarily. I'm certain she plans to have gift certificates."

"Isn't that rather cold?"

"No, not at all. I'd much rather have a gift certificate from Crimson Luxury than a blender as a gift."

Gordon followed her into the kitchen where they began to stack the dishes in the sink. "A blender is the kind of gift a devoted, if misguided, husband gives, Aimee, not me."

They had never discussed marriage, and Aimee was surprised by how embarrassed she was by his off-hand remark. Attempting to hide her blush, she opened the dishwasher, and rinsed the first plate rather than respond, but she could feel him watching her as he stacked the cups and saucers. She did love him, and was confident in his love for her, but the thought of marriage rekindled too many old fears of abandonment and betrayal.

Gordon had noted the change in Aimee's mood and correctly guessed the cause. Wanting to discuss the subject further, he waited until they had loaded the dishwasher, and tossed the tablecloth and napkins in the laundry basket. With his house in order, he started on his life. "Come on, let's go down to the pond."

"You're not worried about an invasion of swamp things?"

"Not in the least." He took her hand and led the way. The night had cooled, and when they reached the pond he stepped behind Aimee and wrapped her in his arms. "This has to be one of the most romantic spots on Earth, or at least in Pasadena."

"Somehow I think a trip to the dry cleaners would be romantic with you, Ash."

"I'm glad you think so." He waited, hoping that she would confide more but when she didn't, he hugged her more tightly. "I think nowadays couples discuss marriage together rather than the woman anxiously waiting for the man to propose. I know you have a lot of doubts, and fears, so I'll wait for as long as it takes for you to be ready, Aimee, but please, don't ever doubt how much I want you for my wife. Whenever you're comfortable with the idea of my being your husband, we'll set the date for the wedding."

The sweet scent of night-blooming jasmine

filled the air, and standing at the edge of the moonlit pond, Aimee found Gordon's reassuring words sublimely romantic, but that did not mean he changed her view of reality. "How did Carol put it, that whenever things are too good to be true, you know they can't last?"

Disappointed by her response, Gordon placed his hands on her shoulders to turn her around. "She said something like that, but while I'll agree there are a great many things we can't control, if you and I want a good marriage, then we're sure to have it. All it takes is the willingness to try. You do seem too good to be true, Aimee, but I'd never back away out of some ridiculous superstition that good things never last."

"Sometimes that's experience, not superstition."

"Well, how about, 'the third time's a charm'?"

"You'd not be embarrassed to be my third husband?"

"Hell, no. I'm sorry I wasn't further up in the order, but third is fine with me as long as I'm the last husband you ever have."

"We've not known each other nearly long enough to discuss marriage, Ash."

"How many times must I remind you we've known each other more than thirty-five years?" Convinced verbal arguments weren't nearly as good as far more persuasive silent ones, he kissed her very slowly, and deeply. "I love you," he whispered before kissing her again. "That's all you'll ever need to know."

Standing in his arms, his vow was so easy to believe. Aimee breathed in the seductive scent of jasmine, and made a decision in an instant she knew she would never regret. "Let's get married in the fall, before JoAnne begins medical school. I hope that isn't too long an engagement for you."

"Sweetheart, anything less than thirty-five years is fine with me." He picked her up off her feet in a boisterous hug, but when he set her down, she jumped. "What's the matter?" he asked.

"I don't know, but I think I just stepped on a swamp thing."

Laughing happily, Gordon took her hand. "Come on up to my bedroom where you're sure to be safe."

As Aimee went with him, her smile was wide. She did feel safe with Gordon, and even better, she felt loved, and even if it were too good to be true, she knew they could make it last as long as they lived.

Casey waited until he and Suzanne were in bed together to bring up one of his favorite subjects. "I know you don't want us to live together,

Suz, and I respect that. The problem is, I don't really need a condo in West Lost Angeles now that I've gone into business in San Marino. I could buy a house close to you, but because I doubt I'd spend much time there, that seems like an awful waste of money. Why don't we just go ahead and get married?"

Snuggled in his arms, it was difficult to argue, and Suzanne knew Casey had planned it that way. Still, she forced herself to sit up. "I'll consider it only if you'll agree to having a prenuptial agreement stating that Aluminum Moons is your business rather than ours. Now I realize you will have begun the business before we married, so technically it would be solely your enterprise, but if, God forbid, we can't make a go of it, I don't want you to ever worry, or stay with me, solely because you're afraid you're going to lose everything again in a divorce."

"What?" Casey sat up and turned on the lamp on the nightstand. "You sound as though you've put a lot more thought into this than I have."

"It never hurts to be practical, Casey."

She was wearing the filmy floral nightgown he liked, and with her curls tumbling over her shoulders she looked anything but practical. "I keep forgetting you've got such a keen mind. I'll bet you're always going to be several steps ahead of me."

Suzanne leaned over to kiss him. "A married couple ought to function as a team."

Casey pushed her down into the pillows. "I think we make one hell of a team. You've got the looks and brains, and I can cook."

"Oh, Casey, you can do a lot more than cook."

Accepting that playful challenge, Casey devoted most of the night to proving just how right she was.

Twenty-two

Matt hadn't expected the party to be so crowded, but apparently Carol and Casey had invited everyone they had ever met. Karen Reis's paintings were big, bright splashes of color that blended shape, texture, and line into explosive patterns reminiscent of kaleidoscopes, but the people filling the cafe were such a colorful group, the festive art was a mere blur in the background. Hugging the wall, Matt attempted to make his way toward the front, but his progress was impeded by the guests discussing the paintings, and he finally had to move out into the slowly churning crowd in the center of the room.

Since coming in, he had tried to locate Carol but feared someone of her diminutive size might not be found until the guests had all left for home. He saw Dan and Janet on the far side of the room and waved, then had a difficult time putting his arm down again at his side. From the bits of conversation he overheard, it appeared a great many of the people present were friends from Russell's, which was understandable, along with Karen's friends who were considerably younger, many dressed in whimsical fashions of their own design.

Casey had decided against allowing guests to sit out front at the sidewalk tables because people driving by would then be likely to stop and want to join in the party. He would welcome them with open arms tomorrow, but tonight, this was a private celebration. Still looking for a face he recognized, Matt headed toward a red-haired woman and was relieved when she turned toward him to see it truly was Suzanne.

"Hi, everything seems to be going well," he greeted her.

"Too well," Suzanne replied. "Neither Casey nor Carol expected so many of the people they had invited to actually come tonight. I'm afraid we've exceeded the lawful capacity of the cafe, but we'll just have to hope the fire marshall doesn't choose tonight to make a spot check. Does Carol know you're here?"

"I doubt it. Have you seen her, I can't find her."

Suzanne stretched up on her tiptoes. "She was over in the far corner a while ago, but I don't see her now. Well, I'm sure you'll find each other eventually."

"I sure hope so."

"Oh, you'll never guess who called me today," Suzanne supplied the answer before Matt could reply, "Sergeant Vasquez. He'd talked with Megan Shank and she told him Jack has gone with her for counseling. He seemed satisfied that she and Jack were doing better and made a rather grudging compliment about the brawl having some good effect."

Matt couldn't think of the reunion without smiling a bit too broadly. "Yeah, that was quite a night, wasn't it? I'm glad things are looking up for the Shanks."

"Maybe that's another of the links you mentioned."

"Possibly," Matt agreed. "I'm going to launch another expedition through the crowd to find Carol. I'll talk with you later."

Suzanne caught his sleeve, and gave him a kiss on the cheek. "Thanks, Matt, for doing such a beautiful job on the kitchen, and for never letting Casey doubt his decision to open his own cafe."

Touched by her gratitude, Matt gave her hand a tender squeeze before moving on. Sighting Aimee, he turned sideways to slip by a heavyset man, and reached her with a minimum of effort. She was talking with two dark-haired young women she quickly introduced as her daughters, JoAnne, and Karen.

"I like your work, Karen," Matt responded. "Of course, it would be a lot easier to appreciate if there weren't so many people here."

"Thank you. I hope everyone who's really intrigued by the paintings will come back next week when there isn't such a crush. I've already sold a couple to some of Casey's friends from Russell's." Hearing her name called, she glanced away, and then broke into an embarrassed smile. "Excuse me, will you? One of my friends appears to be trapped by the front door and I want to speak with him. Come with me, JoAnne."

"Of course." Matt waited until the attractive pair had moved out into the crowd. "You must be very proud of your daughters."

"Yes, I certainly am, but I'm surprised to see Roger here tonight. He's the blond waving. I must say I admire his persistence."

"That's a good quality in a man."

Aimee reached out to take Gordon's hand as he drew near. "I was just complimenting Roger for his persistence, but that's definitely one of your most attractive traits as well."

"Why thank you. Carol just asked me if I'd seen you, Matt. I think she's a bit overwhelmed by the turnout tonight."

"So am I. Where was she?"

"Up near the front. Good luck."

"Thanks." Matt had not been swift enough to follow in Karen and JoAnne's wake and he had to again twist, and turn to navigate through the crowd. When he reached the front, Karen introduced him to Roger who struck him as a nice young man, but Carol was nowhere to be found.

"I was hoping to find Carol up here. Have you seen her?"

Roger shoved a pate topped cracker into his mouth, and hurriedly swallowed. "She was here just a minute ago, but I think she was headed toward the back of the room when she left us."

Glancing down the jammed length of the cafe, Matt didn't look forward to again being bounced around like the silver ball in a pinball machine and shook his head. "Well, I'm bound to find her sooner or later. Thanks."

Seeing his son about ten feet away, Matt guided himself in his direction. Dan and Janet where talking with two other young couples. Believing them to be Karen's friends, he noted only that they were attractive until Dan introduced them as Carol's sons, Rob, and Tom, and their dates, Linda and Sharon. Embarrassed, he had not recognized Rob, he quickly mentioned they had met, and greeted Tom just as warmly. He had been worried about how Dan would get along with two young men who could write "Dr." in front of their names, but obviously Dan and Janet were having no trouble at all making conversation. Relieved, he stayed with them only a few minutes.

"Have you seen your mother?" he asked. "I'm afraid I'm just chasing her around the room and I can't seem to catch up with her."

"Well, she's pretty excited," Tom replied, "so she's not staying in one place very long. She was headed back toward the kitchen when she left, but that's no guarantee that she ever got there."

"Thanks." Adopting a new tactic, Matt slowed his pace to that of the restless crowd and while he was pushed out of his way by a careless elbow a time or two, he made it back to the kitchen in under five minutes. Only a single light was burning, and at first he thought he had missed Carol again, then he spotted her seated on a high stool in a shadowed corner. She was sobbing pathetically into a dish towel and he hurried to her side.

"Carol, what's wrong? It's a wonderful party. Why are you crying?"

Carol peeked over the soggy towel. "I didn't think you were here."

Matt moved to her side and put his arm around her shoulders. He could feel her trembling still, and hugged her more tightly. "I've been here an hour or so and I've been looking for you the whole time. Everyone I spoke with said I'd just missed you. Hey, wait a minute. You weren't sitting back here crying because you thought I wasn't here, were you?"

Dreadfully embarrassed, Carol wiped away the last of her tears. "Why does that sound so silly to you? You made me feel as though I were choosing my shop over you last night, and I was afraid you'd had enough. Deborah didn't have a career, so a woman who owns her own business might not be all that appealing to you."

Matt pressed her cheek against his chest and patted her curls. "I'm going to start calling you Hippity-Hoppity because you jump so easily to the wrong conclusions. You weren't the only one who's been worried. After you left, I was afraid I hadn't been clear enough about what I was suggesting. I know I said I loved you, and hoped you'd want to live with me, but what I should have said was how much I wanted you to marry me."

Carol looked up at him with the wide-eyed look he found so charming. She counted on her fingers. "Let's see, I met you at my house, saw you again when you and Casey were renting tuxedoes, there was the reunion, of course, and then—"

Matt caught her hands between his own. "Stop counting. It isn't how many times we've seen each other that's important. It's how we feel when we're together, and it's more than enough for me." He reached into his pocket for a small jeweler's box. "I should have had this to give you last night. Then you might have stayed with me."

Carol held her breath as she opened the box, then squealed in delighted surprise at her first glimpse of the sparkling diamond solitaire. Then her more practical instincts took hold. "Oh Matt, this is the most gorgeous ring I've ever seen, but I'm sure it was much too expensive."

"What do you think that Victorian house cost?"

She looked even more pained. "A whole lot."

"That's right, it did, and I can afford it too. I started buying real estate in the 1960s when it was still affordable. I'd remodel a house, or duplex, then sell it at a nice profit and buy another. That was my hobby for a number of years. Hell, I could have sent Dan to Harvard with no problem if he'd wanted to go, but he didn't. If it will make you feel better, I'll be happy to provide you with a financial statement, but I sure hope you'll give me your answer now because I won't be able to call my accountant until Monday morning. He doesn't take emergency calls the way I do."

Even in the dim light, the diamond glowed with a radiant fire and captivated by the beautiful ring, Carol couldn't really believe Matt had bought it for her. "I don't have very good luck with husbands, Matt. I try, Lord knows I do, but—"

"You couldn't do it alone, baby. Don't apologize. We'll be starting over together, and that wipes the slate clean. Now how many times do I have to ask the same question? Are you going to marry me, or not?"

His eyes were alight with such a loving glow, Carol knew she had fallen in love with him the instant he had stepped through her front door. "We've already made some awful mistakes, Matt."

"Yeah, and we'll probably make a lot more. So what? Think of how much fun it will be to make up."

"My shop is going to take up a lot of my time."

"Fine, I'll remodel more houses, but I won't mope around and complain I'm being neglected. You do what you love, Carol, and I'm sure we'll still find plenty of time to be together."

Carol looked down at the ring, and then up at him. "You are too good to be true, Matt. You really are."

"Try and look at it this way: I'm a fifty-four-year-old plumber. That's certainly not any woman's dream."

"No, you're wrong. It's mine." She handed

him the box. "Will you put the ring on me please?"

Matt kissed her first, and then slid the dazzling ring on her finger. "I love you, Carol. Now go into the restroom and fix your makeup and we'll go back to the party." He picked her up by the waist and set her on her feet.

"Oh no!" Carol cried. "I must look like a raccoon."

"A very pretty raccoon. Now hurry up. I want to show you off. I like that dress. I've never seen you in red and it's very becoming."

"It's crimson, actually, I was hoping it would bring me luck."

"Guess it did."

Carol took a few steps away, and then came back to hug him. "I do love you, Matt. I really do."

"Thank you. Now go on, hurry up."

Matt was seated on the stool waiting for Carol when Casey came back to the kitchen. "Thank God the party's almost over," Casey moaned. "I couldn't take more than another ten minutes of that bedlam."

Matt nodded. "I'm not fond of crowds myself, but if even half of them patronize Aluminum Moons on a regular basis, you're going to do a tremendous business."

"From your lips to God's ears."

Carol joined them then, and taking Matt's

hand she returned to the party and began bidding everyone good night. The front doors had been unlocked all evening, and Casey pushed them open to encourage everyone to make a prompt exit. By the time all the compliments were paid, promises given to return soon, and all the guests had departed, nearly another hour had passed.

Suzanne collapsed in an exhausted swoon and Casey took the chair beside her. Aimee and Gordon sat down with JoAnne, Karen, and Roger. Dan and Janet, Rob and Linda, and Tom and Sharon, offered to help with the clean up, but a couple of Casey's waiters were there to do that. Tom covered a wide yawn.

"Sharon and I had a great time. We'll tell all our friends about your cafe, Casey, and about your paintings, Karen."

"Thank you. Hope to see you soon."

Carol raised her hand. "Before you leave, let's have a final toast. Is there any more champagne?"

Casey had a full bottle. "I have some right here, but I'm not sure I can swallow another drop."

"You must," Carol insisted. "Matt's asked me to marry him, and I want you all to help us celebrate."

"All right!" Casey shouted. Then fearing that had been too boisterous a response, he adopted a calmer tone. "We'll drink to you first, and then to us. Suzanne finally accepted my proposal last night."

Gordon whispered something in Aimee's ear and when she nodded, he pulled her close. "Aimee and I are getting married in the fall."

Karen and JoAnne gasped, but quickly recovered to congratulate their mother, and Roger gave Aimee a kiss. Reforming in new clusters, congratulations were swiftly passed among the engaged couples and the children present. Dan came forward to shake his father's hand.

"I did all I could to help you, man. I'd glad it finally paid off."

"Hell, you don't deserve all the credit," Matt argued. "I must have had something to do with it."

Surrounded by her sons, Carol was beaming happily. Tom gave her a big kiss. "Way to go, Mom. He's a great guy." Never as enthusiastic a man, Rob was more subdued. "If he makes you happy, then I'm all for it too."

"Thank you." Carol had a kiss for both of them, then locked arms with Matt. Casey poured the champagne and after the three engagements had been toasted, Carol raised her glass again. "Let's have a party here every year on this date to celebrate," she suggested.

"A reunion of our own?" Aimee asked. "What a wonderful idea."

"We'll be here," Suzanne exclaimed, and the others present echoed her promise.

They all had a final sip of champagne, and exchanged a last round of hugs and kisses. With the cafe ready for the next day's grand opening, they left in a warm haze of love and laughter that would last through a great many reunions to come.

Note to Readers

After fourteen historical romances for Zebra Books, TANGLED HEARTS is my first contemporary story and I had an absolutely marvelous time writing it. I once attended a high school reunion without a date hoping to connect with a former classmate who'd want to join me in living out some delicious romantic fantasies. I was sadly disappointed when there were several other single women present, but not one unmarried man. While I enjoyed visiting with old friends, when the dancing began, rather than sit alone, I said my goodbyes and went home.

That bittersweet experience provided the germ for a reunion plot which eventually became TANGLED HEARTS. I love hearing from readers. Please write to me in care of Zebra Books, 475 Park Avenue South, New York, New York, 10016. Include a legal size SASE for an autographed bookmark.